Dear Reader,

The nights are getting longer, darker, and there's a chill in the air as the wind blows the leaves down the street. Soon, ghosts and goblins will walk the streets, though only for one eerie night. Or could it be they're always with us, and it's only for one night a year that we're permitted to see them? Perhaps the rest of the time they live in a different, mysterious world, a world of shadows, a world we invite you to enter now—with *Silhouette Shadows*.

These three stories walk the line between what we know and what we can only suspect. Sometimes there's a rational explanation for what happens—and sometimes there's not. But always you'll find a man and a woman in love, challenging the dark places that haunt every person's soul.

Let Anne Stuart introduce you to "The Monster in the Closet," though the monster may not be who—or what—you think. We all have our demons, some more than most. Sebastian Brand is an extraordinary man, so both his struggle and the woman who loves him must be extraordinary, too.

Helen R. Myers's "Seawitch" will take you to the fog-shrouded coast of Maine, where people whisper about Roanne Douglas and no one believes she will ever find another man to love her after the death—or was it murder?—of her husband. Hunter Thorne is braver than most, but now his life, too, hangs in the balance.

Finally, join Heather Graham Pozzessere for a late-night ride across the English moors to Fairhaven Castle, the darkly brooding inheritance that Alyssa Evans has come to claim. But first she must untangle the riddle of Brian Wilde, a man who may not be what he seems in her "Wilde Imaginings."

Lock your doors, close your windows against the night and turn on *all* your lights. Then sit back and let your imagination roam into a world of shadows—*Silhouette Shadows*.

Enjoy!

Leslie Wainger
Senior Editor and Editorial Coordinator

SILHOUETTE Shadows™

ANNE STUART
HELEN R. MYERS
HEATHER GRAHAM POZZESSERE

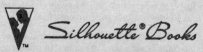

Silhouette® Books

Published by Silhouette Books New York
America's Publisher of Contemporary Romance

SILHOUETTE BOOKS
300 East 42nd St., New York, N.Y. 10017

SILHOUETTE SHADOWS
Copyright © 1992 by Silhouette Books

THE MONSTER IN THE CLOSET
Copyright © 1992 by Anne Kristine Stuart Ohlrogge

SEAWITCH
Copyright © 1992 by Helen R. Myers

WILDE IMAGININGS
Copyright © 1992 by Heather Graham Pozzessere

ISBN: 0-373-48246-9

First Silhouette Books printing October 1992

Printed in the U.S.A.

CONTENTS

The Monster in the Closet

ANNE STUART

Anne Stuart

I've always been drawn to the fantasy of dark, brooding men, terrible secrets from the past and deep, obsessive sexual love that, beyond all rational explanation, holds the only hope for happiness—in books, that is. In real life I'm relatively well adjusted.

I grew up reading Gothics—Victoria Holt's *Mistress of Mellyn* was a spiritual experience for me, and I've never grown tired of all that dreamy, brooding sensuality. I started writing at the end of the Gothic craze, publishing a number of "unsuspecting young female comes to the manor house and meets the cynical master" types before I switched to Regencies and then moved on to contemporary romance and romantic suspense. It wasn't until a personal family tragedy pushed me into writing something both completely different and yet satisfyingly familiar that I returned to my Gothic roots. Lucky for me, the world seemed ready for a change, too. Even Disney cartoons made the move to one of the quintessential Gothic legends of all time, *Beauty and the Beast*.

I think we need the fantasy of darkness and horror redeemed by love. There's something irresistible in not knowing whether the hero will fall in love with the heroine. Or kill her. Or perhaps both. Gothics are the battle between light and darkness, good and evil, but for me the good and evil reside in the hero's soul, not in some nebulous outside force. And the victory is never assured, even at the end. A trace of the blackness still remains, buried in the hero, that could reemerge and destroy them both.

It's a potent fantasy, not for the gentle-minded. It's not a matter of happy endings; it's a matter of life and death, and those stakes can be unsettling. But something in my heart will always respond on the most visceral level to vampires, phantoms, heroes with tormented pasts and black realities. And heroines who can lead them beyond that darkness, into the light.

Anne Stuart

CHAPTER ONE

The house sat alone, silent, waiting, in the midst of all the other abandoned tenements. Of all the houses in all the rows of derelict buildings, only this house still showed signs of life. The windows weren't boarded up; the doors weren't barred. It stood alone amidst the condemned buildings, stern and inviolate.

He stood in the deserted, litter-strewn streets outside, a light autumn rain misting down around his head, and looked up at the house. Several of the windows had been smashed by a vandal's hand, but even wholesale destruction had been too much of an effort for such a depressed area in the city of St. Bart, Minnesota. The house had been left essentially intact, alone, as it had stood for so many years.

They wanted to tear it down, along with the identical row houses beside it. They'd wanted to for years, though he wasn't quite sure what they planned to put in the place of a neighborhood so decayed that it couldn't house anyone but the transient homeless. They probably wanted to bulldoze everything and turn it into a parking lot. And he was the only thing stopping them.

He should sell the house, the one piece of property standing in the way of their revisionist plans. He should give it to them, wash his hands of it, turn his back on it.

He wasn't ready. He'd owned the building for ten years, and today was the first time he'd been able to bring himself to come here, to stand in front of it and stare up at a house that, like all houses, had held its share of joy and pain. And a terror so deep it still made his bones shake in memory.

He wasn't ready to give it up. He'd come here to face it, and face it he would. He and the house and the past would do battle. Heaven only knew who would rise triumphant. Heaven—and hell.

He moved slowly up the steps. The house was unlocked; he'd left word that it should never be locked. He'd hoped the mean streets of St. Bart would rise up and swallow it, that roving gangs would destroy it. But the house had a history and a reputation, and even young gang members kept clear of it. Leaving it still, intact, waiting for him to return.

And now he was back. Ready to face his past.

Ready to face what lay in wait in the darkness beyond.

Ready to face the monsters.

Emma Milsom liked to think of herself as a decisive woman, but at the moment she was in a state not far removed from complete confusion. She'd accepted the job with Teddy Winters against her better judgment, but then, anyone who came within Teddy's exhausting orbit always ended up doing things they didn't want to do. True, she'd been at loose ends. The economy was bad, but never would she have guessed it would reach even the hallowed halls of Shoreham Brothers. She'd been there for five years, since she'd earned her MBA, and her life had seemed safe, secure and comfortingly boring.

And now, a mere three weeks later, she was a thousand miles away from her yuppie life, working for a maverick playwright-director. Gone were her suits, gone were her comfortable income and profit-sharing plan, gone were her condo and her Italian leather shoes.

Now she was wearing jeans and running shoes and cotton sweaters. She was working as a gofer for Teddy Winters while he mounted his ambitious twin productions of *The Tempest* and his own dark reworking of the Shakespeare tale, working for a sum so small it made her laugh, working for no prestige and long hours and the dubious pleasure of having the hormone-laden Teddy chase her around the table when he remembered her existence. All that she had left from her previous life-style was her precious MGB, a dubious memento. It was notoriously temperamental, never started in the rain, shimmied like mad at fifty-five miles per hour, and got lousy gas mileage. And she would sell her soul to the devil before she would relinquish her car.

She'd settled into a single room at the luxury hotel Teddy inhabited, refusing his offer to share his penthouse. Fortunately she was more concerned with her mental health than her finances. Succumbing to Teddy's professional blandishments was bad enough. It would be emotional suicide to believe his romantic overtures.

It had just been her bad luck that the local UPI stringer had chosen to interview her among all the executives laid off by Shoreham Brothers. Her bad luck that so many other papers had picked up the story, and that Teddy, always a voracious reader of magazines and newspapers, had seen it and recognized her name.

Once that happened her fate had been settled, and no matter how hard she'd battled against it, she'd been swept along by the whirlwind that was Teddy Winters. In truth, she hadn't battled that hard. She was in need of a change, of a complete shake-up in her staid life. She'd gotten that, and more, the moment she'd agreed to work for Teddy.

She'd known him for too long, since he was an undergraduate at Harvard and dated her sister. She'd been six years younger and awed by the color and brilliance of his firecracker personality. Her sister had been less impressed, breaking off the relationship, and supposedly breaking Teddy's heart, to marry a premed student. Her sister had never regretted it, even as Teddy grew increasingly famous. He was the enfant terrible of Hollywood, the new Orson Welles, they were saying, except that Teddy was much better looking. A golden boy, too brilliant and volatile for his own good, but glorious, nonetheless.

Some of that glory had tarnished in the last few years. Deals had fallen through, movies had been financial and artistic failures. But nothing seemed to shake Teddy. He'd just managed the professional coup of his life, one that would bring him back to the forefront of the industry. His creative juices were flowing, and the production he was mounting in St. Bart was going to reshape American theatre in the 1990s. Or so he assured Emma.

And she believed him. Not only did he have the script of his new play, *Monsters,* a wonderful, shivery piece of work, and the financial enthusiasm and support of the revitalized city of St. Bart, but he'd managed the unbelievable coup of luring Sebastian Brand from his native England to appear as both Caliban and the Monster. Everything had fallen into place after that, including the addition of Coral Aubrey and her husband, Geoffrey Beauchamps, the foremost young theatrical couple in the business.

Years ago Emma had been star-struck, longing to get involved in the theatre. Unfortunately, she'd been singularly lacking in talent. She couldn't act, couldn't direct, couldn't even manage much in the way of costumes or makeup. She'd been drummed out of the theatre group in college and grudgingly followed her real gifts. Organization. And finance.

Her MBA and her accounting background were her own shameful secrets. Teddy had offered her the job like a magician invoking a spell, luring her to her doom. He knew people, and he knew her—too well. Here was a chance to get the greasepaint out of her system, to find out whether she'd given up too easily so many years ago. She should have stayed in Pennsylvania and polished her résumé. Instead, she'd run away with the circus.

"Darling," Teddy said, bursting into the front office with his customary energy, his silver-blond hair flying out behind him, his blue eyes bright in his handsome face. "I've been looking for you everywhere. The press are on to us!"

Emma looked up from her spot on the floor. She was surrounded by papers, permits, contracts and the like, trying to make some sort of sense of them, and she didn't dare move or destroy her incipient filing system. "Isn't that what you want?" she asked.

"That's what I adore about you, Emma, you're so marvelously tranquil. Of course I want the press. Any pragmatist knows they need the press on their side if they're going to succeed in this fickle business. Explain that to Brand."

Emma dropped an Equity contract on top of the gas bills. "He's here?"

"He's here. I don't know why I doubted him—if anything, the man's unnatural, he's so professional. Punctual to the minute. He said he'd show up on Friday the thirteenth, and show up he has. Unfortunately the press is clamoring, and you know how he is about interviews."

"He won't do them." Emma had done her research before she'd arrived in St. Bart. She'd gathered information on Coral Aubrey and her husband, on Teddy's last few years, but she hadn't been able to find out much about Sebastian Brand, the famous young British horror actor. He'd never given an interview, didn't pose for publicity pictures, and was reticent to the point of outright rudeness when it came to his privacy.

"Exactly. Bloody British," Teddy said. "Your job, Emma, is to convince him otherwise. Failing that, to keep the press at bay."

"I beg your pardon? I thought my job was to organize the office, get the paperwork in shape. . . ."

"That can wait," Teddy announced with an airy wave of his hand. "I've promised Brand that he won't be bothered by the press. All you have to do is get him to make a reasonably polite statement to that effect, hold still for a few publicity shots, and then they'll leave him in peace."

"Why don't you ask him?"

"Hell, Emma, I don't want my head bitten off. I have to work with the man. No sense in starting our relationship off on a sour note." Teddy leaned over, picked up a bill from the caterers and frowned. "Highway robbery," he muttered, ripping the over-due invoice in half and letting it flutter back down. "On your feet, girl. Time's a wasting."

It wouldn't do any good to stall. Teddy would sim-ply drag her in his wake. It also wouldn't do any good to protest that she wasn't particularly enthralled with the notion of getting *her* head bitten off. Teddy didn't respond well to considerations of other people's wel-fare. She really had no choice. She would either have to face the notoriously difficult Sebastian Brand...or she could fake a migraine.

"I have a headache..." she began, not expecting success with that particular ploy.

"No time for headaches in this business," Teddy said, reaching down and hauling her to her feet, send-ing the papers tumbling into disarray around her. "Come along, Emma. Time's a wasting."

In the end even Teddy deserted her, not that she'd expected much in the way of moral support. The small gaggle of reporters in the gutted front lobby was a si-ren call he couldn't resist, and a wide smile wreathed his face as he started toward them. "You'll find Brand backstage, checking things out," he tossed back over his shoulder. "Do what you can with him."

"Teddy," Emma moaned, but Teddy was long gone, working the group of reporters with the exper-tise of a natural showman. She considered returning to the office and barring the door, but she would just be putting off the inevitable. No one could stand in the way of Teddy when he wanted something. They would simply be mown down.

The theatre was deserted. Half the seats were out, being replaced for an astronomical cost. Teddy's plans were so grandiose, his budget so reasonable, that Emma felt the beginnings of an ulcer every time she thought about it.

The stage was empty, only the basic props sat still and silent on the bare floor boards. A table, two chairs and an old-fashioned iron bed.

She scrambled up the ladder to the stage, peering through the dust motes and dimly lit shadows for a human soul. A man was standing by the omnipresent silver pot of Kona coffee, his back to her, and he looked so normal that for a moment she assumed he was part of the over-priced catering concern.

"Excuse me," she said, her voice as unnaturally loud in the stillness as her sneakered feet had been silent. "I'm looking for Sebastian Brand."

The man turned, slowly, and she was reminded of Lon Chaney in "Phantom of the Opera." By the time the words had left her mouth she'd known that this was Sebastian Brand, and she had no idea what to expect when he turned. She'd never seen any of his phenomenally successful movies, and the only photos of him without makeup were distant and grainy.

He wasn't nearly as handsome as Teddy. But then, he was singularly lacking in Teddy's overwhelming charm. Sebastian Brand was a tall man, a bit over six feet, with a lean, wiry build, flat stomach and no hips whatsoever. He was dressed in black—black jeans, a black shirt open at the throat, black leather boots. Even his hair was black, and long, framing his face like a lion's mane.

His face was ordinary and yet arresting—a narrow, sensitive face, with a high forehead, a sharp, distinct nose and a wide, thin-lipped mouth. His eyes were distractingly light in all that darkness, a silvery color, and they were staring at her with patent disdain.

"Who wants to know?" he countered, the tone, even more than the words, insulting in that clipped, British way.

Emma felt a little shiver dance down her spine, and she couldn't even begin to guess its origin. "Mr. Brand," she said, holding out her hand. "I'm Emma Milsom, Teddy's general manager." It was as good a title as any. "He asked me to talk to you about the press."

He didn't take her hand, of course, and she dropped hers, feeling like a fool. "There's nothing to discuss," he said, turning his back to her again and pouring himself a mug of coffee.

Damn Teddy, she thought. "He's talking to the press right now, explaining your position," she pushed onward. "He thought you might issue a statement, though, to clarify matters."

"No statement." He kept his back to her, a fact for which she might almost have been grateful if it weren't so rude.

She took a deep, calming breath. "All right," she said evenly. "Perhaps you might agree to a few publicity shots. Just to sort of quiet them."

"No photos." He turned, and she found she much preferred his back to the intensity of his eyes. "No statements, no rehearsal photographers skulking around. I thought I made myself clear when I discussed this with Winters. We do this on my terms or not at all."

"On your terms," Emma said.

"Emma, darling." Teddy appeared out of nowhere to sling an arm around Emma's stiff shoulders. "I see you've met Sebastian. Aren't we blessed to have him with us on our glorious venture?''

"Blessed," Emma echoed flatly.

"Your *girl* here told me you wanted me to make a statement to the press, Winters," Sebastian said in that icy British voice of his. "And hold still for photos. I thought I made myself clear—"

"Emma!" Teddy said, patently shocked. "How could you have asked such a thing? You know I've told you that Sebastian is never to be bothered by the press. I can't imagine why you'd think to go ahead on your own with such a notion." He flashed an ingratiating smile at Sebastian, his arm still tight around Emma's shoulder. "She's young and enthusiastic, Sebastian. She just got a little ahead of herself. Trust me to make sure she doesn't bother you again."

Emma was shocked into momentary speechlessness. Visions of bloody murder, worthy of one of Sebastian's notorious movies, danced in her head, and she glared up at her boss, mouth open to tell him exactly what she thought of him, when Teddy smiled that same smile down at her. "Back to the office, love, where you belong. She doesn't understand how theatre works, Sebastian. The poor thing was an unemployed accountant when I gave her a job." He made *accountant* sound like the world's oldest profession.

Too angry to trust her voice, Emma jerked and had started toward the edge of the stage, leaving the two men in muffled conversation, when Teddy's voice rang out.

"Wait a minute, Emma."

She had every intention of ignoring him, of ignoring him for the rest of her life, when Sebastian spoke. "Come back here."

The man was an actor, after all. A phenomenally successful one. She'd read his reviews, and through the blood and gore, critics had seen his brilliance; it was no wonder that his quiet, perfectly modulated voice could carry across the stage and stop her cold.

And it *was* her job, she reminded herself. An insulting, low-paying job, but a job nonetheless. And there was no question but that the people she was working with were brilliant. Rude, unstable and manipulative, but brilliant.

She turned, plastering a deceptively polite smile across her face, and walked back. "Yes?"

"Sebastian here is very understanding," Teddy said.

"Very understanding," Sebastian echoed dryly. "Your task, Miss Milsom, is to see that I'm not bothered. By the press, by fans, by aspiring actors and writers and film critics. Your task, Miss Milsom, is to see that I'm left alone."

"That shouldn't be too hard," she said in a dulcet voice.

To her surprise he laughed, almost unwillingly. "I agree. People shouldn't want to be around a bastard like me, but they do. You're to show them the error of their ways. Understood?"

"Understood," she said. The problem with the man, she decided, was that he did have a kind of charm after all. Well, maybe charm was the wrong word. Charisma, perhaps. Not Teddy's facile ease of manner. But something that drew you toward him, pulled you into the hypnotic silvery gray of his eyes, made you want to move closer, then closer still.

As he pushed you away. "Excellent," he said, dismissing her from existence. He turned to Teddy. "Let's get started with *Monsters.*"

And as Emma made her way silently back across the stage, she decided the man had definitely picked the proper profession. Impersonating monsters would be child's play for a rude horror like him. Maybe she'd better spend some time on her résumé this afternoon.

"Sebastian, love, do you have to be so damned pedantic?" Coral Aubrey demanded as she bounced her hundred or so pounds in his lap. "We're not talking Holy Writ here. Half the fun of Shakespeare is reworking it."

"Reworking it," he said coolly, reaching out a hand to steady her. "Not rewriting it. Explain it to your silly wife, Geoff," he called across the stage to the ridiculously handsome man immersed in a racing form.

"You do it, Sebastian," he called back cheerfully, not bothering to look up. "She never listens to me."

Sebastian glanced out over the theatre. She was there again, as she had been for the last three days they'd been in rehearsal. He knew when she entered the cavernous old building and when she left. It was only because of his extraordinary powers of concentration that he never missed a beat or a cue, never betrayed his intense awareness by so much as the blink of an eyelash.

He was aware. Every muscle, every fibre of his body, knew when she was around. He recognized his reaction to her. He simply didn't understand it.

It wasn't as if she were the most beautiful woman he'd ever seen. Far from it. She was tall and a little too skinny for his taste, with a certain coltish grace most women outgrew by the time they reached their late twenties. Her face was unremarkable, framed by a curtain of brownish blond hair; her eyes were an average blue, her features even.

Maybe it was her hands, he thought, shifting Coral's chattering figure around on his lap. She had the most beautiful hands he'd ever seen on a woman, long-fingered, slender hands, with short, unpolished nails. Or maybe it was her breasts, or her hips. Or that wary, irritated, intense look on her face when she watched him and didn't know he was watching her back.

He knew the moment Teddy Winters had spoken that he had put her up to that stupid stunt. Winters was the kind of man to make other people do his dirty work, then shift all blame away from himself. Sebastian had no illusions about the kind of man he was working with, but then, he had no illusions about most people. He trusted very few, the woman on his lap and her husband being two of that select company. Despite their deliberate air of impracticality, Geoff and Coral were two of the most loyal, down-to-earth people he knew. He could count on them for anything.

What he didn't understand was why Emma had taken the rap for Winters.

He'd assumed she was sleeping with him. It was the way these things usually worked—the director-producer would find some love slave who would work for a pittance, content with staring up with adoring eyes and catering to his every whim. Winters was extraordinarily good at getting people to do what he wanted—Emma was obviously one in a line of women ready to fall at his feet and into his bed.

But after three days of involuntarily alert scrutiny, he'd decided they weren't lovers after all. There was none of that sensual awareness, that hormonal smell, to them.

Which meant Emma Milsom was fair game.

He didn't want to think about that. Didn't want to consider that maybe a brief affair would relieve some of the awful tension that had been building up inside him.

It had been months of celibacy since Marcy had left him. He hadn't missed her, but he'd missed her body, her lush, rounded, wonderfully sensual body.

Emma Milsom was too skinny, too vulnerable. She wore her emotions for all to see. There was something about her that drew him, touched him, in ways he didn't want to be touched. He needed to warn her away. Or maybe he needed to warn himself away. It would be too damned easy to reach out to her. Particularly when he had the feeling that she would come to him, despite the doubt in her expressive blue eyes.

He set Coral aside, ignoring her voluble complaints. "You hash it out," he told her. "But no changing dialogue because you have trouble with too many esses." He rose from the uncomfortable prop sofa, walking toward the edge of the stage, slowly, deliberately, giving Emma time to escape.

It took her a moment to realize his intent. A hunted expression crossed her face, and she immediately vanished, heading toward the back of the theatre at something close to a run.

He watched her go, never slowing his steady pursuit. He would prefer to talk to her alone in the office, anyway. Coral was much too curious, and Geoff couldn't control her. He thought about that frightened expression on Emma's face, thought about the look in her eyes. It would be a simple enough matter, frightening her away from him. She was too tempting, and he didn't have anything to spare.

Of course, Marcy would have said he never had. He spent all his energies, his emotions, on his craft. On the monsters he inhabited. And the monsters who inhabited him.

So for his sake, and hers, he needed to warn Emma away. While he still could.

CHAPTER TWO

"Are you afraid of me?"

Emma should have known he would follow her, should have known he wouldn't waste time with polite nothings. She'd managed to land behind the huge, battered desk that was still piled high with papers, barely out of breath, fingers crossed that he wouldn't follow her, that he wasn't really heading in her direction, an intent expression in his eerie silver eyes.

She managed a wonderfully airy laugh that should have fooled him, though she didn't for one moment believe it did. "Don't be ridiculous. Why should I be afraid of you?"

He stood in the open doorway of her office. She could see the carpenters in the foyer behind him, working on the renovations, and she told herself she was being ridiculous, that she had no reason to be uneasy. Until he moved into the room with that dangerous grace she'd observed during the last three days and shut the door behind him.

"Maybe you've seen too many of my movies," he said. "Maybe you really think I'm Slasher Charlie."

"I haven't ever seen your movies," she blurted out before she could judge the tact of that remark.

It stopped him cold. "You haven't?" He seemed genuinely astonished.

"Never a one."

For some reason he didn't seem offended by the notion. "Why not?"

"I'm too gullible."

"I beg your pardon?"

Once again she wished she could pull the words back. There was no way to get out of it, once she'd started. "The problem is," she said earnestly, "that I believe things. I'm not the sort of person who can enjoy a good scare. I see terrifying things up on the screen and I think they're real. Intellectually I know they're just a fantasy. But my mind has nothing to do with it. Deep in my heart I believe in monsters."

He didn't move. He was absolutely frozen, standing there alone in the office with her, dressed in his customary black—black jeans, black T-shirt, his mane of black hair surrounding his ominously still face, where only his silver eyes glittered with some unnameable emotion. "So do I," he said softly. And then he turned and left, closing the door behind him.

Emma sat very still. Her heart was pounding very fast beneath her linen shirt. Looking down, she saw that her hands were trembling, and she clasped them together. "Too much coffee," she said aloud, but she knew she was fooling herself. Sebastian Brand was having the most astonishing effect on her, and she couldn't even begin to guess why.

It couldn't be anything as simple and basic as the fact that she found him attractive. She did, of course. More than attractive. With that lithe, graceful body of his, that mane of hair, that narrow, brooding, arresting face, he was totally mesmerizing.

But just because she found him physically appealing didn't mean she wanted to do anything about it. Even if she wondered what his mouth would taste like, she had no interest in finding out. Too many nasty, biting remarks issued from that mouth. She'd been attracted to men before, sometimes one-sided, sometimes reciprocated, and she was a reasonably healthy, adult woman. She should know how to handle things by now.

But Sebastian Brand was different. She didn't know how to handle him at all, except from a distance.

That brief, enigmatic encounter was part and parcel of the whole thing. She had no idea what he'd wanted, if, indeed, he'd wanted anything other than to disconcert her. For a brief, shocked moment she'd had the notion that he was attracted to her. An unlikely prospect—he thought she was an incompetent fool.

And then he'd turned and left, that imagined awareness disappearing before she could even decide whether it had existed in the first place. Leaving her alone, and more confused than ever.

"What's up?" Teddy breezed into the office, a sweater tied around his broad shoulders, his blond hair artfully ruffled.

"You look like you should be saying, 'Anyone for tennis?'" Emma said in a sour voice. "They're waiting for you onstage."

Unrepentant, Teddy leaned a hip against the littered desk, shoving one organized pile into another. "I take it you're chastising me for being late. You should know, my love, that there's more to getting this production moving than baby-sitting highly professional actors while they do some preliminary character work. Besides, I didn't sleep very well last night."

"Didn't you?"

He leaned across the desk toward her. "You know very well I didn't. Why didn't you let me in last night?"

"It was three-thirty in the morning. I was asleep. Whatever you wanted to talk to me about could wait till the morning." Oddly enough, her hands were no longer trembling. Teddy Winters didn't have the ability to touch her at all, even enmeshed in this difficult conversation.

"I wasn't interested in talking," Teddy said, putting his hands flat on the desk in front of her.

She glanced down at them. For such a tall man he had surprisingly small hands, with wide palms and slightly stubby fingers. "No, Teddy," she said flatly.

"Don't be ridiculous, Emma. You know you've always had a crush on me," he protested.

"No, Teddy. I work for you, and that's it."

He smiled, unabashed. "You should know I don't take 'no' for an answer. I'll be at your door every night."

"I don't think the hotel management will appreciate it."

"It's not the hotel I'm interested in." He leaned back, glancing idly at some of the overdue bills. "So what did Sebastian want with you?"

She didn't know whether to believe his casual tone of voice or not. "I really don't know. He was probably looking for you."

"What did he say?"

"Teddy..."

"I'm not being jealous, Emma," he said, meeting her gaze with an earnestness she had to believe. "You know I'm not the possessive sort, particularly if I hadn't had a chance to possess in the first place. I have a reason for asking. Has Sebastian been making any move in your direction? Flirting with you? Coming on to you?''

"No!" she said, aghast. "For one thing, I don't believe the man's capable of flirting. For another, he has absolutely no interest in me. I can't imagine why you think he would."

"Maybe I give him the credit of sharing my good taste in women."

"Your taste in women isn't good, it's universal," she said dryly. "You still haven't told me why you're asking."

Teddy glanced down at his hands. "There have been ... rumors," he said delicately. "Combined with certain happenings, that suggest that an involvement with Sebastian Brand might not be the healthiest thing in the world."

"What are you talking about?"

"Do you remember hearing about Sally Ryan? No, you probably wouldn't have. She was killed last year on a movie set."

"I vaguely remember something about it," Emma said uneasily.

"It was on the set of *Slasher Charlie's Dream,* and Sally Ryan wasn't just a two-bit actress. She was Sebastian's lover."

That sick feeling in the pit of her stomach was growing. "How awful for him!"

"Perhaps. Especially considering this wasn't the first time."

"What do you mean?" She didn't want to hear this, she knew she didn't.

"Other women have been hurt over the years. Accidents, nothing suspicious." He cupped her chin with one hand, his bright blue eyes dark with concern. "Emma, love, I'm only saying this to warn you. I don't want anything to happen to you. Sebastian Brand is a man with a great many secrets. If I'd realized there was going to be any danger to you, I never would have asked you to work for me."

Emma had always considered herself to be a practical woman. It took all her resolve to shake off the eerie effect of Teddy's words. "I appreciate your concern, Teddy, but it's misplaced. In the first place, Sebastian Brand is not interested in me. Period. In the second, I can't believe you'd listen to tabloid gossip. Someone's just taken a few coincidences and blown them out of proportion. He's an actor, for heaven's sake. He's made a career out of playing monsters. That doesn't mean he *is* one."

Teddy's smile was faintly pitying. "Of course not, darling. I just felt I had to mention it. In good conscience. I'm sure it's simply a few unfortunate accidents that have been exaggerated. But, Emma, I want you to promise me something. If you notice anything, if you have any close calls, you have to tell me. I couldn't live with myself if something happened and I'd gotten you into this in the first place. Please, Emma. Be careful."

The burning in her stomach was full-blown now. She wished she could believe Teddy was just trying to terrorize her, but he seemed far too concerned, too worried, to be putting on an act. "I'll be careful, Teddy. In the meantime, I think you have a cast on the edge of revolt."

He leapt off the desk, his somber mood vanishing abruptly. "Artists!" he said. "They're all a bunch of children. Order in dinner, Emma. We'll be working late.''

Emma watched him leave. At least she'd had her priorities straight, paying the over-priced caterer Teddy insisted upon, then deplored, or there would be fast-food burgers for dinner tonight. She pushed the old oak chair back from the desk and glanced down at the bags she'd hidden at her feet. Maybe now wasn't the best time to decamp from the Clarion Hotel. Not that she believed a word of what Teddy had said, of course. But if there was a faint chance that things weren't quite . . . right, then maybe she shouldn't remove herself from the protection of other people.

She did, however, need to remove herself from the protection of Teddy. He had been slightly drunk last night, thumping on her door and pleading with her to let him in in a voice that was meant to be a whisper but could doubtless have carried to the back row in the balcony. She'd kept the door locked, and she had no doubts about her ability to continue to do so. She just wasn't sure whether Teddy would find another way in.

She didn't want to be around when he found out she'd left the hotel, though God willing it might be several days. His enthusiasms went in waves. Last night he'd been ready to die for her, tonight he would probably forget her existence. That was both the charm and the trouble with Teddy.

She would wait until they were all so involved in work that they wouldn't notice her tiptoeing up the metal steps and catwalks to the fourth floor storerooms. She didn't have that much to carry—a couple of trips would probably suffice for now. And tonight, at least, she could sleep in peace.

* * *

She'd shaken him to his very bones with that off-hand remark of hers. She believed in monsters, did she? Sebastian lounged back in the wings of the theatre, stretched out on an old chaise that must have been a relic of some Oscar Wilde extravaganza, and considered Emma Milsom. She didn't even know what a real monster was.

But he knew, to his lifelong, everlasting sorrow. He'd made his acquaintance with monsters years ago, and they'd hovered at his shoulder ever since, driving him. He thought he'd made his peace with them, thought so until circumstances had joined together to show him just how wrong he was.

Outside in the darkness his house awaited him. He could have left hours ago—Winters was busy with Coral and Geoff, working out details, and there was no need for him to hang around.

Except his interest in Emma's furtive movements. He was an observant man; little escaped him. Unlike Teddy, or most of the actors he knew, his self-absorption was minimal. He could discover things from watching other people, their expressions, their gestures. Their movements.

Emma had been skulking around for the last hour. When she thought no one was looking she'd disappeared up the noisy metal stairs, making as little sound as she could. She was carrying bundles, looking all around to make sure no one saw her.

The rumble of thunder shook the old brick building, and the lights flickered and dimmed for a moment, then flashed back on brightly. He'd forgotten how rainy St. Bart could be in the autumn, if indeed he'd ever noticed. He hadn't spent much time outdoors when he'd lived there decades ago.

His choices were clear. He could leave now, walk home in the rain and thunder. He'd done it before—he liked the sense of being alone with the rain and the violence of nature inflicting its will on a decaying city. It would be the smarter choice, rather than wait to see if Emma would appear once more, looking demure and secretive.

He heard the faint rattle overhead on the catwalk, but he didn't look up, simply walked back onto the stage as if totally unaware of her presence overhead. "I'm going home," he announced.

Teddy glanced over at him, momentarily distracted. "What time is it?"

"Too damned late," Coral said with an extravagant yawn. "I'm taking Geoff away, too. It's always possible, Teddy dear, to be prompt in the morning."

Teddy grinned. "I try not to be predictable."

"If you weren't so damned good," Geoff grumbled, "we wouldn't put up with you."

"Isn't that true for all of us?" Teddy countered.

She'd descended the stairs and now stood not far behind them. Sebastian knew it as well as if he'd watched her. He didn't turn, didn't acknowledge her presence. During the long hours of rehearsal he'd had more than enough time to think, to make decisions. And one of those decisions was that Emma Milsom was exactly the kind of woman he'd always steered away from. And he would continue doing so, particularly now.

"Emma," Teddy said, looking behind Sebastian. "Would you give Mr. Brand a ride home? It's raining buckets."

"I like the rain," Sebastian said flatly. What the hell was Teddy thinking of, trying to throw them together like that? When it was more than clear that Teddy fancied her almost as much as he fancied himself.

"I can't afford to let my major drawing card come down with pneumonia," Teddy said. "We're just getting into the busiest part of production, and I can't have you nursing a cold."

"What do you mean, your major drawing card?" Coral demanded with exaggerated effrontery that wasn't all mockery. "What are Geoff and I, chopped liver?"

"Most definitely," Sebastian said smoothly. "Delicious, free range, diced chicken liver. You can give me a ride home, can't you, Cory?"

"You can walk," she said, sticking her tongue out at him. "Besides, we're already taking Teddy, since he seems to be without a car himself. Be brave, Sebastian. Emma's a nice girl. She's not going to hurt you."

He turned around to look at Emma. She had a mutinous expression on her face, one she quickly wiped away when she realized he was watching her. "I'd be happy to drop you off at your hotel," she said stiffly.

He did want her. It surprised him, realizing it, that he wanted her quite badly. And was just as determined not to have her. "Not a hotel," he corrected her. "I have a house."

She smiled politely. "That sounds a lot more comfortable."

"Not if you've seen his house," Coral piped up. "See you tomorrow, Sebastian. We can rehearse the scene where you murder me."

"With pleasure, Coral," he said. "Murdering women always cheers me up." He could feel Emma's startled reaction to his innocent joke, but he couldn't begin to understand it. She said she'd never seen any of his movies, either the astonishingly lucrative and bloody Slasher Charlie movies, the films that had given him a bank account equal to the gross national income of several of the Russian republics, or his better, more inventive work, playing less bloody but infinitely more terrifying monsters.

There was no denying he frightened her. And that nervous edge seemed to have grown since this morning, when he'd accosted her in her office. He was going to have to get a few things straight between them. She was beginning to disturb even his legendary concentration. He didn't like that prickly awareness that was plaguing him. The sooner he did something about it, the better.

"I'd appreciate a ride home," he said abruptly, and he watched her eyes darken with apprehension.

"Fine," she said briskly. "Let's go."

The rain was coming down in heavy sheets, obscuring the back alleyway when she opened the fire door. "I'm afraid I don't have an umbrella," she called back to him. "You'll have to run for it."

"I can survive a little rain," he said. "Where's your car?" And then he saw it.

Even through the heavy downpour the British racing green of a 1967 MGB was unmistakable. The car of his dreams, the car he'd always denied himself for some perverse reason, and she owned one.

She darted out in the rain, sleek and sure-footed as she skipped over the puddles, and he had no choice but to follow her. If he'd known what kind of car she drove he might have preferred walking through the torrential downpour.

The inside was small and dry and intimate. He glanced at the familiar dashboard, watched as she pulled the choke, fiddled with the keys and kept her gaze straight ahead through the impenetrable rain. ''I sometimes have trouble starting her when it's wet,'' she said diffidently, as the engine made a choking protest.

''M.G.'s are noted for that,'' he said, slouching down in the leather seat.

She cast a glance at him, then quickly looked away, but once again he saw that expression in her eyes, half fear, half awareness. And he knew suddenly that no matter how frightened she was of him, all he had to do was touch her and she would come to him.

He wasn't sure why. She certainly wasn't the sort to fall into bed at a moment's notice—he trusted his instincts enough to know that she had been loved neither wisely nor well nor often. It was making his sudden resolve to leave her alone all the more difficult. It was a typical masculine conceit, that he could be the lover who made a difference, and he did try so hard not to be obvious.

A moment later the engine fired, settling down into the nice throaty purr that a good British sports car should have. ''Take your first right,'' he said, ''and I'll tell you where to go from there.''

He didn't miss any of her reactions when she pulled up outside the house. She'd seemed uneasy when they'd headed into the worst section of town, looking at the litter-strewn sidewalks with surprise. She was lucky it wasn't a clear night. She wouldn't have felt reassured by the kind of people who hung out on the street corners here, looking for business, all of it illegal. The pouring rain made everything dismal and dreary. In the case of the tenement he was calling home, that was an improvement on reality.

She pulled up across the street from the building, putting the car in neutral. "You live here?"

"I live here." Reaching over, he switched off the key, leaving it in the ignition, ignoring her little cry of protest. "We need to talk."

She turned to look at him then, her face still and wary in the shadowy confines of the car. The streetlight overhead didn't provide much illumination in the heavy rain, but he could see enough to gauge her reactions.

"Certainly," she said politely, and he half expected her to add a subservient "Mr. Brand."

"I want you to stop watching me."

Even in the shadows he could see the color deepen on her cheeks. "What do you mean?"

"You watch me. I've seen you. Let me assure you, I'm not the stuff adolescent fantasies are made of. If you're in the habit of sleeping with the male leads in the productions you've worked on, that is one habit you won't be able to indulge this time around. Geoff's happily married. And I'm off limits."

"I don't know what you're talking about."

He stared at her for a long, thoughtful moment. "Don't you? Perhaps not. Let's just agree to keep our distance, all right? You keep out of the auditorium while we're rehearsing unless Teddy needs you for something, you keep the press off my back, and I'll keep out of your way as best I can. Does that sound like a reasonable solution?"

"I still don't know what you're talking about," she said, a chilly edge in her voice. "A solution to what? I promise you, I'm not sitting in the audience weaving erotic fantasies about you. As far as I'm concerned you're a very unpleasant human being. I've been told you're a wonderful actor, but since I've studiously avoided all your movies I really couldn't say. I'll have to take Teddy's word for it. But I'm not about to fling myself at your feet or rip your clothes off for a souvenir. I'm a little old for that, and frankly, Mr. Brand, I'm not interested."

The car was steaming up from the heat of her anger. He'd hoped to make her mad enough to keep away from him, to keep temptation out of his reach. Instead her anger was making him want her even more.

"Good," he said, reaching for the door handle. "Then I'll see you tomorrow." And he dashed out into the rainstorm before she could come up with a scathing response.

Emma watched him go, racing up the scarred and pitted stone steps of one of those depressing buildings, entering without having to unlock it as far as she could see, and slamming the door behind him. She watched as a faint glow emanated from the windows, watched as her hands shook with rage.

"Conceited, pompous prig," she said out loud. "Obnoxious British twit. Stupid, self-centered, talentless moron." The insults didn't help. Particularly when half of them were directed at her.

He'd been far too close to the truth, no matter how hotly she'd denied it. She *had* been watching him. She *had* been weaving erotic fantasies around him as she watched him move around the stage. She did have a crush on him, a stupid adolescent crush on a man with the personality of a python.

Well, she'd been warned, and she would heed that warning. She wouldn't go near the man if she could help it. If Teddy needed notes taken on the production, then he could find someone else to do it. There were any number of people wandering around the theatre, working on sets and costumes, most of them there for the sake of Teddy's blue eyes and persuasive tongue. She would keep to the safety of the office and never have to deal with Mr. Sebastian Brand again.

There was only one problem. Her precious baby, her only valuable possession, her true love, her *car* was going to be stuck here. If she was really lucky it started the first time out during a rainstorm. It never, ever restarted once someone had been fool enough to turn it off.

She made the effort, being careful not to flood the engine. And then she reached over and locked the car doors, looking through the heavy rain nervously. It wasn't the neighborhood she would have chosen to be spending the night in a broken down car. But she would rather face marauding street gangs and murderous drug dealers than Sebastian Brand. Sliding down in the leather seat, she closed her eyes and prepared to wait out the long hours till dawn.

CHAPTER THREE

It was easy to slip into the velvety cocoon of half sleep. The light from the street lamp overhead was pleasantly hazy, filling the car with a cozy glow. If she hadn't been so angry and upset over Sebastian's high-handed dismissal, she would have been sound asleep by the time the sharp rapping came on her window.

As it was, she'd just started to drift when the noise jarred her awake, and she let out a nervous squawk as she twisted in her seat.

The shape at her window was dark, drenched in rain and unrecognizable. She looked beyond, to the open door of Sebastian's row house, and shook her head. "I'm staying here," she said loudly.

She'd forgotten he was an actor. "If you don't come out of that car," he said, his voice carrying through the tightly shut window with perfect clarity, "I will smash the windshield and drag you through."

She believed him. "I can take care of myself," she said mutinously.

"Open the damned door."

She told herself she didn't really have any choice in the matter. She reached over and unlocked the door, and a moment later found herself hauled out of the car. "What are you still doing here?" he demanded through the noise of the rain.

The rain was coming down in buckets, soaking her instantly, and the damned man hadn't thought to bring an umbrella. "You turned the car off," she shouted back at him. "I was lucky it even started in the first place. M.G.'s don't like rain."

She could see his face beneath his slicker, could see the blank comprehension. "Come in the house," he said—an order, not an invitation.

"No, thank you, I was doing just fine." She'd turned away, when his hand caught hers and jerked her around.

"This isn't the sort of neighborhood where you can sleep in your car. You'll be lucky if any of the car is still there in the morning."

"I'm not—"

"You are." He dragged her across the street, up the scarred stone steps of the tenement, and after a moment she gave up pulling back. In truth, she was now thoroughly soaked, freezing and furious. And the more she could see of the neighborhood, the more she was inclined to agree with Sebastian.

He slammed the door behind them, releasing her, and she stared about her in sudden silence.

The inside of the derelict building was a far cry from its exterior. The place had been gutted, the floors stripped down to bare wood, the walls and woodwork painted a stark white. It smelled of fresh lumber, paint and hot coffee.

For coffee Emma could put up with the devil himself. "This isn't my fault," she said. "If you hadn't turned off the car..."

"Stop arguing and get out of those wet things." He'd pulled the slicker over his head and tossed it across a chair, pushing his damp hair back with his eloquent hands.

"What do you suggest I get into?" she countered with acid sweetness.

He hesitated for a moment, and she had the odd feeling he was going to cross the room and touch her, putting the lie to all the things he'd said to her in the car.

But he didn't. "There's a bathroom upstairs, with towels. You'll find clothes in the dresser—help yourself while I pour you some coffee."

The word coffee silenced her last protest. The best she could hope for was to express her utter disdain in the stiffness of her spine, a difficult task when she was feeling like a drowned rat.

There were no longer any partitions in the building, only structural posts left standing, and she was in full view of him as she climbed the white painted stairs. She kept herself from looking back toward him. She knew he was watching her, could feel his eyes on her as surely as if they were his hands. That errant thought made her skin feel suddenly hot, despite the chill of her wet clothes.

The upstairs had been similarly gutted, making it one large, white painted room, with only minimal furniture. The bed was without a frame, sitting on the floor in the middle of the huge space, covered with pristine white sheets and a fluffy down comforter. To one side stood a table and chair; against the wall stood a series of wire baskets filled with black cloth.

His clothes, of course. What else could she put on, unless she had the sudden urge to drape herself in a bed sheet like a toga? The notion of wearing his bedclothes struck her as extremely unwise, and she simply grabbed a soft, black sweatshirt and headed into the bathroom.

At least the bathroom was still partitioned off, the plumbing and fixtures elderly and rust-stained. She stripped off her soaked sweater, rubbing herself dry with the thick maroon towels she found before pulling his sweatshirt over her head.

It smelled like laundry detergent and fabric softener, she told herself, as it settled around her chilled body, against her breasts, with cloudlike softness. There was no reason why she should feel she'd committed an unbearably intimate act. She looked at herself in the cracked, wavering mirror as she toweled her hair, and for a moment she was still, mesmerized by her reflection.

Normally she was an ordinary enough woman, reasonably attractive if you weren't too demanding. Her honey-colored hair usually hung straight around her face, but now it was tousled, ruffled from rain and the towel. Her unremarkable blue eyes looked huge, shadowed, apprehensive. As if she were waiting for something momentous to happen and wasn't sure if she was going to like it.

"Absurd," she said out loud, trying to finger comb her hair back into submission. She wasn't about to use Sebastian's brush—there was a limit to the intimacies she could withstand. She made a face at her haunted reflection. The damnable thing about it was that Sebastian Brand was absolutely right. She *did* have a crush on him, one worthy of an anxious adolescent and not a woman getting dangerously close to thirty.

She would go downstairs and behave calmly, reasonably, drink her coffee and make small talk. She could convince him that her feelings toward him were cool and professional—even if she couldn't convince herself.

She could hear him moving about downstairs, and the scent of coffee was practically aphrodisiacal, particularly combined with the unexpected smell of wood smoke. She was heading back down when she noticed a closet at the top of the stairs.

It was the only part of the interior that hadn't been touched. The section of wall was a grungy, industrial green, the muddy brown door pitted and scarred. Emma stared at it for a moment, then moved across the upper landing, away from the stairs, and put her hand on the old, cracked ceramic doorknob.

It was cool beneath her fingers. And firmly locked. She pulled back, slightly shocked at her own nosiness, and started back down the stairs at something akin to a run. Only to find Sebastian standing at the bottom, watching her.

There was no question that he'd seen her try the closet door. There was no way she could excuse such a shocking invasion of a person's privacy, nor understand it in the first place.

But she could always try.

"Find anything interesting?" he asked, his voice cool and clipped.

He'd stripped down to a worn black T-shirt and black jeans, and his feet were bare. His mane of black hair was damp and pulled away from his face, and he looked still and dangerous. And dangerously beguiling.

Might as well brazen it out, she thought. "What do you keep in the locked closet?"

"My dead wives, of course," he replied, not missing a beat. "What did you expect?"

"I'd forgotten you were in *Bluebeard*," she said.

"I thought you didn't see my movies."

"You were up for an Oscar. I remember thinking how surprising it was for a horror actor to be nominated."

"I'm very good," he said softly. And there was no reason to think there was any hidden meaning in his words.

Except for the way he was looking at her. In the dimly lit hallway they stood in the shadows, but his silvery gray eyes rested on her face with an unreadable intensity. She waited, she didn't know for what, and then he turned away. "Come and get your coffee," he said, and her priorities immediately realigned themselves.

She followed his dark, barefoot figure as he padded through the starkly furnished downstairs area. There was a new, overstuffed white sofa at an angle to the old fireplace, a glass-topped white table with four chairs, and piles of books and magazines all over the place. And absolutely nothing else.

The kitchen was against one wall, a row of white cabinets, a hot plate and a microwave. Two white mugs sat on the Formica counter, and Emma could see the steam rise.

"I put some brandy in it. You looked as if you needed it," he said, reaching for the mugs and handing one to her.

It was warm between her cold hands. She knew she should move away from him, ask him where the phone was so she could call for a taxi, a tow truck, for any kind of help or escape from someone she didn't want to leave. She should at least have walked back toward the fireplace when she was feeling chilled—yet paradoxically hot—and confused as she looked up into his mesmerizing silver eyes.

She took a sip. It was strong and wonderful, and she could feel the brandy curl its way down her spine. "It's very nice," she said weakly.

He took the coffee from her hand and set it on the counter, his movements slow and gracefully deliberate. He set his own beside it, and then he put his hands on either side of her face, cupping it as he looked down into her eyes. He shook his head slightly, and he said something under his breath, something she couldn't understand, something that sounded like "fool." And she didn't know if he meant himself. Or her.

And then it didn't matter, because he kissed her. She'd known he was going to, ever since he brought her into the house, and she'd been waiting for it, longing for it, dreading it.

It wasn't what she'd expected. His lips brushed against hers lightly, and her eyes fluttered closed, shutting the velvet darkness around her. His lips touched hers again, lingered, pressed. And then his mouth opened against hers, his hands tilted her face beneath his, and she could taste brandy and coffee on his tongue.

She'd never been kissed like that. With that much longing and restraint and carefully leashed passion. He kissed her as an artist might paint a picture, delicately, powerfully, thoroughly, so that all she could do was stand there and tremble in helpless response.

She brought her hands up to touch him, and despite the fact that his hands were cradling her face so gently, the iron hard tension in his tightly muscled arms was shocking. The moment her fingers touched him, touched the smooth, hard flesh of his biceps, he broke away, stepping back into the shadows, leaving her suddenly alone.

He picked up his mug and drained it like a man drinking poisoned hemlock. "The tow truck's here," he said abruptly.

"I didn't call..."

"I did."

"Oh." Her palms were damp and trembling. The dimly lit room kept his expression from her, but it served her, as well. "They were very prompt."

"I told them to be."

She smiled wryly. "I imagine you did." She was beyond nervousness, beyond confusion. Walking directly toward him, she reached over and took her abandoned cup of coffee. He flinched for a moment, as if he'd thought she might touch him, and the wary set of his lean, strong body reminded her of some wild jungle animal, part hunter, part prey.

She drained her own mug with far less respect than such a delicious brew deserved, then handed it to him, waiting for him to reach out for it, giving him no choice. Her mouth felt damp, bruised, burning, but she resisted the urge to touch it, resisted the urge to let her gaze linger on his mouth. "Thank you for your hospitality," she said with mock politeness.

He couldn't very well respond with the standard reply of "Any time." He simply nodded, leaning back against the counter, watching her out of hooded eyes.

Sebastian didn't move when he heard the front door close behind her. He didn't move when the muffled roar of the tow truck signalled its departure, presumably with Emma Milsom inside. He'd had to guarantee payment to get them out to such a disreputable neighborhood on such short notice, but it had been worth it. If the truck hadn't arrived when it had, if he'd kissed her again, he would have been lost.

He closed his eyes for a moment, hoping to close out the memory of her startled, expressive face. Instead she swam even more vividly before his eyes. He couldn't begin to understand the impact she had on him, an impact so powerful it overrode his better judgment, his iron self-control. Once he'd realized the inexplicable power she had over him, he'd done his best to defuse it. To warn her away.

Of course, it wasn't going to work if he told her to keep away from him and then kissed her.

Pushing himself away from the counter, he reached for the brandy bottle and his empty mug. And then, like a fool, he set it down, reaching for her mug instead and splashing liquor into it. Maybe he was going to have to resign himself to the fact that where Emma Milsom was concerned, he was going to be a fool. He would have to hope he could scare her away. Otherwise there was no hope for either of them.

And bringing the mug to his mouth, he deliberately set his mouth to the place where hers had been.

The old theatre was still and silent when Emma let herself in through the back alleyway. It was just as she'd left it—the bright ghost light burning in the center of the bare stage, the place quiet, dusty, deserted. The glare of the solitary light bulb sent eerie shadows through the theatre, making it seem ghostly indeed, and Emma shivered.

She'd lost all track of time. It had to be well past midnight, but her watch had stopped working several days ago, and she hadn't had either the time or the money to get a new one.

She glanced up the flights of metal stairs to the fourth floor storerooms. Right at that moment the thought of the clean white sheets and comfy mattress at the hotel was downright hypnotic. Even that ever-present hotel smell of stale cigarettes covered by carpet freshener would have seemed like perfume at that moment.

It was a little late to change her mind. She'd checked out, and all her worldly possessions, including a brand-new sleeping bag and wide piece of foam rubber, were upstairs, waiting for her. She'd made her decision. Now she had to live with it.

It took her hours to make herself a comfortable space. Old scenery was piled against the walls, props and furniture stacked this way and that. She'd opened one window, letting in the rain and chilly breeze, which swept through the room, banishing some of the cobwebs, some of the ghosts. She was too tired to go back down the four flights to the dressing room showers. Instead, she fell exhausted on her new sleeping bag, crawling into it with a weary, blissful sigh. Sebastian's soft black sweatshirt hugged her body; the imprint of his mouth remained on hers. He was absolutely right, she knew that without question. She needed to keep her distance, for her own sake if not for his.

Although she wasn't quite sure why he needed to keep his distance. Unless he simply disliked her. While half of his actions suggested that he found her tiresome, the other half made it clear he didn't.

If she had any sense, though, she would ignore her own helpless attraction. She didn't need to get involved with a man who clearly didn't want any kind of involvement. It would only lead to frustration and heartbreak. He probably had some nice woman waiting for him back in England. No, scratch that. Given his charming manner, he probably had an absolute witch waiting for him back in England. They deserved each other.

No, she would be strong-minded and independent and forget all about her attraction to Sebastian Brand. After all, she was hardly going to end up with a movie star, even one with Sebastian's peculiar specialty. Movie stars didn't fall in love with accountants.

Still, a thought danced through her mind as she drifted into sleep, the man did know how to kiss.

For three days she managed to avoid Sebastian. It was simple enough once she set her mind to it. She woke up at dawn every day, making her way down to the dressing rooms for her morning shower, then out to the closest fast-food restaurant for a prefab breakfast loaded with cholesterol and coffee that was both hot and full of caffeine and had nothing else to recommend it. She was busy in the front office by the time the first workers arrived, and by the time Teddy and the actors straggled in she managed to be so involved with trying to deal with Teddy's creative bookkeeping that she hardly noticed when Sebastian's dark shadow passed her door.

She should have done something about returning his sweatshirt. She'd discovered when she washed it that its cloudlike comfort was no illusion; she knew enough from her previous yuppie life-style to know the designer's name and know this particular piece wasn't from the bargain rack.

Of course, he hadn't done anything about the sweater she'd left behind in his bathroom. She hadn't even remembered it for several days. Of course, it gave her the perfect excuse to go in search of him, to manage a casual conversation. Instead, she decided she didn't need that particular sweater.

"Emma, darling." Teddy breezed into her office late Friday afternoon. Teddy seldom walked into a room, he entered with some bit of stage business. Breezing tended to be one of his favorites, though lounging into her presence was also part of his current repertoire.

"Yes, Teddy?" she said patiently.

"I wondered where you've been recently."

"Right here, Teddy."

"I don't mean during the day. I trust you implicitly, Emma. That's why I hired you. I know you can keep things in order, even when you're dealing with someone as hopelessly disorganized as I am." He gave her a disarming smile that left Emma unmoved. Teddy could organize anything he damned well pleased if it suited his purposes.

"I do my best," she said in a neutral tone.

"Such a good little soldier," Teddy cooed. "Where have you been sleeping? With Sebastian?"

It would have helped things, Emma thought later, if she hadn't blushed. It was hard to be convincing about her lack of interest if she blushed at the very thought of sleeping with him.

"No, Teddy," she said, ignoring the heat in her cheeks, hoping vainly that for once Teddy would be unobservant.

"Then why are you blushing?"

So much for hope. "Because it's an embarrassing question, considering that he doesn't even like me."

"You were at his house three nights ago."

"Teddy!" She sat back in shock. "Are you spying on me?"

"Don't be absurd, darling, I really don't care that much," he said coolly. "I simply like to know where I can find my assistant when I need her. Inspiration doesn't follow a nine-to-five schedule, you know."

"I'm not sleeping with Sebastian Brand, Teddy," she said patiently. "I've simply found a place to stay, on my own," she emphasized, "that's a little more affordable."

"I told you that you could stay in the penthouse with me. There's more than enough room."

There wouldn't be enough room in the state of Texas for Teddy Winters and her, but she was smart enough not to tell him that. "I'm fine, Teddy. And I'm afraid I can't be on call twenty-four hours a day. I'll be here from early morning to as late as you want at night, but after that my time is my own."

Teddy's face went utterly still for a moment, his slightly protruding eyes bulging even more. And then that flash of temper was gone and he was all affable charm once more. "Certainly, dear heart. That's what I came to talk to you about. Could you see if the workmen have done something about the stage lifts yet? We've got scenery coming in, and I want to make sure we're going to be able to move it into place. And there are some reporters coming by later. They probably want another crack at Sebastian, so we'll leave that up to you. Maybe this time he'll agree, seeing as it's you that's asking."

"I'm not asking him for a thing," Emma said sharply. "He hasn't talked to reporters in his entire career, so I doubt he's about to change his mind. When do you want me to check on the lifts?"

"Now, if you don't mind. Sebastian's got several entrances on them, and he was expressing some concern."

She didn't bother to consider why the task suddenly seemed more appealing because she was doing it for Sebastian rather than Teddy. That was a dangerous train of thought, one she usually chose to avoid. "I'll let you know," she said, rising.

"Bless you, dear," Teddy said, blowing her an airy kiss as she went. "Watch your step."

During the three days of her residence Emma had gotten to know the old theatre very well indeed. She knew exactly where the numbered lifts were, right down to their frayed ropes. As far as she knew, no one had worked on them as yet, but she had no objections to climbing down the wooden stairs to check them out. She would have to find Teddy and report her findings, of course, since he wanted to know immediately. And he would certainly be back on stage, the one place she'd avoided so assiduously.

Opening the narrow door to the basement, she flicked on the inadequate electric light. It was about time she allowed herself a small taste of Sebastian's dangerous presence. To prove to herself that she could be immune to him if she tried hard enough. Surely she was strong enough to take the plunge.

Peering through the darkness, she stepped forward onto the first rickety step, which she'd traversed many times before. With a sickening crack it split beneath her, and she felt herself hurtling forward into the darkness.

CHAPTER FOUR

She seemed to float in a dreadful, timeless moment, suspended over the inky blackness of the basement, heading inexorably toward the cement floor thirty feet below. And then suddenly, shockingly, she stopped, slamming up against a lower section of stairs.

She was sobbing quietly, helpless little sounds of fear, as she slowly began to reorient herself. Somehow during her fall she'd managed to catch hold of the sturdy railing, and she was clinging desperately, even as her bruised body rested safely on the remaining stairs.

It took her an eternity to release her death grip, to pull herself into a sitting position, where she sat huddled against the old brick wall, waiting for the tremors to pass. When she was finally able to move she did so very carefully, edging down the remaining stairs. To her surprise they remained firm, not even swaying as she made her way to the bottom.

Her knees buckled beneath her when she reached the cement floor, and she sank down with a groan of pain. Her jeans were ripped at the left knee, her ankle ached abominably, and her side hurt, but apart from that she appeared to be intact.

She sat back on the floor, taking deep, calming breaths. It was odd—she'd never thought of herself as accident-prone, but this was the second time in three days that she'd almost been hurt. The first accident could have happened to anyone. The workmen had moved the protective scaffolding from a large hole in the lobby floor, and the lights had been out. She'd noticed it moments before she would have tumbled down, and it was sheer luck she'd been more alert than usual. Otherwise her close call today would have been moot.

It was all Sebastian's fault, she decided, pulling her wits about her. If she wasn't so obsessed with the man she would pay more attention to where she was putting her feet. The theatre was old, in the midst of major renovations, and if she didn't start thinking with her head instead of her heart, she was going to end up with a broken leg—or worse.

She could see from her vantage point that no one had touched the stage lifts. She hadn't really expected that they had. She'd come on a wild goose chase that had almost ended in disaster. Next time, she would simply ask the workmen.

The measured tread of footsteps echoed overhead, and she heard Sebastian's voice, crystal clear even through the old oak stage, floating down to her. She knew the play well enough to know they were at the climactic murder scene. He was stalking Coral across the stage, and moments from now they would be on the stage bed, where the dance of love Teddy had choreographed would turn into a dance of death. She didn't want to sit there and listen.

Besides, someone might come in search of her, make the same misstep and not end up in one piece. She needed to get out of the basement and get that door boarded up until the workmen could repair the stairs.

The matching set of stairs on the opposite side of the basement was sturdy and safe, and it only took her twelve minutes to climb the one flight. By the time she reached the top she was covered with sweat, her hands trembling, her knee aching abominably.

She could see the stage from her vantage point. Sebastian was kneeling over Coral's prostrate body, and the scene was frozen in time and horror.

And then he looked up and saw her. His eyes narrowed, and he was off the bed, coming toward her so quickly she couldn't escape.

"What the hell happened to you?" he demanded, catching her shoulders as she tried to turn away.

"I fell. The stairs on the right side of the stage are in danger of collapsing." She squirmed, but his hands held her firmly. "I need to speak to the workmen," she said sharply. "I don't want anyone else to get hurt."

"Where are you hurt?" He released his tight grip, only to thread his long fingers through her hair, delicately probing. "Did you hit your head, lose consciousness...?"

She was able to yank herself away, simply because she knew she wouldn't be able to bear it if he kept touching her like that. When she wanted, needed, him to touch her. "I'm absolutely fine," she said firmly. "I just skinned my knee."

"What's happened?" Teddy loomed up behind them.

"Emma's had an accident," Sebastian said, keeping his hands away now, though his silvery gray eyes were touching her instead.

Teddy's reaction was inexplicably extreme. "Darling!" he cried, pushing Sebastian out of the way.

"Didn't I warn you...?" He let the words trail off meaningfully, and it took a moment for Emma to comprehend what he was suggesting.

"Don't be an idiot, Teddy," she said shortly, ignoring the fact that he was ostensibly her employer. Since she'd yet to see a paycheck, and doubted whether her meager salary was going to be considered a high priority, she didn't care if he took offense.

Teddy wasn't a man to be easily offended, however. "I'm taking you to the doctor's office," he said. "I want to make sure you're all right."

"What's happened?" Coral came up behind them, her pretty face creased in worry.

"Not a thing," Emma said, wanting to scream. "I fell on a broken stair, but I'm perfectly fine, and if you'll all go back to work, you'd allow me to get on with my job."

"I don't like it," Teddy said ominously, keeping his worried gaze on Emma's face.

It was a good thing he didn't know about yesterday's close call, she thought wearily. He'd already jumped to enough conclusions for one day.

"I don't like it, either," Sebastian said. "Who are those people?"

Emma turned, looking to the three determined people heading toward them. She didn't need to see the camera to know they were from the local press. She could feel Sebastian stiffen in fury behind her as the photographer raised his camera and aimed it straight at them.

She moved fast, considering that her knee had stiffened considerably, crossing the expanse of stage and shoving the camera down just as he was about to take his first photo. It was a lucky thing for her pocketbook that the photographer used a neck-strap, or the blastedly expensive thing would have smashed on the floor.

"No pictures," she said sweetly. "How did you people get back here?"

"The front door was open," a sharp-faced, too-pretty woman said, moving past her. "We left word we were coming, and we assumed unlocking the door was your way of welcoming us. You can't ignore the media, Mr. Winters," she said, moving past Emma as if she didn't exist.

"I wouldn't think of ignoring the media," Teddy said smoothly, flashing his most effective smile. "We just have certain rules about this production, and..."

She'd already moved past him, homing in on her original target, and Emma found herself clenching her fists. "Mr. Brand, surely you can see how harmless we are. A few words, a few photos, now what would that cost you?" She was speaking in a charming, breathless purr, and was so close to him her generous breasts were almost pressed against him. She was quite abominably beautiful, Emma thought miserably, hating her. She didn't think she could stand it if Sebastian touched the woman.

Sebastian reached out and put his hands on the reporter's shoulders, just as he had with Emma. But in this case he simply spun the woman around and gave her an ungracious shove. And then he stalked away, not even giving her the benefit of the single word, "no."

The photographer beside Emma once more lifted his camera and she smacked it out of his hand without thinking.

"Lady," the man snarled. "Do you realize what this camera costs?"

"I don't give a damn. You try to take another picture and I'll make you eat it," she said fiercely.

She thought she heard Sebastian's muffled laugh from far away, but she couldn't be sure. He was nowhere in sight—she must have imagined it.

"Gentlemen," Teddy said expansively, spreading his arms wide. "And lady," he added, winking at the disgruntled woman, "the rest of us are more than happy to cooperate. I wouldn't be surprised if Miss Aubrey and Mr. Beauchamps would be willing to do a photo session for you, and I assure you, they're both much better looking than the reclusive Mr. Brand."

He was charming them with his usual ease. Emma watched him weave his spell with awe as they moved away, forgetting her existence.

She limped back to her office, stopping off on the way to warn the workmen to block off the staircase. The coffeepot was filled with black sludge, but she needed it quite badly. She was still shaken up by her fall. And even more shaken up by Sebastian's touch.

"How are you doing?" Geoffrey poked his tawny head inside the door, his handsome face wary.

Emma smiled, some of the tension leaving her. Here was one man with no hidden agenda. "I'm fine. I just took a bad tumble, but no bones broken, no stitches needed, no concussion or any of those nasties. I need to watch where I'm going."

He moved into the room, his reading glasses perched on the end of his perfect nose. "You've always struck me as a woman who knows where she's going," he said. "Can I get you anything? Bandages? A doctor? A shot of brandy?"

She thought about the last time she'd tasted brandy. On Sebastian's mouth. She shook her head. "Honestly, I'm fine. Thank you for asking."

"Not that I wasn't concerned myself," he said diffidently. "We all count on you around here to keep things on an even keel. But I was sent to make sure you were okay."

Emma smiled. "Tell Coral thanks."

"It wasn't Coral." He moved over to the coffeepot, poured himself a cup and took a sip without shuddering. "He's not as bad as he seems, you know."

"I don't know who you're talking about," Emma said, lying.

"Don't you?" Geoff smiled sweetly, with the expression that made young girls swoon. "He's not an easy man and never has been. You've probably realized that by now. But he's also a damned good friend, and one of the few people Coral and I really count on in this world. We wouldn't be here if it weren't for him. We've learned to accept him on his own terms, and it's been richly worth it for us. It might be the same for you." He smiled again, a rueful smile this time. "No, scratch that. I don't expect it would be the same relationship for you at all. Anyway, that's all I came to say. Just try to keep an open mind and a tolerant heart. Don't jump to conclusions or start believing what people say."

"Geoff..."

He held up a restraining hand. "Enough for now. I'm really not cut out to be a matchmaker, but I thought I'd do my bit. See you."

She reached for her coffee, but her hand slipped, and black sludge spread all over the papers. Leaping up, she made a vain effort at stemming the mess, then gave in. "I'm out of here," she announced to the carpenter standing in the hallway. "And if anyone asks, I'm not coming back until they're all gone."

"Yes, ma'am," the carpenter said nervously, eyeing her as a man might eye a hungry polar bear. And a moment later she was out in the cool, crisp air of a St. Bart autumn day, limping slightly as she headed down the street.

"I don't mean to interfere, Sebastian," Coral said in her most casual voice.

"But you're about to," he filled in for her, tossing his notebook aside. "Control that evil urge. I don't need advice or suggestions, even well-meaning ones."

"Sweetheart, you're like a dog with a sore paw," she persisted. "I've known you long enough and well enough to realize you've got a problem, and I want to encourage you to do something about it."

"Like what?" he said warily, knowing he was just encouraging her.

"Give in. Honestly, darling, it's just so damned obvious. She's not very good at hiding her feelings. She stares at you like a lovesick calf, and you storm around like Mr. Rochester or something equally Gothic, and it's all so silly. Why don't you just go to bed with her?"

"Coral," he said. "The next time we rehearse the murder scene, I can always be a bit more enthusiastic."

"Save your scare tactics for Emma—they seem to work on her."

"They do, don't they?" he said gloomily.

"And I can't imagine why you're trying to scare her. If a smart, pretty, sweet woman has the good taste to fall in love with you, you might at least be gentlemanly enough to acknowledge it. What harm can it do for you to indulge her fantasies?"

"You don't know what you're talking about, Coral. Cease and desist."

There was a pause. "Oh, my heavens," she breathed. "I don't believe it."

"Don't believe what?"

"She's not the only one in love, is she? The mighty Sebastian has fallen!" she crowed in utter delight.

"I *will* strangle you," he said in a reflective voice. "I'll tell them it was an accident, we were simply rehearsing too realistically and..."

"For heaven's sake, what's the problem? She loves you, you love her, so why don't you do the deed and get it over with?"

"Coral, you never cease to amaze me. Your vulgarity is matched only by your rich fantasy life. I am in love with absolutely no one but myself. Love is an inconvenient emotion, much overrated and a complete waste of time."

"Sebastian." She put her hand on his arm. "Love is never convenient. And it is never, ever a waste."

He leaned back in the chair, eyeing her morosely. "I'm not interested in advice to the lovelorn. Go away, Coral. Maybe Geoff's interested in your fantasy life."

"What am I interested in?" Geoff asked, climbing up onto the stage.

"Sebastian's being bloody-minded again," Coral said. "Where were you?"

"Checking on Emma for the bloody-minded one. She's fine, Sebastian."

Coral turned accusingly. "You don't care about her, and yet you send my husband to check on her? How chivalrous."

"Put a sock in it, Coral." Sebastian rose, striding toward the edge of the stage. "Where is she?"

"Gone out. I saw her leaving as I headed back here. I imagine she's gone home for the day."

"I don't think so," Sebastian said. "Where's Winters? Still trying to seduce the media?"

"I imagine so. You know, you might lighten up a bit. It wouldn't hurt you to give an interview every now and then.... Where are you going?"

"Out of here. I'm not in the mood to work."

Coral let out a gasp of dramatized shock. "And this from the hardest working man in theatre today? The man who'd rather work than sleep? It must be love."

"Bugger off, Coral."

"You, too, darling," she said sweetly.

There was no sign of Emma in the back of the theatre, but he hadn't expected to find her. He was more intent on checking out the basement stairs. There was something about her accident that struck a chord deep within, an uneasy, dissonant chord. He didn't like accidents. Ever since that woman had been killed on the last Slasher Charlie movie he'd been hypersensitive about safety. He didn't want anyone else getting hurt. He most particularly didn't want Emma Milsom getting hurt.

Damn Coral and her sense of humor. It cut too close to the bone, and he'd known her and Geoff both too long and too well to shut them out, to dismiss their well-meaning interference with his usual icy condescension. No one condescended to Coral and got away with it.

But right now he didn't want to think about Coral. He wanted to think about Emma. Not about her long legs and her delicious mouth. About the fact that she'd taken a nasty tumble that could have been even worse. And whether or not it really had been an accident.

It was midnight when Emma finally left the movie theatre. Never before in her life had she spent more than three hours in a movie theatre. She'd been sitting in a sagging seat in the middle of the decaying splendor of the St. Bart Bijou, and she'd seldom seen anything less jewellike in her life. It had been on a whim that she'd paid her meager two dollars and walked in eight hours earlier, but she hadn't been able to resist. A marathon of Sebastian Brand movies, from the first, notoriously low-budget Slasher Charlie movies, up to his highly acclaimed recent films, *Bluebeard* and *Dybbuk.*

She'd expected to be scornful. She'd even accepted the fact that she might be a little uneasy. She'd never expected that she would weep.

The Slasher Charlie movies were sinfully, morbidly funny. *Bluebeard* was impressive. But *Dybbuk,* his latest, was both the most impassioned and the most terrifying. She watched his eerie silver eyes, the only recognizable part of him behind all that makeup. And when she could finally take no more she left, halfway through the final feature, shaken and confused.

The streets were deserted, shining with the wet, chill rain, as she walked the few blocks back to the old theatre. She tried not to look over her shoulder for the caped figure of Slasher Charlie. Her reason was simple: she knew if she looked, he would be there.

There was no sign of life at the old theatre, for which she breathed a temporary sigh of relief. She wasn't in the mood to do battle with Teddy. And she certainly wasn't in any state to run into Sebastian Brand.

She'd known from the beginning she didn't want to see his movies. Why hadn't she listened to her own better judgment? She was gullible. When she saw Sebastian's silver eyes alight with murderous madness, she believed it. When she saw his beautiful hands wielding a butcher knife, she believed it.

Those scenes haunted her as she made her way slowly up the metal stairs. But what haunted her more was the brief, explicit, astonishingly erotic love scene from *Bluebeard.*

"Fool," she said out loud as she reached the top floor. And then she remembered that had been his very word, right before he'd kissed her.

She'd left the window open in the storeroom, and she limped across the room to shut it before dropping down on her sleeping bag. She needed a long hot bath, to soak the stiffness away from her knee, but the dressing rooms at the old theatre boasted only rusting tin showers. She was lucky they were that advanced. She needed to pop some aspirin, make her way back down those rickety stairs and hope that no one had eaten the meager stash of food she kept in the old refrigerator in the front office. Teddy had a habit of devouring anything that wasn't nailed down; she could only hope he'd been too busy charming the reporters to get into her chocolate mint cookies. He'd probably served them to that wretched woman who'd leered at Sebastian.

She leaned over and switched on the reading lamp that sufficed for illumination in her attic apartment. She was sitting on something bulky, and she yanked it out from underneath her, then dropped it with a gasp.

It was her sweater. The one she'd left in Sebastian Brand's bathroom three days ago. And there was only one way he could have gotten up to her secret haven, the place she had thought was safe and remote from everyone.

Unconsciously her fingers caressed the cotton knit, then tightened. She needed to put him out of her mind. If she didn't, she was going to have the most terrifying nightmares. Or, even worse, erotic dreams that outstripped anything she'd ever experienced in real life. That one short scene in the movie had possessed more sensuality than her entire sexual history. It was no wonder she was obsessed with the man.

Once admitted, it wasn't quite so bad. It wasn't true love. It wasn't anything more than your common, garden-variety obsession, intense, unhealthy, but most likely short-lived. Once she left his hypnotizing presence she would be free of it, leaving it only an embarrassing memory.

At least, she certainly hoped so. Maybe she'd spent too much time on this project. Teddy seemed to be bouncing from wall to wall, seldom settling on any kind of consistent work. The three principal actors worked hard, but with little guidance, and the supporting roles hadn't even been cast yet. The production was already over budget, given Teddy's grandiose remodelling scheme, and she hadn't been paid a cent.

She would leave. It would be that simple. Tomorrow—if it wasn't raining, of course—she would load her M.G. with all her worldly possessions and drive off without a backward glance. Nothing would be left to remind her of a week spent in a dreamworld except for Sebastian's designer sweatshirt. She would part with her car before she'd give that up.

The ghost light was glowing brightly in the center of the deserted stage, sending out its bright glare into all the corners of the auditorium. The few pieces of staging cast dark shadows across the floorboards, the table, the straight chairs, the iron bed. She skirted that area, heading toward the women's dressing room and the rusty shower, where she proceeded to use every ounce of hot water the pathetic system could put out.

After towelling herself off, she pulled on the silk chemise she still had from her previous elegant lifestyle and wrapped an oversize men's flannel shirt around her for warmth. Victoria's Secret and L.L. Bean made an odd combination, but it soothed the inconsistencies in her soul. The shirt had belonged to an old boyfriend; it was huge and soft and baggy and it hung to her knees, and it was a ridiculous counterpoint to the fuchsia silk chemise. It was a good thing no one was going to be seeing her.

Her bare feet made no noise as she began to skirt the stage once more. She had an almost superstitious avoidance of center stage—she wasn't quite sure why. If she was going to make it through the night without giving in to nightmares, she needed to get over those stupid notions. Forcing herself, she took a right turn, moving directly across the stage toward the narrow metal staircase.

It was then that she heard the noise. The men's dressing rooms were on the opposite side of the theatre, well away from the shower. She hadn't had the faintest suspicion that she wasn't alone in the old building.

She knew otherwise now. The dim glow of light cast a circle out into the darkened hallway, and the faint clink of noise was unmistakable.

She didn't move, frozen in her footsteps, listening. There was no sound of conversation, no laughter. Whoever was still there in the old theatre was there alone.

Teddy's warnings came to her, and her knee throbbed. Slasher Charlie sped through her mind, followed by the elegant slither of Bluebeard, the horrifying despair of the Dybbuk. Alone in the midnight theatre, the monsters were all around her, waiting to pounce.

"No," she said, a soft, panicked sound. She could turn and run up the flights of stairs, shoving furniture and old scenery behind her to keep the demons at bay. Except that monsters weren't stopped by old furniture. The only thing that could halt the power of a monster was to confront it.

For a moment her muscles wouldn't obey her. When they did, she moved very slowly, walking the rest of the way across the stage to the semicircle of light emanating from the men's dressing room.

She knew *who* she would find when she reached the door. She just wasn't quite certain *what* she would find. But she couldn't run away in terror, much as part of her longed to. She had to face him. Or she would never be able to face herself.

The dressing room was dim. The wall-length mirror ran above the counter, the light bulbs above mostly burnt out, and he stood in the center, staring in the mirror. And then his eyes, his eerie, silvery gray eyes, met hers, and he turned. And her worst fears were confirmed.

CHAPTER FIVE

Sebastian rose to his full height, staring at her for a wordless moment. He was wearing tight-fitting black pants and nothing else, his chest and feet bare. In one hand was a tube of greasepaint.

Beneath his mane of pitch black hair, his face and chest and arms were streaked with red paint, wide swathes of crimson staining his flesh, streaking across his face. He looked savage and bloody, wild and dangerous. He looked like a monster.

Emma stumbled backward in instinctive panic, pulling the oversize flannel shirt around her body. "You've...you've been experimenting with makeup," she said inanely, knowing she was close to babbling. "Is that what you had in mind for the Monster?"

One of the things that both frightened and enticed her the most about Sebastian was his utter stillness. He didn't say a word for a moment, considering, and then he shrugged. "I was thinking about using green, but the red works better. It looks more like blood." He smiled then, a small, wicked smile, perhaps meant to tease. It merely terrified her.

She took another step backward, knocking against the doorjamb. "Very effective," she said, her voice trembling.

That stillness was back as his smile vanished and his eyes narrowed. "Where were you? I didn't expect you back tonight."

He knew where she was living; she couldn't forget that. The presence of her sweater upstairs was proof enough. "Out," she said. "Why are you still here?"

He set the greasepaint down on the countertop. "Experimenting. I suppose I should simply have taken the makeup home with me, but, as I said, I didn't expect you'd be coming back."

"Would it have made a difference?"

He took a step toward her. "It would have been wiser." He frowned as he took in her barely controlled fear. "Exactly where were you tonight?"

"At the movies."

Sudden comprehension filled his eyes, lover's eyes in the devil's face. "You went to see my movies, didn't you? Should I be flattered?"

"I don't think so."

He took another step. "No," he said softly. "I don't think so, either."

She backed up, out the door, using her hands to guide her, afraid to look away from him. "I think I'd better go...."

"Are you afraid of me, Emma?" he asked, stalking her, his body lithe, sinuous, seductive, in the eerie glare of the ghost light.

"You keep asking me that."

"And you never answer. But you don't need to. Your actions speak louder than words. You're scared to death of me, poor baby. What do you think I'm going to do to you? Rip out your throat like Slasher Charlie? Strangle you like Bluebeard?" He kept moving toward her, a threat in every line of his elegant body.

She came up against something hard and immovable. She didn't dare turn around and look; instead she reached behind her and touched the unmistakable bars of the iron bed. "I'm not afraid of you," she said fiercely.

He'd reached her, looming over her, and he put his hands on either side of her body, grasping the iron bars of the bed, imprisoning her. "Of course you are, poor darling. You're terrified, and you're angry." His mouth hovered close, dangerously close, and his silver eyes were bright in his wildly streaked face. "And you're turned on. Aren't you?" he whispered, his voice low and impossibly seductive.

There was no way she could escape. And no way, standing that close to him, that she could lie. "Yes," she said. "Yes to all three."

She saw the triumph in his eyes. "That embarrasses you, doesn't it? It doesn't fit in with your nice little middle-class perceptions, that sex and fear and anger shouldn't have any connection, and you don't understand what it is you feel about me. You only know you feel it." He reached up, touched his redstreaked forehead, then touched hers, smearing the red paint on her brow. "You feel it here," he said in a harsh whisper. He touched his chest, and she could see the gleam of the red greasepaint on his long, deft fingers. Reaching out, he touched her between the breasts, marking her with the paint. "And you feel it here."

She couldn't move. She was hypnotized by his silver eyes and his fierce will, hypnotized by the obsession she'd been fighting for so long. He'd ruled her life since she'd first seen him—every moment had been spent either thinking about him or forcing herself not to think about him.

And now there was no escape. None that she wanted to take. She didn't even know what he was going to do. After eight hours of sex and death on a Technicolor screen, she no longer knew what to expect. And at that moment it didn't matter. All that mattered was that she would die if he didn't put his hands on her.

"The fact of the matter is, Emma," he whispered, his mouth brushing hers so lightly that she might have imagined it, "I feel the same way. Angry." He pushed his body closer, up against hers, his hips pressing against hers. "Turned on," he said, and there was absolutely no doubt of that. "And quite, quite terrified of you." With that he released the iron bars and pulled her into his arms, imprisoning her against his hard, tense body.

He kissed her then, and she was lost. She reached up, threading her hands through his mane of hair, and opened her mouth beneath his. He groaned deep in his throat, his mouth hard against hers, devouring hers, and there was no tenderness, no gentle seduction, simply a fiery hot need that burned brightly within them both.

He shoved the flannel shirt off her shoulders, pushed the thin straps of the chemise down her arms and pulled her tightly against him. She could feel the makeup against her flesh, the heat of his body burning her breasts, and she slid her hands down to his shoulders, digging in tightly as he suddenly scooped her up in his arms.

He didn't carry her far. The old iron bed was hard beneath them, a prop, not a piece of furniture, but neither of them cared. The glare of the ghost light shone in her eyes, and as Sebastian kneeled over her, a huge, distorted shadow danced on the wall behind them.

He put his hands on her shoulders, holding her in place as he watched her, looking demonic in his makeup, his eyes glittering in the darkness. Her breath felt tight in her chest as she waited for him to move his hands down and touch her breasts.

He didn't. He was straddling her body, his black-clad legs another sort of prison, and the soft, supple material of his pants left no doubt at all of the extent of his need. But still he didn't move, didn't touch her, and she felt the tension build in her until she thought she might scream.

"What is it you want from me?" she asked finally, when she could form the words. Her breath felt tight, strangled in her chest; heated desire had pooled in her belly, between her thighs, and she was already far more aroused than she had been in her entire life.

He was watching her out of faintly hooded eyes. And then he released her shoulders and touched her face, gently, pushing her hair away from her eyes. "Fear is a powerful aphrodisiac," he said. "But only up to a point. I want you to tell me I don't really frighten you. That you trust me."

God, but she wanted to. Lying there beneath him, his hand incredibly gentle on her face, she wanted to tell him anything he wanted to hear. She could tell him that she was obsessed with him. That she wanted him. That for whatever perverse reason, she was crazily, improbably in love with him.

But she couldn't tell him that he didn't frighten her. She couldn't lie. He scared her half to death.

He waited, still, eerily patient, until he realized she wasn't going to speak. And then darkness closed over his face, along with a kind of bleak despair.

"Have it your way, then," he muttered beneath his breath, taking his hand from her face, and for one moment the worst terror she knew was that he might leave her without finishing what he'd started.

Instead, he reached down and pulled the chemise from her body, throwing it away from them. He caught her arms and pulled her up against him, and there was anger in his raw kiss, anger and a passion too deep to override.

She clutched his arms, and the greasepaint on his biceps was slick and slippery beneath her fingers. Still she clung, overwhelmed by the power of his kiss. His tongue drove deeply, roughly, in her mouth, and she struggled for a moment, frightened.

He broke the kiss, pulling back only slightly, and he was breathing heavily as he stared down at her. "Isn't that what you wanted?" he asked. "A fantasy screw with the movie star? A little rough, a little scary, and maybe you'll be able to get off for the first time in your life."

The accuracy of that particular thrust made her eyes jerk open. "Damn you," she said. "Let me go."

"This is the way you wanted it, sweetheart. No hearts and flowers. Have a nice roll in the hay with a monster and still get to wake up in one piece in the morning."

"Sebastian," she pleaded, her voice raw with pain. "Don't do this. Don't do it to me, and don't do it to yourself."

He caught her chin in his hand, the fingers long and hard and firm on her tender flesh. "Don't say a word,

Emma. It's too late. Since you won't say what I want to hear, don't say a damned thing.'' And he kissed her into silence, his mouth hard on hers.

He wasn't going to hurt her; she knew that without question. He was trying to push her into sending him away, to stop what was spiralling out of control. And that was the one thing she couldn't do.

Instead, she slid her arms around his neck and kissed him back with all the fierce passion that had lain dormant for so long in her heart.

She could feel his start of shock. And then he slid down, his body covering hers, his fullness resting at the juncture of her thighs, clothed heated flesh against naked vulnerability, as his mouth gentled on hers, almost of its own volition. And then he was wooing her, teasing her, calling her along on a dance of desire on the old iron bed in the darkened theatre.

He moved his hands down to cup her breasts, and she whimpered in pleasure, a sound that turned to a strangled squeak when his mouth followed.

She arched up against him, but his hands were deft, soothing, as he rolled to his side, taking her with him. He was so hot, so hard, that she wanted to burrow against him, to hide from the overwhelming sensations he was arousing in her. But there was no haven, no peace, in his body. He ran his hand down her stomach, moving it between her thighs, and she reached out in sudden panic to stop him. He was moving too fast, and not fast enough.

Catching her restraining hand in his, he placed it squarely on the front of his pants, on the pulsing hardness that burned beneath the supple material. And she was too shocked, too fascinated, to do more than touch him, her fingertips discovering the shape of him beneath the cloth.

He was touching her, too, with a deftness that spoke of too much experience. The fires of arousal were burning, flaring out of control, and she was ready to go up in flames as he stroked her.

"You like that, don't you, my precious?" he whispered, and there was an edge beneath his passion-drugged voice. He slid his fingers deeper, and she clamped her legs around him, reaction rocketing through her.

He took her hand away from him, and she tried to pull back. He wouldn't let her, kissing her palm, biting the fleshy pad beneath her thumb. "There's a limit, love, to what I can take." He rose up on his knees, stripping off his pants and kicking them away. "And your hands are just a little too effective."

"Isn't that what this is about?" she asked, her voice hoarse and little more than a whisper.

His expression was almost tender. "We're doing this my way," he said. "On my terms."

Except that it wasn't on his terms at all. He wanted her trust, and she couldn't give it to him, couldn't give him the words. But she could show him.

He lay back down on the bed, gloriously aroused, and reached for her. But she had her own agenda, pushing him down, her mouth touching his chest, nipping one flat male nipple, distended in arousal.

The greasepaint tasted slick, oily, beneath her lips, the taste and smell of it just two more factors in the strange eroticism of the moment. She moved her mouth down, past the line where the red paint ended and pale, golden flesh began. And she put her mouth on him, needing to taste him, needing him as intimately as she could have him.

He jerked beneath her in shock, his hands threading through her hair, and for a moment she was terribly afraid he would pull her back. Instead, he held her in place, until she was sweating and trembling with reaction, and he was rigid to the point of bursting.

And then he did pull her away, when she was shaking too hard to resist, hauling her up, rolling her onto her back in the center of the bed, pushing her hands up to the iron bars and wrapping her fingers around them.

In the strange and eerie shadows he looked like a monster, a demon from hell. He looked like a man who would possess her, body and soul, and the moment he did, her safe, comfortable life would end. It would be altered permanently, and she faced that knowledge without flinching, more than ready.

"You're a witch," he said, his voice tight with closely reined passion. "You know that, don't you? You think I scare you? Woman, you scare the hell out of me."

He moved then, sliding between her legs, entering her with a deep, hard thrust that made her arch off the bed, clutching the iron bedstead.

His hands reached out and covered hers, holding tight, as he drove into her. She met him thrust for thrust, trembling, heart shuddering, tears streaking her face, as the dance of desire built higher, hotter, deeper, faster, and she didn't know if she could stand any more of it.

The greasepaint had melted over their bodies as they slid over each other, undulating hips, entwined legs, wrapped in each other. She could feel the explosion approaching, and it frightened her as nothing else had.

"Stop fighting it," he breathed in her ear, his own voice ragged, and she knew he understood her body better than she did. "Stay with me, damn it."

She released the iron bars, turning her hands beneath his above her head. He clasped them, driving his hips against her as his mouth crushed hers, and the fear was gone, burnt away in a flashpoint of cataclysmic proportions as her entire body seemed to arch, shatter and dissolve.

She could feel his immediate response, the strangled cry, the arched rigidity in her arms, but for the first time she was more aware of her own tumultuous reactions than her partner's. She knew she was crying, but beyond that her mind simply refused to work, as her body struggled to regain some semblance of normal functioning.

He lay on top of her, her legs still wrapped tightly around his narrow hips, their hands and arms intertwined. His face was buried in her shoulder, and as her own breathing slowed, she could feel the faint, irregular tremors that still shook his body.

She wanted to cling to him, to wrap her body around him and hold him for eternity. She knew she couldn't. When his muscles tightened in her arms, when he began to pull away, she simply released him, unable to rid herself of the feeling that despite the astounding nature of the last few moments, she had somehow failed him.

He sat up, his back to her, and looked out over the empty auditorium. The greasepaint had run down his back, streaking his flat male buttocks, and she glanced down at her own body. Smeared in red, no part of her left untouched. She reached out to touch him, then let her hand drop as she realized he was reaching for his clothes.

He pulled them on with complete, unself-conscious grace. And then he walked away from her, without a word or a backward glance.

She wasn't certain she believed it. Not until she heard the heavy metal door slam shut moments later did she comprehend that he really had done just that, walked away from her without even acknowledging what they'd just shared.

She looked around her for something to cover herself, but the bare mattress had no covering and her chemise was in shreds. The old flannel shirt lay on the floor at the head of the bed, and she fetched it, her muscles feeling achy and shivery and cramped. She needed to curl up against his fiery warmth. Instead, she felt as if she'd been shoved naked into a blizzard, locked away from the blazing fire.

She was freezing as she wrapped the shirt around her. There was red makeup on it, red makeup all over her hands, in her hair, even on her long legs. She needed to pull herself together, go back and take a shower and wash the paint, and Sebastian Brand, from her body.

She wasn't going to. Not right away. She was too exhausted, too overwhelmed. For now she was simply going to climb back up the stairs to her sleeping bag and crawl inside. And maybe after a few hours' sleep she would be able to comprehend what had just happened to her.

Because she'd been absolutely right to fear him. It had happened. The moment she'd given herself to him absolutely, the woman known as Emma Milsom had ceased to exist. She'd died just as surely as if she'd been murdered by one of Sebastian's monsters. That woman who thought she knew what she wanted from life, who thought she knew who and what she was, had gone. And Emma had no idea who had been left in her place.

"Bitch," Sebastian said, walking in his front door and throwing the old coat he'd filched from the theatre across the hallway. He liked the sound of it, so he said it again, louder.

The house didn't answer. But then, the house was so powerful nothing could touch it, particularly not the misery of one poor human being.

He walked barefoot into the kitchen, opened the brandy bottle and splashed an obscene amount into one of the white mugs. His feet hurt, but he hadn't been able to stand being under the same roof with her long enough to find the rest of his clothes, so he'd walked home through the rain-swept streets of St. Bart barefoot and shirtless, with nothing but an old raincoat for protection.

Because if he *had* stayed, he wouldn't have been able to leave her. And the last thing he wanted or needed was to touch her again. Not when touching her the first time had been even more powerful than his adolescent dreams.

"Damn her," he said out loud, draining the brandy and pouring himself an even more generous refill. He hadn't thought it would hurt. He was used to playing the game. Lord knows he could have a new woman every night, from any class, any background, any physical type, including women a great deal more beautiful than Emma Milsom. They all wanted to sleep with him, to tell themselves they'd bedded the monster and survived.

It had always been the same. Even when he'd been starting out, with that dreadful first Slasher Charlie movie, and Geoff had been doing handsome-young-thing roles before he met Coral. The two of them had shared a flat, but the women hadn't been flocking around handsome Geoff. They'd wanted *him*, and they'd wanted him kinky.

He'd obliged at first. But it had grown old fast, and he'd learned to guard his body as well as his privacy. He knew the rules, and he went into a relationship, or even a brief affair, remembering them. He offered the fantasy. They offered his body temporary surcease.

He just hadn't expected it from Emma. He'd let his own stupid fantasies out. It was this damned house, this damned city. He'd vanquished the monsters, found his own way to chain them, to halt their power.

So they'd found a new way to attack. They couldn't attack him through his head anymore. So they were going through the heart.

Or the groin, he reminded himself savagely. "Damn her," he said, trying to shut out the memory of her vulnerable face, the wide blue eyes that a man could get lost in. He slammed the coffee mug down on the counter with an ominous crack, then headed up the stairs.

He paused outside the dark closet with its horrible secrets locked safely inside. He reached out a hand and touched it, then pulled back. The greasepaint on his fingers left a bloodlike stain on the wood, and he shivered in remembered horror.

He stepped into the shower, scrubbing the makeup from his body, scrubbing the memory of her hands, her mouth, from his flesh. Wishing he could scrub her from his mind as well. And it wasn't until he'd towelled off, finished the bottle of brandy and thrown himself naked on his bed that a sudden, uncomfortable thought struck him.

There was a difference between Emma Milsom and the score of faceless monster groupies who'd wandered in and out of his bed. The other women had wanted him because he frightened them.

Emma had wanted him despite the fact. Her fear of him hadn't turned her on. It simply hadn't interfered with the power that flowed between the two of them. He'd been so quick to condemn, his mind between his legs and nowhere else, that he hadn't stopped to think about anything but her body, wrapped around his.

"Damn her," he said again, pain and frustration washing over him. He didn't want to be alone in his bed, his body still aching for her, his soul aching for her. "And damn me."

CHAPTER SIX

"I don't suppose you have anything I could borrow?" Coral Aubrey appeared behind Emma in the dressing room mirror, a disgusted expression on her small, piquant face. Emma jumped nervously, wrapping her sweater tightly around her body.

"I beg your pardon?"

"I've somehow managed to get red greasepaint all over my butt, and wouldn't you know I'd choose today of all days to wear white?" she asked plaintively, surveying the red-stained portion of her anatomy. "Someone got it smeared all over the stage furniture—I can't imagine how."

Half the lights were out in the women's dressing room, a lucky circumstance, Emma thought, considering that her face was the color of the streaks on Coral's clothes. "I can't imagine, either," she said in a hollow voice, remembering the red stains that hadn't responded to soap and scrubbing. Around her breasts. And low on her stomach.

Coral turned from her perusal to glance at Emma. "Funny," she said, "you sound just like Sebastian. When he isn't fuming, that is."

Sebastian was the last thing Emma wanted to discuss at that moment. "I don't know if I have any extra clothing—particularly ones that will fit you," she said doubtfully, sorting through the backpack that served as her purse, briefcase, and overnight bag combined. "I don't think we're the same size."

"Don't be absurd, darling," Coral said with a laugh. "You're a mile taller and pounds skinnier. If you can find me something comfortable with lots of stretch I should do fine. I'd send Geoff back to the hotel for a change of clothes, but heaven knows what he'd end up bringing back. Probably a lace teddy and riding boots. The man's hopeless."

"I can go."

"Nonsense. I know Teddy treats you like a slavey, but I've seen the office and the sense you've begun to make of it. I don't mean to be condescending, but people like us, artists, are usually quite hopeless when it comes to the practicalities of life. We need sensible people like you to make things work, or we'd all be lost."

"Sensible?" Emma echoed dryly.

"Oh, Lord, that came out all wrong, didn't it? It usually does. I'm just trying to say that I don't undervalue you, even if Teddy does. Why, even Sebastian is quite at sea when it comes to the love of his life."

Emma couldn't resist, even though she knew Coral had dropped that little tidbit deliberately. "The love of his life?"

"You've heard of his repertory company, surely? On the other hand, maybe you haven't, given Sebastian's legendary reticence. It's very small, very experimental, near his home in the Cotswolds. They're really doing marvelous things, and Geoff and I can't wait until we can take some time off and work there. Assuming Sebastian can manage to be practical enough to keep it going." She beamed at her, and it didn't take a great deal of imagination to follow Coral's train of thought.

"Then he needs to hire someone," she said repressively. "Some nice, British, middle-aged male accountant to take care of business."

"I thought *you* might need a job," Coral said, not to be deflected from her primary purpose. "Once this project either dies an early death or takes off. It might be sooner than we all think, given the way things are going around here. Is your passport in order?"

"My passport's up-to-date, not that I have any intention of using it," Emma said repressively, tossing a pair of too-short sweatpants onto the counter, and then her hand encountered the sweater Sebastian had returned to her.

"That'll do," Coral said, reaching in and filching it from Emma's reluctant hands. "So what do you think? Haven't you had enough of Teddy by now? Shall I talk to Sebastian about hiring you?"

"No!" It came out with far more force than Emma had intended. "No," she repeated, a great deal more calmly. "It would be a waste of time."

If she'd hoped for Coral's protestations she was doomed to disappointment. "You're probably right. He's been going around snarling all morning, ever since he saw the newspaper. We'd better wait a couple of days to broach the subject."

"I don't want the subject . . . what paper?"

Coral sighed, pulling her red-stained white sweater over her head and dumping it on the floor. "Those reporters yesterday. Teddy didn't manage to do a very good job at heading them off at the pass, which should come as no surprise. There's a full-page article, complete with pictures, about the jinxed production and how tragic accidents have plagued Sebastian's career, which is just so much rubbish!'' she said quite hotly. "But you know how the press can be. Quite ruthless."

"You said there were pictures?" Emma asked faintly.

"Oh, yes," Coral said, slipping off her white trousers and stepping daintily into Emma's. "Including quite a nice one of you and Sebastian. A little grainy, since it was taken from a covert distance, but rather... how should I put it?"

Utter horror filled Emma, as visions of tabloid newspapers danced in her head. Had someone been in the theatre last night, photographing them as they lay on the bed? "I don't know. How should you put it?"

"Romantic," Coral said firmly. "It was taken right after your accident. His hands are on your shoulders, and you're looking at each other with a delicious intensity. Of course, the article made a great deal of the accident. And your quotes were not exactly...tactful."

"My quotes?" Emma shrieked. "I didn't speak to the reporters, except to tell them to go away."

Coral looked pleased. "I didn't think you had. Nevertheless, you're quoted, in quite nauseating detail, about Sebastian and the accidents, and I'm afraid Sebastian hasn't realized that the remarks attributed to you bear a marked resemblance to some of Teddy's weaker dialogue. So we'd best wait to discuss you coming back to England with him."

"I'm not going back to England with him!" Emma shouted. Knowing, quite suddenly, that there was nothing she wanted more in this life, now that it was impossible.

"Maybe you'll have to follow on a later flight," Coral admitted. "I'll work on it. Thanks for the clothes. I think I look charming." She did a little pirouette in front of the mirror, her gorgeous face alight with gaiety. "Lord, I wish I looked like you. Ten feet tall and all coltish grace. Why couldn't I have been born an American?"

She danced out of the dressing room before Emma could react with anything more than astounded disbelief. Coral was fey, interfering, much too nice, and quite obviously pregnant, a fact which came as a complete surprise to Emma. Teddy obviously had no idea—he was counting on a long run. He was going to have one of his patented temper tantrums when he found out. And Emma had other things to worry about.

She found Sebastian offstage, sitting in one of the sagging auditorium seats, his long legs stretched over the seat in front of him, immersed in a thick manuscript. He was fully aware of her approach, but he didn't look up, didn't in any way acknowledge her.

It had to be the hardest thing she'd ever done in her life to approach him, then stand there patiently while he ignored her, looking down at the hands that had touched her last night. With the faint stain of red greasepaint that he hadn't been able to eradicate.

She couldn't do it. She turned, ready to escape, when he lifted his head, his cold silver gaze impaling and immobilizing her. "Did you want something?" His voice was soft and icy.

She was too tough for this, she told herself, feeling the pain crush down around her heart. He couldn't hurt her like this, not if she didn't let him. "No," she said, starting away.

"Not another quote for the papers?" His taunting voice followed her. "Don't you want to elaborate on last night? I'm sure the papers would eat it up. Or maybe we'll have that installment in tomorrow's edition. Perhaps with accompanying photos, with a strategic black strip placed here and there to accommodate your modesty."

She turned back. "I didn't talk to them," she said fiercely.

His smile was very gentle and completely disbelieving. "Now, why do I find that so hard to believe?"

She should have walked away before her pride and her heart were in shreds. She reached out for him, making one last effort. "Sebastian, I didn't..."

His arm was tense, hot beneath her touch, and the muscles jerked beneath her fingers. She half expected him to yank it away from her, but he didn't; he simply gazed at her out of expressionless eyes. "The problem is, love," he said, in a very gentle voice, "that I don't trust you."

She released him as if burned, her face flaring as he threw her words back at her. It was nothing more than she deserved, and all the more painful because of it. She rose, stumbling backward as she tried to absorb the pain, when Teddy called to them from the stage.

"Come up here, Sebastian, I need you!" he shouted cheerfully, his eyes alight with energy. "As for you, Emma, back to the office! The place has been a madhouse since that scandal sheet came out—go do something useful. We'll talk about that shameful interview you gave at a later time."

She stared up at him, openmouthed with shock and fury. Whatever words had been attributed to her could have come from no other source but Teddy himself.

Sebastian rose with sinuous grace, moving past her as if she didn't exist. But he paused just long enough to glance back at her, and his eyes were the color of arctic ice. "And keep the hell away from me," he said softly.

There was a silver lining to the dark cloud of the newspaper article. Teddy was right—the phones were ringing off the hook. Advance sales, which had been admittedly sluggish, were becoming overwhelming, and at least three groups wanted to book benefit previews. Unpaid creditors were surprisingly understanding, a fact that mystified Emma. As far as she could tell, rumors of a jinxed production ought to have made people even more nervous about their unpaid bills. Instead, they seemed to have developed an almost paternal interest in the show.

It wasn't until late in the afternoon that she managed to find a copy of the infamous paper. When she read it she almost threw up. The statements attributed to her had the breathy, inane quality of a beauty pageant contestant, and Emma had never been that fatuous in her entire life.

She was about to crumple up the paper in disgust when she saw the photograph. Coral was right; it was grainy and indistinct. And romantic. Sebastian loomed over her, and to the uninitiated there might have seemed a threat in his posture, in his hands on her shoulders, in his dark hair and clothes and dark expression.

But they only had to look at her to know the truth. A truth she hadn't known when the picture had been furtively taken. She was looking up at Sebastian Brand with love.

"Boss wants you out back," one of the workmen said, sticking his head in the door.

Emma jumped a mile, thrusting the paper beneath the desk. Smoothing it carefully with nervous hands. She wasn't going to let anything happen to that photograph. It captured forever what she'd seen in him, what she'd held for a brief moment last night. What was now gone forever.

"What now?" she said wearily. She was going to have it out with Teddy sooner or later, but right at that moment she didn't feel up to it.

"Didn't say. Just said how I was to tell you to come backstage."

She considered asking whether Sebastian was around, then dismissed the notion. No matter that anyone who picked up a newspaper in St. Bart knew of her idiotic infatuation. She didn't want to give anyone more ammunition. She could face Sebastian, head held high, if she had to. She could also do her damnedest to avoid him, at least until she sorted out her feelings a little better.

The auditorium was deserted and dark. She hummed beneath her breath, something small and brave, not even considering why she suddenly felt nervous. She lived alone in this huge empty theatre, for heaven's sake. It didn't usually make her edgy.

Climbing up on the stage, she searched through the shadows. "Hullo?" she called. "Teddy, did you want to see me?"

There was no answer. He must have flitted off again, she thought wearily, crossing the stage. If only he weren't so damned mercurial. Some people found it charming; she found it a royal pain.

There was no sign of anyone backstage. "Teddy?" she called again, peering nervously into the men's dressing room. If he didn't make an appearance momentarily she would go back to her office and let him find her. She didn't want to risk running into Sebastian again, didn't want to give him another chance to be icily distant.

"Emma?" It wasn't Teddy, it was Coral, heading across the stage. "Were you looking for someone? They've all gone, and I just came back for my clothes...."

It happened so quickly that Emma could scarcely blink. And it happened so slowly that she watched motionless in horror as the seconds ticked by. It wasn't a broken stair this time, or a hole in the flooring.

The only warning was the ominous creak. "Coral!" Emma screamed, rooted to the spot, as a huge section of lighting crashed down onto the stage. Onto the spot where Coral had stood.

And then she moved, racing over the fallen debris and broken shards of glass, screaming Coral's name, horror washing over her.

The quiet moan was her first blessed response. The lights hadn't hit directly—Coral lay pinned beneath a small section, her leg twisted beneath her. She was bleeding from a myriad of tiny cuts, and she looked dazed, shocked. But at least she was alive.

Emma began to yank at the debris, trying to free her. She lost track of the time, she didn't have the faintest idea how long it took for people to respond to her screams, before other hands reached out to help, before Geoff was kneeling by his wife's head, all trace of the golden, indolent prince gone as he stroked Coral's bloody face.

"Get out of the way," someone shouted at her, and distantly she recognized Sebastian's voice. Dutifully she stepped back, allowing them to shift the massive bank of lights from Coral's body, and then she looked up to see Teddy's face, white with shock and anger as he hauled on the debris.

"Don't just stand there," Sebastian shot over his shoulder. "See if the ambulance is here yet."

She moved in a daze, opening the door to the rain-swept night. At least St. Bart had a decent ambulance system—it was there in record time. She stood and watched, drenched in the pouring rain as Geoff followed Coral's stretchered body into the vehicle. Teddy tried to follow, but Sebastian appeared out of nowhere, putting out a restraining hand and shutting the door behind the couple.

"They don't need any more help right now, do they?" he asked, his voice acid.

"I have to make sure she's all right," Teddy said loudly. "I somehow feel responsible. . . ."

"Do you, now?" Sebastian said softly. "I wonder why."

"I'm going to the hospital." Teddy wheeled around, but Sebastian's hand was on his chest, and Emma, caught between the two, could see the iron force in his fingers.

"I'm not sure that would be a good idea," he said, and there was an undertone of threat in his voice. "I'm heading there myself, and I'll be more than happy to give you two a call when I hear how she's doing."

"I'm sure she'll be all right. A bit shaken up, maybe a few stitches," Teddy said, slinging a possessive arm around Emma's shoulders.

Sebastian didn't miss the byplay, even as Emma jerked herself away. "But what about the baby?" she had to ask.

Sebastian's eyes narrowed. "How did you know she was pregnant?" he demanded at the same time that Teddy let out an affronted squeak.

"Pregnant?" he demanded, quivering in outrage. "I was counting on her for a long run. Oh well. Maybe it's just as well this happened before opening, so I can replace her with someone who'll stay the course."

Emma turned to look at him in utter horror.

Sebastian, however, was unmoved by Teddy's crassness. "You do that. You might look for another Monster while you're at it." And he disappeared into the darkening rain with only a last, veiled glance at Emma.

"Bastard," she said to Teddy.

"Don't pay any attention to the man, darling," he replied, misunderstanding. "He doesn't mean a word he says. He'll stay in the play if I say so. He's an artist, he's temperamental, and this has all been a shock."

"Teddy, don't be an idiot!" she shouted at him. "A woman was nearly killed tonight, and you're yammering on about your stupid long run."

"There's nothing stupid about a long run. This production is going to vindicate my career. And you, my dear, are being dangerously obtuse. Didn't I warn you days ago that something like this might happen? First the cellar steps and now this. Coral could have been killed. It makes me shudder to think about it." Indeed, his face was ghostly pale in the rain-drenched light of the alleyway.

"You aren't suggesting this wasn't an accident? You're being ridiculous, Teddy. Everyone was there within moments of the lights falling. You can't make me believe that someone was creeping along the catwalks like a phantom, ready to send the lights crashing down."

"It could have happened," he defended the notion.

"Besides, they fell on Coral, not on me. Unless you think these acts are the work of a madman who's out to maim and murder all women."

Teddy's expression was doleful. "No, darling. I think you're the intended victim. You've forgotten something important. Coral was wearing your clothes. From overhead, a person wouldn't be able to tell the difference."

She was suddenly very, very cold. The chill was biting into her bones, turning them to ice. "Don't tell me that," she said in a dull voice. "Don't tell me that Coral could die, could lose her baby, because of me."

"Not you, darling. Because of someone who's not quite sane, perhaps. Someone who, while he professes to be a lover, is really..."

"I won't hear it!" she said sharply. "You're spinning fantasies again, and sick ones at that. Keep away from me, Teddy. I've had enough."

She ran back into the theatre, past the curious crewmen working on the debris. She almost wanted to shout at them to stop. They were clearing away any sign of a possible crime, and she knew, just knew, that it if hadn't been an accident, it couldn't have been Sebastian's work.

But she said nothing, moving past them on swift-flying feet, out through the auditorium to the office. She paused long enough to get her purse and her car keys. If she was lucky the M.G. would run, at least long enough to get her to Sebastian's rundown area of town. If she weren't, she would damned well walk. There could be nothing more threatening in the derelict streets of St. Bart than what she had faced in the old theatre.

The car started. Beyond that, she didn't dare think. She was going in search of Sebastian, going to the one place where she knew he would show up eventually. She was going to sit there and wait for him, force him to listen to her. She was going to throw her pride and her heart at his feet, and see whether he would throw them back at her.

The worst he could do would be to look at her with those chilly silver eyes and tell her in his clipped British tones that a one-night stand does not a relationship make. And she could shrivel up and slink away, knowing that her instincts had been wrong. That this pull, this powerful thing that stretched and grew between them, that both of them were fighting so hard, was simply a figment of her overwrought imagination.

It wasn't until she pulled up on the deserted street in his derelict neighborhood that another, horrid thought entered her mind. Maybe that wasn't the worst thing that could happen after all, as soul-shattering as it seemed.

Maybe Teddy was right. Maybe the monsters that Sebastian inhabited were part of his soul. Maybe it wasn't her heart and soul that were at stake tonight. Maybe it was her very life.

She stared up at the darkened house. There was no sign of life—Sebastian was probably at the hospital, might not even come home tonight if Coral's condition was uncertain.

She would leave it to fate. If by some miracle the car started again, then she would put it in gear and start driving. Drive straight out of St. Bart, out of this cold, industrial state, back to where she'd come from.

If it didn't start, she would take her chances.

Her hands were trembling when she turned the key, and for a brief, despairing moment she heard a hopeful cough from the engine. And then it sputtered and died, leaving her no choice whatsoever but the one her heart wanted to take.

"Can I help you, Miss?"

She let out a terrified little shriek. A huge, elderly policeman loomed up beside the driver's window. The rain had abated to a light drizzle, and he looked damp, miserable and ultimately safe. "I'm fine," she said faintly.

"Having trouble with your car?" He pushed his cap back, revealing world-weary eyes. "You oughtn't to be in this kind of neighborhood on a night like this."

"I'm visiting a friend." A slight exaggeration. She doubted Sebastian considered her a friend.

"Must be that actor fellow. He's the only one still here. The rest of the houses have been condemned and empty for years. Oh, we get some transients passing through, and I usually turn a blind eye on a cold night, but there's not many who stray down here nowadays."

"I imagine not."

"It wasn't always like this," the policeman continued, obviously in the mood for conversation on such a cold, lonely night. "I've walked this beat for close to thirty years. Could have retired anytime now, but I'm kind of used to it, you know? I remember when this street was just teeming with life. Teeming." He seemed to like that word. "Now they're all gone. Ghosts, all of them."

"Except for that house," Emma said, looking toward Sebastian's tenement.

"Except for that one. Funny about that, too," he mused. "It's the only thing standing in the way of that big urban development project the city's got planned. Can't imagine why anyone would hold on to a place like that."

"How did he manage to buy it in the first place, if the city wanted it?" she asked, rubbing her hands together for warmth.

"He's owned it for years, he has. Ten, at least. When the others were condemned, some overseas lawyer bought it for him. Can't imagine why, unless he liked its history. Hear he's some sort of horror actor. Maybe he likes gruesome stuff."

Emma's chill was getting stronger. She tucked her hands in her armpits, shivering. "Gruesome?" she echoed. She didn't really want to know.

"Bit of a scandal about that house. Not that worse things didn't go on in all of them, but this one made the papers. Gave people the creeps. There was a family living there, mother, father and a young kid. There were fights all the time, but what can you expect? I imagine the father was a bit of a bully. He was from overseas. Australia, maybe, or England. His wife was Southern, sweet as sugar, as nice as her husband was a brute. Back then we didn't check to see that kids were okay. They were considered family property, and the police didn't interfere."

"But you needed to?" she asked.

The policeman nodded, memory darkening his face. "Apparently they used to lock the boy in a closet while they went out drinking. They were always fighting, they were, too. They were killed in a car crash one spring day. They didn't find the boy for almost a week. Locked in the closet."

"Oh, God," Emma whispered.

"He was okay, though," the policeman said, brightening up. "A couple of weeks in the hospital, and then some member of his father's family came and fetched him. Still, it kind of gives you the creeps, doesn't it? Thinking of that boy, locked in the closet, while his parents lay dead."

"Horrible," said Emma. "I think I'll go in now, officer. Could I offer you a cup of coffee or something?"

"No, thanks, miss. I need to make my rounds. You be careful out here. If you see someone hanging around, like as not they're up to no good. Just call 911 if you have any problems."

"I don't think I will," she said weakly. She waited until his burly figure disappeared around the corner. She walked up the steps, slowly, deliberately.

He didn't lock the door, she remembered that. It opened easily beneath her chilly fingers, and she stepped inside. She heard the distant ringing of the phone, and then a voice speaking. She moved farther into the house, leaving the front door open to the night rain, as she listened to Geoff's voice on what must be an answering machine.

"Coral's fine, old man, and the baby's right as rain. Just wanted to let you know. Where the hell are you? Something's going on. Coral's got one of her damned *feelings*. Mind your step."

She lunged for the phone, but he'd already rung off by the time she lifted the receiver. She set it back down, staring at it thoughtfully. Sebastian wasn't at the hospital, so where in heaven's name was he?

She could make some coffee, curl up on the sofa and wait for him. She could start a fire to ward off the damp chill, the musty, dead smell. She could at least close the front door.

But she didn't. She walked into the front hall, put her hand on the doorknob, then turned.

The closet stood at the top of the stairs, and now she understood why it had been left untouched. She also saw, with blinding clarity, that the door was not only unlocked this time, it was ajar.

Bluebeard's closet, she thought, moving up the stairs. What had happened to Bluebeard's last wife? In the movie she was rescued by a handsome prince. But what, God help her, if the handsome prince was Bluebeard himself?

She stood outside the closet as the silence closed around her. In the distance she could hear the falling rain, the creaks and groans of the old house settling for the night. It took all her courage to reach for the handle, pulling open the door.

At first she thought it was empty. And then, squinting her eyes, she stepped closer, peering inside.

The door came up behind her, knocking her into the darkened interior, slamming behind her, plunging her into darkness. She scrambled for the door handle, her hands slippery with panic, and she found it with a muffled sob of relief. Only to find that this time, as before, it was locked.

With Emma trapped inside.

CHAPTER SEVEN

Panic swept over her. She pounded on the door, screaming for someone to let her out, but the noise she made covered any sound of an intruder's retreat. When she finally sank down on the floor of the closet, sobbing in quiet terror, the house, the evil, tragic house, was silent.

With all the strength of will she could muster, she silenced her fearful whimpers. "Come on, Emma," she said out loud, the husky sound of her voice a small comfort. "You've never been afraid of the dark or even the least bit claustrophobic. It's a closet, an empty closet. No ghosts, no monsters." Her voice cracked on the last word, as her bravado faltered.

Maybe there was a light. She stood up, stretching her arms overhead, her fingertips just brushing the ceiling. No comforting light fixture, no blessedly old-fashioned pull-string hanging down. Just bare walls and darkness.

She shivered, though she knew she wasn't cold. She thought of the little boy, locked in here for days and days and days, while his parents lay dead. How many other times had he been locked in here? From how early an age? How could people be so monstrous to the innocent little ones?

Anger swept through her, wiping away some of her fear. If she could think of that poor abused boy, her own situation would pale in comparison. She was an adult, an intelligent, reasoning human being. She knew that sooner or later someone would arrive and let her out. She knew that life had its consequences, and sooner or later everyone had to pay their tab. She wasn't a child to be terrorized by the creatures of the night.

She leaned back against the wall, attempting a brave whistle, but the sound came out as little more than empty breath. She shoved her hands in her pockets, trying to warm them, and her fingers closed around an almost empty book of matches.

She cried then, from relief. She wasn't doomed to darkness after all. Blindly her fingers counted the remaining matches. Three of them. If she was very frugal, they'd get her through her imprisonment. She needed to use the first one, to get a good solid look at her surroundings, to satisfy herself that there was nothing to be afraid of. Just a bare closet, after all, with some tragic memories.

She struck the first match, holding it high, and looked around her. And she knew where Sebastian's monsters came from.

They were all over the walls, the doors, as high as an eight-year-old child could reach, even on the floors. Hideous, horrifying monsters, drawn in crayon in a child's scrawl. They were very old, and at some point someone had tried to scrub them away. But still they remained, the grease from the crayons sinking into the wood, etched into eternity.

The match burned down, scorching her fingers, plunging her into darkness once more. Now it all made sense. She'd known, from the moment the policeman had told her the history of the place, that Sebastian had been the child locked in the closet. Now she knew why he played monsters. They were part and parcel of him, a permanent reminder of his damaged childhood.

She sank down in a corner with a quiet, aching sound. And she sat there and cried. Cried for a little boy, wounded beyond healing. Cried for a man, too closed up to feel anymore. And she cried for herself, and the hopelessness of her dreams.

Sebastian had a very bad feeling, burning between his shoulder blades and in the pit of his stomach. He hadn't gone straight to the hospital—he'd been too disturbed to do anything more than walk through the rain-wet streets, processing what he'd seen and heard in the last twenty-four hours.

By the time he'd reached the hospital Coral was already resting comfortably, her leg in a cast, baby still safely settled in her belly, Geoff by her side. He hadn't bothered going up; they both needed some time to themselves.

As did he. What he suspected was so bizarre that he couldn't quite believe it. But if it was true, the ramifications could be truly disastrous for all concerned.

And most particularly for Emma.

He didn't want to worry about Emma. He didn't want to have to think about her at all, but a capricious, malicious fate had decreed otherwise. He'd tried to keep away from her, but it had been a waste of time. There was something between them, something deep and strong and powerful, almost preordained. Fighting it was simply a doomed effort.

He'd left her back at that theatre with its booby traps. Left her with a man he didn't trust, though his reasons weren't cogent. Maybe his distrust ought to be turned inward. Maybe he was far more of a danger to Emma than Teddy could ever be.

The rain began in earnest when he left the hospital. On impulse he went back to the theatre. He shouldn't have left things like that with Emma. He needed to see her, to touch her, to fight with her, if need be. He needed to be with her.

The theatre was deserted. The debris from the lighting panel lay piled by the doorway, and he surveyed it absently in the bright glare of the ghost light. If there had been any proof of sabotage it would be long gone. The accident would be just one more in a series of jinxes that had supposedly plagued his career.

Odd, that there had been no mention of that before he'd come to St. Bart. Sally Ryan's death had been a shock, one of those isolated tragedies that made everyone a great deal more careful, at least for a while. But the list of other near misses that he'd read in the paper was entirely fictional. He just wasn't sure who was the imaginative writer. That feral reporter? Or Teddy Winters?

He climbed the flights of stairs to Emma's little hidey-hole, fantasizing about finding her curled up, warm and drowsy and possibly naked in that sleeping bag. The room was deserted, the open windows blowing wet rain through the room. He knelt down by the makeshift bed. Even in the darkness he could see the streaks of red greasepaint staining the khaki cover, and a distant, rueful smile curved his mouth. Until he considered where she might be at that moment.

It was late, he'd lost all track of time. But if she wasn't here, the alternative was obvious. She'd gone somewhere with Teddy.

He didn't like the white hot rage that swept over him at the thought. He didn't like the fear that was a strong undercurrent. It didn't matter where she went, what she did, or with whom. If she was off with Winters it was just as well. She was dangerous, distracting.

For the first time he seriously considered his half resignation, made in the heat of crisis. He hadn't finished what he'd come to St. Bart for. Not the performance, but facing his demons, the monsters of his past. He wouldn't ever be free until he'd done so, but in the month he'd been back in this benighted northern city he'd only become more entangled. Maybe now wasn't the time.

Maybe there never would be a time. He should simply hand over the deed to the house, walk away and never look back. He was beginning to have the sense that the only way to vanquish the monsters was to destroy the house where they still lived. If the house were gone, leveled, its secrets crushed to rubble, then he would be free. The closet would be gone, along with its monsters.

He knew that would be his only salvation. He just wasn't sure if he could do it.

The one thing he couldn't, wouldn't, do was go after Teddy and Emma. He wasn't in the mood to enact a drawing room comedy, the outraged lover and all that Noel Coward garbage. If Emma Milsom had any sense at all she would have gotten in that ridiculously impractical car of hers and driven the hell away from both of them.

If she didn't, it was hardly his problem, was it? She was on her own, as they all were. She would survive. After all, he had.

But still that little voice nagged in the back of his head. What if she didn't?

At first he didn't even see her car through the heavy rain. He leapt from the taxi and raced up his darkened front steps, pausing under the dripping eaves to realize that someone had been there. The door was ajar, and a light cast a faint glow into the hallway. He looked behind him and saw the unmistakable shape of the M.G. across the street.

For a brief moment a streak of pure, mindless joy speared through him. She hadn't gone with Teddy. She was there. For him. And then his earlier uneasiness returned, and he stepped inside, closing the door, shutting out the rain behind him.

There was no sign of her. Not in the kitchen, where the coffeemaker was untouched, not in the living area, where the fireplace was cold and dead. Maybe she was lying naked in his bed, waiting for him. He should be so lucky.

He mounted the steps silently. There was no light at the top of the stairs, but he was used to the darkness. His bed was empty, white sheets and pillows and duvet untouched since he'd thrown it together this morning.

His sense of unease exploded. Where the hell was she? Back out in the car, like the other time, shivering in the rain? But his door was ajar; the lights were on. Where in God's name could she be?

And then he knew. With a mounting sense of horror, he knew exactly where he would find her.

The door to the closet was locked, the key that he'd left in the lock nowhere in sight. He pounded on the door. "Emma?" he shouted, unable to disguise his own remembered panic. "Emma?"

He heard her then. The faint sound of misery, and it pierced his heart. "Emma!" he called. "Hold on a second, I can't find the key."

"Sebastian?" Her voice was weak, quavery. How long had she been trapped inside? Even five seconds was too long. She was crying; he could hear it. "Get me out of here."

He kicked down the door. Smashed it with shocking, surprising ease, the old wood splintering beneath his force. She was curled in a fetal ball in one corner, her head tucked underneath her, and behind her he could see his childhood drawings, his talismans to keep the monsters at bay.

He reached in for her, scooping her up in his arms and cradling her shivering body as she wept against him. He kissed her, her forehead, her cheeks, her eyes, as he murmured soft, meaningless comfort, telling her that she was safe now, that no one would ever hurt her again, telling her that he loved her, he would protect her, that it was all right.

He told her everything he'd needed to hear so long ago, and as her panicked tears began to cease, began to trickle off into an occasional, watery shudder, he felt the ice around his heart crack and melt. He'd rescued her. He'd soothed and begun to heal her. And in doing so, he'd begun to heal himself.

The kisses began to change then. When he brushed his mouth against her cheek she turned her face so that her lips were against him, and then she was kissing him back, for comfort first, and then with that growing, mindless desire that burned so hotly between them.

He carried her over to the bed, setting her down on the white duvet, following her down, refusing to release her for a moment, even as her hands clung to him with equal desperation. There was darkness all around them, a warm, safe darkness, and their hands were rough, feverish with each others' clothing, until their hearts were beating against each other, their skin damp with sweat and desire. He kissed her mouth, her throat; he tasted the fullness of her pulse. He kissed her breasts, pulling her sweater up over her head and tossing it away in the darkness. He kissed her belly; he kissed her between her legs, and she arched off the bed beneath him, twisting and writhing, her fingers wreathed in his damp hair as he made her cry out.

He couldn't wait any longer. He'd wanted to gentle her, to soothe her, to make love sweetly and slowly. But he couldn't. He needed her. Now.

He covered her, sliding into her, filling her with a deep thrust that brought a cry to her lips. But her arms wrapped around his back, her long, beautiful legs wrapped around his hips, and she buried her face against his shoulder, against his hair, and her voice was muffled, fierce, as she told him what she needed.

He put his hand between their bodies, touching her, and she exploded immediately, her body convulsing around him. He'd gone into some dark, wild place, beyond sense, beyond reason, and all that existed was her body, her soul, her heart racing against his, her breath panting in his ear, as he thrust into her again and again as she clung to him, sobbing.

Her nails dug into his back, her body shattering once more, and this time he joined her, filling her with his body, his soul, his very life, as the darkness splintered around them.

Time seemed to have lost all meaning. He realized he was lying on top of her, his body still tight within hers, and she was crying. Levering himself up, he brushed the tears from her face, peering down into her eyes. "Emma," he said, his voice hoarse. "Did I hurt you? I'm sorry...."

"Don't," she said in a fierce voice. "Don't say you're sorry. Don't say you shouldn't have done it. Just hold me."

He smiled crookedly. "If I hold you, I just might do it again. You seem to have the most unsettling effect on my better judgment."

"Good," she whispered, turning her head to kiss his hand, and he could feel the tears on her lips. "I want to make love to you all night long. I want to sleep in your arms, I want..."

He silenced her mouth with his, clinging for a moment, tasting the salty tears. Heaven knew, he wanted the same. He wanted to drown his questions, his doubts, in the sweet delight of her body, but the niggling doubt, the sense that something was very wrong, kept him from succumbing.

Instead, he tucked her head against his shoulder and rolled to his side, taking her with him. She nestled against him with a sigh, safe and peaceful, and he thought for a moment that even if she couldn't say the words, her actions were trust enough.

He stroked the hair back away from her face. "What happened?" he asked gently.

She shook her head. "I don't really know," she said in a small voice. "I came here to find you, to talk to you, but the house was empty. Or so I thought." A stray shudder drifted across her skin. "I came up-stairs, and the closet was open. I . . . I looked inside."

"Bluebeard's closet," he said with a touch of grim-ness. "Did you see anyone out in the street, lurk-ing?"

"Only an old policeman."

"Joe. He's been walking this beat for centuries. Or so he told me."

He could feel the hesitation in her. "He's very talk-ative."

"He is that. So I imagine I have no more secrets?" It was a tentative question; he wasn't sure what an-swer he would have preferred.

But he'd learned that Emma had an unfortunate penchant for the truth. "I don't imagine you have many," she said, raising her head to look at him out of sorrowful eyes. "How could they have done that to you? How could parents hurt their child? How could they . . . ?"

"Hush now," he said, putting his fingers across her indignant mouth, stroking her soft lower lip. "It's over, long in the past. I've been luckier than most."

"Lucky?" she echoed in disbelief.

"I was able to work out my own therapy. You must have seen the monsters I drew on the walls. They pro-tected me from my terrors. When I grew up I learned to use those monsters, to inhabit them. And that way they couldn't hurt me. Or at least," he added wryly, "that's what my overpaid therapist told me."

"What did you tell him?"

"Her," he corrected. "I simply said, 'Thank you very much,' paid an exorbitant amount of money and went about my business."

"And that's all there is to it?"

She was also smart, his Emma. "Not quite. She also suggested that sooner or later I was going to have to go back to the past and face the monsters. Or else I was going to spend my entire life fighting them."

"She sounds as if she was worth every penny you paid her," Emma said. "Is that why you're here? To face the monsters?"

"Yes."

She put her head back on his chest, and in the darkness he could feel the heated dampness of fresh tears. "I still can't believe it," she whispered. "I can't understand how your father could do such a thing to you."

A great weariness spread over him, and he pulled her closer, settling her against the bones and planes of his body. "Love," he said, "my father was a decent, good man. He did his best, but it wasn't good enough. It was my mother."

She absorbed that knowledge like a good boxer absorbs a blow, stoically, without flinching. "Is that why...?" She stopped herself midsentence.

But he knew what she was going to say. "Is that why I've been such a bastard to you? Because I hated my mother and now hate all women? No, love. I worked that part out years ago. I've been a bastard to you because I'm a miserable, sour, bad-tempered fool who didn't want to fall in love."

"Sebastian..."

"No more, love," he said, putting his hand over her mouth. "We can work it out in the morning, including who the hell locked you in that closet. For now, you need to sleep."

"Sebastian . . ." she tried again, but he silenced her with his mouth. And then conversation, and sleep, were the last things on their minds.

They had barely had any time at all. Emma lay curled up against his fiery warmth, the cloud soft duvet pulled over their entwined bodies, and tried to hold the moment forever. Never again would it be so right, so perfect. He would regret his words when he awoke; she would regret her vulnerability. But for now all that mattered was his heated body against hers, his arms around her, his hands possessive, protective, arousing, even in sleep.

The rain had stopped, at least for a while, and a faint glow filtered through the windows from the streetlights, throwing shadows in the huge room. The splintered door of the closet hung on its hinges, a mute testament to her panic. She could feel it come again, that bone-shaking terror, and just as quickly it subsided as she sank back against Sebastian's body.

So many questions. So many doubts. And they all boiled down to this. His body next to hers. His arms holding her. All those questions would be answered in their own time. For now they had the night, or what remained of it. They had each other. They had . . .

She jerked suddenly, and Sebastian was instantly awake beside her. "What is it?" he asked, his voice cool and sharp.

"I heard something," she said, wondering if she was being a fool.

"The house makes noises," he said warily, not disbelieving her. "All old houses do."

"It didn't sound like that. And the smell . . ." Her eyes widened, and she sat up. "It's gasoline."

Sebastian's reaction was instantaneous and violent. He flung back the covers and groped for his clothes. "Get dressed!" he shouted, but she was already struggling for her own scattered clothes, infected by his urgency.

"What is it?" she demanded, pulling her sweater over her head, ignoring her long lost underwear.

"This place is about to go up in flames," he said. "I forgot..."

"Forgot what?" Sudden horror filled her, as she remembered the final scene in *Dybbuk*. Sebastian and the lead actress, engulfed in flames of the monster's making. "Sebastian, what have you done?"

The moment the words were out she could have cut out her tongue. In the darkness she could see his stillness, where a moment before he had been all speed. "What?" The very sound of his voice warned her of danger. But she didn't know what the danger was.

"Sebastian," she said miserably, but he overrode her excuses.

"Get out, Emma," he said flatly.

"I didn't mean..."

"Get the hell out of here. Fast."

She still didn't move. He simply crossed the room and grabbed her, his beautiful hands hard and painful on her arms, and shoved her toward the stairs. She half expected him to push her down, and she grappled for the railing just as the room behind her exploded in a ball of flame.

He did push her then, down the stairs, flying after her, the two of them half running, half falling on the old wooden steps. Flames were already flying up from downstairs, devouring the ancient wood of the house with a greedy crackling, filling the place with thick, oily smoke. Emma ran for safety, but the front door, which Sebastian never locked, was immovable.

Sebastian pushed her out of the way, yanking at it himself, but it refused to budge. This was no ancient closet door ripe to be splintered. After a few exhausted tries he stepped back. "We'll have to go for the windows."

His face was brutal, a shifting pattern of flame and shadow, and she was suddenly reminded of the red-streaked paint of the night before.

"The windows are in there," she said, stating the obvious, gesturing to the flame-engulfed room.

"We have no choice," he shouted over the noise of the fire. In the distance she could hear the sound of sirens, but the fire was spreading with such demonic speed that there was no guarantee they would be rescued in time.

Sebastian was stripping off his shirt. "Put this around you and run," he said.

"No!" She shoved it back at him blindly. "You'll be burned...."

"Stop arguing with me!"

"Put it back on or I'm not going anywhere," she said stubbornly.

He cursed her then, pungently, yanking the shirt back around his flame-shadowed torso. "Come on, then," he said, grabbing her hand in an iron grip. "It's only going to get worse."

She would have made it if not for the smoke. It roiled out at her, blinding her, choking her. She stumbled, doubling over for a moment, and then his arms were around her, his body tight against hers, and they were flying through space, through flame, through glass and wood to the street below.

She couldn't see, but she could feel the people surrounding her, hands gentle, nurturing. Someone pulled Sebastian away from her, and she cried out in protest. Her vision cleared, and she batted the oxygen mask from her face.

"Sebastian," she screamed, as medics tried to hold her down, murmuring soothing words to her.

She saw him instantly. He was bleeding from a cut on his wrist, his black shirt was scorched, his face reddened from the flames. She recognized his stance immediately—wary, violent, as he stood a few feet away from Teddy....

"Emma!" Teddy called, his voice loud and rich with relief. "Darling, I was so frightened." He held out his arms, and for a moment Emma was tempted. Teddy couldn't hurt her. Teddy didn't matter enough to cause her pain. Teddy was obvious, dependable, not someone with monsters living in his soul.

"Don't go near him," Sebastian ordered, his voice hoarse from the smoke he'd inhaled. He didn't turn to look at her, simply continued to stare at Teddy with blind hatred.

"Don't be ridiculous, Sebastian," Teddy said, using all his charm. "You didn't get away with it. It's a good thing I decided to make sure Emma was all right or you'd both be dead right now. If I hadn't called the fire department . . ."

"If you hadn't set the fire . . ." Sebastian countered viciously.

"Don't be ridiculous, old man. I'm not blaming you. You've had a string of bad luck. I'm sure it's only coincidence. No one's going to think you're responsible," Teddy said, soothingly, making the opposite very clear. "Just step back, let Emma come to me, and everything will be all right."

Sebastian turned to her then, and she saw the bleak despair in his fire-lit eyes. "Make your choice, Emma," he said.

For a moment she couldn't move. Teddy couldn't have set the fire—it made no sense. Teddy didn't have the demons of the past riding him; Teddy had nothing to gain by hurting his expensive and famous actors.

She hesitated—for one moment too long. "So be it," Sebastian said, his voice flat and dead. And he turned away from her, disappearing into the night.

CHAPTER EIGHT

"Where are we going?" Emma didn't really want to know. She sank back in the front seat of Teddy's BMW and shut her eyes, concentrating on the pain in her throat, the pain in her knee, jarred by the fall, the pain in her heart.

"I'm going to take care of you, darling," Teddy said. "We'll get you a drink, a hot bath, some clean clothes, and you'll feel like a new person."

"I don't want to go to your hotel."

"I have no intention of taking you there. You've been staying at the theatre at night, haven't you? I thought you'd prefer to go back there."

In truth, there was no place she wanted to go. With a moment's hesitation, a moment's distrust, she'd destroyed the one thing that mattered to her. Then and there she simply wanted to curl up and die.

"All right," she said, her voice hoarse and wary. "But I'm leaving, Teddy. First thing tomorrow."

If she expected an argument she didn't get one. "It might be for the best. As long as Sebastian's around, I don't think you're safe, and—"

"Sebastian didn't do a thing."

"Don't be absurd, Emma," he said, pulling up in the rain-soaked alleyway and turning off the car. "You can't be so blinded by love that you don't realize the man is dangerous. There have been too many accidents, too many coincidences. He's been behind everything. The broken stairs, the falling light panel, the fire. As long as you're here, these accidents are going to keep happening."

"What makes you think Sebastian will stay?"

"Ironclad contract," Teddy said smugly, coming around and opening the passenger door for her with surprising concern. "The one thing you can count on with Sebastian Brand is his professionalism. He's never missed a performance, broken a contract, even been late for a rehearsal. He won't walk out on me, much as he might want to. So that means we'll have to get rid of you."

"How thoughtful of you," she said, too exhausted to be more than faintly cynical.

The theatre was cold, empty, silent, only the bright glare of the ghost light breaking the darkness. She glanced at the debris from the fallen light, then looked ahead at the stage bed, and she faltered as misery swept over her.

"He couldn't," she said, more to herself than Teddy. "I just can't believe he's behind the accidents. He'd have to be mad, and I know he's not."

"Emma, Emma," Teddy said, putting an arm around her. "You're infatuated with the man. You need a little distance to put this all together. He's tried to injure you several times. He locked you in the closet, tried to incinerate you. He must have some terrible need to hurt the women who care about him. I suppose it must stem from his relationship with his mother."

A sudden coldness filled Emma, starting at the pit of her stomach and spreading outward. There was no way Teddy could know she'd been locked in the closet.

Unless he'd been the one to do it. "What about his mother?" she asked very carefully.

Teddy shrugged, smiling down at her with great charm. "I haven't the faintest idea. Don't they say that most people's problems stem from their relationship with their mother? Sebastian must have had a doozy."

She fought it, fought his seductive words, holding on to the sudden, horrifying clarity. "Perhaps," she said slowly.

"Besides, what are the alternatives? Either Sebastian has been trying to hurt you for as long as he's been trying to get you in bed, or we have a truly unbelievable series of coincidental accidents."

"There's one other possibility you haven't mentioned."

Teddy wandered across the stage, surveying it with a professional eye. "And what's that?"

"Someone else might be behind the accidents."

He turned back and smiled at her, completely at ease. "That's rather farfetched, don't you think? Who could possibly have a reason for hurting you?"

"I have no idea what the motive could be."

"Then you can't come up with a suspect." He smiled at her with complete sweetness.

"I wouldn't say that." She swallowed, ignoring the terrified racing of her heart. "How did you know I'd been locked in the closet?"

If she'd expected to discomfit him, she was disappointed. Teddy merely blinked, and his smile widened. "You didn't mention it?"

"No one knew but Sebastian and me. And whoever locked me in there."

Teddy sat down on the bed, leaning against the iron railing. "I suppose I'm found out, then."

For a moment she couldn't believe his words. "Is that all?" she demanded.

"Well, it would be a waste of time to deny it. I like to play games, Emma. I've been gifted, or cursed, with twice the intellect of most normal human beings. I like to watch them scurry around while I pull the strings."

"And that's why you've set up the accidents? For sheer malicious pleasure?" She couldn't believe this, couldn't believe his calm good humor.

"Heavens, no. Acquit me of such simplicity! I had very concrete motives, which you are simply too blind to see. I've had a run of misfortune in Hollywood. This production was going to be the revival of my career. I've written a brilliant play, my vision for it is magnificent, and I hired the best actors I could find. Sebastian was a major triumph. Unfortunately, the media was a little slow to realize what an artistic breakthrough was in the making. I decided I needed to get their attention."

"Through the stories of the jinxes. There is no jinx, is there? No series of women hurt and killed in Sebastian's life?"

"Just Sally Ryan, and I gather he barely knew her. But you see how gullible people are. The newspapers printed what I fed them, the wire services picked it up, and suddenly all eyes are on our tiny little theatre. I'm sure if you think about it you'll be sympathetic to my goals. It's a crime to let brilliant work be overlooked. This play is too important to be lost. It's worth any sacrifice."

"Not my life," she said.

Teddy gave her an angelic smile. "I suppose that's a natural thing to believe."

His innocent charm horrified her, and she searched vainly for some way to redeem him. "Why did you call the fire department? You must have regretted starting the fire...."

"Not quite. You see, I hadn't realized Sebastian was in there with you. I needed another tragic, jinxed death, but I couldn't afford to endanger Sebastian. You understand, don't you, darling?"

"I don't understand a thing," she said fiercely. "I'm getting out of here. You can find something else to get your obscene publicity."

"Darling," he said, his voice sorrowful, "I'm afraid not." He caught her before she was halfway to the door, his hands immensely strong, subduing her panicked struggles.

"Don't make this difficult," he panted, dragging her back to the center of the stage. "I would have liked to avoid this, but surely you can see the wonderful, tragic ramifications of it all. The poor, lovesick girl kills herself, hangs herself above the very stage where the show must, of course, go on. The place will be packed. They'll come to wallow in your tragic fate, then leave talking about the play, and Sebastian's performance. You want that for him, don't you, darling?"

She was crazed with terror, fighting him wildly. He reached for something on the bed, crushing her against his body with one immensely strong arm, and she realized with horror that he had a rope in his hand and was wrapping it around her neck as she fought, hysterical with fear, struggling....

"Let her go, Winters!" Sebastian's voice rang out in the darkened theatre, powerful enough to make Teddy's hands still for a moment.

He looked about him, above Emma's head, but there was darkness all around, the solitary light unable to pick up Sebastian's presence. "Don't be silly, Sebastian," he replied, his voice beguiling, the rope still taut around Emma's neck. "Surely you can understand? You can't simply do brilliant work and expect the public to notice. You need publicity. You need a hook."

"Let her go, damn it." There was power in Sebastian's voice. And there was real fear. Emma clawed at the rope around her neck, knowing it was going to tighten, knowing help would be too late. At least she would die knowing that the fear in Sebastian's voice was for her. Even if in her doubt she'd betrayed him, he still cared.

"Can't do it, old man," Teddy said, and the rope began to tighten.

The back door was flung open, and bright, glaring light flooded the theatre. "This is the St. Bart police. Release the woman, Mr. Winters." The voice was amplified by a bullhorn, bellowing through the theatre, using machinery to do what Sebastian could accomplish in a whisper.

For a moment the rope tightened around her neck a fraction more. And then she was released, abruptly, shockingly.

She sank to her knees beside the bed, sobbing in terror, only dimly aware of what was going on behind her. Teddy was being handcuffed, someone was reading him his rights, and through it all Teddy was maintaining a cheerful, upbeat demeanor.

And then Sebastian was there, materializing out of the darkened theatre, standing in front of her. She looked up, needing him, too afraid to ask.

There was no warmth on his scorched face, no forgiveness. "It's a lucky thing the police aren't quite as gullible as you are," he said flatly. "Or you'd be hanging from the rafters."

And then he walked away without a word of comfort, without a touch, a sign.

"Emma, darling," Teddy called over his shoulder as they led him away, an ingratiating grin on his handsome face, "I know you understand and forgive me. Don't you, darling?"

The metal door slammed shut behind him. "Guess again," Emma whispered.

"You're an absolute lamb to help me," Coral said cheerfully as Emma maneuvered the wheelchair through the St. Bart International Airport. "Particularly since I know you wanted to get an early start to the coast."

"I don't mind," Emma murmured, almost truthfully. It had been three days since Teddy had been arrested, the theatre closed down, the project terminated. Teddy was out on bail, appearing on talk shows, facing his eventual trial with his usual insouciance. Coral and Geoff were heading back to England to await the birth of their baby. Of Sebastian there had been no sign at all.

Emma still didn't understand why she'd waited this long to leave. Perhaps it was the stupid, vain hope that he would reappear and forgive her. At least tell her it had been fun while it lasted.

Except that it hadn't been fun. It had been overwhelming, soul-shattering, intense and magnificent. But it hadn't been fun.

But with Coral and Geoff leaving there was no longer anything to keep her in St. Bart. Her mother had called the motel where she'd been staying every few hours, demanding that she come home and recuperate. Friends had called, telegrams had arrived, everyone suddenly wanted to take care of her. It only made sense to give in. Maybe if someone simply took over she would be able to concentrate on healing. And forgetting.

"There's the dear man," Coral said cheerfully as they approached the gate. "And he's alone." For an actress she didn't do a very good job at hiding her dismay.

"Why wouldn't he be?" Emma said sharply.

"Sorry, love, I couldn't hold him," Geoff said, greeting his wife with a kiss on her cheek. "Hullo, Emma."

"Hi, Geoff. Matchmaking again?" she asked in a resigned tone of voice. At least Sebastian had foiled their plans. There would have been nothing worse than being forced to face him when he obviously never wanted to see her again.

"Doing my best and failing miserably. Come to England with us, Emma. Coral needs the company, and you need the change."

"Yes, do," Coral chimed in. "I don't want to spend a six-hour flight surrounded by men."

"Surrounded?" Emma echoed.

"Sebastian's on this flight. If he makes it back in time," Geoff added. "He took off without a word a while ago."

"Don't be ridiculous. Sebastian has never missed a rehearsal, an audition or a plane in his entire life," Coral said. "He'll be here."

"He's already late. That's a first," Geoff pointed out. "So, Emma, you're coming with us?"

He looked so hopeful that she had to laugh. "Of course not. But I appreciate the offer. Even if I wanted to, I couldn't. I don't have my passport with me."

"I put it in your purse when you weren't looking," Coral piped up. "What other excuse can you come up with?"

"I don't want to."

"Sorry, that won't wash," Coral said, reaching up and catching Emma's hand. "You can't let it end like this, love. It's worth fighting for."

"He's coming." Geoff's voice was flat.

Emma felt frozen inside, but she turned her head to watch his approach, her heart lurching inside her.

He was dressed in black, as always. Black trousers, black T-shirt, black linen jacket, his lion's mane of black hair surrounding his face. His left cheek was abraded, burned by the fire, and one hand was bandaged. He looked distant, dangerous, miles away from her, and she could have wept.

Geoff moved first, meeting him across the corridor as they announced preboarding for the first class passengers and all those who needed extra help. Emma watched him give Sebastian a punch in the arm, and then he sped back, scooping the wheelchair away from Emma. "The rest is up to the two of you," he said, wheeling his wife away before Coral could come up with anything more than a distant wave.

Emma watched them go. The boarding continued, and the passengers lined up like sheep for the slaughter, numb expressions on their faces. She wondered if she could manage that same, blank expression when she turned to face the man who now stood directly behind her.

But then, maybe it was too late for secrets or pride. She turned, meeting his enigmatic silver gaze bravely enough. "You're going to miss your plane," she said.

"No," he said. "I'm not." He seemed to hesitate, and she was terrified that he would turn away from her, walk out of her life before she could say what she needed to say.

"Wait," she said in sudden panic.

"I wasn't about to go anywhere." He sounded completely reasonable, but reason wasn't something she associated with Sebastian.

"I have to explain about what happened."

"You don't have to explain a thing...."

"I need to," she said, her voice urgent. "Before you leave, I just need to tell you..." Her face was wet, and she realized distantly that she was crying. She backhanded the tears, not wanting to use them, not wanting his pity. "I need to tell you," she began again, her voice trembling, "that I'm sorry I didn't trust you. Truly, truly sorry. But just because I love you doesn't mean I can read your mind. You never explained, you never said a word, you just expected me to take you on faith, and maybe in a perfect world I could have done that, or maybe if I were a better human being, but I'm not. I'm human, and fallible, and I was just so damned confused, and when it came right down to it, it wasn't you I didn't trust, it was myself." Her words tumbled to an abrupt stop, as he kept watching her, his face still, enigmatic.

"Is that everything?" he asked, his voice soft and emotionless.

She'd blown it. But at least she'd said what she had to say. "Yes," she said. "Except that I do love you, even if it isn't the perfect kind of love you wanted." They were announcing final boarding in the background, and the waiting area was almost empty. "And you're going to miss your damned plane," she added.

The tears were still pouring down her cheeks. He put his hands on her face, his thumbs brushing the tears away. "I never miss planes," he said calmly. "I was late because I went back to the theatre, looking for you. I'm not very good at love, either. Or at opening up to people. If we're going to make this work, I'm going to need your help. I love you, Emma. Will you teach me how to do it right?"

He didn't wait for her answer, because he could read it in her eyes. He kissed her hard and quick on the mouth, and it was a promise, a beginning, a future.

"Last call," the flight attendant intoned, and Sebastian hauled Emma toward the door.

"I can't go with you," she protested.

"Of course you can. I already bought your ticket before I went to find you. We'll have your riduclous car shipped over later. Maybe it'll behave itself and run more smoothly in its native climate." He handed their tickets to the flight attendant as he pulled her tight against him.

"Thank you, sir," the attendant said, passing back the boarding passes. "Best get a move on." He paused. "Say, aren't you that actor? The one who always plays the monsters?"

Sebastian didn't even look at him. He smiled down at Emma, and there was a light in his beautiful silver eyes. "Not anymore," he said softly. "Not anymore."

* * * * *

Seawitch

HELEN R. MYERS

Helen R. Myers

To best tell you why I wrote this story is to share with you that my favorite time of day is between three and four in the morning, when the house is so still, you can hear the air shift as you walk, the refrigerator gurgle and rumble like some giant's severe case of indigestion and somewhere a beam expand or shift, a reminder that our home, like all homes, rests on a living, breathing thing.

From outside come the sounds of other nocturnal creatures, some musical, some bold and a few eerie. If there's a wind, it whispers or moans through the pines and cedars; and particularly at this time of year, the leafless limbs of our hardwoods come together like fragile skeletal fingers applauding nature's mercurial temperament.

In other words, I gravitate toward environments of atmosphere and drama and passion, and let's not leave out mystery—all the things that *Silhouette Shadows* was born to celebrate. If life is about experiences, then *Silhouette Shadows* must be about those dimensions and ideas we've yet to explore or understand even minimally. It's about possibilities, but not the kind you hear discussed by a boardroom full of executives in three-piece suits.

Consider the spectrum: What is goodness and what is evil? How strong is human will when faced with an unknown dimension? Is the power of suggestion a positive or negative force? Are there really such things as ghosts? And what about reincarnation? Is lovemaking necessarily a physical communion, or could it be a mental projection, as well? Can love really remember through the span of time? The questions are endless and compelling.

Science may have taught us not to trust that which we cannot prove, but *Silhouette Shadows* asks only that you exercise imagination. Like those adventurers who once set sail across uncharted seas, and those now being thrust into that perpetuity we call the universe, these are stories about the most courageous, restless and alive individuals I think you'll ever meet.

To be asked to participate in such a far-reaching line was like having prison walls crumble before my eyes. Free, I explored the unknown, where echoes of ancient lore mingle with the whispers of times to come. This was strangely familiar territory, and yet terrifying territory. This is a new beginning. Imagine . . . and enjoy.

CHAPTER ONE

Her fingers were raw and her back was aching after the exertion of so much pressure, but at last all signs of the bloodred pentagram were rubbed off the mailbox she had removed from the picket fence out front. She dropped the steel wool pad back into the basin of soapy water and noticed the shredded sliver on an already short, unpainted fingernail.

"Brats," she said under her breath, biting off the fragment.

The Garrett boys were to blame for this latest vandalizing, she was certain of it. Granted, there were several in town who had caused her this kind of trouble, but those two were forever getting into mischief, and it was no secret "the town oddity" was their favorite target. Besides, the shade of lipstick used had looked incriminatingly similar to the one their mother liked to wear. A garish color for such sallow skin. The woman had no better taste than the boys had manners.

She smiled to herself and decided the matter needed careful study before she chose the appropriate retaliation. Something judicious, something with impact, and yet subtle. Naturally, there were drawbacks to consider, and she would have to take care not to attract the attention of too many adults in the community. No, only young Casey and Tim need understand how far out of their depth they had tread, and how she wasn't at all pleased with having her harmony disrupted. But how they pushed her toward a darker temptation....

A low moan drew her attention and she took a moment to listen to the changing voice of the storm that had started shortly after nightfall. The wind was beginning to sound like a keening woman, as it always did this time of year. Winter wasn't far off; soon the wind's full song would be heard all along this northern coast. In the meantime there were these intermittent laments as gusts drove a heavy rain against the cottage.

If it wasn't for the weather, she would have liked a walk on the beach to relax the stiff muscles earned from a long day of preparing her herb garden for the coming cold. Contemplation of the sea would have helped, too, energizing her spirits. But there was the storm, and so she was no better than a prisoner. It made it difficult to keep memories and doubts at bay... and her fears. Those proved troubling even in fair weather.

Despite the heavy cable knit sweater that covered her to mid-thigh, she shivered and glanced over to the fireplace in the middle of the living room wall. No wonder she felt chilled, the blaze she had created for herself was dying rapidly.

She left the dinette table and crossed to the stone hearth, crouched down and used the iron poker to prod at the crumbling logs. Then she added two new ones from the stack she had brought inside earlier in the day. The heat felt good on her face and she closed her eyes absorbing it. How like a caress, she thought. It had been a long time since she had been touched with anything resembling this tenderness, even longer since she craved being touched at all. Thanks to Drew.

She frowned. First the Garrett boys and now him. It wasn't good to let her emotions dwell so long on the negative; it wasn't safe.

She took a deep breath and willed serenity to return before slowly opening her eyes. The fire licked swiftly, hungrily at the new logs. Long vibrant flames of orange and gold danced and writhed, seducing the eye to continue watching.

Her pulse quickened. A vision was forming between the flames. She saw it. There were lights...headlights...like on a car. It *was* a car. She identified the vaguest outline of its shape, and then a roadway. The area was familiar, she realized, a place barely a half mile from here. The old seaside highway.

The vehicle approached a curve and her heart began pounding even faster because it was the last one before Cliff Point. But something was wrong. The car wasn't slowing as it needed to. She could tell the driver wasn't going to try to make the turn!

He burst through the guardrails as though they were paper, yet she heard metal rip, the sound piercing her eardrums and reverberating through her body bringing shock and pain. And still she continued to stare, to watch the car sailing out over nothingness, hovering above the cliffs, before tipping downward... downward...and then plunging to the rocks and sea below.

"No..." she whispered, rising and backing away from the horrific vision. "You can't. You mustn't!"

Though the downpour was beginning to ease, flashes of quicksilver continued to pierce the BMW's high beams and splatter against the windshield. The largest were droplets dragged from tree branches by a north wind that had Hunter Thorne keeping a tight grip on the steering wheel.

Jagged trees, jagged cliffs and a brutal September wind.... He was indeed in Maine, and within minutes would be arriving at Cliff Point. If only he felt better about returning to his old hometown. Instead, his jaws ached from hours spent clenching his teeth, and his eyes were dry, grainy from struggling to see through the liquid marbling on the windshield. But most of all he was aware of how his hands shook, a result of an overawareness of the infirm-looking guardrail that separated him from a swan dive into the Atlantic Ocean.

What if it happened? he asked himself with his next shallow breath. What if he did tempt fate's affection for him and yielded to the wind beating at his car like an omnipotent fist, let it sweep him over a cliff? Never mind what his intentions had been back in Boston when his partners forced this leave on him; he knew it was useless to think he could change things between him and his father. He was only heading this way because there was nowhere else to go. What an ultimate lesson it would be for everyone if he chose to permanently remove himself, not only from the firm, but from *life*.

It might be a relief to have it all done with; after all, who would miss him? Annoyed as he may be with Cal and Evan, he needed only review his behavior and job performance over the past fourteen months to see how much better off his business associates would be without him, and he had all but isolated himself from his friends. As for his father, did he need another lesson on Leland's indifference to his pain? No, there was no one who would be inconvenienced by his death, and when he coupled that with thoughts of how it would solve everything. . . .

It would stop him from remembering the night he had returned to his brownstone after an evening business function and found all those fire trucks and emergency vehicles blocking his street. No longer would he have to relive the sudden panic he had fought down when he'd raced through the crowd of onlookers, only to discover that the smoke had been pouring from his own home. It would stop the nightmares he had been experiencing, of seeing the two sheet-draped bodies being lifted into the ambulances; stop the guilt he now lived with for racing past Mrs. Oliver's gurney to reach his baby's, his Cady's.

Most of all, it would release him from his perpetual state of mourning. No longer would he grieve for his little girl who would never know her fourth birthday, never know what it was like to ice-skate or sail, to date or to fall in love, or know the wonder of having a child of her own.

Yes, a quick end would cease the sensation that his life's blood was being drained from him drop by drop. But most of all, he would no longer suffer the hollowness expanding inside him. That was the worst. At times like this he sometimes wondered whether he could hear the echoing whispers, the taunts of approaching madness.

As bitter tears flooded his eyes, Hunter blinked against the burning and viciously wiped to clear his sight. *If that's what you want, then do it,* he challenged himself. *Stop whining and do it.*

He gripped the wheel so hard his hands throbbed, and he narrowed his eyes, gazing transfixed on the approaching curve. Beyond the reach of the car's headlights lay oblivion, the great abyss he craved. Out there he could join the fictitious specters of his youth, the spirits of the dead sailors he had heard countless tales of as a boy, victims of sirens who lured their ships onto the deadly rocks below. Unlike them, he needed no temptress to...

"What the—"

It rose out of nowhere, so suddenly he wondered if his eyes were playing tricks on him. A shadow—impossible, he corrected himself—a figure appeared, literally rising out of the darkness and rushing over the guardrail. Certain he was hallucinating, Hunter nevertheless reached out to wipe at the windshield and simultaneously hit the brakes, only to have his stomach drop in a nauseating nosedive once he realized doing the latter was a crucial mistake.

The car went into a spin. Swearing, he fought for control, succeeded somewhat, then lost it again, finding himself heading straight for another section of guardrail.

He jerked the steering wheel to the left, barely missing the thing that had caused him to overreact. As he felt the car skid off the pavement, he had another fleeting, yet distorted glimpse of the shrouded figure, saw a ghostly pale face and clawed hands reaching out for him. Then a huge tree filled his vision.

Impact was sudden, too fast for him to so much as gasp.

Everything that wasn't secured in the car went flying like the ingredients of a giant tossed salad. He fell forward with such violence that his seat belt cut into his shoulder and belly, and forced the breath from his lungs. Then he swung to the left. As his head came in excruciating contact with unpadded steel, his ears popped. In the next instant blinding white lights exploded before his eyes.

Disregarding the fact that he had been indulging in a serious flirtation with his own mortality, he ground out a string of explicit curses at the pain ricocheting through his skull. He lifted a hand to the left side of his head and found a lump that was already the size of a golf ball. Whether he wanted to acknowledge it or not, he was the recipient of a sudden stroke of luck. He just didn't know whether to be grateful or ticked off.

The car sat at a drunken tilt, sounding like something being fed into a grinder. Tired of listening to the clamor, he groped for the ignition key and turned off the engine. In the blissful wake of the resulting silence, he fell back in his seat and waited for everything inside and out to settle.

What the hell had he seen back there? Releasing his seat belt, he cautiously shifted to look out the passenger window, and his heart lurched again.

It was coming toward him.

He blinked furiously and rubbed his eyes. There had to be something wrong with him. He didn't believe in ghosts. Never had, even as a kid, despite the pleasure he used to take in hearing the ghoulish stories the old-timers in town used to tell.

And yet all that was irrelevant; something *was* coming steadily toward him, undaunted by the wind dragging at its shroud. He had to decide fast if he should sit there and wait...for heaven only knew what.

He reached for the door handle, gave a jerk and discovered the angle the car had settled in made it impossible to get out on his side. That left the passenger door as the sole means for exit, except the shrouded figure was already there.

It yanked the door open. He felt the harsh slap of brisk September wind on his face and a sting of pain in his eyes as the roof light illuminated the car's interior, followed by the oddest rush of relief, not to mention surprise.

"Thank goodness. I was in time."

Hunter stared, certain he had misunderstood. "You were what?"

"You're all right."

No, he thought gazing into the mesmerizing eyes of the most stunning woman he had ever seen, he couldn't be. Otherwise, how else could he explain what someone like her was doing out here on a night like this?

She pushed off the hood of the old-fashioned cape that lent her that deceiving shapelessness, and he discovered her hair was long, wavy and as black as her wool mantle. Against it, her fair skin was almost translucent, impetus enough to have sent his imagination into overdrive. Even so, she was a far cry from his imagined ghoul.

Her oval face was a photographer's dream, her mouth wide but temptingly soft-looking, her nose definitive, but delightfully feminine. It was her eyes, however, that captured his interest the most. They were beyond fascinating; they pulled him in deep, until he almost forgot his discomfort, his problems, everything. The term *seductive* might have suited them except for the compassionate and hauntingly sad expression that shadowed their innermost depths. Their color was gray-green, the shade of a forest on sunless mornings when mist blankets the earth, and they were fringed with velvety black lashes that needed no mascara to accentuate their density or length..

For months grief and guilt had been keeping him from allowing himself to dwell on his physical needs, and he didn't consciously give himself permission to feel a sexual attraction now. Even so, that didn't stop every sensory cell in his body from snapping to attention.

Clearly concerned, she began to reach toward his forehead, only to withdraw. "I think you may have a concussion," she told him. "I'd better get you to a doctor. Do you think you can walk or would you prefer to stay here while I go for help?"

Her voice was soft and though what she said was no-nonsense and practical, her tone held a warmth he wanted to bask in. It made up for his being deprived of learning how it felt to have her fingers against his skin. A strange observation, he thought, considering how expert he had become at rejecting any form of human contact.

"You mean you can't utter a chant or something and make someone appear the way you did?" he drawled, bemused.

The shadows in her eyes deepened, cooling some of her initial warmth. "Chants are dangerous things. You shouldn't toy with them unless you know what you're doing, and what it is you're really asking for."

"I meant it as a joke."

"Everyone does." She began to withdraw. "Stay put."

"I can walk!" He knew he sounded anxious, but didn't care.

She hesitated. "Are you sure?"

Not of anything, and that bespoke a definite problem. Besides being light-headed, he felt as weak as a baby. He was also none too certain about his powers of deduction. Had she been serious or was he reading too much into that bit about the chants? And why couldn't he stop staring at her? One thing was for certain, he wasn't ready to let her out of his sight—at least not until he was sure which of them had the more serious head injury.

"Just let me climb out of this mess."

He knew his tone was unnecessarily gruff, but his conflicting reactions to her were bothering him. With an inward sigh, he watched her slip the hood back over her head, and as she backed out of the car, he shut off the BMW's headlights and followed her.

The stiffness already settling in his limbs came as a surprise; so did the puddle of water he stepped into and, ultimately, the blast of cold wind that sliced through his raincoat and the suit he was wearing beneath it. Pulling the raincoat's collar higher around his neck to escape at least some of the frigidness and the needlelike rain, he almost missed hearing the howl that rose from somewhere behind the woman observing his progress.

"What the hell was that?"

"The wind. The sea."

"I don't think so. It sounded like a wolf."

"You must be feeling dizzy."

He was, some, but it couldn't be affecting his hearing. He did, however, have to bend down to hear her above nature's ruckus. She was average in height, yet small compared to him. It reinforced the insanity of her presence and this situation. "Tell me something," he shouted, trying to see her face, almost hidden from view by her hood. "What are you doing out here?"

"Walking."

"That's crazy. Do you realize I could have killed you?"

"Would killing yourself have been more acceptable?"

A chill sliced through him. Feeling as though his legs were about to splinter beneath him, he leaned back against his car. "What are you, a mind reader when you aren't busy directing people to mate with trees?"

"Do you think it took mind reading to see what was on your agenda?"

"That's none of your business." He looked away, more out of embarrassment than anger, and found himself eyeing the evergreen he had struck. It came to him rather belatedly that tonight he had experienced more than one brush with death.

"Maybe Someone's trying to tell you it's not your time."

Hunter shivered and hunkered down deeper into his coat. "Or else that my solution's pneumonia."

His remark brought his rescuer to his side. She directed him to place his arm around her shoulders, then wrapped her arm around his waist. "Lean on me."

If he could remember how, he would have laughed. "You can't be serious?"

"I'm strong."

His frustration mellowed, but not his depression and sarcasm. "Compared to what?"

As she lifted her head, her hood slipped slightly, and for a moment he was once again lost in her eyes. He saw awareness mingle with secrets even more intriguing. Suddenly, he hardly felt the icy water and mud oozing into his shoes. He felt . . .

"Let me help you," she coaxed. "It's all right. Really."

Her other hand lay against his chest. Though reason told him it was unlikely for her to feel anything through all his clothes, he wondered if she had a clue as to the effect those innocent words had on his heartbeat, how he craved for everything to be all right, needed it to be.

"On one condition," he murmured thickly, as he watched her gaze wander to his mustache, his mouth. God help him, she could hypnotize him with those eyes. "Tell me your name."

Her searching look moved like invisible, satin-gloved fingers over his face. What did she see beyond an increasingly waterlogged attorney's conservative image? he wondered. Could she tell his heart had a mighty crack at its core and that it was threatening to shatter into a million pieces? Did she see all the dashed dreams and the guilt devouring his soul?

"Roanne. Roanne Lloyd Douglas."

She said it without flourish or drama, yet in a way that made him wonder why the rain didn't stop or why the clouds didn't part to expose a full, serene moon. He took a deep breath and savored silently the three words on his tongue. Her name sounded old, wise and full of grace. Would she think him crazy if he confided how desperately he needed a little grace in his life?

"I was heading for the Thorne estate." He let his own gaze wander over her pale features. "Do you know where it is?"

"Leland Thorne's home. Everyone does. It isn't often he receives guests."

"I'm no guest. I'm his son."

"How odd . . . I never saw that he had one."

Completely befuddled again, Hunter shook his head. "Saw?"

"A slip of the tongue. I mean knew."

"We've been estranged for some time."

"Why?"

Had anyone else asked, he would have replied it was none of their damned business. But Roanne Lloyd Douglas was drawing a unique, positive honesty from him. "We can't seem to learn how to communicate. It's a long story."

"And a painful one."

They were walking. He glanced around and saw they had reached the roadway. When had she coaxed him to start moving? How? "Does it show that much?" he asked, growing more and more dazed, not to mention curious about her.

"Pain speaks a universal language, Mr. Thorne."

"Call me Hunter."

She didn't respond to the invitation, but somehow it was no less than what he expected from this strange woman. Instead she continued leading him, and soon they were rounding the bend that, he knew, for the rest of his life would leave yet another indelible stain on his memory. Presently, he sighted the small cluster of lights identifying Cliff Point.

In all fairness, he thought, he should release her. The dizziness wasn't so bad now, at least in the literal sense. He was, however, continuing to feel as though he had been launched into a different plane of consciousness, one that was giving him the sensation that she was both his catalyst and his anchor.

"Isn't someone going to be worried that you're out so late?" he asked, unable to contain his curiosity about her any longer.

"No one. I'm a widow."

Her startling openness made him ashamed for not having been equally honest about why he had asked. He tried to make up for it by not offering empty condolences. "Has it been long?"

"Two years. How long has it been since your loss?"

Once again a coldness cut through him. The lady was so acute she was eerie. "I didn't lose a spouse. I mean I did, but it was through divorce several years ago, and no great tragedy to either of us. My daughter was the one who—" As always, the mere mentioning of Cady made his throat tighten.

"That explains it."

"Explains what?"

"It's been horrible for you."

She spoke with such certainty and empathy, he found himself feeling like a dam about to burst. Suddenly, he wanted to share everything with her. "It's been fourteen months and I've been going slowly out of my mind ever since. There doesn't seem to be a reason to go on any longer."

"That's when you have to grab hold tight and hang on."

"To what?"

"Necessary assumptions. The fact that life is worth living in spite of life."

"You can do that?"

"I try. Sometimes more successfully than at others."

"I'm afraid pretty platitudes don't work for me."

"And you think taking the easy way out would? You're too strong a man to submit to self-destruction, Hunter Thorne."

Anger rose, blinding him to everything but an urge to do violence. He was tired of people telling him what he was and wasn't feeling, and how he should think. Wheeling around, he grabbed her by her upper arms. "You don't know the first thing about—" A low growl erupted a few yards away, stopping him cold. "My God. Is that what I think it is?" he demanded, peering into the darkness and drizzle.

"No."

"The hell it's not. 'The wind,' huh?" he muttered, remembering how she had dismissed his earlier question. "What do you call it, then?"

"A friend. Easy, Pontus," she said soothingly to the four-legged creature Hunter could barely make out. "If you don't make any more sudden moves, he won't attack. He's simply being protective. Come on."

Though dubious about turning his back on the beast, Hunter once again complied when Roanne urged him forward. "Why didn't you say you had a dog?" he demanded, as his anger eased enough to give way to chagrin.

"He's not exactly a dog, and he's definitely not mine."

"What does that mean?"

"It means he is part wolf, as you'd guessed, but he belongs to himself."

"He . . . this is getting weirder by the minute."

"You need some rest, that's all."

Was that a smile he heard in her voice? He was beginning to wonder if he wasn't already resting, and would in fact shortly awaken in his own bed and learn all this had been a dream.

They walked in silence for several long moments. Finally he sighed. "I didn't mean to snap at you the way I did."

"I know."

"I'm beginning to think you do—that and a damned sight more. The question is, how?"

"Intuition's a powerful thing. You should learn to trust yours more." She stopped, which prompted him to do the same. "We're here."

To his amazement he discovered she was right. They were at the outer gate to his father's property. Not far beyond them he could see the two-story, modest brick home where an upstairs light indicated the old man was still awake. Suddenly Hunter had his doubts as to whether he would even be welcomed inside.

"Will you be sure to phone for a doctor?" Roanna asked, lingering behind as he stepped toward the security buzzer. "That bruise shouldn't go unexamined."

"My father will tell you that my skull's too thick for serious injury," Hunter drawled, almost reluctant to push the button. Mysterious or not, he owed this woman something hot to drink and a warm place to dry off. But what she didn't deserve was being exposed to the tension he knew was inevitable once those gates parted.

In the end, his selfishness won. He couldn't bring himself to say goodbye, not yet. "I think what we both need," he began, pressing the button, "is a stiff brandy to—" He turned back to her and forgot what else he had been about to say because she was gone. But where? How? He hadn't heard her move. "Roanne? Hello?"

He took a few steps down the road, only to be stopped short by the creature she had called Pontus, who blended so well with the darkness that only his pale eyes were clearly visible. The beast uttered another low growl, then wheeled around and dashed away into the night.

"What do you want?"

The human bark gave Hunter a start. He glanced over his shoulder to the wall where the speaker box was located, and back down the road.

"Who's out there? Damned kids. I'm warning you, keep harassing me and I'll call the police!"

Confused, disturbed more than he wanted to admit, and needing illumination in any way he could get it, Hunter retraced his steps. As he reached for the intercom button, he saw that his hand was shaking again.

He swallowed. "It's me, Leland. Let me in."

CHAPTER TWO

He's coming.

Roanne went still. "Leave me alone," she muttered, not at all in the mood to deal with inner voices, particularly when they weren't *hers.* There were practical matters that needed priority attention.

Already behind with her chores, at the rate she was going, she would never get done. Once she finished dealing with the rest of the herbs she hadn't gotten to yesterday, there were dried marigold blossoms to pulverize in preparation for what would become the saffron substitute she supplied to a natural food shop in Bangor. And that was only the beginning of orders she had to fill for her tiny entrepreneurial business.

No, there was no time for dwelling on nonsensical ramblings; the voice had to be wrong. Hunter Thorne would not come because, like her, he had plenty to keep him preoccupied; nor did she need to let her thoughts linger over how the reunion with his father might be going. It was none of her business. Neither was wondering how badly he had damaged his car. She should just count her blessings that the repair work was sure to be considerable. That alone should keep him involved for days.

But he's been told about you, the whispery voice persisted. *Warned. Can you feel it? How can he stay away now? A man like him?*

She exhaled in frustration and tugged harder, too hard, on the vine of hops, sending dried catkins scattering across her worktable. "There! Are you satisfied?" she demanded, and in disgust, flung the whole mess away. At the rate she was going she would never have enough to stuff those hand-stitched pillows for the client who swore the scented herb helped her insomnia.

This was what she got for her meddling. She should have ignored last night's vision. What right did she have to interfere with someone's life, impose her will on another? Had she forgotten all the warnings of possible ramifications passed on by her mother and even Aunt Lilith in a lucid moment? No less specific were the books she continued to seek out and study to better understand herself and her place in this world. There, too, it stated self-determination ultimately directed one's path.

But, as she kept reminding herself, she also had to consider what the results would have been if she hadn't reacted as she did. Hunter Thorne could have followed the impulse of a weak moment, he could have been dead at this very moment.

She placed her hands flat on the worktable before her. "All right," she told her mental intruder, "it's done. He has another chance. But now I want him and *you* out of my head!"

Too late . . . too late . . . too late.

With a feral growl, she stripped off her protective gloves and flung them on the rough wooden table. As she stalked out of the barn, dusty, aromatic air swirled around her.

The late morning sun proved a welcome contrast to the blustering wind that immediately tugged at her hair, her heavy loose sweater and jeans. A particularly forceful blast blew a handful of black strands into her eyes, momentarily blinding her. She swept them away, then drew in a deep, revitalizing breath. Every molecule of matter seemed to be pulsating with positive energies, and like an unquenchable sponge, her senses eagerly absorbed all they could. But it was the perpetual, turbulent sea beyond the old lighthouse that called to her the strongest. She yielded to its pull and wandered toward the edge of the cliffs.

For as far as she could see the waves continued to rise, cap and sink, though the storm had passed hours ago. Seabirds were out in flocks, taking advantage of the improved weather. Their cries were alternately carried or blocked by the wind, depending on their direction of flight. Several swooped near, shouting calls of greeting, as they had earlier when she brought them their usual bits of bread and crackers.

Her annoyance with herself had just begun to recede, when a snort interrupted her reverie. She glanced to her left, spotting the mass of black and gray fur she had been aware of, but ignoring since exiting the barn. Pontus dropped to his belly and lowered his muzzle onto front paws almost equal in size to her hands. He blinked up at her with uncanny, blue topaz eyes.

"You have nerve sounding reproachful," she scoffed. "Don't you know you've triggered his curiosity, too? How many times do I have to remind you that you unnerve people as much as they bother you?"

In return she received an equally caustic grumble and, mimicking her position of a moment before, Pontus redirected his gaze out to sea. Hardly intimidated, and refusing to be charmed by him, Roanne resumed her own study of the ocean.

She didn't know why she bothered trying to reason with him. There was no changing him any more than she could stop being who and what she was. It was the bottom-line truth in a relationship that was as difficult to define as everything else in her life.

They first met when she had come upon him in a cave down on the beach. He had been incapacitated by a small caliber bullet wound in his right hindquarter. Since townspeople frequently shot wild dogs on sight, it was no surprise to see what had befallen an animal of his genetic makeup. Nevertheless, it had been heartwrenching to see him suffering, and she had set to work determined to gain his trust in order to help him.

Though her efforts were successful on both counts, after three years he continued to retain a considerable independence, sleeping in his cave below the lighthouse—except in the winter and during stormy weather. On those occasions he accepted the coziness of her barn, slipping in and out via the leather-covered opening devised for his convenience. Actually, he never wandered too far away, staying particularly close on those nights she was drawn to the cliffs and the beaches below, to the point she often felt empowered with yet a seventh sense. In gratitude, she made it less necessary for him to hunt by providing him with most of his meals.

Once again he glanced her way and she thought of last night and another pair of eyes that had studied her with similar unmitigating directness. But Hunter Thorne's were a rich brown like his hair and mustache, and so dark she hadn't discerned any delineation between pupil and iris. Intelligent and searching, they troubled her still. The entire man disturbed her.

He had lost a child. The revelation was doing unwelcome things to her defenses, as had last night's involuntary study of his strong, broad-planed features. Noting a sophistication about him that seemed to be as weary as his travel-worn executive attire, her intention had been to dismiss him as one of those driven, wheeler-dealer types who, caught up in his ambitions, had forgotten how to shut down. Even after a near sleepless night she wanted to hold fast to that conclusion. But she couldn't.

If he was truly anything like that, the vision she'd had would never have been so vivid, nor would its affect on her be so profound. No, she had tuned in to his pain and tremendous despair as a result of his being someone entirely different, and that's what was triggering her anxiety. Now *she* needed to be the self-possessed one in order to protect herself from the complex feelings he was stirring within her.

There was no room in her life for this. He had disturbed her rest last night and was destroying her concentration this morning. It had to stop.

She turned to Pontus. "What do you say we go for a stroll down to—"

Before she could finish, the animal leaped up and dashed away. Almost simultaneously, she sensed the presence that explained why. It took great control not to spin around, and she succeeded only by reminding herself she would be exposing the tension humming within her. Instead, she listened to the approaching footsteps while watching the endless series of waves crashing against the rocks far below. Their pounding was merciless, like the fierce beating of her heart.

When her unwelcome guest stopped behind her, she asked, "Have you been away from Cliff Point for so

long you've forgotten that the town itself is in the opposite direction, Mr. Thorne?''

"I've found what I was looking for.''

He sounded tense, almost resentful, and it wasn't
difficult to discern why. She sighed. "You shouldn't
have come.''

"I need an explanation.''

"Didn't you get enough of an earful last night?''

"Is that an educated guess, or did you *see* what
happened the way you do everything else?''

"Don't waste your sarcasm on me, Mr. Thorne,''
she said, determined not to shiver against the rush of
internal and external cold that assaulted her. But she
couldn't keep from wrapping her arms around herself. "I've heard it all before.''

"And how many times have you heard yourself
called a—''

She waited for the word, but it didn't come. Curious to see what expression hid the warring emotions
she felt emanating from him, she did a slow about-
face. "*Witch* is the word I believe you're looking for.''

It shouldn't have impressed her that Hunter Thorne
had the grace to look embarrassed. Among the number of perceptions she had collected last night was that
he possessed a strong sense of fairness. As he glanced
away, she absorbed other insights via the shadows beneath his bloodshot, haunted eyes, the lack of color in
his face. If her night had been restless, his had been
worse. She didn't want to know that. It would be a
critical mistake to let it matter.

He compressed his lips and shook his head. "It's
just...no. No, that doesn't make any sense. It's got to
be my father. He's been living alone for a long time.
Maybe it's affecting his mind.''

"Did you come all the way out here to convince yourself, or to apologize to me?"

He swung his gaze back to her, and she saw agitation and doubt flare once again in his eyes. "What I'm trying to do is understand what's going on. Last night all I did was mention your name and he turned as white as a..."

"Ghost," she supplied calmly.

She could see the hands thrust into the pockets of his raincoat curl into fists. "He said things that were preposterous, and he warned me to stay away from you."

"That doesn't sound preposterous at all. In fact, it sounds like good advice. Why didn't you heed it?"

"Because as unbelievable and bizarre as he sounded, *everything* about last night seemed that way."

"And what you want from me is a reassurance that nothing was quite as unusual as you remember, and that your father's warnings are merely an old man's exaggerations?"

"You've got it." He raked a hand through his hair and then gestured expansively. "I mean, it's laughable. The sun is out, the world is right side up and you're standing there looking—" his gaze swept over her body "—extremely normal to me. So I should write off last night to stress and fatigue, right? To suggest that at first I imagined you'd floated up out of nowhere in front of my car, would earn me an invitation to the nearest therapist's couch, wouldn't it?"

"I don't practice levitation, no. I walked up from the beach along a path cut into the cliffs."

"Good. And it was only coincidence that you were there at all to stop me from doing something that in the light of day seems impossible for me to have considered?''

''I'm glad to hear your survival instincts are back in control.''

''Just answer the question.''

''No, I don't think I will.''

''Why not?''

''Because you've ceased wanting the truth.''

He didn't exactly laugh. It was more of a hard mocking sound, but regardless of his intended censure, the transformation of his face was breathtaking. Roanne saw the man he could be, should be, had fate dealt him a kinder fortune, and once again she felt the powerful pull of attraction she had been struggling to deny from the moment they came face-to-face.

As quickly as he began, he stopped and took a step toward her. ''The *truth* is that I'm tired of feeling as though I've got one arm in a straitjacket. The last thing I need is some beautiful flake playing games with my old man's mind...or mine!''

''Mr. Thorne, in the few years I've lived in Cliff Point your father and I haven't spoken a dozen words to each other, the reason being that he's no less fond of his privacy than I am of mine. As for playing games, all I can say is that such pastimes are a waste of my energy.''

''I wish I could believe you're as honest as you sound. Unfortunately, the numbers don't add up.''

She had been a fool to think she could keep her secrets from him, especially when he had relatives living in this town. A wave of weariness swept over her, and an all too familiar sadness. ''Ask your question,'' she conceded, resigned.

For a man with an advantage, he took his time. "My father says you have visions, that you see things about to occur. Can you?"

"It happens."

"He says you're able to read people's thoughts."

"Sometimes."

"Tell me what I'm thinking."

She didn't want to. What was there was so obvious, so intense, her body grew hot from the fierceness of his emotions. But seeing there was no easier way to put an end to this, she lifted her chin and met his commanding stare. "You can't decide whether to put your hands around my throat and shake the truth—what you *think* is the truth—out of me or..."

"Or?"

"Or kiss me."

He dropped his gaze to her mouth. She saw his chest expand with the deep breath he drew in, stretching the material of his burgundy turtleneck sweater. "That was too easy."

"You think so?"

"We both do. Five minutes around someone as stunning as you and any man would be thinking much the same thing. Try again."

Yes, she thought, taking no pleasure in his description of her, she needed to do something that would ensure he would leave her alone. Not just because she was sensing he had the potential to hurt her as deeply as anyone could, but because he was wrong. Men were easily attracted to her, yet she had never incited passion in any man the way she did in Hunter Thorne. It would be suicidal for her to allow herself to get caught up in such emotion, let alone develop a craving for it.

Focus, she commanded, seeking the calm center of herself. Only when she accomplished that did she look deep, deep into his eyes.

It hurt. Oh, how it hurt. He'd had too much practice at turning his pain inward. As a result, she felt as though she were plunging down a bottomless tunnel, all the while being stabbed by an endless series of razor sharp daggers.

"Well?" he demanded.

She wanted to cry. They stood so close, she wanted to put her arms around him and soothe away the pain and grief, draw him out of the dark, dark despair he had fallen into. But she couldn't be the one; her own world had the potential to be even more frightening, and she dared not let him get too close to it.

"You . . . you wish I did have special powers," she began, straining to force the words out. "You think if it were possible, then I could tell you that Cady is safe now and happy."

Already pale, Hunter Thorne turned ashen gray. He backed away from her as though stabbed by one of his own daggers. As he shook his head, rejection radiated from him in harsh, bitter waves.

"You had to already know her name," he declared coldly. "You heard it from someone, didn't you? Admit it!"

"No. Nor did I know how she . . ." Something interfered. "Why do you keep thinking 'fire' when I only sense smoke around her?"

"Stop it!"

He spun away from her, but not before she saw the overbrightness in his eyes, and the torment. She hadn't meant to actually speak those last words, she only wanted to understand. Poor man. Poor Cady. . . . There was another figure, too, someone older, but the image was less defined.

"I don't know how you pulled that off, but I'm not buying it," he told her, forcing her back to the present. "I don't believe in any supernatural garbage."

"You've never had a precognitive experience? A moment of déjà vu?" she asked, feeling slightly disoriented as she always did after such deep concentration. "You've never received a letter from someone you'd been thinking about or phoned someone who'd been about to call you?"

"Of course. Everyone has."

"But you can't accept that some people are endowed with more of those qualities than others?"

"I believe there are individuals who like to make others think they are for one reason or another. The big question is, what's yours?"

CHAPTER THREE

She stared at him as though he had lost his mind. For a moment he thought she was going to slap him, maybe even push him over the cliff, the emotions flaring in her stormy eyes were that vehement. Instead, however, she tossed her hair over her shoulders and drawled, "Have a good life, Mr. Thorne."

It wasn't until she was a few steps away that he realized she was leaving him. "Hey," he called after her. "We're not through yet!"

"Oh, yes we are."

"I still have questions."

She wheeled around, eyes blazing with green fire. "No, what you have are cheap accusations. You're a bitter, angry man, Hunter Thorne, and you think you're the only one to have ever known grief and hurt, that it gives you a right to lash out at the world at will. You also have a disappointingly *narrow* vision for an educated man. There aren't words in any language to make you hear the truth, so this exchange is over. Find someone else to unleash your self-righteousness on. When it comes to being victimized by *good* people, believe me, my cup runneth over. I'm fed up with the lot of you!"

This time when she walked, he let her go. He had to because, though he may not have understood everything she said, one thing was clear; he wasn't just losing his mind as he suspected, he was turning into a monster.

Hunter groaned inwardly. When had he ever set out to hurt anyone with such determination, and a virtual stranger, no less? As tough as he was in a court-room—where at the first hint of deception, he had no problem being merciless with a hostile witness—at least he delayed going on the offensive until having all the facts. With Roanne, he had nothing. Unanswered questions and allegations repeated by his rambling, slightly inebriated father. Mysteries. It made his behavior all the more reprehensible.

Who was she that she should affect him like this, drive him to such outbursts? With a mere look she pulled the strongest emotions from him—few of them comforting. She touched him on levels he didn't know he possessed. She fascinated him. Heaven help him, she frightened him.

Hunter watched her in her determined retreat. He didn't blame her for stalking away without having made any real attempt to explain or defend herself. Actually, a full lecture had been unnecessary; her parting look was enough of a requital. In fact, he could swear an odor of smoke hung in the air—the aftereffects from her branding her brief message into his soul? Along with her fury, there had been such hurt and hopelessness in her eyes. She was right; he had struck out blindly, unfairly. Why did he do it?

But most of all, why did she have to be so lovely? Her beauty went beyond anything physical, though he had only to look at her and she made him ache. He was beginning to identify a quality about her that was somehow ineffable and serene, yet potent when combined with her natural sensuality.

He had come down here to prove Leland wrong. He still wanted to believe there was some mistake, that it had been too much Scotch making his father say what he did; after all, hadn't their entire reunion been a resounding flop thus far? Instead, Roanne had only fueled his ire by standing there, looking him in the eye and acknowledging she was capable of whatever ludicrousness Leland had imputed. But no one had the psychic abilities she ascribed to herself. Did they?

Then what explains her knowing so much...Cady's name...that she and Mrs. Oliver hadn't been burned, but overcome by smoke inhalation? That you were ready to throw your life away?

Crazy, that's what it was, and he wished he had never come back to Cliff Point, nor had ever met Roanne Lloyd Douglas. More than anything, however, he wished he could get past the notion that the moment he blurted his last statement, he had made a grievous error, one he would rue the rest of his life.

Emotionally and physically drained, and thoroughly disgusted with himself, Hunter dropped back his head and gazed up at the sky. Even there he found no peace. Everywhere he looked he saw clouds, but they weren't the billowy variety that inspired fairy tales and fantasies. To his consternation, each one had the chiselled distorted face of a gargoyle, and each stared down at him with mocking scorn, condemnation and repulsion.

Certain he was hallucinating, he shut his eyes tight, then looked again and saw... plain clouds. There was nothing to see but windswept clouds.

Derisive laughter rose in his throat, laughter that grew louder and louder until suddenly, abruptly, it became something completely different and uncontrollable, almost inhuman. It burst from him in an endless frightening purging. He roared against the unfairness of life, his grief for Cady, his inability to do anything but cause others pain...everything, until at last he had nothing more to give.

Finally, he stood silent, wavering on his feet as the wind buffeted him, more exhausted than he had ever been in his life. But for the first time he was also empty...wonderfully, exquisitely empty.

It had sounded like a dying lion's roar. For the rest of the day and throughout the night Roanne kept thinking about the terrible cry she had heard after leaving Hunter Thorne. By the following morning it was embedded in her consciousness as unforgettably as the near tragedy the night before.

A lion's roar of rage, she thought as she resumed her work in the barn. Only it hadn't been an animal that had made the sound. It was *him*. A part of her wasn't at all surprised; she had an acute understanding of the cycles of mourning and from what she could tell, he was past due for such an outpouring. But another part of her was having difficulties giving a damn.

She wanted to hate him, loathe him, despise him. Why not, after his scorn and innuendo?

She paused in the task of sharpening her pocket-knife and examined the edge. Unlike the kitchen knives she was already finished with, this one had a hard blade and required more work. She reached into the pan beside her and scooped out a small amount of water, pouring it over the gray stone set on the table before her. Then, laying the steel at a slight angle against the moistened block, she continued the methodical circular strokes.

The rhythmic motions were soothing to her grim mood. Thinking about her walk in the woods at dawn helped, too. Her intention had been to search for mushrooms, but she found no edible specimens worthy of picking. What she did come across was the perfect solution for teaching the Garrett boys a small lesson. A smile of satisfaction curved her lips. On the way home she had formalized her plan, and now it was all set in her mind. With some assistance from her friend, tomorrow everything would be in its place and ready for when the young teens returned home from school.

Careful that you don't enjoy yourself too much.

The knife slipped off the whetstone. A trickle of fear raced along her spine.

Was she? She meant what she'd said yesterday; she was tired of being victimized and would tolerate it no longer, but her methods were temperate not cruel. Weren't they?

Whatever you say, my dear, but what about Thorne? Since you're breaking your own rules, he deserves to be punished, too.

Roanne reached up and laid her hand near her heart, where beneath her sweater she searched for and found the heavy silver cross that had once belonged to her mother. As always, its presence, as well as thinking of her mother, reassured her.

"No line has been crossed," she asserted firmly to the voice that had left her blissfully alone since yesterday. She should have known the evil one had merely been biding time. "No real harm will be done to the boys, either. My intentions are based simply on principle, not your wicked methods."

Come to think of it, she added to herself, the boys' mother might end up being grateful in a way, since Casey and Tim's high jinks could stand some serious reform. As for Hunter Thorne, if he kept his distance, that would satisfy her. Reassured with her reasonable thinking, Roanne began working again.

You call that justice? After what he's done?

"Will you—" So preoccupied was she with internal strife, that the unexpected shadow stretching across her worktable gave her another unpleasant jolt. Her mood grew even darker the instant she recognized who else had intruded her space. "Haven't you had enough?" she demanded, scowling at the shadow.

He hesitated a moment but answered with impressive casualness, "If I confess you have me confused about how you do that, may I talk to you?"

"No."

"Roanne…" He sighed. "I came to say I'm sorry."

"Damn you," she seethed, wheeling around with knife in hand. "Go away!"

Hunter Thorne stood in the barn doorway, silhouetted by the midday sun. He was dressed more like the locals today, a navy blue ski vest replacing the raincoat and a slate blue suede shirt and jeans instead of the circumspect suit. Roanne didn't want to notice how his clothes complemented his powerful body, but his stance emphasized the fact, just as it made it impossible to delineate his eyes. No matter, she knew he was staring at her knife; she only wished she read more consternation in his thoughts than growing curiosity and reluctant admiration. She didn't want to entertain him, she wanted him unnerved. The man had too much courage for his own good—and her peace of mind.

"I don't blame you for being angry," he told her, his tone undeniably humble. "I'd even understand if you actually wanted to use that thing on me."

"Don't tempt me."

He didn't. What he did do was scan the rest of the barn's interior and ask, "Am I in danger of becoming a human dog bone?"

"Or worse." Annoyed that he found Pontus a greater threat than her, she went back to work, rinsing off her knife. Once through, she took her time wiping it dry on a towel, hoping the gleaming blade would have some effect on him, since Pontus was off to who knew where and would be of no help whatsoever. Then suddenly she gave in to her black mood and abruptly drove the knife's sharp point into the table. She faced Hunter again, folding her arms to wait him out.

His humility gave way to amusement and he cocked an eyebrow. "Do you expect me to believe you'd use it?"

"Try me."

She shouldn't have underestimated him. It took him only three strides to reach her. Roanne grabbed for the knife, but he was faster. He plucked it up and held it out of her reach.

For a moment he simply examined the sharpness of the blade, with respect not fear, she noted dourly as he folded it back into the handle. But it was when he reached behind her and slid it into her back pocket that she decided he was pushing his luck.

"I'm sorry," he said again, so close his breath caressed her lips.

The appeal in his eyes and the sensuous brush of his fingers against her body created havoc with her nerves.

"Go to hell," she mouthed, fighting a peculiar yearning. She was no neglected seedling that, sensing
warmth after winter, unfolds its shell to reach blindly
for the first glimpse of sunlight.

"What if I told you I'm already there?"

"I'd suggest you stop insisting on showing me the
sights."

"I don't mean to. What I think I want is for you to
show me the alternative."

This was quite a change from yesterday, and Roanne
was anything but relieved by it. "Why the sudden
turnaround?"

He exhaled and bowed his head so that his forehead almost touched hers, and he searched her eyes.
"You tell me. I do well to think at all when I'm around
you."

Roanne averted her gaze, too tempted to reach for
what could only bring her heartache. Too tempted to
even dare ask him how the bruise on his temple felt. It
looked tender, though the swelling did appear to be
going down. "What do you want from me, Hunter?"
she demanded, so tense she didn't realize until too late
that she'd used his first name.

"You want to know something absolutely nuts? I
don't know. I only know that I can't seem to stay away
from you."

"Is that supposed to be a compliment?"

"No, rather a fact I'm trying to come to terms with.
It's somewhat unsettling, though it beats the self-pity
I've been wallowing in." He reached up and touched
her hair. "Tell me the truth, would you really use a
knife on me?"

It was frightening that the thought had even passed
through her mind, especially after months of near

quiet, a quiet that had allowed her to begin to believe she was winning her private battle with the unholy forces that had long been challenging her self-control. The revelation spawned a panic as profound as the sexual tension pulsating between her and Hunter.

"What I won't do," she said, feeling the reckless, ruthless desperation of a trapped animal, "is have an affair with you."

"I don't think either of us is ready for that."

But the tensing muscles at his strong jaw and the passion flaring in his eyes said it had more than crossed his mind. It had embedded itself there, so deeply Roanne couldn't help but mirror what he felt, feel how it would be to have his hands on her naked body, him inside her, full and throbbing. When he sucked in a deep breath and wheeled away from her, she had to bite back a whimper at the almost painful withdrawal.

"Why—um—" He cleared his throat. "—why do you call him Pontus?" he asked, stopping near the animal's water dish and food bowl.

She fought to regain her balance and narrowed her eyes, annoyed with this feeling of vulnerability toward him and how it affected her ability to read his thoughts. Was it his intention? Impossible. First he would have to believe to even attempt creating such barriers, and it was obvious nothing had changed there.

Recovering somewhat, she replied coolly, "Pontus was the one Greek sea god without mythology." She had felt the name suited an animal who had abandoned the forest to dwell by the ocean, but if he wanted to know that, he could do his own homework.

"Do you know he wouldn't let me follow you the other night?"

"I'm a mind reader, remember? I know almost everything."

Hunter grimaced and hung his head. "Can't we forget that and start over?"

"Why?"

"Because I'm ashamed of the things I said yesterday. I had no right to repeat what amounts to an increasingly senile old man's jabber. Believe me, it was a new low in my behavior that really opened my eyes to reality. You were right in calling me what you did. Ever since I lost Cady I've been increasingly foultempered and generally an all-around self-pitying jerk. I've withdrawn from my friends, my partners at the law firm . . ."

"Not to mention your father."

Hunter sighed. "That happened long ago. I guess it goes back to never having forgiven him for remarrying so soon after my mother's death. The marriage didn't last, but the hard feelings between us did.

"Except on the night of the accident, I didn't care about old feuds, I needed him. The last thing I expected when I called was that he might hang up on me. But he did. He never said a word, just listened and then hung up. I told myself it was shock—hell, I was hanging on by a thread myself. But he didn't come down to Boston for the funeral, either." He shrugged. "We haven't spoken since."

This was exactly what Roanne didn't want, becoming enmeshed in his pain and his problems. "Everyone reacts differently to the loss of a loved one," she said, frowning at the new fingerprints she suddenly noticed on the barn window. Miserable kids, she thought, grateful that at least they hadn't got inside and messed with her herbs and recipes—or, thank goodness, the dangerous stuff. Pontus must have been around at some point and scared them away.

"He didn't even send flowers for her grave!"

As he slammed his fist into his palm, Roanne shut her eyes against a wave of queasiness. His anger was worse than what he had exhibited yesterday. What he couldn't know, of course, was that Drew had destroyed her ability to function well in the face of such outbursts of violence.

"Yes . . . that makes sense." She focused on keeping her breathing normal. "You see, he couldn't acknowledge she was gone."

"Odd. That's what he said last night." The anger vanished; in its place came hopefulness, and soon desire once again warmed Hunter's eyes. "He's got to be wrong about one thing, though. You have to be good for me. First you saved my life, and now you're trying to make sense of my relationship with my father."

In self-defense, Roanne turned back to her worktable. "If the end result keeps you away from here, why not?" Let him be momentarily stung, she thought, collecting the rest of her knives and placing them in the basket she had used to carry them from the house. He would get over it. It was her own sanity she needed to be concerned with. "How long before your car's fixed?"

"A few weeks," he replied slowly, his disappointment palpable. "Getting all the parts is the biggest headache. How do you feel about that? About me being around awhile?"

"Why should I feel anything?"

He hadn't heard her. Out of the corner of her eye she spotted him stopping by the open cabinet that held the bottled herbs she kept for her personal use and sold to a select few natural food shops. Roanne dashed between him and the cupboard, shut the doors and set the heavy-duty lock.

"That's none of your concern," she muttered.

"Were those actually homemade medicines and things?"

"They're herbal recipes passed down through my family."

"You're kidding? Do they work?"

The arched look she shot over her shoulder was to let him know the question was nowhere near worthy of an answer.

"Even the things marked poison?"

"*Especially* the poisons."

As before, she sensed his skepticism as he analyzed, reasoned and came to a conclusion. But what that conclusion was had her gritting her teeth even before he verbalized it.

"I think I'm beginning to understand," he said thoughtfully. "You've got the hearing of a cat, you're better than average at reading people and you prefer home remedies to prescription or over-the-counter drugs. So, it's being a bit different and maybe something of an iconoclast that has people like my father so bent out of shape about you, am I right?'

"Not quite," Roanne replied, resigned and determined that he should understand once and for all. "What upsets the fine citizens of this community is that one of their favorite sons not only didn't marry a local girl, but an outcast from a place even more backward than Cliff Point. And do you know what

made me such an outcast? I happened to have been
born to a fey family." When she saw his stark sable
eyebrows draw together and his eyes reflect understanding and shock, she smiled coldly. "Yes, indeed,
your not so senile father was right, Hunter. I'm the
last descendant of a long line of sibyls. In other words,
I truly am a *witch.*"

CHAPTER FOUR

To his credit he didn't laugh outright, but it didn't take any special abilities to discern he couldn't have doubted her more if she had claimed she was an extraterrestrial. Strange how no one around here had a problem believing in her powers, nor had she ever had to explain anything to anyone; she had only to live among them and people understood. But along comes this one urbane, educated *man,* and suddenly she knew a hopeless frustration unlike anything she had ever experienced before.

"So help me," she said, unable to keep her voice from quaking, "if you ask me about a broom or crystal ball, I'll..."

"Turn me into a toad? Fill my bed with spiders and snakes?"

"Go home and make peace with your father, Hunter," Roanne said, wearily brushing her hair back from her forehead. "You've overstayed your welcome here."

"No, what I think I've done is finally seen through you."

That got her attention faster than any apology could have. "What are you talking about?"

"If you're afraid of trying a relationship again, then have the courage to say so," he replied, his own voice none too steady. "I'd have thought you more than any woman I've ever met would resist relying on half-baked excuses. It's a pity to discover I overestimated you.''

This time he was the one to leave, striding out of the barn with his back as ramrod straight as his thinking was inflexible. Her first instinct was to go after him, give him a piece of her mind and prove he understood nothing. Nothing. But how could she when that would only delay his departure?

As her legs began to give, she slumped onto a nearby square bale of hay and dropped her head to her knees. She began rocking back and forth, as though she were sitting in her mother's rocker, rocking to ease the debilitating feeling of vulnerability and loneliness she was all too familiar with.

A cool breeze, like a hand, stroked over her hair. *Don't worry, dear. I'm here . . . and I'll never abandon you.*

As soft laughter echoed through the barn, Roanne shivered and blindly clutched at her cross.

She only managed an hour or two of sleep that night, but Roanne rose early the next morning, dressed, and set off for the woods determined to keep to her plans. Out of necessity, her trek took her close to the Thorne estate and she hurried past it, keeping the hood of her cape drawn over her head to ensure she would better blend in with the shadows cast by the tall trees.

Minutes later, she came to the place she was looking for. Her friend was already waiting. She approached the meandering furry creature with circumspection, and took out the fresh egg she had brought along for a treat. After cracking it into halves, she laid the sticky bounty on a leaf-cleared spot.

"Shh—there's a good boy," she cooed to the animal edging cautiously nearer. "Here's breakfast as promised, and then we'll pay the visit I mentioned yesterday, all right?"

It licked at the egg white, grunting softly when Roanne stroked it's glossy coat. Once it devoured one half of the shell's offering, she checked behind its neck for the wound she had cared for months ago after its nasty collision with a motor bike. She was glad to discover the laceration had healed well.

When it finished her offering, she rose, about to lead it toward town, but the sound of a cracking twig had her spinning around. Before she could reassure her friend, it scampered off into the woods, the white stripe of its bushy tail hoisted skyward in warning like a defiant knight's lance.

"Damn it all," she cried, aware the fragile bond of trust had been temporarily shattered. "Double damn," she groaned, seeing Hunter duck under the last low vine separating them. "I'd hoped I'd finally seen the last of you."

"A couple of hours ago, I would agree that you had. But then I saw you from my bedroom window. I couldn't resist following to find out what you were up to."

"Your lack of willpower is interfering in something that's none of your business."

"Roanne, that was a *skunk*," Hunter said, pointing though the animal was gone. "And it let you pet it?"

She failed to see a need to reply to the obvious. She only tapped her foot, beating a soft tattoo on the moss-covered ground.

Hunter rubbed at his jaw. "All right, let's leave the subject of my willpower and your affection for potentially rabid mammals for a moment. What's this visit I heard you mention?"

"Why should I tell you?" Roanne kept her gaze averted to avoid dwelling on how he hadn't shaved and how it appeared his night had been as rough as hers. "You won't believe me."

"What if I promised to try?"

She didn't want him to try, she wanted him to leave her alone. Though maybe the only way to make him do so was to tell him more of what he found impossible to accept; hadn't it worked before? "He was going to do me a favor," she offered.

Only a muscle twitch shifting one edge of Hunter's mustache gave away his initial skepticism. "Define favor?"

"Some boys in town have been giving me trouble and I decided they needed to be taught a lesson. I was going to put him in the club house in their backyard where they always go directly after school."

When Hunter's entire mouth began to twitch suspiciously, Roanne realized she had only amused him, not to mention increased his curiosity. More than ready to abandon the whole thing, she gestured dismissively and set off on the path leading to town. At least she could do her errands as planned, she told herself. But any hope that Hunter would take the hint and return to his father's estate, soon proved a waste of time once he fell in step beside her.

What now? What had changed from yesterday to bring on this new persistence? She refrained from actually searching his thoughts for the answer, afraid she might learn things she wouldn't be able to deal with.

"Would you like to talk about the kids?" Hunter ventured.

"No."

"Poor tykes. Your—er—lesson would have been a tough one."

Incensed, Roanne halted and declared, "Those poor tykes are thirteen and fourteen. Old enough to know better. Old enough to know you don't break people's windows, damage their fences and rip things from their garden. The other day they drew a pentagram on my mailbox." She began walking again to give her temper an outlet and, again, Hunter was with her. "All I've ever asked is to live in peace, and that's what it's gotten me."

"Ever try talking to their parents?"

They emerged from the woods at the edge of the residential portion of town, and Roanne shot him a droll look before crossing the street. "That earned me a visit from the sheriff who warned me not to threaten anyone in his jurisdiction again. Any other brilliant suggestions?"

She accelerated her pace, and headed directly up the street toward Berry's Market. Bushels of autumn fruit had just been set out to lure the day's potential customers.

She paused before the baskets of apples, painfully aware of Hunter, who stopped and feigned interest in the pears. Even in casual attire he stood out, she thought with an inner groan. Didn't he understand she didn't need the extra attention?

"Are you buying or not?"

She lifted her gaze to meet the wary but stubborn stare of sour-faced Mrs. Berry. Now here was someone who deserved humbling almost more than the Garrett boys, she thought, tempted to tell the overbearing woman once and for all what she thought of her. But indulging in such a luxury would result in her having to do all her future marketing in the next township, too far a commute considering her meager and infrequent needs.

"I am," she replied, suppressing her dislike for the woman. "But there doesn't seem to be a half dozen of these apples that aren't bruised."

"Hmph. They were all fine five minutes ago."

As insults went, it was milder than many she received, but haste was Roanne's current priority. She chose to ignore the remark and drew out her coin purse to pay for the four pieces of fruit she did want. It gave her a sinful pleasure when Mrs. Berry grew visibly disconcerted at how she didn't place the money on the board beside the basket, as she normally did, but offered it into her hand. Like most people, the woman preferred avoiding any physical contact with her. But she wouldn't get away with it today, Roanne vowed to herself, still disgruntled to have had her earlier plans ruined.

Reluctantly, Mrs. Berry thrust out her hand. It was all Roanne needed. She grasped the woman by her wrist and as she passed over the money leaned toward her. "You're not coming down with something are you, Edna?"

Mrs. Berry reacted as though dowsed with a pail of ice water. Her face turned red and her jaw went slack, wobbling like excess skin on an old soup chicken.

"Wh—what do you mean?" she demanded, trying to pull her hand free.

"You don't look at all well." Roanne dropped her voice low so any passerby beyond Hunter wouldn't hear. "It wouldn't be that you're indulging in too many of those fudge cakes you keep hidden back in your pantry? Be careful, Edna. A person with a diabetic condition like yours can't take health for granted."

The heavyset woman choked and jerked loose "How did you—? Get away. Get away from here, you evil thing! Oh! She's done it. I've been hexed. George . . . George!"

As Mrs. Berry fled into the shop in search of Mr. Berry, Roanne placed the apples into the mesh shopping tote she had been carrying under her cape. Well now, she thought, there might be a price to pay later, but this had been worth it.

It would always be like this if you would fully accept your powers.

Roanne frowned at the abrupt and haunting intrusion in her thoughts and headed quickly for the crosswalk. She was barely aware of Hunter's presence as she stepped off the curb.

There are others who would benefit from a lesson from you.

"Not now," she moaned, touching her fingers to her forehead. It had never been her intention to retaliate for all the wrongs done to her since coming to Cliff Point. First because the list was too long, and second because it would only uphold the age-old lesson about how two wrongs didn't make a right.

And yet, doesn't it feel delicious to have such control?

Yes, she couldn't deny it did feel . . . intoxicating.

Why not try it again? Just once more.

The voice, like the clouds overhead, grew less innocent, the wind less casual. Roanne ducked deeper into the protection of her hood and cape, and shivered.

"Roanne."

She found herself on the other side of the street and Hunter holding her arm. "What?" she asked, trying to focus both mentally and visually.

"Are you all right?"

No, she thought, though she nodded to him, she was anything but all right. One more errand and she needed to get home. There was no way she could explain it to him, but the voice whispering to only her was getting beyond intrusive, it was frightening her. A battle of wills was imminent, and she didn't need any witnesses, especially him. What a mistake she had made; to think she could trifle with retribution and keep her spirit pure.

Pure? You lost your purity when you failed Drew.

One last errand, Roanne thought with greater determination, hurrying into Guthrey and Son Hardware. With winter coming she needed to recaulk her window and door seams. But the irony of that, the fact that it emphasized the duality of her entire existence, only added to her growing stress and paranoia. What an anomaly of nature she was, she thought, fighting the strongest urge to burst into hysterical laughter. She had all these powers, yet she still had to rely on practical technology to keep the cold out of her cottage.

At the counter C. Stanton Guthrey was giving change to a customer. C. Stanton, Jr., himself near forty, glanced at her over the rims of wire bifocals and hunched further over the receipts he was tallying. His behavior wasn't anything new to her; even before Drew's death his manner toward her had been wanting. But her growing unease had her wishing he would give her what she needed and let her withdraw to the sanctuary of her home.

"Mr. Stanton," she said as politely as possible, and pointing to a shelf behind him, "if I could trouble you for—"

"I'm in the middle of something, Mrs. Douglas." This time he glanced only as far as the service bell by her clenched hands. "And as you can see, my father, as well. Please wait your turn."

Five minutes passed. Other people walked in and some were helped. Customers who had phoned earlier, she was told, though she didn't bother asking why. She knew there was no point.

"I think you've kept the lady long enough."

Roanne bit her lower lip to hold back a groan of protest. Preoccupied with her own troubled thoughts, she had almost forgotten about Hunter. That was laughable, too, except that it emphasized how deeply worried she was.

When he joined her at the counter, she didn't dare look at him, afraid he would see too much in her eyes. She merely whispered, "Don't."

"They're ignoring you," he replied in kind. "Why put up with it? Why don't you walk out?"

"Because I'd only have to come back another day and then it would be worse."

"Then tell me what you need, and I'll get it for you."

She was embarrassed; worse, her hold on her own temper was slipping fast. Both Guthreys were gawking openly and so were other customers. Desperate, she told him, pointing again to the item. His bemused expression, however, was too much. "Yes, I'm susceptible to drafts and catching colds like normal people," she muttered, glaring back at him.

In the end she decided she would prefer the drafts to this, and she did leave. She all but ran down Main Street, not slowing her pace until she had passed the last residence and started down the wooded path that was a shortcut to her home.

"Hey!"

She kept going. She knew the deteriorating weather was not of any natural origin and how treacherous this trail could become if she lingered. As much as she loved walking through the woods, this latest oncoming battle for her soul would best be fought on her own ground if she could help it, and not with Hunter as a witness—or a possible victim.

"Will you wait!"

He caught her wrist and swung her around to face him. She didn't want to be impressed that despite the stress in his life he had to be in excellent shape to have run all this way. The other day she had concluded he was about ten years older than her own twenty-eight, yet as he stopped to tuck the bag containing the caulk into her tote, she was impressed to see there also wasn't a thread of gray in his wavy, wind-tossed hair.

"Don't you ever use a car?" he wheezed, waving her away as she quickly reached for her purse to reimburse him.

It hadn't been practical because of what she had been up to earlier, but she also couldn't afford to use it; something else she didn't want to get into with him. The car was old and she was trying to prolong its life in case the opportunity ever arose for her to leave here permanently. Not that anything was likely to happen she reminded herself, thinking of the veterinarian who was the last to have voiced an interest in buying her out. But like the others before him, she hadn't heard from him again.

"Put that *away*," Hunter insisted, seeing she was determined to repay him. "Consider this a bribe."

Ever suspicious, she countered, "A bribe for what?"

"A few more explanations."

"You don't like my explanations, remember?" she said, glancing worriedly around at the way the trees were beginning to twist and moan with the intensifying wind.

"That was before I witnessed what happened in town." Hunter placed his hands on his jean-clad hips and swore because he was still trying to catch his breath. Roanne wondered if he had any awareness of what a dashing figure he cut. "Does everyone around here treat you like they did?"

"More or less."

"Why don't you sell out and leave?"

"I've tried. But the local Realtor won't deal with me." She shrugged. "His signs keep disappearing from my yard. There's been some interest in the ads I've placed in various newspapers. But anyone who's gotten serious about making me an offer has been discouraged by townspeople who don't want me to succeed in selling."

"Abandon the place."

"And give everyone what they want? Never."

He could help you, came the voice, stronger than ever. *Use him. He's already infatuated with you. Make him burn with it. Use the power. Use it!*

The intrusion only added to the throbbing in her head. Roanne closed her eyes, barely suppressing a moan. She yearned to keep them shut because when she had these moments, everything grew too focused, too intense and painful.

What she had long feared was beginning to happen. She was losing control, losing her grip on reality. Even the swaying hemlocks and oaks were taking on an energy that was not of this world, and the wind...its wail was more like a ghostly taunt. She had known moments like this before, but never so threatening. Not since...

"What's wrong?" Hunter demanded.

"Nothing. I have to go. The weather—"

"Hang the weather." Hunter forced her back against an ancient hemlock. "Stop pushing me away. Like it or not you've turned everything in my world upside down. You're turning *me* inside out. Want to know all I keep coming up with?"

"Don't say it." She tried to pull free, but he made her efforts ineffectual and she only succeeded in dropping her tote.

"I will. I don't care, do you understand? I'm realizing I don't give a damn what you are, or more precisely what you *think* you are. Whatever it is, it works for me. Whoever you are, I need your faith and your goodness."

She struck at his chest to silence him. "Stop it."

"I can't. I can't do anything anymore...not eat or sleep...I just have this unnatural, impossible need. For you."

"Shut up." Everything was getting so frantic and mixed up. She wasn't good. He was wrong! And yet suddenly, incredibly, she found herself no longer pushing at him but pulling. She gripped handfuls of his sweater as if he were her last connection with sanity. "Shut up... shut up!" she sobbed.

She kissed him to stop herself from edging over into hysteria. She kissed him because what he had been about to ask from her was impossible. Forbidden. But most of all she kissed him because she needed one perfect memory before letting him go.

"Oh, God." His powerful body shuddered under her sensual assault, yet sought more, pressed closer, as though he wanted to absorb every inch of her into him. *"Yes."*

He angled his head and perfected their union, locking his lips to hers and meeting her aggressive passion with a fierceness that within seconds had Roanne trembling as well. And still he tried to get closer. His heat scorched her thighs and burned upward, inward, while her lips, teeth and tongue learned every nuance of his flavors and textures.

Her heart had been barren for so long. Too often human contact had been dismal, and isolation even more desolate. This was her one respite before again cloaking herself in solitude and accepting the mantle of loneliness she was fated to wear.

"I want... I feel..." With a groan, Hunter buried his face at the side of her neck. "You saved my life, and now you control it. Does that make any sense to you?"

Yes, only she didn't want that kind of power over him. But as he searched beneath her cape to explore more of her, she held back the words that would end this bliss. Just a moment more, she reasoned as his gentle but determined hands learned the shape of her aching breasts, bit hungrily into her waist and cupped her hips to lift her against him, until she was melting with desire.

"I need you," he rasped.

No less than she needed him, but that was something he could never know. Brutally suppressing the yearnings of her own body, she whispered, "I'm sorry... I can't."

He stiffened, slowly lifting his head to search her face. His eyes grew wary. "Not here," he agreed slowly. "But soon."

"Listen to me, Hunter." Roanne eased away from him.

No! Don't be a fool. Stay. Take him with you.

Fighting the voice and a temptation as powerful as any drug, she grabbed up her things and clutched them to her chest like a shield. She had to struggle to focus her resistance. "You're wrong about me. You need someone who can teach you to live and dream again. And you'll meet her because you're going to be all right now. But you... you wouldn't be with me."

"Why not?" Though clearly confused, the glint lighting his eyes suggested he intended to convince her how wrong she was.

Fool. Coward!

The wind swelled and the earth moaned. Suddenly, not a dozen yards away, a mighty hardwood ripped free from the ground and fell with a reverberating crash.

Hunter's expression exposed his doubt but growing unease as he searched the sky. Roanne knew what he was thinking; he was trying to understand the speed and fury with which the weather had degenerated, but knew there wasn't a logical explanation.

"That's why," Roanne said, touching his cheek before backing away from him. "Go home, Hunter, quickly. And stay away."

"You don't mean that." ·

"Please. What I don't want is to hurt you, but I'm not sure how long I can avoid it if you don't do as I ask. Stay away," she begged.

Even if he had the sense to listen, she knew he never heard her. At the moment she spoke, her voice was drowned out by a vicious clap of freak thunder. Only she knew from precisely what unnatural source it had spawned, and she ran to keep it away from him.

CHAPTER FIVE

"The woman's become an obsession to you."

Bleary-eyed, Hunter glanced up from his reading and over the stack of books piled on the desk to consider his father's distinguished but stony countenance. "I won't deny that."

"She's making a fool out of you."

Maybe. If being a fool meant calling various friends and experts in Boston over the last several days, who could direct him to serious sources of information regarding the paranormal. Several had responded with silence, followed by a gentle suggestion that he seek immediate medical counsel. But those had been the only moments when he felt he was making a mistake.

Others had asked careful questions before sharing an amazing amount of data and advice. It never occurred to him how many people, people whom any court would judge responsible and intelligent, believed in various and strange phenomena. And now, thanks to a great deal of reading and even more introspection, he was beginning to grasp at least a fragment of understanding himself.

How much easier it would be if he could take his questions directly to Roanne. But she was standing firm on her demand for space. Every attempt he had made to see her since that day in the woods had been unsuccessful. Somehow she either *felt* he was coming and took off, or locked herself in her cottage and refused to answer the door when he tapped, knocked, then beat on it.

He was worried about her. More than worried—and something had to give soon. It was going to drive him crazy if he couldn't at least see she was all right.

"You're driving *me* crazy with all this mumbo jumbo nonsense," Leland muttered, interrupting his thoughts.

How ironic that his father could almost pick up on his thoughts, while they continued to have difficulty managing the simplest of conversations. He watched him reach into the pocket of his fox gray sweater for a pipe. His hair, a matching silver, gleamed in the lamplight as he bowed his head to light the prepacked bowl. Their strong resemblance only made it sadder that the gulf between them remained unbridgeable.

"Want to talk about something else?" he asked, though he knew what answer he would get. "I've told you from the start that repairing old wounds was the first reason for my visit."

"But not your primary reason for staying now," Leland replied, watching smoke curl upward creating a veil between them.

"Not any longer, no." Hunter felt an ache for their lost years, but he couldn't change what he didn't understand. He raised his hand when Leland began to speak. "We won't discuss Roanne, either. No matter what the gossips say, she's helped me as no one else has. Look, given that the repairs on my car are taking longer than anticipated, you aren't able to have the isolation you prefer. Say the word and I can get a room in—"

"Who said anything about what I prefer?"

"Every look and gesture is like a silent testimonial."

"Just because I'm not an outwardly emotional man, just because I was raised to control my feelings..."

"Hide, Leland. Let's give things their proper names. You *hide* your true feelings. You always have. You did it all the while Mom was sick and you did it when Cady died."

"You call this talking? Dragging up the past and rubbing my nose in my failures as a husband and father and grandfather?" Leland shot back. "Yes, I made my mistakes, but apologizing can't change anything, so what's the point?"

"Maybe I'd finally understand. They say with understanding comes forgiveness. Neither one of us is getting any younger. Are we going to carry all this to our graves?"

As he closed his eyes, a spasm of pain crossed Leland's lined, but still handsome features. "You make your decisions and then you live with them. That's all there is." He opened his eyes and went to the bar. "It's getting late. I only came to get myself a nightcap before I retire to my room. You want anything?"

"No, thanks," Hunter replied, yielding to bitterness. "One of us should stay sober in case there's an emergency."

His father had already poured two fingers of Scotch into a heavy crystal tumbler, and after that remark poured a third. Then, without any further comment, he walked out.

"Very progressive, Thorne," Hunter muttered, though he wasn't certain whether he spoke to his father or himself. At least they hadn't started a shouting match this time.

His concentration shot, he knew there would be no more reading tonight and shut his book. As he pushed himself to his feet, he felt momentarily drained, as tired as when he crammed for his toughest cases. It would do him good to turn in at a reasonable hour for a change.

But once he showered and crawled naked beneath the covers of his own bed he found sleep the furthest thing from his mind. Pillowing his head with his laced hands, he gazed up at the moonlit ceiling and let his thoughts return to Roanne.

What was she doing now? Was she thinking of him, remembering those few precious moments he had held her, caressed her and tasted her as he had been craving to do? How could she bear locking him out like this? *How?* He shut his eyes and bit back a groan as his body reacted to his tormenting memories.

He wasn't sure what made him reopen them or when, or that he really did. A part of him was convinced he must be asleep, had been for a while, because there was something different about the shadows in the room. As it came to him that he need only check the travel alarm on the nightstand to be certain, he saw her.

She stepped out of the deepest shadow. With a grace that made her seem to float, she came to the foot of the bed and watched him sleep. He *was* asleep! It was as if he could see it with some third eye.

Dazed, delighted, but also disconcerted at the bizarreness of it all, he tried to move and found he couldn't. His entire body felt leaden, useless. Only his heart and lungs seemed operative; too much so, he discovered when to his amazement and pleasure, she began lowering himself over him.

Her movements were slow and as subtle as a current of tropical, exotically scented air. Blacker than any night, her long mane became a veil enclosing them in a cocoon of heightened sensitivity. He had no words to describe her phantomlike weightlessness; it didn't stop his body from going instantly hard, feverishly hot wherever she touched him. And when she brought her lips to his, he groaned, and drank greedily from her.

As parched as his throat felt, his soul was countless times worse, a dry wasteland. He wondered if he could ever get enough of her, fill himself, drown in her sweet, moist kisses. Determined to try and aching to break his arms free of the invisible shackles that kept him from crushing her to him, he found it impossible.

"This has to be a dream," he groaned, gripping at the bed sheet as she began raining kisses down his body.

"Don't make me go," was her only reply.

Actually, her voice wasn't exactly a voice but a distant awareness, like the echo of the sea well beyond his bedroom window. But the sea, he reminded himself, was real. She couldn't be anything except fantasy, a seawitch who had somehow filtered into his imagination when sleep had lowered the defenses of his conscious mind.

"Let me stay. You want me."

Yes, he wanted her... her hands and her mouth... and the oblivion, ecstasy and peace he knew he could find buried deep inside her. But not, he insisted with a last lucid, desperate corner of his mind, if she was merely a figment of some lustful dream.

"You're not real!" he rasped, and pushed himself upright.

Sweat was pouring from his body, his fully aroused and achingly hard body. Every breath he took was labored...and he was alone. That above everything else shocked and pained him the most. *He was alone.*

Grief-stricken and in physical agony, he tossed back the covers and lunged out of bed. He made his way to the bathroom, indifferent to the darkness. Lights weren't important right now; besides, he had no great desire to face himself in the vanity mirror.

The water pipes groaned in protest when he wrenched on both the hot and cold shower taps, and reality became a sharp taskmaster as he wasted no time stepping under the needlelike faucet spray. The icy sting won a harsh gasp from him, but he braced his hands against the tile wall and accepted the assault.

Finally, however, the water grew warmer. Relieved, he raised his face to the downpour. Yes, this was reality, he told himself, waiting for the rest of his fever to subside and his body to relax.

But instead there came again the lambent caress of her scent. It teased his nostrils seconds before her presence surrounded him. "Sweet madness," he whispered an instant before feeling her actual touch.

Damn it, he was awake! The bathroom was real, the water pounding at his body was real, and these were his hands he was curling into fists as—he shuddered reflexively—as her mouth took over where her hands had stopped.

Believing his legs would buckle, and gritting his teeth against the explicit, desperate words he wanted to shout, he pressed his head against his forearm.

"Roanne." Her name came torn from somewhere deep inside him. "Sweet . . . *Roanne.*"

Mere heartbeats later, and in defiance of any law or logic he knew or ever hoped to understand, she drove him to a violent, unbelievable release.

He didn't know how long he stood there after he felt her presence slowly diminish and recede. Eventually, he became aware he had used up all the hot water and was shaking from cold as much as anything else. It was only then, with his legs so weak he had to hold on to the wall to stay on his feet, that he exited the shower, grabbed a towel and stumbled back to bed.

Throwing himself face down on the rumpled bedding, he dragged the pillows to him and clutched them close with a fierceness that made his arm muscles ache. He tried to think but couldn't; he wanted to understand, but didn't. All he knew was that he believed. In the end his overwhelmed mind resorted to sheer survivalist instinct. It shut down and he slept.

It was late the following morning when the front door of Roanne's cottage opened and Hunter stepped inside. She could see his surprise that it wasn't locked, the way it had been during his last few attempts to see her. What he couldn't know was the reason, namely that she needed to see him for her own sanity's sake.

"Hi," he murmured, no smile softening his tense features.

She didn't need smiles, the aura of his relief and pleasure was enough. But afraid she might give away too much and cross the boundaries she had carefully set for herself and this meeting, she resumed kneading the oatmeal-nut bread she made weekly for herself. "Help yourself to a cup of coffee."

It broke her heart how it took him two tries to get the gruff, "Sure" out. So prepared had he been for rejection, he had no response for anything better.

How good he looked. He was dressed casually again, a red shirt and jeans under the now familiar vest. For once he had slept deeply, easing some of the shadows under his eyes. It was gratifying to see. She was grateful for these stolen moments.

"I caught you on a busy day?" he ventured, coming to stand on the opposite side of the central counter where she worked.

The electricity between them was so potent, it was a wonder the air didn't crackle. "There's always something to do around here," she replied, aware he was eyeing the various bowls scattered about. "Besides marketing my herbs, I support myself with my special recipes. Things like jams and relishes. I also sew. All of it goes to various specialty shops."

"It sounds like a tough way to make a living."

"I don't need much."

She was melting under the intense intimacy of his gaze, and would have been thrilled it it weren't all hopeless. "The reason I—" she began.

"I came to—" he said at the same time.

To avoid wringing her hands, she wrenched the bread dough into two halves and began kneading again. "Sorry. Go ahead."

"No, you first."

"I only...I wanted to ask if you're all right?"

"Don't you know?" he asked softly.

She had known this wouldn't be easy, but it was proving to be torture. "You've been busy yourself," she said, deciding to focus directly on her agenda before he lured her into more dangerous territory. "But

I think you made a mistake with your current course of study. It isn't helping the situation with your father.''

Hunter set down the mug, uttering a shaky laugh. "I can't get over how easy it is for you to crawl into my head."

"It's your own fault, you're too open to me. If you were more like Leland, it would be harder. I'd at least have to be in your immediate physical proximity."

"If I was more like him, I doubt I would have come back here." He shook his head. "Do you have any idea what's going on with him? What it is he's keeping from me?"

"No. As I said before, sometimes getting close helps, but not always." She had tried to probe, but Leland Thorne was a brick wall to her. The image of a wall flickered before her eyes and she shivered.

"What?"

"Nothing. Well, I'm not sure. Just be careful, all right?"

Hunter frowned. "Are you getting a premonition?"

"I'm not sure."

"Does it have anything to do with that day in the woods?"

"That has nothing to do with you." Not as long as she kept him at a safe distance. "Anyway, it's under control again, so don't worry about it."

Flippant words for such a close call. For days she had been a total recluse, barely going out, except to bring meals to Pontus and to tend to a raccoon who had come with an infected paw. Otherwise, she had closed herself in her house and curled up in her mother's rocker, spending hours gripping her old Celtic cross and whispering the prayers her mother had embedded in her memory well before teaching her any of the white magic.

"Nothing to do with me?" Hunter came around the counter and, taking hold of her shoulders, forced her to face him. "Roanne, why do you think I'm scouring two states trying to find everything in print on the mystical sciences? I want to understand. I want you to feel comfortable talking to me. I want—"

"Will you *listen*." Roanne twisted away from him, but in doing so the back of her hand struck the bowl of cooked cranberries cooling nearby. The contents rolled back and forth like a rampant tide spilling over the edge and onto the pristine, white counter.

In growing horror she watched the juice turn to blood, its source not a ceramic bowl but the scalp of a curly-haired youngster who lay ominously still on the edge of a cement play area. Behind her an empty swing rocked back and forth in silent testimony to the girl's misadventure.

"What's happening? What do you see?" Hunter demanded, stroking her hair.

Nauseous and half-blinded by the pain the child felt, she groped for and found Hunter's hand. Strong and warm, it was the ballast she needed. "I heard you arrive by car. Will you drive me to the elementary school? No, the library...it has to be the library first."

"I...of course. When?"

"Now, and...oh, God...hurry!"

CHAPTER SIX

She let Hunter take control for a few minutes, force her to pause and put on her cape against the cold and secure her seat belt himself. She needed the time to regain her balance and her composure, because it was a child she had seen.

Despite her annoyance with the Garrett boys, the truth was she adored children and had wanted one of her own desperately. But that was before she knew the full truth about her Aunt Lilith and had married Drew. It was doubtful she would ever allow herself to bring a baby into the world now; that's what made her all the more protective of the children around her.

"Who's at the library?" Hunter asked, once he had his father's sedan turned and headed toward the main road.

Roanne leaned back against the headrest and willed her strength to return. She would need every ounce to help those who were too superstitious, too afraid to accept her aid. "Rosemary Shelton. It was her daughter, Marcie, I saw." When he told her he remembered a Rosemary from his early school days, she briefly described her vision to him.

Hunter swore softly. "Do you feel everything they do?"

"Sometimes, especially with the children." She turned her head toward the passenger window, hoping he wouldn't ask her more about that.

"How much time do we have?"

"Not enough. Hurry, Hunter."

Rosemary Shelton was a small, athletically built woman whose hair was several shades darker than her daughter's, but whose natural curls and facial features were a distinct if older version of her child's. Roanne had never spoken to her because she rarely went into the library, and she was grateful that Hunter took the initiative to introduce himself and draw her aside.

"Marcie's at school today, isn't she?" he began.

The woman's expression turned wary and her gaze moved quickly to Roanne. "Of course. Why? What's *she* doing here?"

"You have to go to her," Roanne replied urgently. "Keep her from playing on the equipment—I'm sure it's the swings—during recess."

"What? Why would I want to do that?"

"Rosemary," Hunter injected. "Try to stay calm. Roanne only—"

"There's no time for this!" Roanne cried glancing up at the clock. She grabbed Rosemary Shelton's arm. "Your daughter is in danger of being hurt. Come *now* or deal with the guilt later!"

It took another precious two minutes to get to the school. At the gate to the playground, where children were already racing about, they were blocked by a teacher acting as security attendant. Unfortunately, she was a substitute who didn't know Rosemary Shelton, let alone Hunter or Roanne. Before anyone could convince her that they needed to get inside there was

a high-pitched scream followed by several screeches
and cries.

"My baby!" Mrs. Shelton cried, bursting through
and racing toward the fallen child. "Marcie...
somebody call for an ambulance, a doctor!"

Like everyone else, Roanne and Hunter ran to the
scene and eased through the children blocking their
way. Roanne crouched and said, "Mrs. Shelton,
maybe I can—"

"Get away! Oh, haven't you done enough?" the
woman wailed.

"But I—"

"Made this happen because I was afraid to talk to
you. I've heard about you and how you threaten people. Everyone at the library heard you yell at me.
You're a horrible woman to use a baby for your mischief. Horrible!"

Roanne felt herself lifted and drawn away. Stunned
by Rosemary Shelton's rebuke, she belatedly recognized Hunter.

"Take the car," he said gently, "and go home. I'll
stick around to see what I can do here and follow
shortly. It'll be all right." He kissed her on the forehead. "It'll be all right."

But he was wrong.

*Do you see? No one appreciates you. They don't
understand. But we do. Join with the power. Exalt in
yourself.*

Along with the evermore forceful whisper, the wind
gusted and billowed inside Roanne's cape. She spun
away from the sea and the beckoning. She had not
come out here to listen to this. She had come down to
the beach to get away from her misery, from herself.

After hours of walking, however, it was apparent she had been wasting her time. There was no relief here, no escape. Her thoughts and emotions remained turbulent, while the voice was gaining strength.

Not even the call earlier from the veterinarian had lifted her spirits. Empty words, that's all the man had given her. Regardless of what he insisted, she doubted he would come back to talk seriously about her property. Why should he be any different from the others who had come before him? Why would he want to be a part of this miserable community?

A stronger wave struck the single towering rock protruding from the shoreline, attracting her attention. Water arced in hundreds of directions like an exploding fireworks rocket before falling to join the incoming foaming tide.

Roanne felt a particular kinship to that rock. She, too, was alone, and being assaulted from almost every direction. Even Hunter had sent her away. He had been right to, of course; it wasn't wise to be continually seen with her, especially when his was one of the oldest, most respected families in the area. Never mind that it had still hurt.

Can you blame him for being cautious? Look what loving you got me.

The taunt, the different voice, had Roanne gasping and wheeling around to search the darkening horizon. It wasn't possible . . . was it?

"Drew?"

It was dusk and the demarcation line between sky and water was fading fast, creating a new dimension, while intensifying old fears. The effect was chilling, dizzying.

Roanne . . .

The wet sand became an accomplice plotting against her as it shifted and sucked at her booted feet. She swayed, yet fought the manipulation. She would not succumb to this latest attempt to break her will. She would not yield her independence. But as she resumed her walk home, she pulled her cape more tightly around herself.

Where was Pontus? He had been with her when she first came down here and now... *Ah,* she thought gazing upward, her pace faltering. She should have known.

At the top of the cliff she spotted a man silhouetted by the last hint of pink and violet in the western sky. His broad-shouldered and lean-hipped stance clearly identified him, and Roanne couldn't help the rush of longing that recognition brought. The problem was he was too late; he had been from the first.

"I was here earlier, but not seeing the car threw me," Hunter said, when she reached the crest of the cliff. "You didn't have to bring it back to my father's place."

She pretended not to see the arm he stretched out to assist and embrace her, and concentrated on her footing. "I thought he might need it. Besides, it wouldn't be wise to let it be seen sitting in front of my house for too long."

"What's that supposed to mean?"

"Exactly what I said. If you had any doubts before, you shouldn't now."

When she tried to walk past him, he stepped before her. "Are you upset because I sent you home? I was trying to keep you from being hurt any further! Hell," he muttered, trying to calm himself. "I didn't come to argue with you, I came to let you know that we got

Marcie patched up. She has a mild concussion, but she's going to be all right."

"You don't think I *know* that?" The urge to snarl, to hide and lick her wounds was growing inside her. "What's more, I don't need a protector."

"Well, I disagree," he said, mimicking her low, intense tone, while passion flared in his eyes. "It bothers me that the citizens of Cliff Point don't appreciate the guardian angel in their midst, or what she suffers to protect their children."

Roanne shook her head, not wanting to hear. "Don't make me out to be what I'm not, Hunter. You read a few books and you saw me try to do the right thing for a change, but you don't really know me or what I'm capable of. Rosemary Shelton was right."

"That's ridiculous and you know it."

"Do I? Then why didn't I tell you to drive me straight to the school? It was a dangerous waste of time to talk to her. What if way down deep, I really meant to make a point to everyone that they'd better start watching how they behave toward me? And think about what I did to Mrs. Berry and what I'd planned to do the Garrett boys."

"That old hag was rude. You only put her in her place."

"Don't underestimate the power of suggestion."

"Bull. As for the rest, do you call that skunk revenge? Those two punks should have their hides tanned for all their vandalism. But what were you going to do? Force them to take a bunch of long baths. Wow, that's really brutal!"

He refused to see the emerging pattern that was disturbingly clear to her. As much as she wanted to love him for it, she didn't dare. "Go home, Hunter.

All your rationalizing isn't going to change anything. There's nothing for you here.''

Hunter took hold of her upper arms and drew her tight against him. ''How can you say that?''

An abrupt and familiar growl stopped her from replying. Roanne didn't want to admire how Hunter's gaze never wavered from the challenge of hers.

''Tell him to back off,'' he commanded, his tone taking on a smoothness and confidence that had her narrowing her eyes.

She muttered, ''I should let him have you as dinner.''

''Go ahead. But you'll just get more upset and spend the rest of the night patching me up, won't you?''

Was she becoming that transparent? He was right; it would devastate her if anything happened to him. Breaking her own rules, she did something she wouldn't ordinarily risk in front of another human being, she looked at Pontus and signaled him telepathically.

The animal uttered a parting low bark and dashed away. As she anticipated, Hunter had expected a more conventional communication.

''If you're trying to impress me, you've succeeded,'' he said. A muscle twitching at his jaw exposed the depth of his tension. ''But then you seem to prefer using unique methods to make your point. Breathtaking, but definitely a style apart from the norm.''

''I don't know what you're talking about.'' It was a weak hedge, but she was getting desperate, aware of what he was leading to.

"Roanne." Hunter slipped his hand into her hood and closed his fingers around her long, wavy hair, gently but firmly drawing her head back. "You said you didn't play games." Using his other hand, he framed her face, stroking his thumb across her cheek, and down the length of her throat. "Are you going to start now? Or did you start last night when you came to my room and made love to me?"

It was there between them, a palpable thing; the memory, the heat and desire. If she reached out to touch him now, Roanne knew she would find him as hard, as aroused as he had been last night. "I—" Her mouth turned dry from the fever beginning to burn in his eyes. "—I've never been to your room."

"The hell you haven't."

She lowered her lashes and focused on the five o'clock shadow beginning to form along his jaw. "Any psychiatrist would tell you that what you experienced was a product of self-induced hypnosis. Wishful thinking."

"But we both know that would be a bunch of crap, don't we?" His grip tightened. "And you know it's the reason I came to you this morning. I'd intended to confront you, but you had that vision. Now we're going to stop beating around the bush, understood? What's also going to stop is this determination you have to scare me away."

"Hunter..."

"Nothing you can say will undermine my resolve." He drew her closer, forcing her to meet his searing gaze. "Do you think I can walk away from you? It's too late. All I can think about is last night...everything you did to me...and how I want the chance to do the same things to you. Read my mind, Roanne and skim the first layers of what I want to share with you.''

In the distance came the distinct lonely howl of Pontus. It was no less sorrowful than the cry gathering in Roanne's heart. "Haven't you been listening? It's not a matter of wanting. It's a matter of what is.''

"That sounds arbitrarily oblique.''

"I can't give you what you want, Hunter.''

"What am I asking for except that you be a woman? *My* woman,'' he added, his tone deep and coercive. "There's something between us and it's defying the rules. Don't you think a positive thing like that deserves a chance?''

High tide had progressed while they had been standing there, and the one wave that came close was an unpleasant surprise. Like skeletal fingers, it reached for them, dousing them with icy water. Below, the roar of the sea was eerily reminiscent of a moaned name... *her* name.

Roanne saw Hunter listen, frown and reject the notion.

"No, hear it!'' She was as determined as she was afraid. "By wanting me, you're inviting that on yourself. You call that positive?''

"I don't know what it is.'' He drew her further back from the cliff. "But I know my choice where you're concerned.''

"No!''

"Yes!'' he insisted, crushing his mouth to hers.

His touch was everything she remembered and determination made him all the more virile. For a moment Roanne gave herself up to the sheer magnificence of it, of him, kissing him back as though she were starving, and she was.

But there was no avoiding the inevitable. The more she wanted him, the stronger the sea protested and the wind threatened.

"Please," she moaned, finding the strength to push him away. "Stop denying the truth. I'm becoming an extension of that. I'm dangerous. I'm *evil.*"

"And I'm telling you you're wrong!" Hunter roared.

"Think! How did your father say my husband died?"

He frowned, clearly not pleased to resurrect that of all subjects. "He said his boat went down in a squall," he admitted, when she gave him a look allowing no vacillation. "But the man had no business going out in questionable weather."

"He didn't know there would be any, Hunter. That's my point. Maybe if he had known as I did, he wouldn't have taken out the boat. But I didn't tell him. *I didn't tell him.*"

Everything bright and hopeful died in Hunter's eyes. "What are you saying?"

"I killed my husband."

CHAPTER SEVEN

"I've heard enough." With impressive swiftness, Hunter swung her into his arms and carried her toward the cottage.

Yielding control twice in one day wasn't something Roanne had done in a long time, and it reinforced her doubts about her weakening frame of mind. She used the time to protect what fight she had left by closing her eyes and withdrawing into herself. All the while Hunter walked, unimpeded by what she knew had to be the considerable weight of her heavy cape and boots.

By the time he pushed through the front gate and strode to her door, she expected him to be winded, but his breathing had barely altered. She could, however, sense his racing adrenaline and hoped it was a result of anger, that he would set her down and be on his way. What she discovered was that there, too, his determination rivaled her own.

The inside of her house was dark and cold. After a quick glance around and muttering something about living as "sparsely as a nun," Hunter set her on her mother's rocker and went to the fireplace, where he used the kindling and logs she had stacked earlier to encourage the coals glowing amid whitecapped mountains of ashes. When at last the embers ignited into flames, he retraced his steps and bent to unlace her boots.

She chose to draw the line at being treated like a child. "I'm not helpless."

"Sit still or by God I won't be answerable for my actions," he growled, brushing away her hands and resuming the task.

Roanne fell back in her chair, too surprised to argue. Why was he angry? If anyone had the right to be perturbed, she did.

"Do you have something strong to drink around here?"

"I don't want anything," she replied testily.

"Well, I do."

As soon as he had her second boot unlaced and removed, she flung off her cape and sidestepped him to go the kitchen. "I have a bottle of whiskey and some honey wine I make myself."

"Whiskey's fine."

She poured a modest portion and brought it to him, trying not to give too much significance to his removed vest. It was bad enough to note how the firelight gave him an untamed look as it shot gold and red highlights through his wind-mussed hair, and that with his bowed head, his shadowed face bore an almost volcanic expression. Equally disturbing was the way the firelight emphasized the breadth of his shoulders and the way his chest rose and fell on each deep, controlled breath.

"I've had this forever so it's probably strong," she warned, handing him the glass. She couldn't help being aware of his gaze sweeping over her black tunic, matching slacks and sock-covered feet. Without shoes, she barely reached his chin, and along with his scrutiny, that awareness accentuated the electric current crackling between them.

"The stronger the better." Hunter downed a third of the liquor in one gulp, only to frown when he saw her wince.

"Drew used to drink like that," she explained, wrapping her arms around her waist.

He considered her stance and his steely countenance softened somewhat. "I'm not leaving until you explain. All of it."

She had concluded as much herself and, in a way, she wanted to get this behind her. But where to begin?

"I met him after my mother died," she said, staring into the flames. "We lived north of here on one of the small islands. I never knew my father. He'd passed away shortly after I was born, but my mother said he was special and understanding. What he wasn't was successful, so ours wasn't an easy life.

"For as long as I can remember, people had always shunned us, and after my mother was gone the situation grew worse. They treated me as though I had some terrible communicable disease."

"Is that why you married him? To give yourself a way out?"

While he didn't sound outright critical, Roanne could tell he was having to struggle with his doubts. "I won't deny that," she replied, aware her unabashed honesty might prove difficult for him to handle. "But I did believe I could grow to love Drew ... in the beginning." Sadness filled her as she remembered his laughter and humor in those earliest days. "We'd met when his boat developed some mechanical problems and he put into our island for repairs. I was supporting myself much the same as when my mother was alive, by baking bread and pastries for the local guest house. He was there the day I made the deliveries.''

"If you don't mind, I think I'd like to skip over the parts about your happy courtship days," Hunter said, saluting her with the glass before taking another swallow.

"The sarcasm isn't necessary."

"Oh, that's not sarcasm," he countered grimly. "That's unadulterated jealousy." His hard smile vanished as quickly as it had come. "How long was it before you married?"

"Four months."

"Did you sleep with him prior to your wedding night?"

Roanne stiffened. "I don't see how that's any of your business."

"Isn't it?"

His challenging look sent an unfamiliar but bewitching heat coursing through her. "On my wedding night I came to him a virgin . . . and he made me regret it." She felt more than saw his shock and dismissed it with a one-shoulder shrug. "I made the mistake of keeping the truth about my abilities and my ancestry a secret. A foolish decision considering everyone else on the island knew. But I was young. I thought given time, he would understand I wasn't really any different than other women. I could laugh, cry . . . bleed." She closed her eyes, the memory of her humiliation as vivid as if it had all happened yesterday.

"It never occurred to me that after the ceremony he would want to stop over at the local pub to celebrate. It was there people let him know how much of a dupe they thought he was."

Hunter stared into his glass. "How did he handle it?"

"I'm not sure because I left. But hours later when he arrived at our cottage, so inebriated he could barely stand, he demanded that woman or witch, I perform my wifely duties. Later he made it clear that the only 'magic' I was ever to dare exhibit was that of trying to learn how to please him in bed."

Hunter downed the rest of his drink and set the glass hard on the fireplace mantel. "He sounds like someone out of a Dr. Jekyll and Mr. Hyde type of story."

"Actually, I think I became the monster." The memories made her hug herself tightly. She felt more than naked, it was as if every inch of her civilized veneer were being scrubbed away.

"After that, our relationship never had a chance. He brought me here and laid down his ground rules. I was to keep to myself. I was to care for his house, and I was *not* to let anyone know about my abilities. But that was impossible," she cried, in the same desperate way she had made her plea to Drew. "The visions couldn't stop because he wanted them to, and I wouldn't keep silent if it meant letting people get hurt. It made him furious, because rather than help anyone, they grew frightened and resentful of my presence in their community. Drew's frustrations deepened when animals started coming to me seeking help. And...sometimes things happened, situations I had absolutely no control over. That upset him most of all."

"You mean like what just went on outside and in the woods the other day?" Hunter asked, his mouth a grim line beneath his mustache.

Roanne moistened her dry lips, aware she was about to subject him to yet another, stranger, dimension to what already had to be an impossible tale to comprehend. "Yes. As I mentioned before, for generations the women in my family have been what some would call white witches. They preferred to describe themselves as healers, advisors, but the terms mean nothing. What I want to impress on you is their strict discipline about using their powers. They almost never succumb to doing anything negative."

"Almost?"

"There was one who was an exception. Lilith. She was my mother's older sister and she . . . she was lured to the dark power. Because I'm the last Lloyd, she's determined to merge my power with hers. Hunter . . . Lilith died a few weeks before I married Drew."

Hunter was trying to decide whether he wanted to know exactly what the *dark power* and *merge* meant, when a sudden downsurge in the chimney put a violent end to their discussion. Flames shot into the room along with smoke and ashes. Thinking the damper had accidentally jammed shut, Hunter reached for a poker intent on leaning into and up the firebox to check.

"No!" Roanne pulled him back. "It won't help. Damn her!"

She ran to a weathered armoire before he could ask any questions, and there took out an exquisitely carved box. From inside she snatched up a length of what appeared to him to be plain old rope and, as she raced back to the fireplace, she began whispering. Hunter had heard chants before—there had been an entire decade when he couldn't get through an airport or city

park without tripping over one zealous group of cult-
ists or another—but he had never heard this language
before, nor had he ever seen anyone tie knots quite like
the ones she was tying into the rope.

Once the interlacing was completed, she placed the
rope on the floor before the fireplace in a pattern creating a circle, and sat cross-legged in the center of it.
Hunter couldn't believe his eyes. She was so close,
another blast of flames like those first few would sear
her. Nor was he coping well with seeing her engulfed
by smoke. It brought back such horrific memories, he
was a hair's breadth away from grabbing her and carrying her to safety. He was stopped by realizing that
while he was gagging, she seemed in a trance, oblivi-
ous to everything.

About to open the doors and windows to at least
ensure he could get her out fast, he saw her begin untying the knots one by one. What followed happened
so quickly, it was more than he could intellectually
accept.

He wasn't certain where the blue light came from.
It simply appeared around her and grew brighter and
brighter until—he told himself it wasn't possible—it
fanned out like great wings engulfing the smoke and
flames. Effortlessly, it began pushing everything back
into the fireplace and up the flue. Within seconds fire,
smoke and ashes were cleared from the room. By the
time the last knot was released, the only remaining
evidence was a slight scent of sweet fruitiness lingering in the air.

"Mooncakes," Roanne said, her voice an odd
monotone and barely audible. "Lilith liked to eat
them all the time. I remember the scent used to linger
on her breath when she bent to kiss me."

Hunter looked from the cheerfully crackling fire to
Roanne sitting slumped forward so that her head
rested against her updrawn knees. He was torn between snatching her up for fear she was about to faint
and grabbing his vest and getting the hell out of there.
The trembling of her hands as she reached up to cover
her head made his decision for him.

Retrieving his glass he went to where she had placed
the bottle of whiskey and poured another portion.
When he returned, he sat down beside her on the floor.
By then she had recovered enough to where she was
methodically refolding the rope.

"It's the untying of the knots that releases the
power," she said in a voice sounding disconcertingly
weak to him. "But the blue light . . . Hunter, did you
see the light?"

"It was rather hard to miss, sweetheart."

"That was a hopeful sign. You see, I'd never tried
this spell before. It was reassuring to see I managed it
and was able to withstand her intrusion."

"You mean that was *Lilith?*" So that's what she
meant when she'd said "Damn her." Hunter shot a
look at the fireplace. "Here, take a sip of this. Take
it," he insisted, raising the glass to her lips.

She did, but only one. Then she studied him as
though seeing him for the first time. "Why aren't you
afraid?"

"Don't look now, but my back is soaked with sweat
and it's not a result of the room being as hot as a fur-
nace."

"The point is you didn't run." She bowed her head.
"I wish you hadn't witnessed that. I've spent years
avoiding any use of the magic, but Lilith's been forcing the issue."

"How can she . . . come and go like that?"

"The spirit world is all around us, Hunter, like memories, like air. That's why you have to be careful with how open and receptive you are. Dark spirits relish creating mischief or outright evil on the vulnerable. It's through those methods or their promises to their victims of gaining more power that they win new conquests or converts. That's what I was trying to tell you before. Lilith took advantage of my problems with Drew and my growing unhappiness with him."

"I'm not sure I understand."

"There wasn't a day that passed when I didn't hear her encouragement to rebel, to be my own person, to defy his rules. It's impossible for me to explain what it can be like."

"I'd appreciate it if you'd try," Hunter said, before taking a swallow of the whiskey he had intended for her to finish.

"It's a whisper that's her voice, but in my head. Other times it comes from somewhere around me, particularly the sea because she knows how much I love it. Sometimes, and this is what's most terrifying, she uses different voices. Like tonight she used Drew's. That's when I'm not sure she hasn't merged with a greater darker entity." She met his gaze. "I know. You're thinking it sounds completely schizophrenic."

"Somewhat," Hunter admitted, brushing the back of a finger across her cheek. "But if you insist on crawling around in my head, kindly read about how I believe you anyway, because I know what I saw happen with my own eyes . . . and what I saw those other times. So go on."

Instead Roanne averted her head. Confused, Hunter reached over and forced her to face him again. That's when he saw the suspicious brightness in her eyes. Wanting to kiss her so badly he ached, he forced himself to let her go. "Finish," he coaxed.

"Lilith made sure Drew heard me talking back to her," she managed, though her voice was husky. "It infuriated him. He thought I was mocking him, and he punished me to make me stop."

"Punished how?"

"He was physically abusive."

He wanted to swear, he wanted five minutes with Drew Douglas himself, but most of all he wanted to crush Roanne close and try to make her forget. Afraid he couldn't keep his hands to himself, he got up and began pacing around the room, eventually finding himself staring into her bedroom. He groaned silently and swung back to her. "Why didn't you leave?"

"He said if I tried, he would find me and commit me to an institution. Once I made the mistake of telling him Lilith died in one, and how the idea of ending up the same way terrified me."

"There was *no one* who could help?"

She shook her head. "People around here saw him as hard-working, congenial and level-headed. If he sometimes drank too much at the local bar, they believed he was entitled to it considering what he had married." Roanne wiped the moisture lingering beneath her eyes and stood to put away the rope and box. "It's not all his fault, you know. He wanted me, and he hated himself for not being able to stop. That's a powerful conflict for anyone to deal with. The unforgivable one is me. In the end I think . . . I *know* I used his hate against him."

Hunter scowled. "Don't start that nonsense about having killed him again."

"I'd had a vision," she continued, ignoring him. "I saw his boat caught in a storm and going down. I knew when and I knew where it was going to happen. Hunter... I never told him."

Though he felt a nauseous lurch in his stomach, he replied firmly, "He should have paid attention to the weather forecasts himself."

"I told you before, there were no advance warnings. That's why he was planning to go out. He'd had the boat in dry dock and money was tight, so he needed the work. The night before he was edgy and he drank to stop thinking about his creditors and all his other problems. I should have gone to bed when I saw what he was building himself up to. But I didn't. Knowing as I did that when he drank, my mere presence was like gasoline on an already out-of-control blaze, I stayed because a part of me knew I had to warn him about what I'd seen."

"There. You see?" Hunter said, relieved she had finally admitted as much.

"It's not that neat," she replied sadly. "For the first time in ages I didn't remain silent when he got ugly. When he came at me, I refused to cower. Do you understand, Hunter?" With a half laugh, half sob, she raked her hair back from her face. "The next thing I knew it was morning and he was gone. I'll never know if I maintained my silence because I'd come to despise him or because I threw away my chance to tell him."

"*I know,*" Hunter declared, unable to bear the distance between them any longer. He reached for her. "You never warned him because he didn't let you. Believe it, Roanne, because whatever you are, you're not capable of the evil you're suggesting."

"What if I am?" she sobbed.

She was killing him. Did she have any idea what he was seeing in her eyes? The goodness and fear, the sweetness and loneliness. The aching misery. Hers weren't the eyes of a woman who would submit to evil under any circumstances. "I'll stake my life that you aren't," he said outright, in case she wasn't paying close attention. He drew her against him so there was no mistaking his true feelings. "Do you understand? *My life.*"

"Hunter, don't do this," she moaned, yet pressed closer and buried her face against his shoulder. "My defenses are crumbling where you're concerned."

"It's about time." He forced her to lift her head and receive his searching mouth. "You came to me as my fantasy. Now come to me as a woman."

CHAPTER EIGHT

Some things were meant to be, and this was one of them. Roanne realized that the instant his lips touched hers.

They had been building to this from the moment they met, maybe before. As a young woman she had dreamed in her innocence and naïveté that there was someone somewhere who had been created to make her thrill, ache and burn. The looks, the kisses and the dreams she had shared with and of Hunter had sealed her belief that she had found that man.

But it was a bittersweet discovery. Only she understood how fragile the dream was. In her heart of hearts she knew this one night was all they could have. Yet perhaps the time Hunter had spoken of wasn't necessarily something to be gauged by years, but in hours, minutes... heartbeats.

Knowledge, her mother had often said, was freedom, and hers allowed her to rise on tiptoe and reach for what she wanted. She had never boldly offered herself to a man; now she pressed her body against his and parted her lips for his unhesitant exploration. She had never responded with total honesty to the passion she knew she was capable of, now it flowed, a warm wine merging with the blood running in her veins and heating it to something more feverish.

"Yes, touch me," Hunter murmured, as she led her hands in a restless eager exploration to get inside the barrier of his shirt. He held still long enough for her to undo the buttons and then ripped it off himself before once again reaching for her.

He was every bit as powerfully built as she had imagined. She buried her face in the soft mat of dark hair bisecting his chest and ran her fingertips and nails over his already taut nipples. The shudder of pleasure that ran through him encouraged her to take her time in tracing each muscle, each rib in a downward journey that brought her fingers to the buckle of his belt.

But when he sucked in his breath in anticipation, instead of loosening it, she hooked her fingers around the leather and brass and gently tugged. "Come with me," she murmured, backing toward her bedroom.

After Drew's death, she had been compelled to burn whatever was in the room that carried his scent and his touch, then she had scrubbed down the place and finally herself. It was now her sanctuary, austere but pure with its white plaster walls, linen curtains and cotton sheets. At the dresser, she lit three candles and they illuminated a wooden tray where silver lidded jars were filled with various liquids and dried petals. In the center above another candle, which she also lit, was a shallow copper dish.

From a silver and glass decanter, she poured a small amount of liquid into the dish before meeting Hunter's gaze in the dresser mirror. "Seawater...water being my astrological element." She then lifted the lids on several jars. "My ancestors believed incense added another depth to your energy. To influence love, for example, a number of flowers and herbs were used including rose petals...strawberry leaves...vervain."

She smiled. "The Romans' Diana was said to be particularly fond of vervain."

As the water heated and the floral scent began to permeate the room, Roanne reached up and, holding Hunter's rapt gaze, released the one button at her left shoulder securing her tunic. With a brush of her fingers it slid down her arms, barely a whisper in its descent to the floor. Next, she unfastened her slacks and stepped out of the rest of her clothes.

Until this instant, she had never thought much about her body; she found, however, that she relished Hunter's gaze on her. She wasn't voluptuous, but he made her feel that way. He made her feel beautiful, and his thoughts . . . the things he wanted to do to her, with her, filled her with a tingling excitement and a hunger to experience them all. So vivid and distinct were they that when he came up behind her and reverentially brushed his fingertips over her breasts, her nipples roused to an aching hardness shooting frissons through her entire body.

Sensing his attention on her necklace, she turned and lifted the ornate object so he could more closely examine the fine engraving around the moonstone. "It's been passed from mother to daughter for generations. Silver is said to ward off evilness. Tonight," she added, slipping the chain over her head and setting it on the tray, "you'll keep the darkness at bay for me."

"Tell me what you need, what you want," Hunter said, sliding his hands deep into her hair and kissing her. When he raised his head again, candlelight illuminated the beauty of his strong features and the desire burning in the bottomless depths of his eyes. "Anything. It's yours."

"I only want to please you." She lowered her gaze to his chest and ran her splayed, worshipful fingers over each pronounced contour. Bending forward, she awarded kittenlike strokes to his nipples and followed the hair arrowing down toward his belly. This time her fingers worked swiftly and deftly to unbuckle his belt, open the fastenings of his jeans and release him into her hands. "I want to burn the remembrance of this night beyond your memory, straight into your soul, so that no matter where you go or who you're with, you'll think of me."

Hunter's breath caught as she slipped to her knees to finish undressing him and repeat the sensual exploration that had haunted every hour of his existence since she insinuated herself into his mind and heart. At last, an unintelligible oath bursting from his lips, he pulled her up and off her feet.

"I'll remember because you'll be with me," he muttered, encouraging her to wrap her legs around his waist. He carried her to the bed, where he lowered her to the cool crisp sheets and covered her with his body. "I want you to be the last sight I see at night and the first in the morning. I want to leave this life with your name on my lips and rediscovering what it's like to see desire light the emeralds in your eyes every time I touch you here . . . and here."

A delicate, unrestrainable trembling began in Roanne's body as Hunter proved to her that even with his own desire reaching its plateau, her pleasure was paramount in his mind. His was an urgent but thorough journey. He drew his hands over her hot, damp skin, deftly determining what made her moan with yearning, and what made her gasp, what made her writhe beneath him and what made her press closer and reach for him.

When his lips found the secret place that no one had ever explored before, she felt him pause and she opened her eyes to meet his watchful gaze. She saw there a challenge and a power she had previously underestimated. He would be tender, but not controlled. He would give, but in giving he would take something of her for himself. Did she understand that vulnerability? Did she dare edge that far out onto the psychological and emotional precipice they had chiselled for themselves?

One night, Roanne promised herself and arched her hips to accept anything, everything he would offer and, oh, yes... take.

The world went out of focus after that as she knew it did in the most turbulent of storms. When Hunter finally rose over her and slipped into her, all that was identifiable were the emotions, the insatiable hunger, the breathtaking pleasure, and the gut-wrenching terror of reaching for something she knew neither of them were sure they would be able to satisfy. And then they were there with nothing to do but hold tight and ride the force of the explosion upward and higher; until oxygen was thin and consciousness was a dimension of irrelevant usefulness.

He thought his heart would explode before it had a chance to calm its frantic beating. Blood pounded in his head, behind his shut eyes, to the roots of his teeth. If this was possession, she could have him, he told himself, seconds before remembering that she could access his thoughts the way typhoons sliced through rice paper. He groaned.

A tiny gushing sound, as close to a laugh as he thought he was likely to get from her, broke from her lips. Then she inched closer under his chin where he had tucked her. "It's a flattering offer," she murmured, "but what makes you think I have the stamina?"

He wasn't certain whether he felt amusement or disappointment. He wanted ... he didn't know what beyond this moment to never end. That was his problem; he was afraid she might be, could be, taking this more lightly than him.

"Don't," she said, touching a finger to his lips and then letting it slide down his chin to his chest. "Doubts are worse than regrets. Just savor what is."

He wanted to. He was trying, he told her with his mind while gazing up at the white ceiling and the subtly shifting pattern the candlelight made. But having lost his world once, and expecting never to feel anything beyond bitterness and despair again, his impulse was to cling tightly to this new miracle in his life.

Feeling her slight withdrawal in the way she, too, shifted to gaze up at the ceiling, he quickly asked, "Do you remember when you were first aware that you were telepathic and ... special?"

"Would you remember the day you discovered you could fly without a 747 wrapped around you? I was four and we were in the dry goods store on the island. I found myself answering a shopkeeper at the same instant she asked me a question. At the time we were newcomers, so you can imagine how my mother all but dragged me out of the place and home so she could explain what was going on." She grew quiet for a moment before adding, "Actually, it's the expression on her face I remember more than anything else. She looked excited, but also resigned. I've often wondered if it's the same feeling a mother has when her daughter begins to menstruate for the first time."

Hunter planted a kiss on the top of her head. "And are you comfortable with it now?"

She raised herself up on an elbow and eyed him quizzically. "It's all I know. You don't turn this off like a water faucet. The magic, the power... as I said, I've tried to leave that alone for the most part, but you can't stop the rest."

"Have you ever considered moving somewhere that would allow you to work with people who would appreciate your abilities?"

The lashes he both admired and resented lowered like battle shields. "You mean be a laboratory specimen? I think not," she replied, her tone brisk and uncompromising. But just as quickly she grimaced and bent to nuzzle his shoulder. "That's not entirely true or fair. I have been invited to join a special university group in Boston. When I was ten I had a trance experience. It hasn't happened since and neither my mother nor I could determine what happened, but anyway, because it occurred at school and they couldn't rouse me, they transferred me to Boston for observation. That's how the doctors found out what I could do. One man in particular—he's getting on in years now—has been keeping tabs on me ever since."

"And?"

"And nothing. Most aren't like him. We've developed a friendship of sorts through letters. Sometimes I help him by offering recipes for remedies when modern medicine has come to a dead end. A few times he's asked me to assist in police investigations, but that proved very hard for me, debilitating and...depressing.'' She sat up and tossed her hair behind her shoulders in a way that made him think she was casting off the bad memories.

''The point is I don't like routines, I don't care for performing for an audience, and I *don't* like the atmosphere that surrounds modern academia. Think of it, after hundreds, thousands of years has their collective attitude changed toward anything that's different and unique? Of course not. The standard is still, 'if it drowns, burns or dies when you sink, ignite or torture it, then maybe, *maybe* it was legitimate.''' She uttered a low growl. ''Dealing with the average human being is punishment enough, thank you.''

I didn't mean to upset you, Hunter told her silently. *I only want to understand, so I don't make the mistakes others have.*

Roanne rolled over to lean on his chest, her touch gentle as she stroked him, moving her fingers over his body as though she were reading a book by braille. ''Never mind. Tell me what it's like to be a successful attorney in Boston.''

''What makes you think I'm successful?'' he asked, becoming as effortlessly aroused by her beauty as he was by her touch.

''Your natural aura is a rich blue. I've seen hints of it beginning to reemerge. Remember when I told you that you would be fine? Back on the night of your accident it was an extremely unhealthy gray, and I've noticed when you're torn between decisions or beliefs, it edges toward a violet.''

''If I'd heard you say that a few days ago, I'm not sure I would have believed you.''

A delightful gleam lit her eyes. ''You're not buying it completely yet, but it's nice to be given the benefit of the doubt. Now answer my question, are you pleased with your life's work? Do you feel you make a difference?''

"I used to believe I did," Hunter replied, growing thoughtful. Amazingly, when his thoughts turned to Cady, the pain was softer, bittersweet, of course, but for the first time he was able to recall with amusement instead of grief special occasions, as when he used to take her to his office. "I'm beginning to think I can again," he added with surprising conviction. He studied Roanne's soulful, mysterious eyes.

"You did it yourself," she insisted, answering his unasked question.

He grasped her by her waist and drew her completely over his body, reaching for her mouth with his. She responded eagerly, a soft moan rising from her throat. He had meant the kiss to be tender, a physical worshipping of all he was grateful for and with. But the heat and yearning returned with stunning speed and soon they were caught in the throes of something far more intense. They rolled over and over the bed, harmonious in their determination to give and take.

Suddenly Hunter broke the kiss. "Come back to Boston with me," he rasped, his tone urgent. When she simply stared at him, he felt panic rush him toward further explanation. "Not to work with any research group. I'd never ask you to do something, unless you wanted it."

"That's not the point."

"Right, the point is we haven't known each other for long," he guessed, "but look at it this way, we know the important things."

"Hunter, I wouldn't fit in your world. You need someone who likes city life, and entertaining, and..."

"We could move to the coast, it wouldn't be a bad commute, and who said I like entertaining? I'm a trial lawyer and my free time is spent either researching my next case or getting over the stress of the last one. I push the PR stuff off on my partners who are involved with corporate law and trusts." He drew a breath, starkly aware how his body was once again aching to seek a home in hers. "Are you going to deny we're good together?"

"I can't believe you're even suggesting this."

He overpowered her attempt to slide out from beneath him by locking one of his legs over both of hers. It was no contest, but he wasn't interested in fairness at the moment. "Why? Because you're not like other people? Maybe I wasn't being reasonable about that at first, but I've been trying—"

"It's not just that. I have responsibilities, Hunter. There's Pontus...my herbs...my workshop in the barn."

"All of them details that could be taken care of. For one thing, we could take Pontus with us."

"How long do you think he would last in that environment? Besides, I told you he's not a pet. Even if I wanted to take him, he's not mine to uproot." She turned her head away. "And you're forgetting the most important point of all."

Hunter grasped her chin and forced her to meet his angry gaze. "Don't say it. Don't you dare."

"It's not something I'll ever be able to disprove to you, Hunter. Maybe you can overlook it now, but what about a few years down the road? What if my behavior grows more erratic and you can't explain it away as neatly as you did Mrs. Berry and the Garrett boys? What if you find yourself unable to close your eyes at night because you're not sure you'll be opening them in the morning? Don't forget Drew.''

"I know you're determined to hurt me in order to push me away," he muttered, the sting of her words effectually drawing the blood she had obviously intended, "but you're wasting your time if you think I'm easily scared off."

"Then you're a fool."

"My choice."

She closed her eyes for a moment, then opened them. There were no emerald fires burning in their depths now, only the muted grays of someone too used to grief. "I'll never have children, Hunter. I promised myself the line ends with me. I won't subject a daughter of mine to what I went through."

"You could already be pregnant."

A spasm of something—pain?—flared in her eyes and was gone. "No witch gets pregnant unless she wants to," she replied, with a quiet finality.

As he recoiled, she used the opportunity to free herself and try to scramble off the bed. But in the last instant, Hunter grabbed her around the waist and dragged her back against him. "Fight me," he growled. "Curse me. Try to run away from me if you believe you can. Only don't think you'll be fooling me. And don't think you'll ever be able to deny either of us *this.*"

He was as hard as she was moist and he slipped into her slick heat with a breathtaking precision. Her gasp sounded torn from her and, as he flattened one palm low over her abdomen and used his other hand to tease her breasts into pouting ripeness, she dug her fingers into the bedsheets. But her hips . . . sweet heaven, her hips were pressing back into him as though, like him, she couldn't get close enough.

More... faster, he told her, as he matched every thrusting motion with a desperate one of his own.

"Hunter... stop it. I can't!" she sobbed.

He knew what she was protesting, not his driving her to a climax she wanted to resist, but the claim he knew she was afraid to admit he had on her heart, her soul. "You can. You will. You're mine now," he rasped, feeling her crest. "Just as I'm yours." As she cried out, his own release followed more powerfully than before. With a groan, he buried his face in her hair and poured into her. "Mine," he whispered again and again.

Somehow, he vowed, he would make it come true.

CHAPTER NINE

Roanne stared at Pontus as he nuzzled the white German shepherd. "I can't believe it," she told the man, who was trying to hide his sheepish grin by ducking his head and adjusting his wire-framed glasses. "He's tolerant and occasionally curious about the animals that come by for food or help, but he's never been this friendly."

"It's just as I told you the first time I was here," her visitor replied with a warmth as reassuring as his appearance was unthreatening, "not only was I serious about coming back, but Sheba is the girl to handle your friend."

Roanne remembered the conversation well; however, she was only beginning to believe his assertion held any validity. As the two dogs played, leaping at each other and dashing off toward the path leading to the beach, she shook her head and turned to the man drawing a cashier's check out of a worn leather billfold.

Dr. Reeve Burton had been the last person on her mind when she'd heard a vehicle pull up outside. In fact, for an instant, she had been afraid she'd misjudged and it was Hunter, determined to press his case, as he had been for the last two days. He had convinced the garage to have his car ready, no excuses acceptable, by tomorrow. He planned to leave town that afternoon and, treating her protests as minor technicalities, declared his intention to take her with him. Between him and Lilith and Drew, she didn't know how much more she could take.

"I don't know what to say," she told the man she guessed was a few years older than herself. In his clean but worn baggy slacks and oversized shirt he appeared in need of a hearty meal as well as a new wardrobe. Not a reassuring candidate for a business transaction, she mused, until she noted the keenness in his eyes and intelligence in his fine-boned face. No, she would make no casual conclusions with this one. "You're serious about this?"

"Absolutely." He swept a few errant blond hairs off his face, blown free from his ponytail, before spinning around, arms flung wide. "This is what I've been wanting since I convinced my father I wasn't joining the family business, but pursuing veterinary medicine. It's away from town so barking won't be a problem to the community, yet close enough to attract clientele who may be going elsewhere for their pets' medical help. Besides, I'm crazy about the view," he added, his wistful gaze drawn to the ocean.

She understood *that* only too well, but a mutual love for the sea didn't mean the check he held was for the full amount of the price she had set on his first visit. Especially when he looked like someone who survived on optimism and was driving a station wagon every bit as travel weary as it was overpacked. She forced herself to point out the fact.

"I see what you mean," he replied, as he considered the car. "Well, on the other hand, could you see the logic in me chauffering sick animals in a Mercedes or BMW? It might reassure you if you'd take a look at this check and hear me out. I couldn't make you an outright offer before because I wasn't sure how long it would take to sell my boat and motorcycle and leave my place in Connecticut.''

It was Roanne's turn to look sheepish. The check was not only in the amount she had quoted, it was a percentage higher.

Minutes later, she asked herself if she should dare take his offer. He was ready to buy her out now; go to town to have the deed transferred before witnesses. The higher price was inducement to let him take possession of the place within days, if at all possible.

Pontus seemed agreeable. From the direction he and Sheba had gone off in, she guessed he was already showing the German shepherd his private cave. A sale to the good doctor would also mean she needn't worry about her other four-legged friends who might wander by. How much more of a sign did she need?

Dare leave and see what happens.

She shut her eyes against the malevolent voice that had the subtlety of a rapier to the heart. Ever since the night she and Hunter made love, the intrusions had been growing in intensity and frequency. Would leaving change any of that?

Never.

"Are you all right?" Reeve Burton asked, a concerned frown knotting his sun-bleached eyebrows.

Roanne wondered what he would say if she told him the truth. "Yes," she said instead, "I... it's just a migraine."

The gamble had to be made, because if she stayed, her will would be whittled away like a knife tearing at a meager willow branch. What's more, she could leave even sooner than the doctor had asked, timing it in order to be gone before having to face Hunter again. Preparations would be hectic, and she would have to leave behind more than she would like; but if it meant avoiding the drawn out pain of a long goodbye with Hunter, it would be worth it.

Be warned.

"Dr. Burton, there's one other matter," Roanne said, fighting to ignore her heartbreak along with her mounting fear. "As I told you before, if I sell to you, you would hear things from the townspeople that could make you have second thoughts about your decision."

He kicked at some gravel with his athletic shoes. "Well...people will always talk about something. But Mrs. Douglas you forget I've been inside your barn and I've watched you with Pontus."

"Meaning?" she asked, impressed that he wasn't the easy read she had imagined.

"Live and let live, I say. Would it reassure you to know some of my ancestors on my mother's side were Icelanders? I missed being born there myself by three months when my father took my mother back there to visit. To them spiritism and mysticism are taken as facts of life."

Roanne hadn't cried in front of another living soul for longer than she could remember, but his easy acceptance made her want to weep. "Doctor," she said, swallowing the lump in her throat, "I—I think you have yourself a deal."

Hours later Roanne stood at the door of her house looking at the few boxes holding her personal belongings and finding a new value in not being a material person. Dr. Burton had leased his Connecticut home furnished and explained the remainder of his generous check was to purchase whatever furnishings and dishware she cared to leave behind. Except for her meager wardrobe, her most valuable supplies from the barn and her mother's rocking chair, she was ready.

She could leave tonight, in hours, if that was what she wanted, though Reeve, as he had asked her to call him, was emphatic about how his own enthusiasm shouldn't pressure her. A deal was a deal, he kept insisting, and assured her that he could happily unroll a sleeping bag in the barn for a night or two if she needed more time. But her business in town was complete—traveler's checks purchased and safely tucked away, and arrangements made for the rest of her funds to be wired to her whenever and wherever she settled.

A half hour later, shutting the front door behind her and eyeing the boxes weighing down her old car, she headed for the barn, knowing she would have to be strict with herself in the rest of her packing. Perhaps she could store what else she would like to keep and make arrangements with Reeve to forward it to her later—if he would promise to be discreet about her whereabouts.

Her mood was fluctuating and she bounced between contradictory feelings of relief, pensiveness and outright fear. How much more reassuring this moment would be if she wasn't so aware of the impending crisis hanging overhead like a ticking bomb.

In anticipation of trouble, she had hidden an amulet behind the bed to ward off evil so that Reeve would be protected during his most vulnerable moments, and with a knife she quickly carved a word of power on the top of the front doorframe. That along with the hollow stone talisman she would offer him later was all she could do for him in case trouble arose once she was gone. She suspected, however, the attacks against this house—both by spiritual forces as well as the human variety—would cease once she was gone.

But that meant the oppressiveness she was picking up was something more. Unfortunately, stress and the voices crowding her mind were making it difficult to pinpoint what was wrong.

At the doorway to the barn she heard barking and glanced back to see Reeve way off in the distance walking along the cliffs. Sheba and Pontus were with him, continuing their flirtatious romping. She allowed herself a fleeting moment of jealousy. Like her, Pontus had lost his heart without intention or choice. But in his case, his story would have a happy ending.

She would have to arrange for a few minutes alone with him before she left. He wouldn't enjoy being made a fuss over; contrary to his current behavior, he didn't respond well to too much touching. But she would never have survived these years if it hadn't been for him. She needed to let him know that while she had always been prepared to say goodbye to him, she would never forget. Not ever.

Steps away from the locked cabinets, a wall flashed before her eyes and she instinctively stopped. The image vanished as quickly as it had appeared, but she stayed rooted in place, familiar with the pattern of disclosure if not the material itself. She had glimpsed it before, yesterday, soon after Hunter had arrived. Aware she would have to relax her conscious mind to access her subconscious, she began the deep, calm breathing to accelerate the process.

The wall appeared again, only for a second, but this time the image was clearer. What upset her most was

how she seemed to have been rushing toward it at a
great speed.

When nothing else came for another few moments,
she shook her head and proceeded with her boxing.
The bottled items were easy to sort through. She left
a few spices she would offer to Reeve and the rest she
packed, insulating each with a handful of hay. She
also went through a mental list of her clients she would
have to notify and how she should go about it.

Busy with carrying a full, taped box to the car, she
was ill-prepared for the horrific blow she received to
her chest. The force and pain of it knocked her backward and the box flew from her grasp. As it tumbled
to the ground, Roanne pressed her hand to her
pounding heart, gasping for breath and staring at the
scene playing out before her eyes. Though the pain
was physically hers, the image was of Hunter in his
car, smashed into the brick wall of his father's estate.

Another wreck? She had been compelled to warn
him yesterday to be careful, but the need to impress
the importance of the matter was now beyond a com-
pulsion to her. Only how could she do it? She couldn't
risk going to him; she was afraid he would see too
much. What if she asked Reeve to deliver a note for
her? There was time. Hunter's car wasn't going to be
ready until tomorrow. Yes, it seemed like a reasonable solution.

But what if he ignored the warning? There was a
distinct possibility he would if it was delivered sec-
ondhand. There was also the consideration, once he
understood why Reeve was delivering it and understood the ramifications of her abrupt departure, that
he might do something more reckless, like come after
her.

Or what if the car had been repaired earlier than anyone anticipated and she was tuning into something about to happen?

"Please, no," she whispered. Disregarding the fallen box she was about to inspect, she took off at a dead run for the Thorne estate.

She had never run so fast. At least it made her less mindful of how much chillier it was in the woods and how the clouds obliterated most of the effects of the late-afternoon sun, emphasizing the matter all the more. Nevertheless, she was aware of how ridiculously underdressed she was in her cable knit sweater and jeans.

The first thing she saw as she raced through the opened gates of Leland Thorne's home was Hunter's car idling part way down the drive. The scene sent her racing heart plummeting. Not only had her fear come true about the car being ready sooner, but Hunter was about to drive off somewhere.

Both he and Leland were outside. Hunter stood by the driver's side, his back to her. That forced Roanne to read thoughts and emotions, and what she was gleaning added to her concern. Leland seemed particularly distressed. He was breathing heavily and leaning on the trunk for support, and because his line of vision made her vulnerable, she ducked behind one of the huge hollies, which provided enough cover to give her the moments she needed to figure out what was going on.

"Have you gone completely mad?" Hunter demanded. "You could have a heart attack chasing after me like that."

"I don't care about me," Leland wheezed, "it's you. You can't leave."

"For crying out loud, I'm going less than a mile down the road to see Roanne, not driving to Boston. In fact, I would have been there hours ago, except those fools at the garage called and said they were bringing the car over, but then took forever to show up."

"Yes, yes. That's not what I—"

"I made it clear last night what my intentions were toward Roanne, Leland. You're not going to break your word about being at least civil to her, are you? Because I'm warning you, no matter what our differences may be, I won't stand for you being cruel or rude to her."

"I said I would honor your decision, didn't I?" the elder Thorne declared, the flush in his face deepening again. "This has nothing to do with that. Not in the way you think. It's all...it's all...oh, God, forgive me. I don't know how to tell you."

Roanne didn't hear if he said anything else, she was taking in too much from the barriers that were falling in his mind. The thoughts and information rushing forth like a flood had her clasping her hand to her mouth and gave her no option but to step clear of her hiding spot.

"Hunter," she ventured, when she was only a few yards behind him. "Be patient a moment and listen to him."

At the sound of her voice, Hunter had spun around and his expression was an endearing mixture of pleasure and apology. "Roanne. Damn, I'm sorry. You shouldn't have to hear this."

She dismissed that with a brief shake of her head. "Listen to him, Hunter." Then she focused on Le-

silently willing him to accept her strength and reassurance. "It's all right now, Mr. Thorne. There's nothing to be afraid of."

"I can't," he moaned.

"Believe me, I understand," she replied gently. Without taking her eyes off the older man, she said to Hunter, "Get into the car."

"What?" Hunter demanded.

"Get in and shut off the ignition. Put it in neutral and release the emergency brake. When the car begins to roll, steer onto the grass to keep your speed down."

"What's going on, Roanne?"

"You'll see. And, Hunter, this time . . . try to remember to fasten your seat belt."

She knew if nothing else got his attention, that would. In her vision, she had seen he hadn't bothered fastening it. Because he had been out of the car when she arrived, there was only one conclusion he could make of that.

It was as much a test in his professed faith in her abilities, as it was for her to prove her point. She could feel his frustration and unease, but slowly, reluctantly, he did as she asked.

The driveway was on the slightest of inclines and the car began to roll the instant the emergency brake was released. In accordance with her directions, Hunter steered onto the grass and aimed for the wall.

Roanne felt the leap of his pulse when he realized what was wrong; she actually felt his heartbeat skip as he tested his brakes and, after two or three taps and a harder push, found them practically useless. But what impressed her were his quick reflexes. Without further delay, he spun the wheel and the car veered away from the wall in a hard left, and rolled straight into a dense patch of junipers. A number of branches snapped upon collision, but the car, and more importantly Hunter, were fine.

She and Leland had almost reached him by the time he overcame the first wave of shock and climbed out of the car. His pale face and stunned expression alone told Roanne he had put two and two together and come up with the obvious answer; somehow, the mechanics at the garage had failed to properly secure all the car's hoses and valves and much of the brake fluid had leaked away between the garage and here. If he had driven much farther, the results could have been lethal. But she could tell he didn't yet realize there was more.

To Leland, she said gently, "The premonition you had of this was as stark and as upsetting as the one you had the night Cady died, wasn't it?"

Tears brimmed in the old man's eyes and spilled down his wind-stung cheeks. "I—I couldn't believe it," he confessed. "Both came as dreams. The first time I thought it was only a nightmare, a result of overindulgence during dinner... the room being too warm that night... I don't know. I needed to grasp at any explanation. And then Hunter called with the news." His voice broke and for several long moments he fought losing control.

"I knew then how I could have, *should* have done something," he continued at last. "But I was so ashamed. I wasn't able to admit the truth to myself let alone my son. Exile was the solution... and the least punishment I deserved."

"Am I hearing this right?" The rage in Hunter emphasized the veins at his temples and neck. "You *knew?* You had a precognition and you kept it to yourself?"

His harsh voice startled birds in a nearby tree. With cries of alarm, they flew away. Leland's attention, however, was focused wholly on Roanne.

"I'm so sorry," he whispered. "How...how do you bear it?"

She offered a smile, though she knew it was tremulous at best. "You do the best you can. I think it's easier for me, because it's all I know. For you it requires a leap of faith, a departure from the norm. It's small consolation, but my heart goes out to you, Mr. Thorne."

"Well, mine doesn't," Hunter ground out. "Damn it, I lost my *daughter*...your *granddaughter.* You should have grabbed a phone and yelled bloody murder. I don't care what kind of a fool you were afraid it would make you look like!"

"Hunter," Roanne cried before more irreparable damage could be done, "he did what an ordinary human being with ordinary human fears and doubts would do." She spun away, wishing she could find the words to make him see. Did he have any idea how excruciating it had been, *was,* for his father? How terrifying? She could feel it all, everything, now that Leland let her see.

Furious that the man she had lost her heart to should be so unyielding, she whirled back, "Oh, Hunter, listen to yourself! How did you ever believe

you could have dealt with me, with what I am, when
you aren't even willing to understand what a strain,
what an inconceivable burden this was on your own
father?"

CHAPTER TEN

Why the tears? They aren't because you'd begun to believe you had a future together after all? Ah...and now he's tarnished his armor.

With Hunter's shout of her name ringing in her ears, Roanne ran through the woods disregarding the path she usually took back to the cottage. She couldn't go there yet. Reeve might be back from his walk and she didn't want to be seen like this.

Roanne...Roanne...foolish girl. It would never have worked.

"I never said I thought it would," she muttered, as angry as she was sick at heart.

Because at your core you're beginning to understand you're just like me.

"I'll never be like you. Never!"

Don't look now, my dear, but you're talking to yourself.

"Leave me alone!" she screamed, pressing her hands over her ears.

Her cry was lost in the moan of the evergreens as they rocked with the wind, great giants that seemed to be mourning with her. She gazed upward wishing their armlike branches were reachable; how blissful it would be to climb into them and be held, soothed. The pang of loss, of acknowledged defeat was so sharp in its newness, she felt drained of strength and any will to go on.

Just as she faced the reasons why she could never have a future with Hunter, she accepted the reality that she had seen him for the last time. The way he had rounded on his father, his anger and quick judgment only emphasized the necessity of such a decision. For herself, she would prefer a lifetime without him to the prospect of failing him, and she would eventually fail him, that was becoming clearer by the minute.

She sank to her knees on the soft carpet of moss and peat and pressed her clasped hands to her lips. There didn't seem to be an end to the racking sobs that rose from deep inside her. They felt as though they were being torn from her flesh, one by one. She cried for all the acculumative hurts, the injustices of life and for the beauty she had been allowed to experience, only to have it ripped away.

When she grew too tired to cry, she sat and stared at the spread of ground before her, barren because the sun couldn't reach it. This was a reflection of her future, her due, she told herself. Her mother had been wrong to think it could be otherwise.

Yes.

Her worst fears were being realized. She had proven to herself that at her core she wasn't pure as her mother had been, and her mother, and all the mothers before them.

Say it.

"I'm like you, Lilith."

Rise and meet your power.

Numb, beyond lethargic, Roanne struggled to her feet and continued the rest of the way through the woods. When she emerged, she found herself north of the old lighthouse. Some vague instinct suggested she make a right turn and head for the cottage, but she yielded to the pull of something stronger and walked toward a less familiar break in the rocks leading down to the beach.

The closer she came, the darker the sky grew, the rougher the sea. The seabirds soaring about cried out fearfully and raced for cover, until the only sound was the pounding sea and the baleful moan of the wind.

Roanne lifted her face and let it bathe her. On some level she knew it was growing bitterly cold and that she wasn't dressed for such weather, but on the surface she was strangely unaffected.

Look.

In the distance the clouds and sea converged into a boiling mass. Violent but beautiful, it rose and twisted. It was like watching an artist work with dry ice and mercury.

Amid the mass a figure emerged, huge even while hunched on its four long legs. It would make Pontus appear like a pup in comparison. But no sooner did the beast show its form than there was another transformation; limbs lengthened further, torso broadened and lizardlike tail drew inward, inward until . . .

Roanne blinked at the figure of a man who emerged and stood upright.

With her words ringing in his ears, Hunter realized the instant Roanne had disappeared beyond the gates that he had made another crucial mistake. But this time he was determined not to take so long in rectifying the error.

He turned back to Leland. The resignation in his father's eyes made him feel all the more ashamed and

he closed the few yards between them. "Leland...
Dad..."

His father shook his head. "Don't let that one get
away. I think we both need her."

Relieved, buoyed, Hunter gave into a startling impulse and hugged him. "I promise we'll talk soon."

"Yes. I'd like that." He cleared his throat. "Now
move it."

Hunter moved, sprinting down the path leading to
Roanne's cottage. He found it odd that he didn't catch
up with her and less reassuring when he reached the
cottage and saw the unfamiliar station wagon and the
stranger.

"Can I help you?" a casually friendly man said,
emerging from the house.

"Who the hell are you? Where's Roanne?"

The stranger accepted the harsh demand with barely
a lift of an eyebrow. "Um, I take it you're not the local minister or welcoming committee person?" When
Hunter took a threatening step toward him, he held up
his hands. "Easy, friend. I'm only trying to get a grasp
on the situation. Apparently, she hasn't filled you in
on things?'

"What things?" Hunter shot back, feeling as
though he had stepped through some time warp.

"I've bought the place." With impressive conci-
sion, he filled Hunter in on his deal with Roanne.
"I'm Dr. Reeve Burton, the new vet," he said, offering his hand.

Hunter went through the social niceties, too relieved to be embarrassed for what he had been thinking. The guy was fairly good-looking in a laid-back
kind of way and for a few moments he had allowed
himself to believe he was meeting the real reason

Roanne had been keeping a wall between them since the night they'd spent together.

But what did all this mean and why hadn't Roanne told him anything? Her car looked about ready to go and he had a sickly feeling she may have been planning to leave without as much as a goodbye. "Is she inside?"

"No, as a matter of fact I'm a little concerned." Reeve paused to turn to the two dogs that raced from the barn barking and romping. "Hey, you two, keep it down will you?" Seeing Hunter's incredulous stare, he laughed. "Roanne was blown away herself. I think it had a lot to do with her decision to sell to me."

Yes, Hunter thought, aware he would be happier if he knew what else was going on in Roanne's mind. "You said you were concerned. Are you saying she isn't here?"

"Exactly. I was off walking with the dogs and when I got back I found a box that looked as though it had been dropped, but no sign of Roanne."

"She just left me," Hunter replied, half to himself. "I thought she was headed here. She was upset and..." He shifted his gaze to the ocean. Of course, he thought, reassured.

"The sun will be down soon. Would you like the dogs and I to help you look for her?" Reeve offered.

"Not yet, but thanks," Hunter called over his shoulder, already jogging toward the path leading toward the beach. He saw Pontus cease his play with the white German shepherd and take a step toward him. Man's and animal's eyes met and Hunter could have sworn a question was being posed. "Stay," he ordered quietly. "You've found your happiness. It's up to me to find mine."

* * *

The water figure glided over the waves toward her. Fascinated and horrified, Roanne could neither scream nor budge. The cold had rooted her in place and terror kept her vocal cords frozen. She wanted to grasp her cross, but her arms felt cemented to her sides. She wanted to pray but the words were lost in her memory.

You could if you really meant it.

As the figure reached the beach, Roanne forced out the whispered, "Who are you? What demon are you?"

You know me. I'm the husband you murdered... the aunt you turned your back on... I'm what you dream of being in your deepest slumber. Come with me and fulfill your destiny.

As he—*it,* she insisted with her last shreds of sanity—passed her, it caressed her cheek. Roanne gasped at the rush of sensations—warmth and reassurance and something unnaturally sexual—that permeated her body. Compelled to watch, she followed its ascension to the rocks. It was heading for a cave.

Come.

"Roanne, don't!"

At the sound of Hunter's voice, Roanne felt another wave of dizziness and disorientation and she stopped. Strange, she thought, she hadn't realized she had begun to follow the thing. She became aware of more around her, too; the tide was coming in, and she was getting drenched. The water was already up past her shins. But awareness had a price; she was losing her feeling of warmth and well-being, and she wanted it back the way a drug addict wanted his next rush.

Suddenly, Hunter appeared before her. "Roanne, the tide's coming in," he said urgently. "We have to get out of here before we're trapped."

"Safe...up there. The cave."

She tried to look around him, to point, but he stopped her in both instances. "No! Don't look at it. There's nothing up there for you. God, I'm not even sure I believe what I'm seeing, but I am telling you this," he added fervently, "it's not here to help you, understand?"

The shivering became uncontrollable. "Go away. Leave me in peace."

"To do what? Die? Become like Lilith? You'll have to kill me first," he said, folding her into his arms.

The waves fought his hold and the wind threatened to knock them both off their feet. "P-please," Roanne moaned against his chest. "This is what I am. I'm tired of fighting the truth...so tired. I belong up there. It—he's calling me."

"It," Hunter emphasized. "Don't give it a persona. And it's not real if you don't want it to be!" Hunter gripped her by her shoulders and shook her hard. "Concentrate, Roanne. Hold on and concentrate. Only you can empower it, do you understand? You're tired. You're hurting. But you can't let that defeat you."

"I killed Drew."

"No!"

"They all said I did."

"Listen to me, darling." Hunter held her tight and whispered into her ear. "I believe each of us has the power of good and evil inside us and that we're put here on earth to wage a lifelong battle of choices.

Which we choose is our decision, but it *is* a decision, Roanne. You have a right to choose."

Roanne didn't want to hear any more. Every word was a blow to her senses. "I'm not like other people, Hunter."

"No, my love. You're not like anyone else on earth, thank heaven." He groaned, moving his hands up and down her back. "You're beautiful and kind and forgiving. No one else would have stuck their neck out for me the way you did that night on the highway, and ever since then I've watched you again and again prove your affirmation and respect for life."

She wanted to believe him, but she was afraid she wanted to be free of the cold and the hurting more. "I wanted to strike out," she reminded him.

"Everyone does sometimes. It's human nature, the survivor's first instinct. Do you think I'm not ashamed of the hell I put my father through? Roanne," he said, excitement brightening his voice, "do you know what you've done? Dad and I are going to talk. Before I came after you, we hugged." With a groan he rubbed his cheek against hers and stroked her hair. "You've given me back my ability to touch . . . to love. *You.*"

Roanne raised her head and for the first time let herself indulge in the pleasure of searching his face. "Oh, Hunter . . . I wish . . ."

"No, *want*," he declared, his own voice growing raw from the cold. "You have to want it. It's the only way we can make our future. I want to spend the rest of my life with you, because I love you. Do you hear me, Roanne? *I love you.*"

It wasn't just passion, it went deeper. Nor was it fragile or fleeting; it spoke of life beyond the boundaries of time. Roanne touched his lips, afraid she had imagined the words, but determined to at least speak what was in her own heart. "I—I love you, Hunter. With all my soul."

No! Choose him and you choose death.

A huge wave knocked them off their feet. The pull of the tide undertow was deadly and Roanne knew she would have been swept away it if wasn't for Hunter's unyielding grip on her. He fought the dangerous current and inch by inch dragged them both to their feet.

"We've got to get out of this inlet or we'll drown," he yelled.

"It's too late." Devastated to think how she had jeopardized his safety, she tried to think of a solution. "If you let me go, you can save yourself."

"No way! From here on out, we're in this together." Pressing a kiss to her temple, he began inching his way toward higher ground while keeping her locked to his side. But each wave seemed to grow more brutal in its assault. Again they fell, and then again. The fourth time Roanne's heavy cross struck him on his chin. He grabbed it. "How much power do you think this has?"

"With the right incantations, the power of generations," Roanne replied, beginning to understand. Along with understanding, however, came sorrow. "Hunter, if I do it wrong, we've nothing else."

His eyes burned his message into hers. "I told you, we have the power of love. Always. And don't you forget it. Now give it your best shot, Seawitch."

He placed the medallion into her hand and then closed his around hers. It took Roanne a moment to collect herself. She wanted to weep with gratitude at his faith, but tears were a luxury they couldn't afford at the moment.

Drawing a deep breath, she slipped the chain from around her neck and, bowing her head, began mouthing the appropriate phrases. The cry of rage that rose around them was terrifying. In response Hunter's arm tightened around her waist nearly squeezing the air out of her lungs, but Roanne continued.

At last, she raised their joined hands in the direction of the cave.

Damn you!

"Now, help me throw it out into the water as far as possible," Roanne directed. "Ready?"

The cross flashed like a silvery white star as it sailed through the air, arcing high before plummeting into the churning waves. In the instant it hit, a howl erupted from the cave.

Roanne and Hunter turned, and Hunter whispered an oath as up on the edge of the rocks the watery figure writhed under the assault of the very waves it had risen from. Then, to their amazement, it began melting before their eyes, seeping away down the wall of granite to be swallowed up by the assaulting waves. Slowly, the waves withdrew, and the clouds lifted from the sea, until finally, the last rays of the sinking sun beamed over their heads, turning the water a serene gold.

"The sea is both giver and taker," Roanne murmured, her vision blurring from the tears that came softly, easily now. "Rest in peace, Drew... and you, Lilith." And with a cry of joy she threw her arms around Hunter.

He uttered a moan of relief and kissed her with aching tenderness and a promise of much more. "Shall we go home now, love," he said when they reluctantly parted for a much needed breath, "before we catch a cold that interferes with our honeymoon?"

As far as proposals went, this one was rather assuming, but Roanne didn't mind in the least. She lingered back, however, when he tried to lead her down the beach. "Home. Hunter, I just remembered... there's something I haven't told you."

"There's an understatement. I met your Dr. Burton when I came looking for you. Remind me to thank him for making things all the more convenient for us."

"But where will we stay tonight? I'm not sure your father—"

"Oh, yes, he will. You were barely out of the gates when he gave me firm instructions not to let you slip away. Face it, darling, we both need you."

Roanne glanced back out to sea. "And the rest? There's no guarantee that we'll always be free of this threat."

"No one ever is," Hunter replied, somberly. "Remember what I told you? But I believe that as long as we have faith in what we feel for each other, I don't think we'll have much trouble." He, too, glanced out to sea. "Would it be breaking an oath of some kind to tell me what those words were that gave you such power?"

"The Lord's Prayer." When his eyes went wide, she laughed, laughed freely for the first time in years. "I may be different, Hunter, but I'm not a complete pagan."

In reply, he swept her off her feet and whirled her round and round. Their laughter was soon joined by the returning seabirds that dived low over them to join in the frolic.

After yet another long, soulful kiss, Roanne sighed dreamily and laid her head against his shoulder, while he continued walking. "This is sheer insanity you know," she couldn't help but warn him.

"No doubt."

"Your life will never be the same again."

"Lord, let's hope not."

She stroked his cheek. "I don't even know what you like for breakfast."

Her husband-to-be stopped at the path leading up to the cottage and smiled down at her. In a flash of clarity Roanne suddenly saw through his love for her, their future . . . their sons . . . and daughter.

"Well?" she whispered, tremulously.

Lowering his head, he brushed his lips against hers. "You . . . and I hope you don't keep me waiting until morning."

* * * * *

Wilde Imaginings

HEATHER GRAHAM
POZZESSERE

Heather Graham Pozzessere

Ever since I can remember, I loved to read. I'm grateful to my parents, because they loved to read, too, and because there were always all sorts of books around my house. With my father, it was World War II, books about ships, a lot of nonfiction. Through my mother, I discovered Victoria Holt and Mary Stewart and Phyllis Whitney and other authors, and I looked forward to each book almost as if I could swallow it whole.

When I first went to college, I began as an English major, then became a Mass Communications major, and finally a Theater Arts major. Then I got out of school and used my training in a manner so many people did—I bartended!

Actually, I did some dinner theater, a few commercials and some modeling, and I loved it all. I really was once tied to some railroad tracks for a publicity stunt; I have been a tap-dancing waitress—and I like to think that it all built my character! Anyway, then along came Jason, then Shayne and then Derek, and with them came the opportunity to sit down and write. It was something I had always wanted to do, and my husband, Dennis, suggested that I quit saying it and try to do it.

Well, I *did* want to write. More than anything in the world. And when I sat down to do it, I was glad of everything I had done that had seemed so odd at the time, because I think it all helped. I wasn't an instant success, but I was very determined. Majoring in theater and all those constant auditions helped me persevere in the face of rejection, and so I kept plugging along, and in two years my first book was published. English helped, theater arts helped, everything helped—but I still think the most important love for any author is the love of reading. It doesn't matter where you come from or what you've done, just as long as you love the written word!

I've continued to love what I do. Now there are numerous books out there, and here at home we have Bryee-

Annon and Chynna to go along with the boys. Yes, it can be hard to work with that many children! But they've also been invaluable, introducing me to all kinds of intriguing people—teaching me baseball!—and adding to the wonderful pool of emotions that is so necessary for writing! I could never have done any of it without Dennis and all of them.

Now, as for *Silhouette Shadows*...! I'm extremely excited about the line. As I said, I started out with Victoria Holt and loved all her wonderful romantic suspense. I'm a big fan of mystery, and I'm one of those people who just loves to wonder about the possibilities in life. I don't definitely believe in ghosts, but since I do believe in God, then I believe that there is an afterlife, and that spirits might roam those misty shadows in between. There are all manner of mysteries in our world, some real, some imagined, and, once again, some in between! One of my favorite books to write dealt with a past that infringed upon the present, an old passion that threatened the new. Of course, in my world, love conquers all—or at least puts it in its proper place. I'm looking forward to all the wonderful paths that can be explored in *Silhouette Shadows,* and I sincerely hope you enjoy my story! Thank you!

Heather Graham Pozzessere

CHAPTER ONE

"Allyssa!"

The husky sound of her name, more a statement than a question, caused her to catch her breath. It was not that she was afraid of the darkness or the mist, or even of the man.

It was just that he had appeared so suddenly before her in that misty darkness.

She stopped, trying to see through the field of swirling fog. At first all that she could fathom was that he was tall and carried himself with a certain arrogance, his hands planted firmly on his hips, and he was watching her from a distance, coming no closer.

He was the kind of man who waited for people to come to him.

Then a breeze came shifting softly by her, touching her cheeks, cooling them and seeming to roll away some of the mist.

He wore his hair slightly long. It curled at his nape, while one lock fell rakishly over his forehead. It was dark hair, nearly black, gleaming in the dampness of the night. His face was handsome, with masculine, ruggedly sculpted planes and angles, a broad, sensual mouth, and large, wide-set eyes that seemed to glitter. They were hazel, she realized, and in the curious light they seemed to have a touch of gold about them. He was clean-shaven, broad-shouldered and tightly muscled. Even with the distance that still lay between them, Allyssa sensed that he was a man accustomed to constant physical action. He seemed to be in excellent shape. His clothes emphasized the taut-muscled, athletic quality of his build. He was wearing black pants that hugged the leanness of his hips, high black riding boots, and a loose white cotton shirt that made a deep V at his throat and had sleeves that flowed until they were cuffed at the wrists.

Had he ridden here? she wondered. Perhaps it had been the only way to come, the storm had been so bad.

Yet she hadn't been expecting him.

"Allyssa?" This time his voice was softer, huskier. Perhaps more of a question now, and then again, maybe the sound was just reflective and even a little amused.

He had been studying her in turn, and she was just a little bit the worse for wear. She had rather plummeted into this trip to the moors. Actually, she had decided less than forty-eight hours ago to leave the safe harbor of her home in Maryland and come to England.

And she had certainly never planned for this kind of rain or mist, or the fact that she would arrive and find no transportation, none at all, at the minuscule train station in the ancient town of Fairhaven.

And there had indeed been nothing at first. Nothing.

When she had first arrived she had stood in the cold and the wet and the near darkness, shivering, watching as a thick mist slowly rolled down from the hills just beyond the station. She hadn't expected the town to be big, and she certainly hadn't expected to be greeted by any of her very distant relatives.

But she hadn't expected it to be so very silent and dark, either, when her train had chugged into the tiny station. Surely there should have been someone around, but there wasn't. The train had stopped, depositing her with her baggage, then chugged on into the night. Within seconds it was gone, swallowed up in the darkness, and the great rolling mass of steel might never have been. Like the indistinguishable shapes looming at her in the fog and darkness, it might have been a phantom vehicle, a trick of the imagination. All that was real here were the darkness, the cold, the swirl of the fog around her, the phantoms of the night. . . .

She was letting her imagination run away with her, she'd told herself. The platform beneath her feet was very real. The station itself was real; there had just been that note on the door to the small office stating that office hours were from nine to six seven days a week, with time off for tea from two to three. There was nothing in the least ghostly or frightening about the night. The only difficulty had been her own foolishness. She hadn't come from the largest city in the world, but Baltimore was certainly cosmopolitan enough.

And it had never, never occurred to her that she might come here and find nothing.

Nothing . . .

Until now.

He was here now. The tall, dark stranger with the powerful build who seemed to know her.

Was he a trick of the light? Or the lack of it?

Full darkness had come quickly once she had arrived. When the train had been slowing for the station, it had still been light. Oh, not very light, but light enough. She had seen the beautiful, rolling hillsides. The grass had been beautifully, deeply green, truly creating an emerald splendor. The sheep on the hillsides had appeared very white against that deep green background. The scenery had been incredibly lovely. Lonely and even haunting, perhaps...

"Allyssa! Are you frozen there, girl?"

This time the tone was impatient. Aggravated. She had grown accustomed to the sound of English accents, as diverse as those in America, since she had boarded her flight at Washington International Airport for her trip into Heathrow. This man's was different still. Light, yet his tones were deep and resonant. He spoke with a sure sense of command, as if he were a man accustomed to handing out orders and to having them obeyed. Who was he? She tried to remember the habitants of Fairhaven the solicitor had described to her. Was this her very distant cousin? She hadn't asked to be picked up—she hadn't had the good sense to do so, she reminded herself curtly—so how had he known when to come for her?

How had he known that she was coming at all? She had never written or phoned, never even agreed that she would definitely come.

What difference did it make? He was here. The night was as wet as a river, and surely he intended to take her to the castle, a far more pleasant prospect than trying to find a way to stay dry and warm beneath the eaves of the tiny train station.

"Yes, yes! I'm Allyssa Evigan," she said quickly, hurrying along the concrete path toward him. For a moment she was afraid that she had imagined him, created him from the wealth of mist and darkness, but as she hurried he remained right where he was without disappearing. He continued to stare at her, certainly real enough.

When she reached him, she paused again, waiting. He was studying her more intently. Those sharp hazel and gold eyes quickly ran the length of her, judging, assessing.

What did he see? Under normal circumstances, she thought that she might have put forward a decent enough appearance. She was a medium five feet six inches in height, a bit thin, maybe, but her curves did exist. She had her mother's features, fine and small, and her father's eyes, large and green. Her hair was a soft natural blond that she wore layered far past her shoulders. Brandon had always told her that she had great eyes and magnificent hair, that he would have wanted to marry her for the color of either her hair or her eyes alone....

But that was a long time ago now. And her magnificent hair was sodden and damp and clinging to her cheeks. She had worn jeans, anticipating the long, hard hours of travel, but she had also worn a silk blouse, and beneath the crush of her trench coat, she was certain that it was wilted and the worse for wear, too.

She should have spent a night in London, she chastised herself. She could have caught up on her sense of jet lag. She could have arrived here looking if not dignified, at least a bit more human!

But it was too late for that. And, really, she didn't owe this man anything. Since he didn't mind being rude, she could respond in kind.

She arched a brow. "Are you frozen there, sir?"

He smiled. A handsome smile, meeting the challenge. Then he laughed out loud, and it was a pleasant, provocative sound. She felt somehow warmed. Angry still, but warmed. He was blunt, he was bold, but he had a definite charm about him. Very masculine and seductive, she thought, somewhat amazed.

"Well, now, you're the newcomer, you know. You're going to be looked over often and well," he told her.

Well, that was true enough. And blunt, too. She wondered if she should have come at all—whatever was happening in Fairhaven couldn't really concern her. She'd never even heard of the place until the strange little solicitor had appeared on her doorstep three weeks ago, informing her that her great-grandfather—she hadn't even known she'd had a great-grandfather—had died, and that it was imperative that she come to the reading of his last will and testament in Fairhaven.

She might have simply offered the man coffee or tea and then forgotten all about him, except that she could never, never forget the way things had been when her mother died. She could never forget holding her and listening to her cry softly, nor could she forget the things her mother had said....

Well, she was here now. She had told herself that she wasn't coming, but she was here. The reading of the will wasn't for another week, but Mr. Sheillan, the solicitor, had assured her that all the heirs of Padraic Evigan were assured a place in the castle, so there would be time for her to see the fine estate and the countryside—and to get to know her kin.

Well, if this man was kin...

Distant kin, she reminded herself. Her great-grandfather, Paddy, had been one of three cousins and had inherited the estate from his grandfather. But his cousins had heirs now, too, one, at least, who lived at the estate. Darryl Evigan.

This must be him.

The man before her suddenly pointed to the dark sky. "Can you see them? Just the ghost of them. Storm clouds are coming back in. The rain will start up again soon. We had best get going."

She nodded. "That's fine, thank you. I'm so grateful that you're here. I hadn't expected anyone to meet me. I hadn't written or called. I didn't realize that it would be quite so small a place. No taxis or—"

He reached over and with a strong grasp took her small overnight bag from her fingers. The rest of her luggage had been set against the wall of the station by the porter.

"Too small for you, is it?" he asked her. The words were polite enough, but the tone held just an edge of contempt.

"I never said that."

"Ah, but were you thinking it?"

"I was merely thinking," she said evenly, "that I was glad you came along. There are no taxis here. A cold station is not a nice place to spend the night."

The hazel-gold of his eyes flicked over her again. "No, it's not, is it?" he said softly. Then he reached out and touched her chin, causing it to rise. She longed to wrench it away from him, but for some reason she remained still while he searched her eyes and studied her once again.

"But you know," he said softly, "perhaps you won't be welcomed here."

She did pull away then. "I don't know why I should be welcomed. I've never been here before. I never even knew the place existed."

"Until you heard about the will."

"Until I heard about the will."

"Mmm, a gold digger," he said. He was smiling. She didn't know if he was serious or teasing, for there did seem to be laughter behind the words. Yet they might well be very serious. . . .

He was blunt. She would have to be equally blunt. "Perhaps you wouldn't mind insulting me and assessing my motives once we've reached the castle? It really is wet out here, and I'm freezing."

"Of course, of course! How remiss of me. It's just that I really don't feel the cold. You've more luggage?"

"Yes, down there. I'll just run—"

"No, we can't manage it tonight. Someone will come in the morning."

"But—"

"It will be perfectly all right. This is a very, very small place, as you've commented. Come on now. I can't take your luggage, the way that I've come. Especially if you can manage with this?" He lifted her small leather case.

"Yes, I—"

"Good, let's go."

He took hold of her elbow with a definite authority. He wasn't accustomed to anyone refusing him, she thought resentfully. But since it was very cold, not to mention so miserably wet, she would wait until tomorrow to start firmly setting him in his place, she determined.

When they got down the small brick steps that led to the back of the station and the platform, she narrowed her eyes against the darkness, looking for a car. She didn't see one. She heard a shuffling sound and looked quickly in the direction from which it had come.

A massive black horse stood there. Very tall, nearly seventeen hands high, and beautifully lean and muscled.

She looked at the man at her side, thinking that the two were very similar, both very tall, both tightly muscled. Both lean and sleek.

"A horse?" she murmured. Well, of course, he was wearing riding attire. She had thought, when she had first seen him, that he must have been riding.

"The roads are mire. It would have been impossible for anyone to get a car through tonight Do you ride, Allyssa Evigan?"

She nodded. If he was waiting for her to become upset about his mode of transportation, he was going to be disappointed. "Yes, I ride. My father taught me, when I was very small."

"Ah, yes, he would do so! Evigans always know and love their horses! Come on, then."

He whistled softly, and the beautiful black horse came right to him. Allyssa had never seen anything quite like it.

"I'll give you a hand," she heard, and before she knew it, strong arms were around her and powerful hands were lifting her by her waist, swinging her upward. When she was seated in the saddle, he tied her overnight bag behind it, then leaped up behind her. He kneed the horse lightly, and they started away from the station.

She could see very little in the darkness. The storm clouds seemed to have covered the world. All that she could feel was the warmth of the man behind her, the force of his arms around her. It was a pleasant feeling.

I don't even know him, she thought. He's rude, and thinks himself some great lord, to the manor born!

And still . . .

Still, there was something about him. Something that had made her feel things she hadn't felt in years. Stirrings of excitement. Warmth . . .

She wasn't welcome here; he had said as much to her. He had probably come for her because she did have her legal rights and he was trying to deal with the situation properly. She really didn't mean to infringe; she had come to find out about her parents. What had made her father so determined to move away? And what had been so terrible that it had haunted her mother's last moments of life?

"There, see?" The soft, husky tone of his voice was stirring as he spoke to her, just behind her ear, his breath teasing her senses. "See there? The clouds are lifting just a bit."

And they were. The two of them were moving through a fairy-tale village, a beautiful, charming little thatched-roof place where Shakespeare would have felt completely at home. The houses were set well apart, most of them on little rises or knolls in the rolling landscape. She imagined the color of the grass again, so endlessly green. The natural beauty of the landscape, combined with these quaint houses. They were passing through the center of the small village now. There was the Rose and Thistle pub, a haberdashery, a tobacco shop, an inn and a large restaurant. No loud, large signs proclaimed each place of business, just very small placards set in the windows, except for the pub. A sign with a coat of arms hung from the eaves.

Yet even the pub was quiet as they rode through the streets. There truly was nothing here this night.

"And there," he told her. "There now, look up."

She did so. There was Fairhaven Castle. It rose majestically out of the landscape, tall, turreted stone, gray in the night and mist. Ramparts stretched from tower to tower. Light gleamed from windows that were little more than narrow slits. It was harsh; it was wonderful. She felt the most curious rush of emotion as she stared at it. Yes! It was her heritage, incredible and magnificent....

Sweet Lord, she'd never even seen it before! And here she was coveting a pile of stone in the darkness!

"Yes, you feel it!" he whispered. "I can feel it in you, the rush of desire! It does that to all of us, doesn't it? It's in the blood."

She gritted her teeth, twisting within his hold. "This is extremely diluted blood, don't you think? What could we still have in common? I've been told our great-grandfathers were cousins. I could be more closely related to anyone on a London street!" Maybe that was an exaggeration, but she didn't like the way he had read her emotions so quickly.

He laughed, a husky and seductive sound. "I would have been disappointed if you hadn't felt it!" he assured her.

She was about to turn and tell him that he was imagining things, but he chose that moment to set his knees to his horse once again, and suddenly they seemed to be sailing through the night. She leaned low against the horse, her fingers entwined in thatches of mane. He was reckless, wild, she thought.

No, he was just an expert. And he knew that she was a capable rider. Knew that they would be all right, racing through the darkness . . .

The cool, damp air caressed her cheeks as they rode hard, climbing the mound to the castle. She closed her eyes momentarily, then opened them.

It loomed before her. Fairhaven Castle. Huge, stark, forbidding. No—it was forbidding only to those who did not belong! she thought whimsically.

Ah, but she did not belong. She was not welcome here. He had told her so.

Perhaps it had been a moated castle at one time, but it was moated no more. A bridge sat over dry land, surrounded by brush and flowers. The bridge was lit and led into a courtyard that also seemed to be a bastion of light against the night.

He brought her only to the bridge, dismounting from the horse in an agile leap and reaching up to her. She could have dismounted on her own, and she should have done so, but his eyes seemed to glitter with gold. She felt their pull again and marveled at it.

Then, to her surprise, she accepted the arms reaching for her. She slid slowly against his body as he lowered her to the ground.

"Go on in, Allyssa," he told her. "Just inside the courtyard, take the massive door to the first tower. There's a fire burning in the hearth. Warm yourself."

"But where—"

"I've the horse to see to for the night," he said, handing her her overnight bag. "Go on in. Be warmed. And, my dear . . ."

"Yes?" She had turned toward the castle, but now she turned back to him. His eyes seemed like fire, he was studying her so intently, so passionately. She nearly stepped back, afraid.

But even afraid, she felt his power too keenly. She remained where she was, watching him.

"Be warmed, but be wary!" he warned her. He reached for her once again, drawing her near. She felt the quick heat of his kiss against her forehead. Then he released her, thrusting her toward the castle.

"Go!"

She started toward the tower door, then gasped as the wind suddenly picked up with ferocity. She hugged her coat around her, clutching her bag, and ran for the door. Despite his instructions to enter, she started to knock.

The massive door swung inward.

Tentatively, she entered the tower.

There was a beautifully carved stairway almost in front of her, leading to the upper levels. She turned from it and saw a large, octangular room. A massive hearth covered all of the far wall, and a fire was burning brightly and beautifully against the night. She set her bag down and hurried toward it. She warmed her hands, then turned. There was a large table in the center of the hall. It would easily seat twenty. The feet were composed of carved lions. It was a wonderful piece, but the hall seemed strewn with equally magnificent antiques. There were large Queen Anne wing chairs in front of the fire, with marble-topped tables before them. Ancient draperies covered the three window seats far across the room from the hearth. Coats of arms and crossed swords covered the walls.

Allyssa slowly slipped off her trench coat. There was a small cherry table with a decanter and glasses around it. She walked to the table and lifted the decanter, uncorking it, sniffing thoughtfully. Brandy. She could use a swallow against the chill.

She poured herself a glass, then walked slowly to the fire. A sheepskin rug lay directly before it. She sank down on it, fluffing out her wet hair, sipping the brandy.

Yes, this was beautiful! She had to be glad that she had come, if only for the chance to see this room! She stared into the flames. They were hypnotic, and she felt very warmed and comfortable, ridiculously at ease.

"May the saints preserve us!" she heard suddenly, along with a loud clattering and the sound of shattered glass.

She leaped up quickly, her sense of security and comfort as shattered as the glass. She stared across the room. A very proper butler in white gloves and black tails had come into the room. He had been carrying a tray.

The tray now lay on the floor. Brown liquid oozed over the stone. Glass lay in chunks and slivers.

The man, tall, blue-eyed, white-haired and very dignified, was staring at her as if she were a ghost.

"Who—who...? How did you get in here?" he demanded.

Puzzled, Allyssa frowned. Surely, if someone had taken the time and made the effort to come and get her, he would have warned the household.

"I'm Allyssa Evigan," she said. And she waved a hand in the air. "I've just arrived. I was told to come on in by the fire."

He continued to stare at her for a moment. "I'll get the master," he said, then turned swiftly and was gone. Allyssa turned to the fire and watched the flames. They danced in myriad colors, yellow, blue, magenta.

"Yes?"

She whirled around. A man was standing before her. Nicely tall, trimly built—his hands on his hips. Allyssa looked him over swiftly from head to foot. His hair was a deep sable brown, his eyes a light green. He was fairly young, certainly handsome. . . .

And not the man who had picked her up at the station.

She sighed softly, smoothing her hair. "I'm sorry I seem to have startled everyone. Darryl Evigan picked me up at the station. He told me to come on in, so I have. I am sorry if I've distressed anyone."

The man came closer, pausing on the way at the brandy decanter, where he poured himself a glass, still staring at her.

Very perplexed.

"Look, I'm sorry—" Allyssa said.

"No, no, please!" he murmured. "I'm glad that you're here, it's just . . ."

"What?" Allyssa asked.

"Darryl Evigan did not pick you up from the station."

"But he did—"

"No, no, Allyssa. I'm certain of that."

"But how?"

"Because I'm Darryl Evigan."

CHAPTER TWO

"Oh, my God!" Allyssa gasped. "Then who—I'm sorry!"

"No, please don't be sorry," he told her, frowning. He walked closer to her. "I had no idea you were coming. It seems, though, that someone did. This person who picked you up—did he say that he was Darryl Evigan?"

Had he said that? No, never. She had assumed that he was because Darryl Evigan lived at the castle and would surely be the one to come for her.

She shook her head slowly. "No, when I think back on it. I really am sorry."

"Well, you must stop being sorry," he told her, quickly offering her his hand. "I suppose that I should just be grateful that someone *did* see you there and bring you home to us here." His handclasp was warm and firm. She found herself studying this man in the firelight. His smile was charming, his manner warm. She felt a slight trembling, wondering how, after all this time, she had managed to meet the first two men in ages to make her feel alive in the same night. "Welcome to Fairhaven Castle!" he continued, his fingers lingering on hers. "Our little American cousin! Come home at last."

She smiled, but a curious sense of unease suddenly snaked its way down her spine. "Be warm, but be wary!'' another man had warned her. She wasn't welcome here.

But she didn't even know who the man who had picked her up from the station had been. And now that she was inside the castle, safe and warm and meeting this very normal man with his pleasant manner and easy, infectious smile, she felt a growing sense of anger. One of the villagers, feeling in a mischievous mood, had seen her, and in such a small place they had probably known that she was the American cousin, and it had seemed a fine joke to pick her up and deposit her at the castle doorway with no word of explanation.

"I'm not so terribly sure that I've come home," she told Darryl, extracting her hand from his at last. "Home is really a much smaller place on the outskirts of Baltimore. But I am glad to be here. The scenery has been spectacular. The castle is magnificent. It's wonderful that I do have a relative—however distant—who lives here."

He smiled, suddenly seeming very close. "We'll have to work on not being such distant relations!" he said huskily. He stepped back just a shade with a sigh of regret. "Let me call Gregory in here. I'm sure he's already seen to it that Eleanor, our live-in maid, has prepared a room for you. He can escort you up, and you can have a nice long bath. Then we'll meet again for supper, if you're not too weary."

"No, that would be lovely. Thank you," Allyssa murmured.

He didn't need to call Gregory—the butler was standing right behind him just seconds after he spoke. He assured Darryl that a room was indeed ready for

Allyssa, then bowed his head and asked her to follow him.

She picked up her overnight bag and did so, thanking Darryl and telling him that she would be down quickly.

"At your convenience, please!"

The room Eleanor had chosen for her was in the same tower, just above the place where they had been talking before. It had the same exquisite old charm as the grand hallway below. There were window seats, although she couldn't tell what the windows looked out on as yet; the night was too dark. There was a massive old four-poster bed with a canopy and heavy brocade curtains. There were heavy Tudor chairs before the lit fire, huge old mirrored armoires and a cherry table set before still more windows. The windows were small—original arrow slits, she imagined—but even so, they must let in the morning light, and it was probably beautiful at daybreak.

As she looked around, Gregory cleared his throat. "There's a modern bath added, Miss Evigan, to your right. Eleanor assures me that whatever amenities you might require are there. If there's anything else . . ."

"No, no, I'm quite fine, thank you, Gregory," she told him. She could see the bathroom; the door to it was slightly ajar. There was a massive claw-footed tub, and she was dying to crawl into it. If she could just be lucky enough for the castle to have steaming hot water . . .

The minute Gregory was gone she hurried into the bathroom and turned the hot water tap. For a second nothing happened, and she was ready to say that the devil could take intriguing old castles. Then there was a sudden rush of water, deliciously hot and steaming.

She gave a glad cry of satisfaction, then added just a touch of cold, so she wouldn't scald herself.

While the tub filled she dumped the meager contents of her overnight bag on the bed, finding her makeup case and toiletries and taking them into the bathroom, then shaking out the one other set of clothing she had in the bag, a denim skirt and cotton blouse. The cotton had wrinkled, but she had a travel steamer with her. She found padded hangers in one of the armoires and quickly hung up her blouse and steamed out the wrinkles while she waited for the tub.

Finally it was filled, and she got into it. The heat of the water was heavenly. She sank down, dousing her hair as well as her body, deliciously glad of the heat after the chill and the rain. She scrubbed her hair and her flesh, then leaned back, loath to leave such wonderful comfort.

How strange the evening had been! she mused. It had seemed so horrible at first. She had imagined that she might well be sleeping beneath the eaves of a train station, through no one's fault but her own. Then the mysterious stranger had appeared, bringing her here. And then Darryl Evigan had proven himself to be a very charming gentleman. And now this heavenly bath...

She started suddenly, thinking she had heard a movement in the bedroom. She tensed, her fingers curling around the edge of the tub. "Who's there?" she called out.

No one answered, and she heard nothing more. Slowly the tension eased from her. She was hearing things. Maybe she was still dealing with jet lag, or maybe she just had an overactive imagination.

She leaned back again. It still seemed so incredible that she was here. She had always known, of course, that she had been born in England. But when she had been very young, she had been led to believe that her parents had come to America as the great land of opportunity. They had never even mentioned that they still had relatives back home.

She had lost her father when she was ten. Not quite fifty, he had succumbed to a heart attack. She and her mother had become very close, dealing with the painful blow together.

She had never really thought about England. Even when she had been in college, ready to spend a summer abroad with friends, they had all opted for Paris, maybe because it was the City of Lights, maybe because it seemed such an appropriate place for students, and maybe because it had just seemed so romantic. She had never realized that her mother had been incredibly relieved about her choice, not until a year or two later, when she had caught that terrible fever. Nothing the doctors had been able to do had made any difference. Jane Evigan had died of pneumonia, but not until the fever had brought on delirium and she had whispered hauntingly of England over and over again. "I wasn't guilty, I wasn't!" she had cried.

And Allyssa had tried to reassure her. "Of course not, Mother, of course not!" she had said fiercely. No one had ever been a kinder, more caring person than her mother, and Allyssa had loved her fiercely.

"Guilty of what, Mother?" she had said later, when the words had poured out again. "Guilty of what?"

But Jane had never said. Later, the doctors had told Allyssa that in Jane's state of mind, she might have been talking about stealing a cookie when she was a child. "But she is at rest now, safe and serene," they had said.

And that was true. No pain, no fear, no worry, would touch either of her parents again.

She had gone on. Baltimore was a wonderful city, and she had used her love of languages and American history to forge a career as a specialized tour guide in nearby Washington, D.C. She loved her work, loved history and loved the way that the former continually allowed her to delve into the latter. It had been when she was taking a group of new politicians through the White House that she had met Brandon McKee, Kentucky's newest, youngest, freshest congressman.

She closed her eyes for a moment. The helicopter crash that had taken Brandon and several other promising young men hadn't been even three years ago. Sometimes she still felt numb. Sometimes she simply felt as if she had been alone forever. Friends told her she was insane to still be grieving, to be in mourning. It wasn't that. She knew that she was young, that she had a lifetime ahead of her. It was just that after Brandon, it was so hard to meet anyone she really wanted to become involved with in a romantic way....

And so she had been drifting. Working. Fixing up her house. Going through the motions. Then the solicitor had come, telling her about that great-grandfather she had never known existed. Darryl Evigan might never believe it, but she really didn't care if there was nothing in the will for her at all except some kind of a token, perhaps. Coming here had been important. The questions her mother had left behind had plagued her for a long, long time. She was blessed with many friends, good friends, but her life had still seemed empty.

The trip here had been like wiping a slate clean and going back to the very beginning, all in one. And it was already proving to be fascinating, she thought with a wry smile. Now the world seemed full of mysteries. Just what was it that Jane Evigan had not been guilty of?

And who was the handsome villager who had determined to be such an enigma, sweeping her from the station and setting her down at the castle—to Darryl Evigan's vast surprise?

She smiled, rising from the water at last and wrapping herself in the giant white bath towel that had been left for her. She stepped before the mirror over the sink, picking up her brush and starting on her wet hair.

She frowned suddenly, certain that she heard a noise from the bedroom.

"Who's there?" she called out sharply.

There was no answer. She set the brush down carefully and tiptoed into the bedroom, hoping to catch the intruder in the act of intruding.

But the bedroom was empty.

"It's a castle, and it's a dark and stormy night!" she told herself out loud. Then she dressed quickly, suddenly realizing that she was starving.

Besides, her long lost and very distant cousin was waiting for her downstairs.

When Allyssa came down, Darryl was waiting for her. He was sipping a brandy, staring idly at the fire. He looked up and smiled as soon as he heard her coming into the great hall.

"Well, you look a good deal refreshed. However, you still must be exhausted from the trip. We'll eat quickly, then you can make an early night of it."

"That sounds lovely. Thank you for being so considerate."

"Come on, then. I'll show you the family dining room." He walked across to where she stood near the foot of the stairway and offered her his arm. She accepted, thinking that she liked the way he was dressed for supper, not fussily, but handsomely, in a tweed jacket and a tailored shirt, but open-necked, and casual fawn trousers.

He led her into a room that opened off the great hall to the left. It had apparently been a passageway at one time, she decided, but it had been a very broad passage. Now a more intimate table than that in the great hall—one that would seat eight, at the most—had been set near one wall. The decor had been continued from the great hall, though. Swords and coats of arms covered the walls, along with a very old and handsome tapestry between two windows.

"Well, what do you think?" he asked, seating her.

"I'm impressed."

"And just think, we're quite small, as far as castles go."

He sat across from her at the warm mahogany table. Plates had already been set before them, and even as they sat, Gregory seemed to melt out of the stonework to wait on them. He poured wine, then reappeared almost immediately with serving dishes of fish and lightly seasoned vegetables. The food was delicious. Darryl was tremendously entertaining, describing the building of the castle in the late thirteen hundreds and the life of the village today.

"It is an interesting phenomenon," he murmured, sipping his wine. "We Evigans survived off sheep all those hundreds of years ago, and we're still surviving off sheep. Of course, things were very different then. There were servants by the score, and, I do assure you, the financial possibility of that has long since passed us by."

"I really hadn't thought about it," Allyssa murmured. "It must be difficult to keep the place up."

He shrugged. "In past years, we sold off land when the going got rough. But we're coming to the end of that option, if we want to stay in business at all."

Allyssa edged a piece of broccoli around on her plate. "Did changing times bring all this about? Or was Paddy a poor businessman?" She set her fork down and leaned across the table. "Was he a tyrant? What was he like? Whatever happened that made my parents leave this place and never even mention that it existed?"

He lowered his lashes quickly and seemed to be fighting some inner struggle. Then he stared at her hard across the table. "Yes! Paddy was a tyrant. He wanted to dictate to people, and he never wanted to give them anything. He could have turned the estate over to your father—or to mine!—but no, he couldn't do that, he had to hold on to power, and to whatever money there was. It was his way of keeping people in line."

Allyssa lowered her lashes quickly, startled by his outburst, and torn by it. She was sorry for Darryl, living beneath the iron-fisted rule of a dictator.

But she was sorry for her great-grandfather, too. Had no one been with him to love him when he died?

And what about her mother's dying words?

She sipped her wine, trying to sound as casual as she could. "Why did my parents leave? Do you know?"

"I wasn't even ten years old when they went," he said softly. "And you—you were just a little bit of a thing. Just turned three. Even then, you had your own little pony. I remember you on it. You were just as stubborn as you could be, and everyone in the place bowed down to you almost as deeply as they bowed to Paddy!" He smiled, taking the sting away from the comment. "You were beautiful then," he said softly. "But you're far more beautiful now."

She flushed uneasily. The compliment had been spoken with a deep sincerity. "Thank you. That was very sweet."

"You don't remember being here at all?"

She shook her head. "Not a thing."

Gregory materialized again, bringing them coffee and delicate little cakes. Allyssa chewed gingerly on hers, not hungry anymore, but fascinated to learn whatever she could from Darryl.

"So I lived here until I was three?"

"You did."

She smiled. "Were we friends?"

"The best. And you didn't even recognize me."

"Did you recognize me?"

"I must admit, I did not." He smiled, his fingers curling over hers where they lay on the table. She felt a sense of warmth enveloping her. It was comfortable.

But just a little bit uneasy, too.

She withdrew her fingers and sipped the last of her coffee. The caffeine wasn't doing a thing for her. "Will you tell me more tomorrow?" she asked him.

"Whatever you want to know," he assured her. "But you had best go up and get some rest." He stood, then came around politely to pull out her chair before offering her his arm again.

"You know," she murmured, "you really don't have to see me upstairs."

"I'll just see you to the stairway, then."

And he did. He walked her to the stairway, then touched her chin lightly with his knuckles, raising it. "Welcome home, cousin. It's good to have you here."

"Thank you," she said softly.

His lips just brushed her forehead. She turned from him then and hurried quickly up the stairs to her room. She entered quickly, closed the door behind her and leaned against it, eyes shut, breathing deeply. He was a very handsome man, and a charming one. She had been hurting for so long, and now she had come here, to a strange country, where it was so easy to accept the comfort he was offering. It felt nice, but she didn't really want more....

How could she know what she wanted? She'd only been here one evening.

"Ah, girl! 'You were beautiful then. But you're far more beautiful now.' What a crock, I daresay!"

Allyssa's eyes flew open in amazement as she heard the words.

Dear God. He was there. The impostor who had swept her up from the train station on his black steed to bring her to the castle.

There! Right there in front of her. Casually stretched out on her bed, his arms behind his head, fingers laced together, while he relaxed comfortably on a pillow. Thick, inky dark hair slightly askew and rakish over his forehead, black lashes heavy over the half-closed eyes with which he observed her.

Later she would tell herself that she should have had the good sense to be frightened, except that she was instinctively certain that he did not intend to harm her. She strode over to him, fists clenched tightly at her sides, and stared at him.

"Who the hell are you, and what in God's name do you think you're doing in my bedroom?"

His wicked hazel eyes opened wide. "Your bedroom?" he inquired politely.

"While I am a guest here, this is my room!"

His eyes narrowed again quickly. "I warned you. You must take great care while you're here."

"And I'm warning you—you had better get out of my room before I scream. Loudly!"

He smiled, and she backed away just a bit as he coiled his taut-muscled form and prepared to rise. She really wasn't afraid of him. It was just that he was awfully good-looking. Wickedly so. Like a pirate from an old-time movie. He certainly had the power to mesmerize her, because she should have screamed by now.

And yet she hadn't.

He stood before her, his hands on his hips once again.

"Out!" she commanded.

"Ah, yes, Allyssa, my love! I'm—"

"I'm not your love. And you're a deceitful wretch, whoever you are! If I catch you in here again—"

"What?" he asked, taking a step nearer.

She lowered her voice to a warning tone. "I don't know what your game is! Do you work for Darryl? If so, be warned! I'll tell him—"

"Alas! So you've come so close to him so easily! 'Tis true—there's no fool like a woman!"

"Thank you. Thank you very much. You've called me a fool and laughed at the idea that I might be beautiful. If you'll just—"

"Oh, no!" he said softly, huskily, coming closer. He took her hands in his, and still she didn't scream. She merely stared into the glittering hazel of his eyes as he murmured, "I didn't laugh at the idea at all. I find you very, very beautiful! I'm dismayed that you fell so easily under the spell of a man such as Darryl, that and nothing more."

She pulled her hands from his quickly. "Out!" she whispered. She couldn't listen to such things, not when she was living in her distant cousin's household, not when he had been so kind. She really didn't know why she didn't scream and have this offensive charlatan thrown out of her room.

Maybe because she doubted whether anyone she had seen in the castle—including Darryl—would be capable of throwing him out.

She rubbed her wrists, staring into his eyes. Then she hurried past him, walking toward the bathroom. "I don't know who you are or just what you're after, but I want you out of my room. Now!"

She stepped into the bathroom and closed the door behind her, then stood very still, listening. But she didn't hear anything.

Damn! He'd looked very casual and comfortable on her bed! And to think the English were supposed to be more conservative than Americans!

Comfortable...

And dry, she thought. How curious. He hadn't changed clothing, but his hair and clothing had dried

after the rain and the mist had dampened them
both....

Well, she had left him quite some time ago. He must
have spent his time in front of a fireplace.

Right. Hers.

No, he had spent some of his time spying. He had
repeated Darryl's comment to her, word for word.

And he wasn't leaving! She hadn't heard a sound,
not the opening of a door, not the closing of it—
nothing.

She threw the bathroom door open. This was it. He
could leave or she would have him thrown out, even if
she had to phone the police herself!

But when she threw the door open, she discovered
that he had gone. Silently.

She walked across the room uneasily. Yes, she was
alone.

Still uncertain, she threw open the doors to the armoires. She looked under the bed, then sat on it, baf-
fled.

He was really gone.

She leaped up and ran to the door, bolting it securely. Then she changed for bed and crawled in beneath the cool clean sheets and warm down coverlet.
Who was he? What was he doing...?

The question would plague her forever, she thought.

But in fact it wouldn't. Jet lag very quickly got the
best of her, and she slept.

She awoke to the loud and discordant strains of an
argument. A fierce one.

For a few minutes the noise was only an undercurrent in her sleep. Slowly the sound became more def-

inite, and she realized that she wasn't dreaming, that she was really hearing voices.

She leaped up and unbolted the door, opening it a crack. Yes, she could hear the argument. Darryl was involved. So was someone else. A male someone else, judging from the deep, husky tones that drifted her way.

She bit lightly on her lower lip, trying to make out their words. Despite how loudly they were fighting, she couldn't quite do it.

Then the noise level suddenly dropped. They were still arguing, but someone must have reminded them that she was sleeping upstairs. The argument was still going full steam ahead, just at a lower level.

She closed her door thoughtfully, trying to remind herself that she didn't really have anything to do with this place.

But she did. It held the answers to the haunting secrets of her past.

She rushed into the bathroom, quickly brushed her hair and teeth and applied a lick and a promise of makeup. She slid into her blouse and skirt, then hopped across the room in her hurry to slip into her shoes. She threw open the door quickly, hoping that the argumentative stranger would still be there.

He was. The argument was ensuing. It had something to do with sheep and land and the historic trust, she thought, hurrying down the stairs.

They were both at the table in the great hall. Darryl was at one end, facing her. She quickly saw that his handsome face was taut with anger.

She couldn't see the visitor at first. He was standing at the other end of the table, staring at Darryl. All she could see was a set of very strong, broad shoulders and a cap of ebony dark hair. And she could hear his voice, strong and irritated.

"It's not half so difficult as you imagine. It's the way of the new world, and if we can't be reasonable and rational and get with it, it will all be over for everyone involved!" the stranger stated angrily.

"I want no part of it!" Darryl retorted. "How much plainer can I be?" He must have noticed Allyssa then because his eyes were suddenly riveted on her, and he pushed back his chair, standing. "Allyssa. Well, we did manage to awaken you. I'm so sorry. But now that you're up, you might as well meet Brian Wilde."

"Brian Wilde?" she murmured. She remembered the name. Brian Wilde. Along with Darryl and herself, he was the last of Paddy's surviving kin. But he didn't live in the castle. The solicitor had told her that he lived in a hunting lodge not far away.

The man at the end of the table moved quickly and impatiently to meet her. "So you've come back, Allyssa," he said. Then he was staring at her, and she gasped softly. He was the man who had come for her last night.

He was the dark, haunting stranger at the train station.

The man who had been in her room—and on her bed.

"Why didn't you tell me who you were?" she whispered.

He frowned, staring at her. "What?"

"Why didn't you—" she began, then stopped, staring at him in return. He was going to deny that he had met her anywhere, she realized.

"Why didn't I what?" he demanded.

What was he doing? For the moment she would play it his way, but she meant to find out what was going on.

"Nothing," she said.

He stared at her as if she were insane, his hazel eyes very intense, golden in the firelight. "Everything must be a question to you," he said. "I'm sure you can't remember very much. You were what? Three?—when you left here, and now Darryl has reintroduced us. All these years. Imagine. Not a word from you. But now you're here. For the reading of the will. How lovely."

He thought it was anything but lovely, from the sound of his tone. She almost felt as if she had been slapped.

But he didn't give her much time to reply. "I am truly sorry to have awakened your guest, Darryl. I'll leave you both to your happy reunion. I've work to do." He started out the door, pausing, his eyes raking her up and down. Then he walked past her and was gone, slamming the door sharply behind him.

"Allyssa, his behavior is atrocious. I can only apologize for him—" Darryl began.

But Allyssa shook her head, already in motion. "It's all right. Just a moment. I have a word to say to him myself!"

She raced after Brian Wilde, catching him just before he could mount a tall roan horse awaiting him on the old bridge.

"Wait!" she commanded, running up to him. She must have done so with a certain authority, because he stopped, watching her darkly as she approached. "You son of a bitch!" she snapped. "How could you do it? Last night, picking me up, appearing in my room—and then pretending you've never seen me before."

"Oh, I've seen you before," he said.

"There! Now you admit—"

"I admit that you were the most willful three-year-old I ever met!" he told her, his eyes flashing. He pushed back a wayward lock of his ebony hair, but it stubbornly fell over his eyes, again creating the image of a handsome rake. He pointed a finger at her. "You led us all a merry chase. A pretty child grown into a fetching woman. Still collecting and breaking hearts, I wager."

"What can you possibly know about me?" she cried furiously.

His eyes swept over her again. "They broke Paddy's heart when they took you away, that's what I know."

"I was a child! I wasn't given a choice!"

He took a step toward her. A menacing step. "Ah, yes, but you've been grown up a few years now, eh, my girl? And Paddy's dead and buried, and here you come."

"I didn't know—"

"Didn't you?" he demanded.

She stared at him, astonished. He was judging her without knowing a single thing about her life since she'd been three years old. And his manner had changed. Incredibly so. Why hadn't he gone through this tirade last night?

"No, I didn't know!" she snapped. Furious, she took a quick step toward him, then lashed out swiftly, slapping him hard across the cheek. "That was for last night!" she told him, spinning around to leave.

"Allyssa!" he hissed. Her heart pounded. For a moment she was certain that she had behaved not only impulsively, because of her temper, but dangerously, as well. He was going to follow her, spin her around and strike her.

But he didn't. Compelled, she paused and turned.

He was staring at her from his regal height with his gold eyes flashing.

"I'm telling you for the last time. You've gone daft, girl. I didn't see you last night. And you can play with Darryl all you like, but strike me again, Miss Evigan, and you'll pay the price." He leaped on his horse with a swift, sure move, collecting the reins. Then he edged the animal closer, looking down at her. "I promise you that!" he vowed.

And then, to her astonishment, he rode away.

CHAPTER THREE

Darryl spent a large part of the morning with Allyssa, but by afternoon, he excused himself, saying that he had work to do, but she should make herself at home.

Allyssa thought about telling him that she would feel more at home if he would let her share a little of the work that went with the place, but she decided it would be tactful to wait—and not appear as if she was attempting to take over the castle. Darryl had old-world ways, some of which were very nice. He never sat until she was seated, and he never failed to open a door, but sometimes his courtesy reached the point that he seemed to be treating her like a hothouse flower. When she had first returned to the castle after her argument with Brian Wilde, she tried to find out what the two men had been fighting about. But no matter how tactfully persistent she became, he was more so—he was determined not to tell her what the fierce argument had been over.

She was going to have to find out on her own.

Several times when they spoke casually, when he walked her out to the garden, when he pointed out a piece of furniture he thought she might remember for some reason, she thought about blurting out the fact that Brian had picked her up at the station—and that he had draped himself all over her bedroom. Except that Brian had denied it so vehemently....

What was going on? Just a matter of old rivalries?

If so, Mr. Brian Wilde certainly deserved a swift kick for keeping her in the dark about their old fights, playing disappearing tricks on her the way he did, and then denying it all!

She never did say anything about Brian to Darryl. And that afternoon, once he had gone off to do whatever it was that he had to do, Gregory suggested that she might like to ride around the estate. There were six horses in the stables, from old Betty, who could scarcely outrun a turtle, to Cignet Sam, who came quite close to being extraordinary stock.

The idea of riding around the estate appealed to her very much, and since Gregory had brought the rest of her things from the train station early that morning, she quickly donned a cotton shirt and a pair of jeans and headed out to the stables. A young man named Liam was working there with the horses and the tack, and he suggested that Lady Luck might be the best mount for her—she was surefooted over the somewhat rocky terrains Allyssa would find in places; she could jump hedges and hurdles like a champion; she could definitely beat a turtle in a race, but she was no wild, galloping killer. Allyssa thanked him and agreed with his choice. While she watched the red-haired, freckle-faced youth head into the barn, she stared out across the property. The stables were set to the rear of the castle. Fields rolled and stretched in every direction. On a distant hill she could see a flock of white sheep. Closer to where she stood were paddocks with neat fences.

"Where the shearing goes on," Liam told her, grinning, as he returned. He gave her a rueful smile. "Ye've really got to work to keep a castle up, these days. We've chickens, too, in the back barn there. And don't tell no one now, but we've been known to raise a pig or two, even in the twentieth century. The castle is really a very fancy farm, Miss Evigan."

"Allyssa," she told him, smiling. Gregory could be so stiff and correct, and she had scarcely seen any of the other help in the castle, so she was glad of Liam, who seemed not only friendly, but normal, too!

He gave her general directions. "The castle property runs to the north and the west, and there're some beautiful trails through the woods along the way. If you were to head due south, ye'd come upon the village, such as she is. The inn is a right fine place, though, for a pint of ale, if ye've a mind to stop. Mrs. McKenzie runs the place, and she's right friendly, though she'll be curious as a cat's meow, if ye can imagine!"

Allyssa thanked him and started out, noting from his look that he seemed just as curious as Mrs. McKenzie could possibly be, but she liked him anyway: everything about him seemed so open and honest and friendly.

Lady Luck handled like a dream. She was spirited but obedient, and Allyssa soon gave in to the temptation to canter her across one of the beautiful open fields. This morning, the landscape didn't seem so green. Oh, the emerald shades were there, but they were interspersed with glorious lilacs and earth tones, more beautiful than ever.

Running through the field was a wonderful sensation. Lady Luck raced along smoothly, her gait as graceful and easy as Allyssa could have hoped. The air was cool, blowing through her hair, whipping cold and refreshing against her cheeks. She reined the mare in as soon as she saw the forest looming before her. As Liam had told her, she saw an enchanting little trail that led into the green canopy of the trees.

Lady Luck seemed to dance into the trees at first, reluctant to give up her run. But Allyssa loved the scenery she discovered, broad branches that met over her head, parting just enough to allow a dazzle of sunlight on her here and there. The ground seemed to be carpeted in softness, with a layer of moss stretched over it.

She was startled when the trees suddenly broke and she found herself in a huge clearing. A sprawling, thatched-roof house sat in the midst of the clearing, surrounded by rose gardens. Behind the house and to the left were stables nearly as large as the dwelling itself. Smoke puffed cozily from the chimney that stood high atop the golden thatch on the roof of the house. It was so charming that it had a fairy-tale quality about it, almost as if it weren't real. The house resembled many of the smaller, Shakespearean-style dwellings she had seen in the village, but this one was much larger. It was nearly the same size as the castle, yet so secluded here in the forest that it was modest rather than grandiose.

As she sat on Lady Luck, staring at the house, she nearly jumped, startled to hear a voice behind her.

"Ah, what do we have here? Our American cousin. Spying for the Yanks, Miss Evigan?"

She must have nudged Lady Luck in her surprise, because the mare leaped forward. "Whoa!" she cried, reining the mare in. She patted Lady Luck, calming her, then whirled the horse around.

It was Brian Wilde.

He hadn't been riding. He came out of the forest as if he had materialized from it, from the mossy, green magic of the trees and the softly carpeted ground.

But he walked toward her in very modern jeans and a cotton work shirt, his hands on his hips, his eyes, as always, gold and assessing.

He stopped before her horse and grinned at her. "Slumming, Miss Evigan?"

"I don't even know where I am," she told him curtly. "And if these are English slums, you have it all over us poor Yankees."

He lowered his lashes briefly, then smiled at her again, patting Lady Luck's neck. "Well, I deserved that one. I'm sorry to say that we have atrocious English slums. I meant, Wilde Cottage must be a letdown after Fairhaven Castle."

"It's not a letdown at all," Allyssa said honestly, studying the house again. "It's enchanting."

"Mmm," he murmured, watching her. "Well, the history of the place is interesting, at least. It seems that the lord of the castle during Henry the Eighth's day was in love with a nobleman's daughter. For various reasons—such as the fact that they both already had spouses—they were unable to wed. He was a very wealthy man, having helped to get Henry's dear dad, Henry the Seventh, on the throne, so he built this house in the woods for his beloved mistress. It was very convenient, I imagine. He would just tell his wife, 'Honey, I'm going hunting with the boys,' and ride right through the forest from the manor to his cottage."

"You're making that up for shock value," Allyssa said coolly.

He started to laugh. "No, Miss Evigan, I'm not."

"It doesn't matter. It's beautiful."

"In a way," he murmured, "it does matter. And it should be beautiful, more beautiful than the castle. The castle was begun as a defensive stronghold by the Normans—they wanted to protect their rumps from the Saxons. While the house was built with love in mind. Illicit or not, it tends toward greater beauty, don't you think?"

She didn't know what to think; he was never the same from one minute to the next. He was watching her now with that familiar golden glitter in his eyes. Amusement? She could never be sure.

"What were you and Darryl fighting about this morning?" she asked him.

"Why don't you ask Darryl?"

"I did. He won't tell me."

He reached up suddenly, his hands fastening around her waist, and lifted her to the ground before she could protest. For a moment she was pressed tight to his body again. He felt so hot and tense that she nearly jumped. A fire seemed kindled in her own flesh by the glitter in his eyes.

Then he eased her down until her feet at last touched the ground. "Come in, come in. I'll show you the place, and I'll try to answer your question."

He caught hold of her elbow and started to lead her toward the house.

"Lady Luck—" she began.

"That mare is very much at home here, don't worry. She'll eat up my lawn and be waiting for you whenever you're ready. Right, Lady?'' he called softly to the horse.

The mare seemed to understand him. She lifted her head, throwing back her mane, and whinnied. Allyssa arched a brow to him.

"I've a knack with animals," he said with a shrug.

"Especially those of the female sex?" she heard herself asking.

His smile deepened slowly. "Maybe. Come on. I'll show you the house."

She followed him along a beautiful garden path between the rows of roses. "Pete Tomason has been keeping them up as long as I can remember," he commented as she gently touched a few petals. "Do you remember old Pete?" he asked, studying her eyes again.

She shook her head. "I don't remember anything at all about being here. I was a toddler when I left."

He shrugged. "Maybe a person doesn't remember things from that age. I couldn't possibly judge, could I? I've been here almost all my life."

Allyssa stopped short, so angry at his tone that she spun to face him, poking her finger into his chest. "Would you please quit that! It seems as if you're always implying something, and I have simply had it with your rudeness! You have some nerve! Showing up in my room, making snide comments, then trying to pretend you were never even there! How dare you? How dare you—"

The finger she had been thrusting suddenly curled back into her hand, and what she pounded against his chest became first one fist, then both. He quickly caught her wrists, jerking her swiftly against him.

"What is it with you?" he demanded angrily. "I was never, *never,* in your room. Trust me, Miss Evigan, if I had been, we would both remember it—very well!"

His eyes seemed like pure, hot metal. She opened her mouth to protest, to deny everything that he was saying, as she gathered her strength to break away from him.

But before a single word could leave her mouth in her own defense, she saw that his head was suddenly, and fiercely, lowering toward her own. And then his lips were on hers.

She knew she should fight him. She didn't even know him, not really, and what she did know about him should have steered her completely away from him.

But such thoughts meant nothing when the rough feel of his lips against her own was the most exciting thing she had ever known. He kissed her as if it was something he had wanted to do from the first moment he'd seen her, as if it was something he had been fighting, something he had been dying to do. . . .

Hard. Forceful. His tongue wedged apart her lips and teeth. Hot, liquid, intimate, it seared into her mouth, into her soul, into her being. She should have been pounding her fists against him again, but instead her fingers were curling into the cotton of his shirt as she was assailed by delicious sensations. She was tantalizingly aware of the tremendous heat and energy emanating from him, keenly aware of the rippling muscles of his torso. His scent filled her nostrils, rich, masculine, a mingling of leather and aftershave and the subtle, individual scent of the man himself. But it was a kiss, just a kiss. . . .

Never just a kiss. Never had a kiss made her feel so explicitly what she wanted to do. Never had she simply molded herself so swiftly and naturally against the body of a man. The force itself was exquisite. . . .

As his fingers threaded through her hair she pressed closer and closer until she could feel the length of him, flesh and bone and sinew and more.

Then suddenly, as swiftly as his touch had come, it was gone. His fingers were still tangled in her hair, but his face was high above hers, and he seemed angry, incredibly angry. "I told you—neither of us would have the least doubt that I had been there!" he snapped huskily.

She wrenched herself away, spinning and heading almost blindly toward her horse. To upset her further, the mare spooked and ran several feet away from her when she moved to take the reins.

Behind her, Brian whistled. Lady Luck turned as obediently as a lamb and trotted to him. "Miss Evigan?" he said politely.

She walked over to him and snatched the reins from his hands. She would have mounted on her own power, but he was too swift. His hands were on her waist again, lifting her, setting her down. She gathered the reins quickly, staring at him, in a hurry to be gone.

"You didn't see the house," he told her.

"Get out of my way."

He arched a brow. "Running? I didn't think you were the type to be easily scared."

"Move!" she snapped.

"You still don't know what the argument was about between Darryl and me."

"I don't care—"

"Oh, yes, you do. And I'll tell you. The sheep just can't cut it anymore. We can't hold on to these places without changing our ways. The National Trust wants us to open them both to the public, two afternoons a week. It would give us all kinds of government credits and, quite bluntly, it would save our butts."

"Well, Mr. Wilde," she suggested irritably, "why don't you open your own house to the public and let Darryl do whatever he wishes with his?"

He shook his head, still holding the reins so that she could not move, still studying her eyes. "You don't know, do you?"

"Don't know what?"

"They're linked, you see. The way Paddy saw it, there were three heirs to his grandfather's estate, those being Darryl, you and me. I loved the cottage from the time I was a child. You were gone—no one knew if we would ever see you again. The cottage came my way, the castle fell to Darryl. But there are numerous legal ties. Neither of us can sell without the other's permission. Neither of us can make changes—like signing with the National Trust—without the other. That's how it was set up during Paddy's life. But then again, sweet distant cousin, everything could change. After all, the solicitor did find you. And, after all these years, you're back."

"Gold digging," Allyssa said sarcastically, trying to jerk the reins from him. "Let me by!"

"Why? Are you in such a hurry to run to the castle and commiserate with Darryl?"

"Despite whatever faults *you* may see in him, Brian Wilde, the man is a hell of a lot nicer than you are!"

He instantly released his hold on the mare, stepping back. "And your names are already the same! How convenient for you!"

Allyssa decided not to reply, now that she was free of him. She set her knees to Lady Luck's ribs and bolted from the clearing.

Despite her anger, she had the good sense to slow the mare's gait as she made her way through the trees. Still, she headed for the castle as fast as she dared, racing once again when she came to the open fields.

Darryl was still out when she arrived. She learned that he would be very late, but that dinner would be served whenever she chose. She thanked Gregory for the information and hurried up to her room.

As she stripped, she kept her gaze nervously on the bedroom, thinking that Brian Wilde might appear again. But he didn't. Still, she stared into every corner of the bedroom, checked under the bed and peered into the armoires, then bolted the door firmly.

Then, as she sank into another deliciously warm bath, she closed her eyes in comfort....

Suddenly she bolted up in horror. Oh, no! She had been *hoping* that he might appear again in her room.

She gritted her teeth, leaning back once again and lifting a washcloth to drip hot sudsy water slowly over her arm. Why? What was it about him? He was rude, he was insulting, he was...

Exciting. She wanted to deny it, but she couldn't. He was nothing like Brandon, she assured herself. Brandon had been so soft-spoken, so dedicated to his ideals. He had loved her so gently, so tenderly.

And she had never known anyone like Brian Wilde. She'd never even imagined anyone like him. Just be-

ing held the way he had held her... The feel of his
lips...

The nerve of him, sweeping her up like that! The
nerve of him, period. What was he doing? Trying to
tease and torment her into leaving?

Then why had it seemed so...?

Natural, she supplied silently. Wild. Passionate.
Unbearably exciting. As if he had hungered for her for
so long. As if he had needed her touch and was remembering it now as she remembered his. She brought
her trembling fingers to her lips. It was so easy to remember. Too easy...

She thought she heard a noise in the bedroom. She
dropped the washcloth and nearly catapulted from the
tub, grabbing a towel and quickly wrapping it around
herself before hurrying to the bedroom, refusing to
confront her own emotions.

The towel fell, but it didn't matter. She was chasing
phantoms. The room was empty.

She ate alone in the family dining room. Then she
read for a while before returning to her room and
crawling into bed, where she lay awake for a long, long
time.

And it wasn't until just seconds before she finally
fell asleep that she realized what she was doing.

Waiting...

Darryl was downstairs the next morning when she
arose, waiting for her in the great hallway. There was
a full array of breakfast offerings set up on a buffet
near the huge banquet table, and he poured her coffee himself while she fixed herself a plate of poached
eggs, bacon and potatoes.

"I do apologize for leaving you alone yesterday," he told her. "It was awfully rude when you had so recently arrived, but the Flemish buyers were here, and I had to spend time with them."

She waved a hand in the air, smiling ruefully. "Don't apologize. I know your life has to go on."

"Yes," he said quietly. "But I rather like the fact that it's going on with you here. Do you feel like another ride today? I can take you into the village to meet some of the locals if you can bear my company for a few hours."

"That sounds wonderful."

"Aha! What sounds so wonderful?" a deep voice suddenly demanded.

Darryl made a sound in the back of his throat as Brian Wilde strode into the hall, smiling, just as if he belonged there. He walked straight to the buffet table and helped himself to a plate. "What, no salmon, Miss Evigan?" he asked her in mock horror. "Why, Fairhaven is famous for its breakfast buffets when guests are in residence! Come now, eat up, have a hearty appetite, girl."

"Brian," Darryl said sourly, "to what do we owe the honor of your company?"

"Why, how can I stay away? Our beautiful American cousin has arrived. She's here at the castle, preferring grandeur to charm!" He brushed Allyssa's cheek with the backs of his knuckles, arched a brow, then proceeded to the table with his plateful of food. Allyssa fought the temptation to slap him soundly on one smug cheek.

"We're going riding," Darryl said bluntly.

"How convenient! I rode here."

"You weren't invited," Allyssa said coolly, keeping her eyes away from his.

But, oh, she felt his gaze! And as angry as she wanted to be, she had to steel herself to keep from looking at him. She'd already noticed his hair was newly washed, falling at a rakish angle over his forehead. His eyes, with their hazel and gold sizzle, seemed to touch her like wildfire. He was rude, crude, abrasive...

And she wanted him to ride with her.

But she would die before she said it! she insisted to herself.

However, he was equally determined to come, and somehow he managed to make it happen. They started into the village together, Brian and Darryl going on with what must have been their never-ending argument.

"I certainly don't want a pack of strangers prowling about the place!" Darryl insisted. "How do you know who might be in one of those groups?"

"I'd rather have those groups arrive—and I don't give a damn who might be in with the lot—than lose the place altogether, which is a very real threat!"

"Well, now, it might not be up to you at all, soon, eh, cousin?" Darryl asked. He cast a triumphant eye in Allyssa's direction.

She frowned.

"A two-to-one vote can cancel out anything I've got to say," Brian informed her pleasantly. "But then again, none of us really knows what's going to be in that will, do we? So maybe we should forget the whole subject for the afternoon?"

"How strange. We share a single great-great-great-grandparent, and here we are!" Darryl murmured.

"Strange, indeed!" Brian laughed. "We could be almost as closely related to some stranger on the street!" He winked at Allyssa, who was reminded of the way he had behaved that first night, when he had swept her up from the station.

When he had teased her, so negligently, from her bed.

"We could make an effort to get along, for Allyssa's sake," Darryl said.

"Ah, yes, but why fool the poor child with extraordinary behavior?"

"I'm not a child," she said irritably.

"Ah, yes, of that I'm well aware," Brian murmured. She felt his gold eyes rake over her, their touch making her warm.

Making her remember.

And making her want...

"If he fails to be polite, ignore him," Darryl instructed her. "I've been doing it for years now."

Brian smiled, his eyes shifting away from her at last. "Race you over the next rise, cousin!" he cried to Darryl.

The two instantly kneed their horses and went plunging wildly forward. Lady Luck followed automatically, and Allyssa gave her leave to do so, galloping wildly in the others' wake over rises and hills. She was a good rider, passing Darryl and pulling abreast of Brian just as he reined in.

He pointed down the next hill. "See? What a vantage point!" And it was. Far down the hill she could see the village nestled in the valley. It was a beautiful sight. "The people are just as magical," he said softly, watching her. Darryl reached them then. "Share a pint, shall we, cousin?" Brian asked politely.

"Several, maybe!" There was just a touch of acid in his tone, as if the polite veneer he'd been attempting to maintain was beginning to crack.

They rode down to the inn, where Mrs. McKenzie ushered them into the pub area. She talked a blue streak, provided them with glasses of dark, foaming beer and chips with vinegar, then left them. Both Darryl and Brian were on their best behavior, managing to discuss music and movies and offer opinions on British politics. There was a dart board, and the two wound up in a game, yet the rivalry seemed a friendly one. They tried to include her, but she'd never thrown a dart in her life and was afraid she might hit one of the other patrons.

Sipping her beer, she watched them and felt a little fluttering inside. They were both such strikingly good-looking men. Of course, they were her relatives....

But she might well be more closely related to some stranger she passed on the street, just as Brian had said.

Which was good, of course, because she never should have felt such stirrings as she did with...

Brian. She bit her lower lip. What was the matter with her? Brian was curt, rude and harsh. And there was that little matter of his denying he had been in her room and insisting that if he *had* been there, they both would have remembered.

The fluttering came again, and she quickly looked down. Yes, he was tall, dark, very handsome. Taut muscled, hotter than a flame, quick-tempered, aggravating, exciting. She was still a fool! Darryl was the one who seemed to give a damn about things. He was trying his best for her.

She looked up, feeling guilty. She was going to do her best to be more concerned for him. To let him know that she appreciated his manners.

After the two men finished their game they had one more beer. Then Brian paid the bill, and they left, mounting up quickly to ride back.

Brian rode with them as far as the castle. But once there, he didn't dismount.

He looked at the sky, as if searching for something. "I think there will be quite a moon tonight. What do you think, cousin?" he asked Darryl, his tone full of some hidden meaning Allyssa was unable to decipher.

Darryl scowled. "Yes, I imagine there will be!"

Brian smiled, then touched his forehead lightly to Allyssa. "Take care, cousin," he said, and turned his horse to ride away.

"The devil take him!" Darryl muttered. Then he looked quickly at Allyssa. "Sorry. But this has been going on for years."

"Even brothers squabble. It's probably natural that cousins should, too."

"We're not that closely related," Darryl reminded her. Then he grinned. "No—we just dislike one another."

She smiled, and they rode to the stables, where they left the horses with Liam.

Once they were inside the house, he apologized to her again. "There's a matter I forgot to take care of yesterday. I realize this is incredibly rude, but I have to be gone for supper again. I promise I'll make up for it."

"There's no need. You mustn't worry," she assured him.

He moved a step closer to her, cupping her chin in his hand. "Allyssa, you are extraordinary. So beautiful, so intelligent. So sweet."

She smiled and wished that she would feel something for him in return. But she couldn't. Not anymore.

Damn Brian. He had ruined something for her yesterday when he had kissed her.

She backed away. "You're pretty fine yourself, cousin," she said softly.

"Well, we've time, and we'll make up for any that we've lost," he assured her.

Unable to find the right words to say to him, she smiled and turned quickly, then ran up the stairs.

In her room, she decided on a hot bath. As she leaned back in the tub, she muttered aloud, "You really are an SOB, Mr. Brian Wilde! And I hope you're out there to hear me!"

But once again he wasn't. Her room was empty, cold.

She dressed and went downstairs. The sun was just setting. Gregory told her that she could dine whenever she wished, and she nodded, then told him she wanted to see the sunset. She slipped outside and began to walk idly toward the rear of the castle.

She spotted an ancient graveyard. She hadn't noticed it earlier, and now it looked both beautiful and mysterious in the waning light. Even from a distance she could see that there were beautiful new angels to mark the recent graves, as well as broken stones and ancient relics of carved sarcophagi. There was even a large stone structure—the family vault, she imagined. Against the setting sun, the cemetery was as lovely and quaint, as picturesque, as everything else she had found here. And yet there was something . . .

She frowned suddenly. Somebody was entering the large crypt. She narrowed her eyes to see better against the setting sun.

It was Darryl.

She started to walk toward the cemetery, but the distance was greater than she had imagined, and she started to run.

Suddenly she tripped over a broken stone, that seemed to rise from the ground to block her way. Winded, she got to her feet and kept going, but the sun was setting fast now. Darkness was coming.

At last she reached the vault. The name "Evigan" was deeply etched in the large marble cross atop it. A shiver swept down her spine.

"Darryl?" she called softly. There was no answer.

The door was open. A breeze shifted, and the door at the bottom of the stairs moved just a little, creaking in the night air.

It was nearly dark now. She looked around, then told herself to stop being a fool. She walked down the steps and through the door into the unknown.

Down below, the darkness wasn't as complete as she'd expected. She could make out shelf after shelf of coffins and freestanding stone slabs supporting even more coffins. In the dimness, the details escaped her. An eerie feeling crept along her backbone.

"Darryl!"

But he still didn't answer. The shapes around her seemed to shift, to turn molten and begin to writhe.

She was losing her mind. . . .

No, there *was* something in front of her. Then, as suddenly as it had appeared, it was gone.

And then she heard something. Behind her. She tried to spin around, but before she could complete the movement there was a sharp, searing pain at the back of her head.

And suddenly the darkness was complete. She crashed down to the cold stone floor, images of death fluttering wildly along the black corridors of her mind....

CHAPTER FOUR

Strong hands were on her, lifting her. She could just barely feel them. There was a cool touch against her face. Fingers moved gently over the back of her skull.

"You'll be all right." She heard the words, spoken softly. At least, it seemed that she heard them.

She might have been dreaming. She thought she opened her eyes, but she was in the mist again. She couldn't see very clearly, although she struggled to.

He was there. Smiling tenderly. He was in those black riding breeches again, knee-high black boots and a white cotton shirt. His fingers stroked her softly. "You'll be all right."

She tried to see his face. Tried to make out his features. The bump on her head had done things. Nothing was clear. Was she imagining this?

"You'll be all right!"

She heard the words again. A promise on the air? Real or imagined? She was rising, drifting, spinning.

And she *wasn't* all right. She couldn't keep her eyes open. They fell closed once again.

Maybe it was seconds later, maybe eons. She heard her name being called. "Allyssa! Dear Lord, what in God's name...?"

She struggled to open her eyes, struggled against the blackness that had claimed her.

"Brian." His face was very clear now. The hard, rugged planes of it, the gold of his eyes. She tried to smile. The world was clearing. "Brian."

"What happened to you?"

His hands were on her once again, touching her cheek, seeking along her skull for damage. Holding her.

She blinked and tried to focus. He was wearing black jeans and a V-necked red sweater against the chill of the night. "You've changed," she murmured. "You've changed your clothes."

"You're rambling!" he said anxiously. He rose, lifting her with him into his arms. "Come on. You're coming home with me. Then you can tell me what happened."

"The castle . . ." she murmured.

"We're not going to the castle," he said. He hesitated, searching her face. "Perhaps I should take you into the next town, to the hospital."

"No, no!" she murmured, her arms tightening around him.

"All right. We'll see," he agreed. He started walking, carrying her from the family crypt. His horse was obediently waiting for the two of them. He lifted her up, setting her carefully in the saddle, holding her for a moment lest she should lose her balance. Then he leaped up behind her. "Are you all right?" he asked her.

She leaned against him. No, she wasn't all right. She had a pounding headache. But the world had cleared. She was going to be fine. And no matter how frightening things seemed right now, she wasn't afraid. Not when he was behind her, the wall of his chest so secure against her back, the warmth of his arms so tight around her.

"I'm fine," she murmured softly. "This is just like the night we met. How strange."

He didn't answer her, though he seemed to stiffen ever so slightly.

He nudged the horse, and the animal picked up a slow trot. Darkness had descended, but both man and horse knew the way, with or without the light. Woozily she noticed that there was no sign of the moon he'd predicted earlier. Soon they were traveling through the inky green darkness of the forest, and after that, they emerged by the cottage in the woods. Brian slid from the horse and reached for her, bringing her down to him. He searched her face again, but sighed. "I've got to get you inside. There's not enough light out here to see your eyes."

"My eyes are fine."

He gave his horse a smack on the haunches. "Head on into the stall, boy. I'll tend to you in a bit." The horse obediently trotted off. "Think you can make it into the house this time?"

But Allyssa was looking after the horse. "My Lord! Is he always that well-behaved?"

"He knows there's hay in his stall," Brian said. "Now, come on!"

"I'm quite sure I can make it," she said indignantly, "if you can just keep quiet!"

He muttered something that she couldn't quite make out. She followed him along the pathway until she stumbled over one of the flagstones. He muttered again, turning to sweep her into his arms.

"I can walk," she said.

"I'm not so sure."

She shrugged, a slow smile curving her lips. "Fine, then. Carry me."

He did so, pushing the front door open with his foot, then closing it the same way once they were inside the cottage. With her arms around his neck, Allyssa tried to turn to see the place. It was beautiful. More than beautiful. It was as quaint and rich in history inside as it was outside. The fireplace mantel was made of magnificently carved dark wood. There were wonderful crown moldings surmounting the walls, and huge exposed wooden beams. A copper kettle hung over the fire. The room was vast, but very warm, with massive filled bookcases, a large curving stairway and heavy, comfortable furniture. Big handsome chairs sat before the fire, and that was where he took her, sitting her down, kneeling in front of her, then rubbing her wrists.

"Cold?" he asked.

She shook her head, studying him. "Why do you change so from one minute to the next?"

"I don't change at all," he said.

"But you do. You behave as if you don't want me here—"

"I *don't* want you here," he said flatly.

"Why?"

"Because I don't want you to get hurt. I was worried about things to begin with, and then you go falling down the crypt stairs, bashing your head—"

"I didn't fall down the stairs!" she protested, amazed to realize that he thought she had. "Someone struck me!"

"Who?" he demanded, his eyes narrowing.

He doubted her, she realized, fighting to control her temper. "I don't know. I followed Darryl into the crypt—"

"And Darryl hit you?" he demanded sharply.

"I never said that! I don't see how he could have. He wasn't there."

"You just said you followed him in."

"Yes," she said, "I know. But I must have missed seeing him come out and go somewhere else or something. Because he wasn't in the crypt when I got there."

Brian rose from his knees, sitting down in the chair beside hers and watching the flames reflectively. They mirrored the color of his gaze.

"I—" she began.

But he spun on her before she could finish. "I've got it. One of our dear departed relatives got up from his coffin to give you a good wallop on the head."

Angrily, Allyssa leaped up. It was a mistake. Her headache, which had been fading, began to pound again. "I certainly never said anything of the kind!" she snapped angrily.

"Oh, will you sit down!" he responded, equally aggravated. He rose, grabbing her by the shoulders. She didn't have the energy to resist, so she sat down again, gritting her teeth.

"Someone very much alive and well struck me on the head with something," she said stubbornly. "Why do you find it so difficult to believe me?"

He hesitated a long while. Too long. "Why?" she demanded again.

"Because," he said softly at last, "your imagination seems to work overtime, cousin!"

"What are you talking about?"

"I never picked you up at the station. I never came to your room."

Allyssa stared hard at the fire, fighting the sudden sting of tears at the backs of her eyes. What was going on here? Had she lost her mind since she had come to England?

Or was he lying to her? Was Brian himself the greatest danger she had come across?

She stared at him hard, determined not to give in to her emotions. "Then you have a twin running around in riding breeches and a white shirt. *Someone* picked me up at the station. *Someone* appeared in my room, mainly to warn me about Darryl—"

He interrupted her with a snort. "Well, that was certainly wise."

"Oh, was it?" Before she knew it, she was on her feet again, staring at him. "All I know is that Darryl does not mysteriously appear and disappear—"

"Neither do I," he said, his eyes narrowing.

"Well, something is happening!" Allyssa insisted. Behind her, the fire snapped and crackled. "I know what I saw—"

"Well, you didn't see *me!*"

She whirled around, staring at the flames. Then she turned back to him. "There are a number of options here, you know."

He nodded. "Yes. One, you might be imagining things. You were very tired, and you had traveled a very great distance. Then there's option number two. Someone is out to get you—for an unknown reason. Option number three—"

"Brings us back to you!" she exclaimed softly, leveling a finger at him. "You're the one who's out to get me! You're trying to make me believe that I'm going insane!''

He stood up, furious now. "For what possible reason?" he demanded harshly. Suddenly his hands were on her arms, dragging her hard against him. "For what possible reason?"

"I don't know, but I am *not* going mad!" she retorted. "So if you consider that as an option . . ."

"Did I hit you on the head tonight, too?" he demanded sarcastically.

"Well, I didn't fall down the damn steps!" she insisted. "And you were there—"

"I was there *when?*" he roared, his fingers tightening, his eyes burning deeply into hers.

She started to tremble. Was it fear of his rising temper, of the way he was holding her?

Or was it a reaction to his warmth? A desire to keep being touched?

She forced herself not to struggle against his hold. To stare at him with all the disdain she could muster. "Let go of me," she said coolly.

"Allyssa, I'm telling you—"

"Let go of me," she repeated.

"I can't accept—"

"You can't accept the fact that I'm telling the truth."

His fingers tightened around her arms for a moment. "Damn it!" he said heatedly. "Damn *you!*" Then his hold eased. Finally he released her altogether, thrusting her from him and turning away, fighting some inner struggle as he stared into the flames.

She swung around to leave him, blinking against the sudden moisture that sprang to her eyes, blinding her.

She started for the door, intent on escaping him, no matter how far she had to travel on foot, no matter how dark the night.

"Allyssa!"

She heard him raggedly cry out her name and turned back. He was approaching her with long, determined strides. Before she knew it, she was being held tightly against him again. "I will not let you go back to that castle alone tonight!" he told her, his gold eyes glittering with passion. "I will not!"

She stared at him, as furious with him as he seemed to be with her. But then she exhaled in a soft gasp as he suddenly pulled her closer, then closer still. At last, with hunger and relentless purpose, his lips touched hers. With urgency, with force, with fever and will, he caused her lips to part against his.

Fight! she told herself.

But the will to do so escaped her like fog drifting into the darkness. The force he'd used moments earlier turned to sweet seduction. Heat rippled into her with every movement of his mouth and tongue, with his every caress, with the very way he embraced her to him....

If he had been in her room, he had told her, neither of them would have had any doubts that they had been together.

No, she could never, never doubt this man now. His burning kiss seemed to last forever, to take her to distant lands, sailing upon clouds, then touching the earth in the most elementary way. When his mouth rose from hers at last, she stared into the dark gold passion of his eyes. Wordlessly she touched his cheek, then lightly threaded her fingers through the ebony darkness of his hair.

When he swept her into his arms she didn't say a word, nor did she demur as he carried her up the long stairway. She remained silent as he walked along the shadowed hallway, thrust open a door with his foot and carried her inside. They were in darkness, yet she could see, for the moon had risen at last, seeming very bright and full, and cast its ivory illumination into the room. But the details of the place were sketchy in her mind. There was a bed, a huge four-poster, with draperies pulled back and tied at each post. There were massive windows. There was a fireplace, but no fire burned there at the moment.

And that was all she saw, for she could not tear her eyes from his. He stretched her out upon the soft down coverlet, following her seconds later. His weight was sprawled half over hers, and then he was kissing her again. Kissing, tasting, exploring, touching, kissing again. Dazed, she kissed and parried in return, felt the fabric of his sweater, felt the excruciating heat and ripple of muscle and flesh beneath it. He pulled away from her and hastily wrenched the sweater over his shoulders. Moonlight made his shoulders very broad, his chest sleek and shiny, enticing to touch. She reached out, savoring the feel of naked flesh beneath her fingertips, the vibrance of his body, the heat, the fire. She felt his lips on hers; then they moved, touching her throat, lingering there. Button by button, her blouse was falling open. The hot sweeping caress of his breath moved with a tantalizing slowness down the length of her. And here and there, he touched... touched her nakedness with a kiss, the worship of his tongue, the sweetest savoring of his lips. Then that heat again, touching her, touching her...

She tried to rise, but he pressed her back firmly. She heard the slow rasping sound of the zipper on her jeans and closed her eyes. His fingers were on the waistband now, slowly tugging the fabric from her hips. Ah, his lips again. Touching, touching. His breath, bringing new fire. There was a soft thud in the darkness as her jeans fell to the floor. He rose. Bronze and majestic in the shadows and ivory light. Again the rasp of a zipper sounded. His black jeans followed hers to the floor. Naked, agile, determined, he returned to the bed, the fire of his nakedness covering her, radiating into her. His fingers eased beneath her bra strap; his lips touched where fabric had been. With a deft touch, he slipped free the clasp, then caressed the breast thus exposed to him, his palm working over the fullness of her flesh brushing, teasing the crest. Then his mouth touched her. Covered her. She gasped in ecstasy, her fingers clutching the muscles of his shoulder, touching him in return. The weight of his body eased off her, and his lips teased her lower abdomen, the juncture of her thighs, over the narrow silk barrier of her panties. His breath, hot, so very, very hot, teased her....

Then his fingers were on the elastic band of her last fragile covering, and in seconds nothing stood between her flesh and his caress. Deep within her, deep in secret and intimate places, she felt the hot explosive coil of desire winding more and more tightly. She let out a soft cry, reaching for him, thirsting for him, needing to touch, to kiss, to caress in return.

She found herself on her knees, with him kneeling before her. Her lips moved over his shoulders; her teeth grazed his flesh; her tongue loved silently over each and every tiny hurt. She pressed against him, using the fullness of her body, amazed not only that she could feel so hungry, but that along with her hunger she could feel so deliciously secure. Yes, she wanted him. There was no hesitation. No thought. No fear. She wanted the feel of his palms moving down the length of her back, over her buttocks. Wanted his kiss against her lips. Against her breasts, her throat, her lips again. She wanted to...

To fall beneath him. To look up and see his eyes, gold even in the moonlight and misted with his passion. There was nothing to see but that gold, for it seemed that the mist of the night rose around them, and then there was nothing but the bed, the moon and the man with searing gold desire in his eyes.

He stared at her for one long moment. Then, at last, he touched her, entered her, still staring into her eyes. She cried out at the sudden invasion, no matter how sweet. She closed her eyes, even as her body closed around his. For long seconds he held entirely still, allowing them both the exquisite introduction.

And then he began to move.

The coil of desire within her wound tighter and tighter. At first she was nearly still herself, just aware of the wonder of the feel of him. Then instinct brought her to life, and she rose against him. Again, again. Undulating, writhing, wanting more and more.

Receiving it.

She bit his shoulder lightly, trying to endure the tormenting ecstasy. It had been so long. So very long.

And never like this. Never this demand. Never this blinding force of passion. Never this constant, increasing rhythm that asked so much—no, demanded it—relentless, giving, seeking, allowing no quarter...

None. Not even when the sweeping feeling sought to drown her. It was unbearable. She fought against him, strained against him....

Then cried out as her climax swept through her, as blinding as sunlight, as volatile as thunder. She clung to him still, shaking, trembling, slipping slowly downward again, downward into the mist, out of the light, but still feeling. Oh, yes, still feeling so much. Brian, the sleekness of his skin, the strength of his flesh. The hair-roughened quality of his legs, his belly, his chest. The texture of his cheeks. The force of his heartbeat. The ragged heaving of his breath...

He eased down beside her, still gasping. She curled against him, her eyes closed, her head lowered. Reason was rushing upon her swiftly now. She had just made love with Brian Wilde, a man she hardly knew. She had wanted him so badly, so instinctively, that she hadn't thought about Brandon for a second, though she had never been able to forget him for a full minute in the company of another man. She had never even thought to go so far with any man since Brandon had died.

Brian Wilde.

The man who made her think that she was losing her mind.

She groaned suddenly, and his fingers touched her hair. "What is it?"

"We shouldn't have done...this."

"Why not?"

"We're not that...well acquainted."

"I dare say we are now."

She sat up, staring at him. She wished she didn't like the way he looked quite so much, his hair tousled, his fingers laced behind his head, his chest and torso damp and appealing. "I should be afraid of you," she whispered.

He smiled. "Why? Because you might lose your virtue?"

"There's my sanity," she said softly. "Or my life."

He sat up suddenly, his smile vanishing. "Oh, my Lord, I forgot!" he murmured in dismay. "Your head—"

"My head is fine. Honestly," she murmured.

"Is it?"

"Yes."

He lay down, studying her. His face was in shadow, but the moonlight touched her own, she thought.

Once again she didn't know what was truth and what was not....

And Brian Wilde did.

She shook her head suddenly. "I shouldn't be here. It's really very rude. I—"

"Making love is rude?" he queried politely.

She felt a flush cover her cheeks. "That's not what I meant, and you know it! I have to get back. If Darryl has returned—"

"Darryl left you," he reminded her irritably, his eyes narrowing. "And Darryl is the man you followed into the crypt. How do you know he's not the one who clunked you over the head—assuming you *were* clunked over the head?"

"I'm telling you—"

"All right! But you needn't rush back. You shouldn't go back at all. You should stay here."

"Wonderful! Stay with a man who seems to think I should be committed to an asylum!"

"What?"

"Well, you continue to doubt my word—"

"You started this, worrying about Darryl."

"Damn it, Brian Wilde, all we ever do is fight!"

He reached for her suddenly. "Come here!" he commanded.

"But—"

He pulled her relentlessly against him. "I know a way to keep us from fighting!" he whispered huskily against her lips.

"But—" she began again.

She never finished. His lips touched hers. One thing led to another.

A silver mist seemed to roll in upon them once again. The taste of ecstasy was too rare, too sweet, not to be savored one more time.

Perhaps she *was* losing her mind. She shouldn't trust him.

She shouldn't . . .

But in the silver magic of the night, it didn't matter in the least. There was only one thing she knew for certain.

Whatever she should or shouldn't be doing, she absolutely couldn't deny him this.

CHAPTER FIVE

Two days later, Allyssa stood in the center of the family crypt again.

It was broad daylight outside. She had made sure to come at noon, when the sun was high in the sky. She wasn't sure what she had expected to find, though whatever it was, she wasn't finding it.

The crypt was well cared for, though it was an eerie place, even by daylight. Some of the coffins were incredibly beautiful. Some might well fit in museums—minus the family corpses, of course. Numerous knights, in stone and in wood, lay side by side with their ladies, holding tightly to their swords and lances. The faces of some were hidden by the visors of their helmets; others were bared to the world, with rich mustaches and beards in place. The Victorian coffins and sarcophagi were heavily carved with skeletons and death's heads, many adorned as well with elaborate poems about the deceased. In the twentieth century the coffins became much simpler. She found her great-grandfather's—he was the most recent inhabitant of the tomb. His coffin had been carved from a very simple, off-white marble sarcophagus adorned only with his name, Padraic Michael Evigan, etched directly into the marble in broad letters. Someone apparently still loved Padraic, for wildflowers had been scattered over his coffin, while the rest of the crypt was barren of them.

The place was huge, she thought, trying to estimate its size. At the least it was about three thousand square feet, with several smaller rooms breaking off from the main tomb at the foot of the aboveground stairway. The first room contained both the oldest coffins and the newest ones, with all the years between having been interred deeper in the crypt.

Allyssa had been afraid to come, yet afraid not to come. She knew she hadn't fallen down the stairs.

Options...she had options, she reminded herself, and with the thought a little pang seemed to tear at her heart. She had made Brian take her home the other night. He had been bitter and mocking, but he had played her game. At the castle she'd told Darryl that she and Brian had had dinner together, and that was all. Brian had watched her, as if waiting for her to say more. But she hadn't. She had merely stared at him, silently imploring him to remain silent himself, and he had done so. But she hadn't seen him since.

Darryl had gone out of his way to be charming, riding with her around the estate, taking her to Mrs. MacKenzie's. In the taproom, she had met a number of the local people, who had welcomed her, cheerfully assuring her that the castle was haunted, as any ancient castle should be.

Haunted... She wondered if she should add that possibility to her options. What would Brian say? Either I *am* losing my mind, she thought, or someone is playing a trick on me, or you really are an evil man trying to make me think I'm insane—or the place is haunted.

But she wasn't able to put that possibility before him, because he made no effort to see her. The solicitor had stopped by to make arrangements to read the will on Friday morning; some of the neighbors, the parson and his wife, and the local doctor, had made calls, too.

But Brian had kept away.

She sighed, sinking down on the slab by Paddy's coffin, then shivered suddenly and looked around, feeling eerily as if she weren't alone anymore.

She wasn't alone, she reminded herself. She was here with dozens and dozens of dead relatives. But she wasn't losing her mind; she was a sane and logical person, and she didn't believe in ghosts. The door to the stairs and the outside world was wide open. There was actually a bright sun in the south of England today.

And she was alone. She had walked around the entire place, sliding her fingers along the stone wall to find some other entry or exit, and she had discovered nothing. Other than the fact that, even in daylight, the inner rooms were dark and musty and smelled like...

Death.

Once again she shivered. It was time to get out of this place.

She slipped off the slab by Paddy's coffin and started for the stairs, but when she reached the doorway and looked up, she froze.

Someone was coming. Someone dark and towering and huge against the sunlight was staring at her. She threw up an arm to shield her eyes against the glare, amazed at the fear racing through her. Whoever he was, he had only to come down those stairs, press her back and lock her in with the dead forever. Perhaps he was one of them, come to make her stay....

"What in God's name are you doing in there?"

She let out the breath she had been holding, and her heart seemed to shudder within her chest, as if it had stopped right along with her breathing.

It was Brian. "What are you doing?" he repeated angrily, striding down the stairs and coming to stand before her.

"None of your damned business!"

He walked past her into the crypt, staring around as if he expected something to be changed. "How do I know you're not some little gold digger, willing even to rob the dead?"

She stared at him, locked her jaw and swung around, but before she had taken a full step he caught hold of her shoulders and swung her back again. Another tingle of fear swept through her.

He had been the one to find her the last time. How could she be sure that he wasn't the one who had cracked her on the head? He was the one who kept appearing... and denying his every appearance.

"Did you follow Darryl here again?" he demanded.

Her eyes widened. "No. Why?"

"What are you doing here, then?"

"Communing with the dead," she retorted sharply. The gold sizzle of his eyes swept her. "And I'm quite finished doing so," she continued. "If you don't mind, I'd like to go back above ground now."

He stared at her without moving.

This was it, she thought. The end. She'd been an absolute fool. She'd fallen for this man. She'd fallen for the look in his eyes, the seduction of his touch.

Fallen for the husky tone of his voice and the hungry way he looked at her. She'd trusted him blindly against all reason, and now she was going to pay the price.

His eyes left hers at last, and he looked around the tomb once again, then sighed deeply. "All right. Let's get out of here." He caught hold of her arm, pushed her forward, then led her up the stairs, away from the tomb.

A pair of flying, trumpet-playing angels guarded the stairway from either side of the tomb. Allyssa found herself sinking down on those steps, in the shadow of an angel. Brian did the same.

"So how is cousin Darryl?" he asked her.

"Fine."

"Still certain you're a pillar of virtue?"

Allyssa stared at him, feeling color stain her cheeks. "What did you want me to tell him? 'I'm sorry, you were busy, so I went to the tomb and got myself conked on the head. But Brian found me, so naturally I went home with him and...'"

Her voice failed her, right when she had intended to be flippant.

"You're ashamed? You have regrets?" he demanded.

"It just..." she began.

"Oh, that's right. It's rude to sleep with one man while you're living with another."

"Oh, would you stop!" she cried. Leaping up, she started away from the cemetery with long strides.

"Wait!" he snapped, catching up with her in seconds and taking her arm again. She tried to shake him off, but he refused to let her go. "Excuse me for having found you so damned fascinating!" he seethed, spinning her around.

"I—"

"Let's get lunch," he said. Without giving her a chance either to agree or refuse, he started walking so quickly that she couldn't do anything other than try to keep up. To her surprise, she found that there was a car in front of the castle, a small BMW. He led her to it.

"Yours?" she murmured.

"I do drive upon occasion," he said curtly.

Apparently he didn't believe in speaking while he did so, either, she reflected sourly a little while later. Nor did he just drive down into the village. They traveled for nearly thirty minutes until they came to a small town with a delightful open-air restaurant overlooking a tiny creek where black swans swam.

He suggested the lamb, the first words he'd spoken since leaving the castle. "The Dover sole is also excellent here," he told her.

In the end, she opted for the fish. It was nice to be out and away, she reflected as they waited for their food. He had ordered dark beer for both of them, and she sipped hers, becoming accustomed to the fact that it was served warm. Then she leaned back and watched the swans.

"So what were you doing in the tomb?" he asked her.

She brought her gaze from the swans to his eyes. Hard and gold, they assessed her. "You brought me to lunch just to get an answer to that question?"

"I brought you to lunch because I wanted to see you away from the damned castle again," he said.

She smiled, then lowered her lashes quickly, not wanting her eyes to give away too much. She had wanted to see him again, too. No. She had wanted much more than just to *see* him again. She wanted the magic of that night again. Not just the shimmering excitement, but the warmth, the tenderness. The way she had felt when he held her. So coveted, so secure.

"I was trying to find . . ." she murmured.

"What?"

She lifted her hands, palms up. "I don't know, exactly. Another entrance or exit. Is there one?"

He arched one brow. "I don't know," he said at last. "I never thought about it. I certainly never looked for one."

"Well, I don't think there is. I looked, and I didn't find one."

Brian leaned back, staring at her sternly now. "Stay out of the tomb."

"But it was broad daylight—"

"And it's still underground, dark and dank, and you found yourself in danger there once before."

"According to you, I fell down the stairs."

"I don't know what happened. Neither of us really knows what happened. I thought we agreed on that?"

She smiled again, her lashes lowered. "I don't think we ever agreed on anything. I think you just did your best to convince me that you weren't *dis*agreeing with me—at least for the moment."

He reached across the table. His hand, large and bronze, covered hers, and her heart began to thud. "Want to try to reenact the night and find out just what we did and didn't agree upon?"

Yes, she did. . . .

Their waitress arrived with the sole, and Brian abruptly removed his hand from hers. "Ah, but, we don't want to be rude to poor Darryl," he muttered.

"I wish you'd quit that!" she said.

He shrugged. "And I wish you'd quit playing games."

"I'm not playing any games!" she assured him. "I don't know what's going on. I don't really know either of you. I—"

"You don't know me?" he inquired softly. She gritted her teeth, not replying, and he leaned closer, ebony hair falling over his forehead, eyes flashing. "You damned well ought to know me. And you should learn to trust your own instincts."

"Right! You never seem to believe a word I say, but I should trust my own instincts! I'm telling you, I don't know what's going on here. I still can't begin to understand what my mother was talking about—"

"Your mother?" he interrupted, suddenly curious.

She stared across the table at him. "When she was dying, she kept saying she wasn't guilty. That she hadn't done something she had been accused of doing. I couldn't understand her, and she was so ill, I didn't want to press her to explain. But the things she said nagged at me. They were what compelled me to come over here once the lawyer reached me. I honestly didn't remember anything about this place. Anything at all."

Brian sat back again, his eyes on the swans this time as he ran his finger up and down his beer glass.

"I remember. Vaguely," he said after a moment.

"You do?" Startled, she leaned eagerly across the table.

He shrugged. "They'd been doing some digging in the wine cellar at the castle. They happened upon a passage, and a number of relics from the Norman days. One piece was a very fine cross, estimated to be from the time of William the Conqueror."

"And?"

"And it disappeared. Your mother had absolutely adored it, and Paddy, being Paddy, threw out all kinds of accusations. Aunt Jane, your mother, was in tears, and your father was furious. He told Paddy in no uncertain terms that he wouldn't allow his wife to be treated so."

"Good for my father!"

Brian smiled. "I thought so, too. I was about eleven at the time. I loved Aunt Jane. My mother died when I was an infant, and I always thought that Aunt Jane was beautiful and kind and wonderful, so I was delighted to see the way that James—your dad—stood up for her. I think Paddy made his big mistake then. He probably should have apologized, and maybe he even wanted to. But he was a stubborn old coot, even then, so he kept silent. Your father threatened to leave, and when Paddy failed to apologize, James carried through on his threat and went to America, where I gather he lived very happily."

"Until he died," Allyssa said softly.

"Mmm. I think Paddy actually found out where you were right after James died. But, of course, there was no way on earth he could convince your mother to come home. Your father had always been his favorite, though, you know. I knew that you would be left something in the will. Maybe that was his way of bringing you home."

Allyssa moved her fish around on her plate. "Thank you for telling me this. I asked Darryl, but he didn't remember."

"Darryl remembers. Darryl and I are the same age. He couldn't have missed what was going on!"

"Then he didn't want to tell me," Allyssa said. "He probably wanted to spare my feelings. Maybe he's afraid I'll believe my mother was a thief."

"Who the hell knows?" he said, suddenly irritable. "Such a magnanimous gesture seems out of character."

"Why are you so hard on him!" Allyssa flared.

"Because he's been a spendthrift, a parasite and a wastrel all his life," Brian said flatly.

"Oh, really? And you think he's frittering away something that should rightfully be yours?" she asked sweetly.

"Damn it, no, I—" He broke off. "All right. Have it your way, Miss Evigan. Stand up for him if you want!" He leaned close. "But take care! I can't guarantee that I'll always be in the right place at the right time, especially when you're so damned careless!"

"I don't know what you're talking about!"

"And I pray that you never do! Are you done? Maybe we'd best get back before poor Darryl misses you."

Oh, yes. She was quite done. She threw her napkin on the table and rose, walking out of the restaurant and leaving him to pay the tab.

He was silent on the ride back, saying nothing until he pulled to a stop on the bridge over the empty moat. She reached for the door handle, but before she could touch it, she suddenly found herself in his arms. Furious, she tried to protest his touch, but her resistance lasted only seconds. The thrust of his tongue was too seductive for her to resist. There was no way to feel his arms, his lips, and not remember . . .

And not feel the heat, the hunger, steal into her body.

Then, as abruptly as he had taken her, he released her. When he spoke, his words were a caress against her lips. "Remember, there's much more where that came from. Waiting for you whenever you can tear yourself away from poor dear Darryl!"

She gritted her teeth, then pushed him away with a vengeance and slammed out of the car. She ran across the bridge, but even then, she could hear his laughter. Furious with herself, she touched her lips, swollen now, bruised and awakened by his kiss.

She found Darryl in the great hall, reading the paper, waiting for her.

He rose quickly when she came in. "I was getting worried," he told her. "Of course, I've been such a poor host. But I thought that you might enjoy a movie. There's a cinema in the next town over. They do a nice double feature. Then we might have dinner."

"That sounds...wonderful," Allyssa told him. She wished she could shake her feelings for Brian. Darryl was so courteous, so considerate! And she felt so guilty.

Was she a fool, as well, trusting a man who meant her only harm? She didn't know. Something deep within her kept warning her that Brian was the one who kept mysteriously appearing...

And then denied that he had done so. Yet who could look so much like Brian, talk like him, except Brian himself? And yet some other part of her kept crying out that she had to trust him. So where was the truth?

"I'll get my coat," she told Darryl. "It might get cold later."

"Great," he said. "We'll have fun. We do well together, don't you think?"

She nodded a bit jerkily. "I'll just be a moment."

And it *was* a nice evening. The first movie was very funny, and then there was an intermission, when tea was served. They stopped for fish and chips on the way back, and talked about everything but the estate. When they reached the castle once again, Darryl took her by the arms and drew her to him. Perhaps she stiffened; perhaps he simply sensed her reserve. He merely kissed her tenderly on the forehead.

"Good night, Allyssa," he told her huskily. Then he whispered, so softly that she wondered if she really heard it, "Just give me a chance."

She saw little of him on Thursday—and nothing at all of Brian.

But at ten o'clock on Friday morning the three of them, a number of the servants and the solicitor gathered in the great hall for the reading of Paddy's will.

It was long. Very long! There were bequests to this one and that one for long and generous service. Paddy might have been a stubborn old coot, but he had also been a thoughtful one, in his way. He hadn't forgotten a single soul in his employ.

The solicitor's voice droned on and on. After a while Allyssa ceased to pay attention. She stared first at the flames in the hearth, then at the swords and coats-of-arms on the walls.

Then suddenly she realized that there was absolute silence in the room.

And everyone was staring straight at her.

"What?" she murmured.

Darryl stood up. "Excuse me," he muttered darkly. Stepping past her, past them all, he strode across the hallway. The heavy ancient door slammed in his wake.

"What?" she repeated, staring from the red-faced solicitor to Brian. "What is it?"

But Brian stood, too, then leaned over her chair, his smile icy. "Why, Miss Evigan, weren't you listening? Paddy decide to leave everything to you. Oh, there are conditions, of course! But the bulk and bundle are really yours. Isn't that what you came for?"

He straightened away from her, and a second later the heavy door slammed a second time.

This time it seemed to slam against her heart.

CHAPTER SIX

By the following Monday afternoon her head was pounding. After Darryl and Brian had left, the help had all walked out, too, each and every person staring at her as if she were the wolf who had come after the three little pigs. The solicitor hadn't even had time for her then, he had told her to come to his office on Monday morning, when he would do his best to explain everything.

She had found Darryl that night at the supper table and tried very hard to apologize. He had simply waved a hand in the air. "You didn't do it, Paddy did. And I don't mind that you're the one in charge, I really don't." He offered her a bitter grin. "I'd much rather you than Brian! It's just that I lived with Paddy, stayed with Paddy, all these years. I kept this damned place going all these years! I'm hurt by the way he treated me, don't you see? But, Allyssa, you mustn't be distressed. I'm sorry I walked out this morning, truly I am. If you don't mind, though, I'd just as soon be alone at the moment."

Miserably, she'd gone to bed. On Saturday he'd avoided her, though she'd attended church services with him on Sunday, and she'd seen Brian there, too.

He had stared long and hard at her, then offered her a mocking bow. He hadn't waited to talk with her after the services, either. She'd spent the Sunday afternoon by herself, riding.

Pausing in the cemetery and looking down the stairs to the family crypt, she'd wondered, Paddy, what were you doing? Trying to make up for what you did to my mother and father? But you can't imagine what you've done to me now!

In the morning, while she was pondering a way to ask Darryl for transportation to the solicitor's office, a car arrived for her, sent from that very office. Then she spent the next three hours trying to understand the stipulations of the will. The castle was to be home to all of Paddy's descendants for as long as they desired, but all decisions concerning its upkeep were to be hers. Care of the cottage was Brian's. Care of the stables and business was to remain with Darryl, if he so chose, but he was to draw a salary. The remainder of the profits would be hers. She couldn't sell anything without agreement from Darryl and Brian. If she should die, control of the castle would revert to Darryl, with absolute control of the cottage then falling to Brian. It was extremely confusing and complex, and by the time she returned to the castle, she wanted to either lie down and fall into a deep sleep, or drink herself into a stupor.

Gregory informed her coolly that Mr. Evigan would be out for the evening, but that he himself would be delighted to see that she was served dinner upstairs.

Gregory would simply be delighted not to have to see her, she knew. But she would be equally delighted to dine upstairs, so she thanked him and suggested that he also bring her a bottle of Chablis.

He did so. She dined on a meat pie, trying to read a mystery novel but having little success. She sipped her first glass of wine before she ate, her second during the meal and her third when it was over. Then, for good measure, she drank a fourth before deciding that a hot bath might make her just as tired and help her avoid the agony of a hangover the next morning. She turned off the lights in her room. The fire that some kind-hearted staff member had built her was just burning low in the hearth. She filled the tub with hot, steaming water and sank into it.

The steam filled the bathroom like a mist. She laid her head back. The bath was working. It was so hot and relaxing that, despite the turmoil in her head, she nearly dozed off. Afraid that she might drown and therefore end the difficulties over the will, she crawled out of the tub, wrapping herself in a big towel. She started toward the bedroom, then stopped.

It was dark, of course, with just the fire's glow, and spooky, with the steam from the bathroom streaming out into the other room.

A man was standing there. Tall, dark, towering. Hands on his hips, watching her.

The steam cleared slightly.

Brian.

She bit her lower lip, clinging to her oversize towel, then walked out of the bathroom and straight to him. He stared at her without a word. There were so many things she wanted to say. She wanted to be flippant, to tell him that he ought to learn to knock. She wanted to ask him if he had crawled through the window.

Most of all, she wanted to ask him if he would remember being here tomorrow....

But none of those things left her lips. Though she parted them to speak, no words came. He seized hold of her harshly, and his lips fell upon hers, hungry, questing. She wanted to protest, but, far more than that, she wanted to feel him. He kissed her endlessly, until her knees grew weak. Then he lifted the towel from her shoulders, let it fall to the floor, and then his lips touched her shoulder. His hands fell to her breasts, caressing them. He kissed her again, whispering against her lips, "You taste like wine."

"Lots of it!" she whispered in return, and he smiled crookedly. He lowered himself against her, his lips falling first to the rise of one breast, then taking the fullness of it into his mouth, his tongue laving and caressing the nipple. Her breath caught, and her knees threatened to give way, but his arms came around her, supporting her. He lowered his body still farther, his kisses and caresses drying the last of the dampness from her skin. His fingers curled around her buttocks, bringing her close against him. Lower and lower against her abdomen he caressed her. Her fingers dug into his shoulders as he brought her closer, closer, his touch more and more intimate....

She cried out very softly. The mist and the wine seemed to be swirling together. She was going to fall from the effect of each searing ecstasy. But she didn't. He swept her up and carried her to the bed. And there he made love to her. Once, twice...

And into the night. Violently, tenderly, tempestuously. Firelight touching them, turning them golden. The mist of the night swirling around them, adding a touch of magic. He rose above her again and again, the gold of his eyes igniting a blaze, the touch of his fingers, his every caress, creating new desire. She shuddered against the force of his body, felt the sweeping wonder of it filling her. Touched heaven again and again.

She should have spoken. Oh, she should have spoken. But it was too beautiful a night. He had made it so. And finally, when they had reached the heights yet again and she lay against him, spent, content to feel their naked flesh just touching, she slept at last.

She awoke with a start. Daylight was streaming through the narrow slit that served as a window. It must be very late. She pressed her head into her hands. It was pounding.

The wine! That horrible wine.

Then she remembered. . . .

She stretched her hand out. He was gone. Of course he was gone. What had she expected?

She bit her lip, looking at herself. She was naked. She pulled the covers up. He had been there. He *had!* She was *not* losing her mind! She was going to find him, and she was going to accost him, then and there.

She leaped up, then hurried into the bathroom. Quickly, she bathed and dressed.

Darryl was not to be seen downstairs. She left the house and found Liam by the stables. He cheerfully asked her if she'd like a ride, and she told him yes, please, and asked him to saddle up Lady Luck for her.

She watched him as he did so. "At least you seem to be speaking to me, Liam."

He nodded. "Right so," he told her.

"Why?"

"Because I knew Mr. Paddy Evigan, miss. And I'm certain he knew what he was doing. Coming between the two of them—it's the best thing I can imagine. We'll find out what's what around here now, I daresay! Here you go, Allyssa Evigan. Lady Luck all ready for a ride."

"Thank you, Liam. For Lady Luck, and for the vote of confidence. Actually, though," she said, accepting his hand for a boost up onto the mare, "I told the attorney—the solicitor—yesterday that I'd like him to find a way to get me out of Paddy's will. I..." She hesitated. "I've learned what I needed to learn here. The things I felt that I needed to come home to find out. I really didn't come for anything else. Certainly not to take anything away from either Darryl or Brian."

"We often get what we don't think to ask for, don't we now, miss?" Liam said. He waved a hand to her and started toward the stables. Allyssa nudged Lady Luck and started out across the fields for the trail through the forest that would lead her to the cottage—and Brian.

When she was halfway across the fields, she reined in for a moment, certain she saw a rider near the woods. Then the figure disappeared into the cover of the trees. Brian, she wondered, out already?

She gave Lady Luck free rein, as both she and the horse loved a fierce gallop across the open fields. Riding felt so wonderful. The sharp chill of the air against her face, the magnificent feel of the beautiful horse racing beneath her. Leaning low against Lady Luck's neck, she felt the wonder and the freedom of their motion. She closed her eyes for a moment, to better hear the thunder of the horse's hooves.

Someone was yelling. Her eyes flew open. Brian. He was racing out of the trees to her left, yelling at her.

Damn him. She was a fool for caring. They fought every single time they were together. He chastised her constantly, denied his own actions, and made her furious.

And then he stepped into her bedroom, leaving her without a word to say.

She looked straight ahead, determined to ignore him. When she was ready, she would slow her gait and speak to him, but not until then.

But suddenly she realized that the earth was trembling beneath her. She turned back. Brian, with a hard look on his face, was bearing down on her. Lady Luck was a strong, big-striding horse, but Brian's dark steed seemed to be more than her match. Allyssa urged Lady Luck onward, but Brian came closer and closer, thundering up behind her.

"Stop!" he commanded her.

When she didn't, he suddenly came leaping off his horse, flying at her. She screamed, stunned breathless at the impact of his body thudding against hers. They went flying into space, then crashing down hard upon the earth. The shock was startling and painful. Brian had managed to twist so that his body was mostly beneath hers, but still she had to gasp for breath, had to struggle to roll away to discover whether she was still in one piece.

"You stupid, arrogant fool!" she cried, beating her fists against his chest in her anger.

"Son of a bitch!" he cried in return, catching her wrists, wincing as he thrust her back and rolled over her, straddling her. "You little fool! Don't you ever listen? I was trying to save your life!"

She stared at him, thinking he'd clearly gone insane. Save her life! He had nearly killed her, throwing them both from their horses at that speed. Even if he had taken the brunt of the fall, they would probably both be a mass of bruises from head to toe.

"What—" she began.

Then she heard a squeal from Lady Luck. She broke off, staring at Brian, then pushing at him. "What was it? What happened?"

He rose, taking her hand, pulling her to her feet.

Across the field, just before the place where the trail led into the trees, Lady Luck was down. She had tripped and fallen and rolled. She was half up now, snorting, terrified, the saddle twisted beneath her belly.

"My God!" Allyssa breathed. "I don't understand. What happened?"

"Someone stretched wire across the riding trails," Brian said sharply. "I'd just discovered it when I saw you. God forbid you should listen to me! Excuse me, will you? I'm going to see if that poor horse is going to survive this!"

He started walking toward Lady Luck. Allyssa ignored him and followed quickly behind him. "Easy, girl!" Brian said softly to the horse, who had collapsed on the ground.

She whinnied, her dark eyes rolling. "Let me, she's come to know me," Allyssa said. She started talking to Lady Luck, moving closer and closer to her. She reached the horse and patted her nose and her neck, still talking very gently. Brian came along beside her and told her to go on. One by one, he ran his hands over the horse's legs.

"Get her up now," he told Allyssa.

She nodded and urged the mare up. With a heave, Lady Luck got to her feet. She swayed at first, but then she took several steps before obediently standing still. Allyssa looked anxiously at Brian. "Is she going to be all right?"

He nodded. "It seems so. Come to the cottage. You look as if you could use a stiff drink."

She shook her head. "I definitely don't want anything to drink!"

"Then I'll give you coffee, or tea."

She hesitated, and he smiled. "Mrs. Griffin, my housekeeper, is there. You'll be perfectly safe."

She walked Lady Luck along behind him. At the cottage, they left the horses in a paddock and went into the house. The fireplace reminded her of the last time she had been there, and she sat nervously in front of it. He seemed to sense her unease and quickly called, "Mrs. Griffin!"

A plump, rosy-cheeked woman in her late fifties or early sixties appeared. She smiled, walked over to Allyssa and took her hand. "How nice to meet you, love! I've been hearing so much about you!"

Allyssa wasn't sure what she had been hearing, given the way Brian had been acting, but she smiled in return. Mrs. Griffin promised them coffee and biscuits right away, and she was true to her word. It was delicious coffee, too. Maybe the British were known for their tea, she told Allyssa, but coffee had actually been around much longer, and she could make it quite well, thank you!

When she was gone, Brian and Allyssa sat uneasily across from one another by the fire. Finally Allyssa looked at Brian. "So," she said, trying to keep her tone light, "is someone trying to kill me?"

He leaned forward, close to the fire, brooding as he sipped his coffee. At last he looked at her. "What do you think?"

She leaned back. "I don't know what to think!" She bit her lower lip, then said softly, "Honestly, I don't know what to think! Someone cracks me on the head—and you're there. I'm nearly thrown to my death—and you're there."

"So!" he said, and the word sounded harsh. "You think I'm trying to kill you? Why save you, then?"

She shook her head. "I don't know. Maybe you're just trying to prove that I'm insane. Wouldn't the property revert to you and Darryl in that event, too?"

He exhaled slowly. "Probably. Has it occurred to you that I might *not* be trying to kill you *or* make you appear insane? And that if I'm *not* doing it, then perhaps someone else *is?*"

She nodded. "Options," she said softly.

"You need to go away."

"I can't!" She leaned toward him suddenly, anxiously. "Something is happening. I could never leave now—I would never know!"

"Damn it, Allyssa! I can't guarantee that I can always be in the right place at the right time!"

"You always have been," she told him.

He gritted his teeth. "Allyssa! I was not at the station the night you arrived! I was not—"

She leaped up. "I know! I know! You weren't at the station! And you weren't in my room that first night. And damn you!" she whispered, trembling. "You weren't in my room last night, either, right? I'm sure you'll deny that, too!"

She spun around, determined to leave. She had reached the door before he called her name. "Allyssa!"

She stopped, her back stiff and straight. She felt more than heard him coming after her. He caught hold of her shoulders and spun her around. "I wasn't in the train station the night you arrived. And I wasn't in your room that first night, either.''

"Let me go!" she commanded him.

"But I would never, never deny that I was in your room last night. It was, beyond a doubt, one of the most wonderful nights of my life."

She started to tremble as he held her, lowering her eyes. "Why did you disappear?" she whispered.

"I know how you feel about being rude to Darryl. I didn't think that you'd want me there once morning came."

She raised her eyes to his glittering gold ones once again. "How did you know I'd want you there in the night? After the way you've behaved—"

"Can't you understand?" he demanded, his voice suddenly harsh. His eyes searched hers. "No, I guess you can't. Not yet." He stepped back, releasing her. "There's nothing I can say. Not when you don't trust me."

"I—I do!" she protested. "I think I do!" she amended softly. But was it a lie? True, he *had* been with her last night; he had admitted it. But there were things she didn't know. Who had come to the station? Who had come to her room? Who had knocked her out in the crypt, and who had strung the wire across the trail?

Who would benefit from her death?

Darryl Evigan—and Brian Wilde.

"I have to go," she murmured.

"Fine, run," he told her. "Just be careful where you run, Allyssa! Be careful who you choose to run to!"

She threw open the door and hurried from the house, down the path between the roses and to the paddock, where Lady Luck was patiently awaiting her.

She rode carefully to the castle, avoiding the wire.

Exhausted, she hurried up to her room after leaving Lady Luck with Liam. She fell asleep nearly as soon as she lay down.

Dreams plagued her. Dreams in which a tall, dark man kept coming to her. He wore Brian's face and Brian's smile, black riding breeches, a white cotton shirt and high black boots. "Take care, Allyssa, take care!" he warned her. She twisted in her sleep, dreaming that she opened her eyes to find him there, standing guard at her door. "Rest," he said softly. "I'm here."

She closed her eyes in her dream. And after that all dreams faded, and she slept deeply and well, curiously secure.

She woke with the room nearly dark, full of shadows. Anxious, she leaped to her feet. It was nearly suppertime. After quickly bathing and changing into a soft red knit dress, she hurried downstairs.

Darryl was there, waiting for her. "Sherry?" he asked. "Or perhaps something else to drink?"

"A sherry would be fine, thank you," she told him.

"Actually," he said ruefully, "I shouldn't be offering you things that are yours."

She placed a hand gently on his. "Darryl, please. I find the terms of the will very distressing. This is your home. *I* am the guest here. I don't know what to do. I may just go home, and perhaps I should—"

"Perhaps you should marry me!" he said suddenly.

"What?" she gasped.

"Oh, I know that sounds awfully rushed, doesn't it? I apologize with all my heart. I shouldn't have spoken. It's just that we've done well together here, haven't we? My God, being together, living together, has been wonderful. I've been falling in love with you, bit by bit, ever since that first night when I walked in and saw you by the fire. You were so sodden, but so beautiful with your wide eyes and mane of hair! I am talking foolishly, aren't I? It's just that I was so certain that you were growing fond of me, too—''

"I *am* fond of you!" Allyssa assured him awkwardly. "It's just that this is so—''

He pressed a finger to her lips. "No, please. I spoke out of turn. I've given you no time at all. Let's just forget everything I've said. Let's start fresh, all right? Give me a chance to start over—and be subtle this time!" He grinned engagingly.

She lowered her lashes quickly, feeling both terribly guilty and ashamed. He had no idea that she had been seeing Brian. No idea of just *how* she had been seeing Brian.

Falling in love with Brian...

"You're very kind and considerate, Darryl," she murmured softly. "I—''

"Don't say anything now!" he implored her.

"I want you to know that I think you're wonderful," she insisted. "Brian told me that Paddy accused my mother of stealing a cross. He said that you must have known, too. I know that you were trying to spare my feelings when you said you didn't know anything about it, and I want you to know how much I appreciate it."

"Brian shouldn't have told you," Darryl said.

"But he did."

He shrugged. "I never believed that your mother stole that cross," he said. "And they're all gone now, anyway, your mother, your father, Paddy. Let's start over, shall we?''

She nodded, and he offered her his arm. "If you'll join me, Miss Evigan, I believe that our dinner is being served."

Feeling uncomfortable after his earlier outburst, she joined him, but he said nothing more even remotely intimate during the entire meal.

She still felt guilty. She had to tell him. She would never marry him. She was sleeping with Brian Wilde.

Falling in love with Brian Wilde.

But Darryl had already suffered one bitter disappointment because of her. She just couldn't say anything that would be cruel right now. She smiled, talked and laughed during the meal, careful not to let him know how hollow her laughter really was.

She was grateful, after the meal ended, when he told her that he had to go out. She fled up the stairs to her room and stayed there until she heard the great doors closing downstairs. Only then did she go down, restlessly prowling the great hall.

Sunset was coming. It was still so beautiful. On impulse, she left the house, sensibly telling herself that she would stay safely near the castle.

But she had scarcely left the house before she paused, catching her breath.

She could see the cemetery. And she could see the family crypt.

And she could see Darryl going down the steps.

She looked at the sky. Surely the daylight would last a bit longer!

No, she would be a fool, an idiot, to follow him!

But she had to! She had to know what was going on. She had to know if she was losing her mind, if she was falling in love with a madman, or if Darryl might be out to kill her. . . .

She bit her lower lip, then, throwing caution to the wind, went running into the dusk. She reached the darkening cemetery with its broken stones, its angels and its virgins. She passed by them all, running until she reached the family vault.

The door was open. She tiptoed down the steps and slipped inside.

The darkness almost overwhelmed her. She could barely discern the looming shapes of the coffins of her ancestors. Then she heard something, a noise from one of the back rooms. She hurried silently toward it, straining to see in the near total darkness, bracing herself against her fears.

There was light, a beacon of light coming from a tunnel. There *was* another exit from the crypt! It was behind a large, angel-covered monument to a fifteenth-century knight. She couldn't quite ascertain how the doorway had been opened, but she took a quick guess that it had something to do with the large marble statue, since the tunnel stretched out behind it, lamps lit at intervals along the dark stone walls.

She wasn't going to go any farther. She wouldn't be so foolish. She would just take a peek, then leave the crypt. Someone in the village could tell her how to get hold of a constable, and she could let him find out what was going on. She squinted, looking down the artificially lit tunnel. It seemed to stretch forever. Where did it lead? Why had Darryl disappeared down its length?

Something—a rustling, a shiver—alerted her, and she turned. A scream caught in her throat. A body was rising from one of the coffins.

"No!" she shrieked as a foul-smelling sack was thrown over her head.

She was swept up into ruthless arms. Though she tried to scream, to fight, she was tangled in the cloth, and her cries were muffled. She could scarcely move her arms and legs, so strong was her captor's grip. She struggled and wriggled and still tried to scream, but all to no avail.

She was being carried ruthlessly down the length of the tunnel.

Ready or not, she was going to discover where it led.

CHAPTER SEVEN

Allyssa couldn't begin to tell where she was being taken, only that she was moving at a swift rate and that they were heading down, deeper and deeper into the earth. Her efforts to fight became less frantic as she realised that she was quickly losing her breath, suffocating beneath the sack that had been thrown over her head. She went dead still and tried to inhale deeply.

It was then that her attacker came to a halt at last. And she heard his voice, whispered, frantic. "She found it this time. We didn't stop her fast enough. She found it—"

"And you brought her down here!" another voice exploded.

Allyssa strained to determine who the voices belonged to. They were muffled by the sack over her head, and they echoed eerily off the stone walls.

"You fool! Aren't you listening to me? She found the tunnel! There was nothing else I could have done! And what does it matter? You knew she had to be taken care of one way or another."

Taken care of... Dear God! What did they intend to do to her?

Who were they?

"I had my own manner of taking care of her in mind."

"Then you're a bloody idiot on that issue, too. She's been seeing Brian Wilde right cozy since she's been here. She'd not have married you."

Her heart began to sink. She'd been the idiot. Darryl Evigan was here in the tunnel. She didn't know what he was doing, except that it had to be illegal, and that now he intended to do something to her.

"Put her down," she heard Darryl say. Now that she knew who he was, she wondered how she'd missed recognizing his voice before.

She was more or less dropped to the floor. She struggled to free herself from the thing that had been tossed over her head. It was a Victorian coffin cover, with fine fringe all along the edges. She threw it as far away from her as she could and studied her situation.

It seemed grave. She was on the floor of a large room, with a number of boxes strewn around.

She looked up from the floor. There was Darryl, looking very grave as he stared at her. He was properly dressed, a silk shirt, casual jacket, neatly pressed trousers, every inch the country gentleman.

Even while he was in a cold, dank graveyard tunnel, doing God knew what and now planning an evil end for her, he managed to look calm and well-groomed.

The coldness of fear swept through her with that thought, and she leaped to her feet, fighting the panic that assailed her, determined not to go down like a scared, silly little idiot.

"What the hell do you think you're doing?" she commanded furiously, then gasped.

Gregory, the wonderfully proper butler, had stepped into sight. *He* was Darryl's accomplice?

Once again she stared at Darryl, hoping that a show of bravado might bring her through. "I repeat, wha the hell do you think you're doing? Distant relation or no, Darryl Evigan, I should press charges for thi outrage! Gregory! How could you put that—tha thing!—on my head?"

Bravado was getting her nowhere. Darryl and Gregory just stared at one another, then at her. "I'm sorry, Allyssa, I really am," Darryl said softly, a wry smile curving his lips. "I really was falling in love with you, did you know that? But Gregory says that you've been seeing Brian. Is that true?"

"That's none of your damned business!" she replied icily.

"So it is true. Well, it doesn't matter. I couldn't trust you now in any case. You'd show him or someone the tunnel, and my way of life would be destroyed. And you can't just come over from America and destroy everything, Allyssa Evigan! If only you'd stayed there..."

"Look," she said, trying to sound very patient. "I'm willing to forget this whole thing. I'm sick and tired of this country. I don't give a damn about any of it—I just want to go home. Now, I'm going to turn around and walk out of this tunnel, this crypt and this cemetery, and get a train into London. Then—"

"I'm so sorry, Allyssa, but I don't think so," Darryl told her, starting to move toward her.

"Look!" she cried out, "I really don't know what you're doing. I—"

"You really don't, do you?" He paused, cocking his head, the charming inquisitor. "How odd. You should. I started this when I was very young. When your parents were still here with you. It all began with that Norman cross. A man in the village offered me what seemed like a small fortune for it. Of course, I was really grossly cheated, but I was too young to know its real value at the time. Anyway, things worked out perfectly. Your mother was accused, I made my money. And every once in a while, the man would come back for more, though he never got quite such a good deal from me again. I learned how and where to dig on my own property, and how and where to dig elsewhere, and then how to smuggle all the artifacts through this tunnel to the river, across the Channel and onward to France. It's an incredibly lucrative business. I mean, what did you think? It's impossible to keep up a castle these days without some kind of a sideline!"

He might have been speaking about moonlighting as a bartender, his confession was so casual, but she was reeling. Her mother had been innocent, as innocent as she had claimed. Darryl had nearly destroyed her parents' lives! Damn him!

But he hadn't succeeded, because they had loved one another. Her father had given up his home and family to defend her mother against all odds. Darryl had gotten the cross, but her mother had ended up with everything that really mattered.

But still . . .

Her temper suddenly snapped. "You slimy, treacherous, disgusting son of a bitch!" she whispered. Then she flew at him, hands pummeling, nails raking. She was such a whirlwind of fury that she brought him crashing down to the cold stone floor before he even guessed her intentions.

"Damn it! She's like a wildcat! Help me!" Darryl commanded.

Gregory's effete looks were deceiving. He clutched Allyssa by the shoulders with painful strength. She whirled, trying to fight him, too. He turned her around, jerking her right arm backward at an angle that threatened to snap it. She went still, white with the pain, clenching her jaw.

"We're wasting time!" Gregory warned Darryl.

"Don't rush me. This has to be done carefully."

"I say we just tie her up, gag her and leave her," Gregory said.

Darryl nodded. Allyssa frowned, wondering what they meant to do with her once they returned from conducting their business. "What about rope burns?" Darryl asked.

"We won't leave her struggling," Gregory said. "But we've got to hurry. The water will be here soon."

"The water—" Allyssa began.

"The water," Darryl said, coming toward her, his hands behind his back. "What a pity. I had to do this once before. You thought it was Brian, didn't you? Sorry, my dear, distant cousin. Truly, truly, I am."

She saw his arm move swiftly. He was holding something in his hand. Some kind of a marble statuette.

Another relic he was planning to smuggle from the country, she thought briefly.

Then she wasn't thinking at all. Darryl had learned how to strike people very well. The blow was swift, hideously painful. Then the pain faded. The world blackened.

And she crumpled silently at his feet.

It was a strange night. A silver mist had begun to roll in just moments after Allyssa had left.

Brian leaned against the doorway to the cottage, staring at the forest, watching as the mist began to settle over the earth.

Why couldn't she see? he wondered, a hollow feeling gripping him. He couldn't bear seeing her walk away, but he didn't have the words to stop her. And every time she left, he was afraid of what might happen to her.

Paddy had been afraid of something, too. That much had been obvious from the will. Paddy hadn't wanted to leave his beloved estate to Darryl. He hadn't wanted to disinherit him completely, either, but he had suspected something.

Well, hell, so did he, Brian reflected. Darryl was up to something, had been up to something.

Whatever it was, he wouldn't hurt Allyssa.

Yes, he would. Someone had struck her on the head....

Or had she fallen down the steps? He had been so certain she had fallen, because that was how he had found her. And there had even been times when he wondered if she'd already been in league with Darryl when she'd come here, accusing him of having picked her up at the station. She seemed determined to mistrust him as much as she did Darryl. Or did she really? It was all very strange.

He closed his eyes. He really didn't give a damn about the cottage or the castle. Not anymore. Since Allyssa had come, he had discovered that all he cared about was her. The words had hovered on his lips so many times when they were together. I love you.... So plain, so simple. And so very difficult when so much lay between them.

A cold breeze suddenly picked up. The mist swirled hard before him.

Go to her....

The words almost seemed to have been spoken out loud, causing the chill that he felt to cut deeper. Darryl wouldn't hurt her, Brian thought again. He wouldn't dare....

Danger...

Once again he could have sworn he heard the word spoken aloud. But no one was nearby. Mrs. Griffin was gone for the day. Jimmy, who helped with the horses, and Mary Merks, who helped Mrs. Griffin, had gone for the evening, too.

He was alone in the coming darkness and the swirling mist. Neither frightened him. He had known the darkness and the mist forever. Except for his years with the RAF and the brief stint he had spent in London, he had lived here always. He had loved the landscape, and he had loved Paddy, and he had been able to stay because with the cottage he wasn't dependent on Paddy or the land. He had never been afraid. He loved the darkness and the mist....

Icy fingers suddenly seemed to close around his heart. A cold hand seemed to shove him urgently from behind. It was the wind. The wind...whispering, crying out...warning him?

He was afraid. He was in love with her, and he had tried to make her realize that she was in love with him. But he had been angry, and he had let her go back to Darryl. And to danger?

Oh, you fool, you fool! The voice was his own, mocking him inside his own mind. He had been so determined to be wary of her. After so many years she had returned, and he had been sure she was back for nothing more than what she could drain from the place. But he had been wrong. He knew it in his heart. And if he were to lose her now, life would never be the same again. She had touched him with her wide eyes and her innocence. There had never been anything he could do to prove his own innocence to her, and yet she had loved him anyway, whether she knew it or not.

"Allyssa!" he cried suddenly. His voice carried, echoing in the night. "Allyssa!" What a fool he'd been. Suddenly, and without doubt, he knew that she was in danger. Deadly danger. He started to run.

She came to because of the water.

At first it just delicately touched her cheek where it lay against the stone. It touched her leg, her hip, her ribs, her arm. She managed to open her eyes. Her hand lay sprawled out before her. She saw the water as it rose over her fingers. Rose quickly. She sat up, her head reeling. She pressed her hands to it, trying to remember where she was and how she had come to be here. It was dark. Only the faintest hint of moonlight, seeping in from some distant opening, allowed her to see at all.

The tunnel. She gritted her teeth against the thudding pain in her head. She was in the tunnel. She had followed Darryl here. He had struck her on the head, though apparently he hadn't bothered to tie her up after all. He was a criminal. A handsome, polite, charming, well-dressed criminal.

And he had tried to kill her.

Not only that, he stood a very good chance of succeeding.

The water was rising all around her. It had come up six inches as she had struggled to sit up, and another six as she had tried to clear her head and assess her position. She staggered to her feet, but by the time she reached them, the water came to her knees.

The horror of her situation filled her. The tunnel flooded at high tide. That was the trick to the place. The tunnel ran to the river, and the river led straight to the ocean, and the place flooded every morning and every night at high tide. She didn't know when it had been built, but it was clearly ancient, and she was certain that in the past, the Evigans had helped their political friends and hindered their enemies with it. And now...

She didn't dare think. The water was rising so quickly! It was past her knees. It was cold, frigidly cold. It would numb her soon, keeping her from thinking, keeping her from moving. Oh, yes, she would be taken care of! She would drown, and all that Darryl and Gregory would have to do would be to move her body from the tunnel to the river. Her lungs would be filled with water, and the coroner would rule that hers had been a death by accidental drowning.

The darkness was confusing. She turned, trying to fathom in which direction the family crypt lay. She decided that it was to her left, and she started walking that way.

The water had risen to her hips.

She tried to hurry, but it was almost impossible to move quickly through the icy water. And it was rising, rising.

To her rib cage now. Coming faster in a sudden rush. To her shoulders. She began to swim, urging her frozen limbs to obey the signals from her mind.

Higher, higher...

It rose above her head. She treaded water, taking a deep breath from the airspace above her head, then plunged forward, swimming hard. Breath! She needed another breath! She rose to the surface again. The cold was so fierce. Her limbs didn't want to move. Her mind didn't want to obey. Perhaps it would be easier to give in to the numbing power of the cold. How did one drown? It would be awful. She would be desperate, her lungs burning, her head pounding. She would breathe in, the freezing water would fill her lungs... and she would die.

She made it to the tiny pocket of air at the top of the tunnel. Would that soon fill with water, too? She gasped in a breath, listening to the loud wheezing of her bid for air. She inhaled, exhaled, inhaled again. Oh, no! She had forgotten the direction. In the darkness, in her terror to breathe, she had become confused....

My hand! Take my hand!

She blinked. Fingers, long, strong fingers, reached out to her. Brian. Not Brian. She didn't know. Someone trying to save her? Someone trying to kill her more swiftly, more mercifully?

The fingers curled around her own. Hard, strong, sure. She felt as if she was sailing through the water. Perhaps this was death. Perhaps this was how one died.

She closed her eyes against the sting of the water. The fingers! She had lost hold of them. She was alone again, scrambling to the surface, seeking air, air....

Something was in front of her now. A wall. She crawled up against it, gasping, heaving, as she found an inch of air and inhaled deeply. "Help me! Dear Lord, help me!"

Something moved beneath her fingers. She was sinking again, falling, falling into the water. She heard a distant splash.

And felt a touch again. Hard, strong, sure. Arms swept around her. Arms dragged her up. Arms wrapped around her tightly and securely, arms so warm that they would surely never let her go.

A strong kick and surge brought them both up together. She was being dragged up, up. Then she was suddenly on firm ground, the cold stone floor of the crypt. She rolled slightly, still gasping for breath. She had reached the secret exit from the crypt. Looking downward, she could see the slope of the tunnel.

It was completely flooded now, the water lapping into the crypt but rising no higher.

She closed her eyes, feeling those strong arms again. She began to cough, and her eyes opened very wide. Brian. He was drenched from head to toe, his dark hair plastered over his forehead, his sodden sweater clinging to the muscled wall of his chest. His eyes, though, were warm. A burning gold that offered such a ray of heat...

"Oh, Brian!" She threw her arms around him, and he clasped her tightly, rocking her. They were surrounded by the hard wooden coffins and the marble sarcophagi of the family, but nothing seemed eerie or frightening to her now.

Brian rose, sweeping her up in his arms. "I've got to get you warm."

"How did you know?" she whispered. "How did you find me? How did you know where to come?"

"I don't know," he told her.

"Oh! You've got to watch out! Darryl did this. He's been smuggling artifacts out of the country. He's been doing it for years and years."

"And Paddy must have guessed," Brian mused. They had reached the main entrance to the tomb, and he stopped and stared at her. "You're trembling!" he whispered. He hugged her more closely to him. "My God," he said huskily, "if I had lost you ... My God, what am I doing? I've got to get you warm." He started up the stairs from the crypt, his eyes still locked with hers.

"I love you, Brian," she said very softly. She was trembling, with cold, but her voice would have quavered anyway. "I love you," she whispered again, as he stared at her with a burning gaze.

"How touching! How very touching!"

Brian's gaze flew from hers, and they both stared up the steps at the man who had spoken.

Darryl was there. Waiting for them. With a gun.

Allyssa inhaled sharply. Brian set her down on the lowest step and started up the rest of the way, staring at Darryl. He seemed to be ignoring the gun.

"Brian!" she cried out sharply.

"Stand still, you fool!" Darryl warned him. "I'll shoot you in the blink of an eye—"

"Well, isn't that what you're planning on doing anyway?" Brian asked curtly. He paused for the barest fraction of a second; then he made a flying lunge.

The gun went off.

Allyssa screamed, racing up the stairs to see what was happening. The gun was nowhere in sight, and both men were still alive. They were rolling over one another, knocking into the ancient gravestones, coming to rest beneath the kneeling angel.

"You son of a bitch!" she heard Brian rage to Darryl. She heard the crunch of one blow, then another. There was no contest anymore. Brian was the stronger man to begin with, and he was furious. He dragged Darryl up, then knocked him down again.

It was over. All over...

Except that Darryl hadn't been alone. From her vantage point near the top of the steps, Allyssa could see that Gregory—the ever faithful servant!—was coming silently around the crypt, carrying a long, wicked-looking kitchen knife, intending to sink it into Brian's back before he could turn to defend himself.

"Brian!" she cried out in warning. Her fingers closed over something on the ground. Shaking, she looked at it. It was the marble statuette Darryl had used—twice!—to knock her out. She picked it up, then gasped. Gregory had turned away from Brian when he had heard her call out. And now he was coming toward her.

She threw the little marble statuette with all her strength, catching Gregory in the forehead. He fell backward, right into Brian's arms. Brian snatched the knife from his grasp, then let him fall to the earth with a thud.

Brian looked from Gregory to Allyssa. "Bravo!" he commended her.

She smiled, but she was shaking more and more severely. She was trying to stand, but she was faltering. He swept her up once again. "I've got to take you to the castle. Call the constable. And warm you up," he said tenderly.

She leaned back in his arms. "Darryl stole the Norman cross," she told him. "My mother was innocent."

"I never thought she was guilty."

"Do you think even Paddy somehow knows now that she was innocent?"

"Yes, I think so." She leaned back, smiling. It was so comfortable to be held.

Within two hours the constable and his men had come and gone. Brian and Allyssa had done all the explaining they could do. Then Darryl and Gregory had been arrested, and they had done the rest of the explaining. The constable had been a very happy man. "We've been trying to figure this one out for years and years, Miss Evigan. You and Mr. Wilde have done us a tremendous service this night. We knew artifacts were disappearing. We just couldn't begin to fathom how!"

Allyssa hadn't needed to see Darryl again, and she hoped she never would. The constable assured her that her distant cousin would be locked up for a long, long time.

By the time midnight came, she had soaked in a scalding bath, Brian had prepared them both hot toddies with lots of lemon and whiskey and sugar, and she had sipped hers and felt wonderful. Wrapped up in a huge towel, she lay in his arms in her bedroom in the castle, touching his cheek.

"You were wonderful. You came into the depths of the tunnel to find me!" she whispered.

He frowned. "No, you were wonderful, my love. I was frantic! I didn't know where to search. Not until I heard you calling for help behind that false door."

Allyssa frowned. "But you led me to the door!"

He shook his head.

"But..."

"Let's not discuss the tunnel," he said firmly "Let's get back to where we were before we were so rudely interrupted by Darryl and Gregory."

"Where were we?"

"You were saying that you loved me. Say it again.' She shook her head.

"You don't love me?"

"I would very much like to hear it from you before I start repeating myself," she said primly.

"I love you," he said huskily, kissing her lips, then her forehead, then her nose, then her lips again. "I love you. I think I might have fallen in love with you the moment I first saw you. I don't know. I tried not to. But I do love you. Very much."

"Oh, Brian, I love you so much! We'll get the castle put in your name. We'll find something to help us survive here, other than the sheep—"

He pressed a finger against her lips. "I don't survive on the sheep," he told her.

"No?"

"They're awfully pretty on the green hillsides. That's why I keep them. But for a living, I write mystery novels."

Allyssa started to laugh, then leaned against him "Well, you aren't after my inheritance, then!"

He shook his head. "Sorry!"

She frowned again. "But, Brian, someone did pick me up—"

He groaned softly. "Let's not argue. I love you, Allyssa. I love you with all my heart. I'm dying for you to marry me, to live with me, to be my wife You're safe now, and I'll never let you go again."

She was safe. She was in his arms. And maybe some things didn't matter. Maybe some mysteries were best unsolved.

"Never?" she murmured, trembling slightly, feeling the gold heat of his eyes on her.

"Never," he promised. "You're still cold!"

"No," she murmured.

But she was glad she had been trembling, because he was rising over her with a definite sizzle in his eyes.

"I promised to warm you," he said softly. "And right now I intend to make you very, very warm."

She smiled and wrapped her arms around him. "I love you!" she whispered again.

"And I love you!"

And then, just as he had promised, he saw to it that she was very, very warm indeed.

EPILOGUE

Brian and Allyssa could think of no reason to wait fo their wedding. They made arrangements with th church, and eight weeks from the day Allyssa had firs come to the castle, she and Brian hosted their ow wedding reception there. The ceremony had been ce ebrated in the fourteenth-century chapel in the vi lage, and though they were going to have a number o guests staying at the castle—mainly Allyssa's friends who had flown over from the States, and a few o Brian's friends and business associates from Lon don—they had chosen to make their home in the cot tage.

They had talked about everything together, mulle over all the options. Because it should be done fo historical reasons, and also because it would make lif easier for both of them, they had decided that the would open both places to the National Trust two af ternoons a week—different afternoons, of course, jus in case they needed privacy, though of course mos rooms would never be opened to the public. The fu ture seemed suddenly bright and beautiful. Travel ap pealed to both of them, and they looked forward t taking off at the slightest whim.

They were also both looking forward to starting family. A year alone sounded nice to both of them, bu Brian was several years past thirty, and Allyssa fel that she was fast approaching the three decade mark herself, so they felt comfortable knowing they could start their family any time.

She had never imagined being quite so happy.

Their honeymoon would take them to Paris for a few days, then down to the Italian Riviera for a few more, but their plane wasn't scheduled to leave Heathrow until noon the following day. Because of that, they had decided to escape the wedding crowd in the castle and spend their first night as man and wife in the place where they had felt the first stirring of passion for one another—in the quaint old thatch-roofed cottage they intended to call home.

They left the castle in a storm of rice and flowers. In Brian's BMW, they pretended to head for London, then turned and drove straight home. Mrs. Griffin would be leaving from the castle for her holiday at Bath, and the day help had been given time off, too, so no one would be around to intrude on their solitude.

Brian lifted Allyssa from the BMW and carried her, in her elegant and traditional white gown, along the path between the roses and over the threshold of their home. In the doorway he held her tight, kissing her in a very long and leisurely fashion. Then he groaned softly. "I've got to put you down!"

She laughed, sliding to her feet. "Oh, no, I think the honeymoon is over, and it hasn't even started yet!"

"Is that so?" He swept her up, laughing when she protested that he ought to put her down again, then carried her up the stairway, his eyes locked with hers.

But when they reached the second floor landing, she
found that her gaze was suddenly drawn from her
husband's.

There was a painting hanging on the wall, a nearly
life-size portrait of a man. Tall, dark, remarkably like
Brian.

He was wearing tight black riding breeches, a white
cotton shirt and black knee-high boots, and carried a
quirt. Behind him, against the backdrop of the fields
and the castle, stood a horse. A huge black horse. The
man seemed to tower there, handsome, arrogant, his
gold eyes examining all those who would pass him by.

"What is it?" Brian asked her.

For a moment she couldn't speak. Then she lifted
her arm from his shoulder to point to the painting. She
was still struggling for breath.

"Who—who is that?"

"The painting?" he inquired.

She nodded wordlessly.

"That's Paddy. Painted in his younger days. He was
in his late nineties when he died, you know. I'd say
that must have been painted when he was about
thirty." There was a curious pride in his voice that
touched and warmed her.

He might have fought his battles with Paddy right
along with everyone else, but Brian had loved the old
man.

And maybe, Allyssa thought, in his way, Paddy had
loved Brian far more than her husband would ever
imagine or believe.

"Allyssa, you're so pale! What's the matter?" he
asked anxiously.

She shook her head, smiling at him and stroking his cheek tenderly with her knuckles. "You resemble him. A lot."

"You think so? He was your great-grandfather, not mine."

"Well, then you must both look like his grandfather!" Allyssa said, then drew his head down to hers and kissed him tenderly.

How strange. The great-grandfather who had caused her parents so much torment had loved them, too.

And he had also loved her. In the end, he had given her everything. Not just the family heritage, but something far more important. Love. Brian.

Brian was studying her, his expression worried. She smiled. "I think we should go on to the bedroom while you're still strong enough to get me there," she teased.

"I have plenty of strength left!" he promised indignantly. Then his mouth lifted in a promising smile.

"Oh?" she murmured huskily. "Care to show me?"

He started to carry her again. Over his shoulder, she stared at the man in the painting.

She blinked, certain she had seen the man wink, then stared hard again. No, it was just a painting...

Paddy. She had a sudden sad feeling that she wouldn't be seeing him again. He had accomplished all that he had stayed behind to do.

"Thank you!" she mouthed to the painting.

"What?" Brian said.

She leaned back and met the golden eyes of her husband. "Thank you!" she whispered softly.

And then his footsteps were hurried, taking them to his bedroom. Their bedroom.

It was, after all, their wedding night. And Allyssa was convinced that they were quite alone. Nothing would ever haunt them again.

Nothing . . . but the power of love.

*   *   *   *   *